Praise for the Vera Stanhope series

'Nobody does unsettling undercurrents better than Ann Cleeves'   **Val McDermid**

'Cleeves sets a good scene, this time in Northumberland during a heatwave, and she brings a large cast to life, shifting points of view between bereaved relatives, victims and suspects in a straightforward, satisfyingly traditional detective novel'   *Literary Review*

'Ann Cleeves . . . is another fine author with a strong, credible female protagonist . . . It's a dark, interesting novel with considerable emotional force behind it'
Spectator

'Cleeves has a way of making unlikely murders plausible by grounding them in recognizable communities. In this world, neighbours are close-knit, and close ranks'
Financial Times

'Cleeves weaves an absorbingly cunning mystery and fans of Vera, the messy, overweight, man-less heroine of this crime series, will soon have a face to put to her, as the actress Brenda Blethyn takes on her endearing character in a forthcoming television series, *Vera*, based on the books'   *Daily Mail*

'Ann Cleeves is a skilful technician, keeping our interest alive and building slowly up to the denouement. Her easy use of language and clever story construction make her one of the best natural writers of detective fiction'
Sunday Express

Praise for the Shetland series

'*Raven Black* breaks the conventional mould of British crime-writing, while retaining the traditional virtues of strong narrative and careful plotting'   *Independent*

'Like a smoky Shetland peat fire, this elegantly written, slow-burning intrigue shrouds you in mystery and crackles with inner heat'   **Peter James**

'Beautifully constructed . . . a lively and surprising addition to a genre that once seemed moribund'
Times Literary Supplement

'*Raven Black* shows what a fine writer Cleeves is . . . an accomplished and thoughtful book'   *Sunday Telegraph*

'Ann's characterization is worthy of the best writers in the field . . . Rarely has a sense of place been so evocatively conveyed in a crime novel'   *Daily Express*

'In true Agatha Christie style, Cleeves once again pulls the wool over our eyes with cunning and conviction'
Colin Dexter

'The setting is Fair Isle, full of birds and beauty, but, in Cleeves' hands, deeply sinister'   *The Times*

'A most satisfying mystery set in an isolated and intriguing location. Jimmy Perez is a fine creation, and I hope Ann Cleeves' Shetland series will be with us for a long time to come'   **Peter Robinson**

THE CROW TRAP

Ann Cleeves is the author behind ITV's *Vera* and BBC One's *Shetland*. She has written over twenty-five novels, and is the creator of detectives Vera Stanhope and Jimmy Perez – characters loved both on screen and in print. Both series are international bestsellers.

In 2006 Ann was awarded the Duncan Lawrie Dagger (CWA Gold Dagger) for Best Crime Novel, for *Raven Black*, the first book in her Shetland series. In 2012 she was inducted into the CWA Crime Thriller Awards Hall of Fame. Ann lives in North Tyneside.

www.anncleeves.com
@anncleeves
facebook.com/anncleeves

Ann Cleeves

THE CROW TRAP

PAN BOOKS

First published 1999 by Macmillan

This edition published 2016 by Pan Books
an imprint of Pan Macmillan
20 New Wharf Road, London N1 9RR
Associated companies throughout the world
www.panmacmillan.com

ISBN 978-1-4472-2446-4

1 3 5 7 9 8 6 4 2

A CIP catalogue record for this book is available from the British Library.

Typeset by Intype Libra Ltd
Printed and bound by CPI Group (UK) Ltd, Croydon, CR0 4YY

Visit **www.panmacmillan.com** to read more about all our books
and to buy them. You will also find features, author interviews and
news of any author events, and you can sign up for e-newsletters
so that you're always first to hear about our new releases.

Prologue

If you were to look for Baikie's Cottage on an Ordnance Survey map you would not find it mentioned by name, though Black Law Farm is. It is marked by an open square and named in small print on Map no. 80 – THE NORTH PENNINES, KIMMERSTON AND THE SURROUNDING AREAS. It is hard to find because it falls just where the paper folds. The track which leads from the road is shown by a dotted line as a public footpath. The farm is surrounded on the map on three sides by blocks of pale green. These blocks are superimposed with tiny computer-drawn Christmas trees which indicate a forest. On the fourth side the page is white, apart from brown contour lines, until the burn is reached. The burn is wide at this point, shown by two dark blue lines, coloured in with a paler blue. The lines are squiggly, a child's drawing of a river. This is the Skirl burn. Beyond that the contour marks are very close together showing that the slopes are steep. The tops of the hills are marked by symbols like small clouds. These are rocky crags and they are named: Fairburn, Black Law, Hope. Between the burn and Hope Crag another feature is marked in brown lettering. This says simply LEAD MINE (DISUSED).

From the bedroom at Black Law Farm Bella looked out at Fairburn Crag. There was still snow on the tops. She saw the dark shadow of the forest, the grey stone buildings beyond the yard. She turned away from the window to her dressing table. With a steady hand she applied lipstick, rubbed her lips together, then pressed them on a piece of tissue. In the mirror she saw Dougie in bed. She caught his eye. The lid twitched so she fancied he meant to wink at her, to say: My, you look bonny today, lass. After the stroke they had said there was every chance his speech would come back but it never had.

'I'm just popping down to Baikie's,' she said. 'If Rachael calls I might be a while. That'll be all right, will it, pet?'

He nodded, smiled lop-sidedly, patted her arm with his good hand.

'Do you want the telly?'

He nodded again. She leant over and kissed him. 'Bye then,' she said.

In the kitchen she changed into wellingtons and put her black patent leather shoes into a carrier bag. Outside an east wind blew scraps of straw in eddies round the yard and took her breath away.

PART ONE

Rachael

Chapter One

Rachael turned off the metalled road, then stopped with a jerk. There was a new tubular steel gate and she'd almost driven into it. One of the Holme Park tenants trying to impress. A ewe with a tatty coat and mucky behind nuzzled up to her as she got out of the car to open the gate. The ewe was fat. They didn't lamb up here until the end of April. The steel of the latch was so cold that it seemed to freeze to her fingers.

The track was worse than she remembered, pitted by frost. She drove slower than walking pace with two wheels on the verge. Still the exhaust bumped against a rock.

A mile on she realized she had taken the wrong track through the forest. She should have come out from the trees into open countryside, should by now have reached the ford. Instead she was on a sandy path, not so uneven but very narrow. On either side conifers blocked out the evening light. She drove on, hoping for a place to turn but the track divided into a footpath, the trees meeting over her head.

She had to reverse back to where the track forked. Branches scraped against the paintwork with the noise of chalk on a wet blackboard. The bumper hit a stone bank hidden by undergrowth. She pushed the gear into first and moved forward with a jerk before reversing again. When she reached the main track it was almost dark and she was shaking.

At the ford she stopped the car and got out to test its depth. Five years ago a student on his way back to Baikie's after a night in the pub had drowned, his car turned over by the force of the flash flood. The car headlights reflected from the surface, making it impossible to gauge the depth. It had been a dry spring so she decided to risk it. The water steamed and hissed as it hit the hot engine but she pulled out easily enough on the other side.

The track was blocked again by a gate, this time of wood. It was too dark to read but she knew there was a sign. Access to Black Law Farm and Baikie's Cottage only. She left the engine running while she opened the gate. The car was parked on a slope so the headlights shone up at an angle onto the open hillside. A movement must have caught her attention because she looked up and saw, caught in the beam, the silhouette of a figure, dressed for walking in a Gortex jacket and hood. There was a flash of reflected light and she guessed he was carrying binoculars or a camera. She was certain it was a man though the figure was too far away to tell. He turned and disappeared into the gloom.

She had the unpleasant sense that she had been watched for some time. As she drove the last half mile to the cottage she wondered who could be foolish enough to be out on the hill with so little light left.

Rachael decided not to call at the farm. It upset Dougie to be disturbed without warning. Bella would hear the car and come down to the cottage when

Dougie was asleep if she got the chance. There was a light in the farmhouse kitchen but the curtains were drawn. The dogs barked loudly and chased from a barn into the yard. The noise seemed to echo round the hills and Rachael thought: that's good. She'll not miss that wherever she is. Then she saw the light upstairs and thought Bella was probably settling him down for the night.

She drove on through the yard which was scraped and clean. Baikie's Cottage was at the end of the track with a view of the valley, surrounded by trees which had been planted over the years to give some shelter from the wind.

The key was where it always was, under an ornamental chimney pot near the back door. Inside she groped for the light switch. The house smelled damp but she knew it was clean. She had come in November, after the last of the students, to scrub out. Bella had arrived with a couple of bottles of homemade wine and they'd made a day of it. They'd ended up in the farmhouse drinking Dougie's whisky. She slept in the guest room – Neville's room as Bella called it, though as far as she knew Neville hadn't been there for years – and had woken with the worst hangover of her life. It was the only time she'd ever slept in the farmhouse.

Rachael switched on the Calor Gas cylinder outside then went into the kitchen to put on the kettle for coffee. The kitchen was tiny – a modern extension so narrow that she could touch both walls at once. She plugged in the rusty fridge, shut the door and was relieved when it began to hum. The gas flame spluttered but the kettle wasn't even warm. While she waited

7

for it to boil she walked through to the living room and shut the curtains to keep out the draught. Once they had been grey velvet but the sun had faded them in strips and now the pile was quite smooth. There was a sofa covered with an Indian bedspread which Rachael had brought the year before from home, a couple of armchairs which needed something to hide the stains, books spotted with mildew and in one corner a fox in a glass case. The surroundings were so familiar that Rachael took no notice of them. She thought only about getting warm. Even inside it was so cold now that her breath came in clouds.

The grate was laid with paper and kindling but there were no logs in the basket on the hearth. There were matches on the mantelpiece but they were damp. After several attempts to strike one Rachael twisted newspaper into a spill and lit it from the gas flame in the kitchen. She nurtured the fire, remembering old tricks from the last time. The kettle squealed and she made instant coffee from an emergency jar she had brought in her bag. She drank it crouched over the fire, tending it until she was certain it would not go out.

She emptied the car then put a pan of water on the stove. She'd have pasta for supper, and a glass of the wine she planned to have with Bella later. She took out the basket to fetch some logs. They were stacked at the back of a high, open-fronted shed, which also housed a rusting tractor and some piled bales of straw. The lights from the house didn't reach that far and she carried a torch. Outside it was clear and icily cold. The stars in the wide sky, unpolluted by street lamps, seemed brighter than at home.

Bella had arranged her suicide as efficiently as she

had done everything else in her life. In the torchlight she swung, hanging from a noose made of strong, nylon rope. Her face was white. She had prepared for the occasion by putting on lipstick and the silk top Rachael had bought her as a thank-you present after last season. Her black shoes shone so the torchlight reflected from them. She'd pulled two bales away from the wall and climbed onto them to tie the rope round a beam. Then, when she was ready, she had kicked one away.

Of course there was a note. She had thought of that too. It was addressed to Rachael and apologized that she had to be the one to find the body: *I couldn't put Dougie through that and I knew you'd cope.* It went on to remind Rachael that the kitchen door of the farmhouse was open so she'd be able to get to the phone without disturbing anyone – meaning Dougie again. But there was no real explanation for the suicide. She just said that she couldn't take any more. She had known that Rachael would find her before the end of the evening because she had left the log bucket empty. Rachael had always realized that Bella was a clever woman.

When Rachael saw Bella, swinging, recognizable by the silk top, the smartly permed hair, the lipstick, but not really Bella, because Bella had never been that still in her life, she was furious. She was out of her mind with anger. She wanted to use the body as a punch bag, to thump it in the stomach. She wanted to climb onto a bale and slap the white, lifeless face. Because Bella had been a friend. So what right did she have to do this without discussing it with Rachael first? And because, since she heard that the project would go ahead, Rachael had been looking forward to this evening.

She'd imagined sitting in Baikie's Cottage with Bella and sharing a bottle of wine and a bucketful of gossip.

But she didn't hit the body. Instead she turned and punched the bale of straw, over and over again until her knuckles were scratched and bleeding.

Later she realized how long she must have been in the tractor shed. When she went back to the cottage the pan of water was boiling and it had taken half an hour for that lousy gas flame even to get the kettle warm.

Chapter Two

The cottage, which had come to be known as Baikie's, was bought from the farm soon after the war by Constance Baikie. She had been a naturalist and illustrator, a spinster. Once she had walked the hills in search of inspiration but obesity soon restricted her ramblings. She had taken to sitting in an armchair and only drawing the birds, plants and insects she could see from her window. This was her most prolific period. The original plates from her books sold for surprisingly large sums. A London gallery took her up and organized an annual exhibition. No one knew exactly what she did with all her money, she lived very frugally. For diversion she wrote spitefully funny letters to learned magazines ridiculing the research of her colleagues.

Dougie, still fit and active then, brought all her supplies from Kimmerston once a week in his Land Rover. She never offered to pay him for this service but each year at Christmas she gave him a sketch of the farm or the surrounding hills. Later Bella found them stacked in a pile in the drawer of his desk and had them framed. Miss Baikie wasn't lonely. She received visitors graciously but expected them to bring gifts – cream cakes, biscuits and bottles of whisky.

In 1980 Miss Baikie died suddenly. Dougie, calling

one morning with the milk, found her sitting by the window. She had been there all night. In her will she launched a charitable trust to encourage environmental education and research, and donated the cottage to that. She stipulated that the trust should not benefit anyone under eighteen. She had always disliked children. Undergraduates used Baikie's as a base for their fieldwork. Rachael had spent the previous spring there to complete her MSc. When the committee decided they needed new blood she was elected a trustee.

The cottage was much as Constance had left it. The furniture had all been hers. Fanciful students imagined that they saw her ghost, late at night.

'Not if it was moving,' said a lecturer who'd known her. 'If it moved it couldn't have been Connie. So far as I remember she never did. Not while I knew her.'

Rachael didn't believe in ghosts.

That's what she told Anne and Grace the next day when they fussed over her. Rachael had planned to start work immediately on the mapping but she was made to go over it all again. It was her first time as team leader and in one sense she resented the distraction. As it was she was nervous about taking charge. They were at Baikie's for the survey and not to chat, but when Anne and Grace turned up to start work she had to tell them what had happened to Bella.

Anne was a local woman and Rachael had worked with her before. She was older than Rachael, very confident, and Rachael wasn't sure how she'd take to being told what to do. Grace had come highly recommended, but Rachael had never met her before. She'd had no say in the zoologist's appointment, which still rankled.

Grace was pale and thin and news of the suicide seemed to drain her of the little colour she had. It seemed an overreaction. Bella, after all, had been a stranger.

Anne wanted to know all the details, however.

'How dreadful!' she said, when the tale of the discovery of the body had been told. 'What did you do then?'

'I went back to Black Law and used the phone.' She'd gone in quietly, not wanting to scare Dougie, though realizing he'd probably expect Bella to be banging around. She'd been unnerved to hear voices coming from upstairs and wondered for a moment if she'd imagined the whole thing. She'd crept up the stairs thinking: God, I'll look a real fool if Bella comes out and catches me. Then there'd been a loud blast of music and she'd realized that the voices were coming from the television in Dougie's room.

'I don't think I'd know who to call in the event of a suicide.' Anne's voice was sympathetic but slightly amused which annoyed Rachael. Christ, she thought, I hope we're not going to get on each other's nerves already.

'I dialled 999. I didn't know what else to do. The operator put me through to the police and they arranged for a doctor to come. I should have thought Dougie would need one anyway.'

The doctor's name was Wilson. She'd worried that he would get lost on the way but he'd visited Dougie before and anyway he knew the area. He was driving a Range Rover and wore walking boots and breeches, and looked like a vet.

'He said Bella'd been dead for at least two hours,'

she said, 'then a policeman turned up. They arranged for an undertaker to come out from Kimmerston.'

She'd offered to drive out to the fork in the track to show the undertaker the way. Mr Drummond had been very sweet considering the dreadful drive and the time of night. He had a round cherubic face and specs and said that suicides were always very upsetting. Then the doctor had to send for an ambulance to take Dougie away. He couldn't stay in Black Law with no one to look after him. Perhaps the doctor was waiting for her to volunteer but she couldn't face that, even for a day. She thought it would almost have been nicer for Dougie to go out with Mr Drummond and Bella, but she could hardly suggest it.

'How was Mr Furness?' Anne asked. 'Did you have to tell him?'

Rachael thought Anne was enjoying the drama. She'd always been a bit of a drama queen.

'Of course,' she said. That was what Bella had wanted.

'Did he understand?'

'Oh yes.'

'How did he take it?'

'He cried.'

'Did you tell him that she'd killed herself?'

'No. Just that she was dead.'

She and the doctor had stood outside the farmhouse in the freshly scraped yard, watching the ambulance drivers lift Dougie out on the trolley. The doctor was shivering though she had stopped feeling cold.

'I suppose it was the strain,' Wilson had said. 'Living all the way out here. Keeping the farm going and caring

14

for Mr Furness. It's not as if she was born to it. I suppose something just snapped.'

'No,' she'd said firmly. 'Really. It couldn't have been like that. Bella loved Black Law. She enjoyed every minute of her time here.'

Then he gave her a pitying look, because he thought she couldn't face up to the reality of the situation. For the first time she wondered what Bella had meant by not being able to take any more.

When the ambulance, the doctor and the undertaker had driven away in convoy she was left with the young policeman. He watched the tail lights of the other vehicles disappear into the darkness with a sort of wistfulness, as if he were being abandoned, then he said:

'Do you know if there's any booze in the house?' She could tell he was eager to get inside, but that didn't seem very professional even when he added: 'I expect you could do with a drink.'

She found a bottle of whisky in the cupboard in the living room. They sat in the kitchen where it was warmer. He poured himself a drink without waiting to be asked and passed the bottle to her.

'What are you doing all the way out here?'

'Working.'

'You work for the Furnesses?'

'No, for an environmental agency. Peter Kemp Associates. We're doing an Environmental Impact Assessment. We've been given permission to use the cottage down the track as a base.'

He looked blank.

'You've heard about the proposed quarry in the National Park?'

'Yes.' But his voice was uncertain. He sounded like a boy, optimistically trying to bluff his way through an unlearned lesson, so she told him. About the quarry, the planning application, the legal requirement for a survey to assess damage.

'We've been hired to do the survey and the report.'

'You stay all the way out here on your own?'

'Only tonight. My colleagues arrive tomorrow.' She looked out of the window at the lightening sky. 'Today.'

'That'll be Peter Kemp.'

'No. Peter doesn't do much casework now. Anne Preece is a botanist. Grace Fullwell's a mammal expert.'

'Three lasses?'

'Three women.'

'Oh aye.' He paused. 'And you have to go out in the hills. Counting things?'

'Something like that. There's a recognized methodology.'

'Isn't it dangerous?'

'For women you mean?'

'Well, for anyone.'

'We leave a record of our route and the time we expect to be back at base. If there's a problem the others can organize a search.'

'I'd not want to be out there without a radio.' He shuddered as if he felt suddenly cold. 'I'd not want to be out there at all.'

She saw that he was prolonging the conversation so he didn't have to set off up the track alone in the dark.

'You're not a country boy,' she said.

'Does it show?' He grinned. 'No. Newcastle born and bred. But Jan, the wife, thought the country would be a better place to bring up the bairn so I put in for transfer. Best thing I ever did.'

Though now, here in the wilds, he didn't seem so sure. She'd guessed he was married. It wasn't only the ring. He had a well cared for, pampered look.

'Shouldn't you be getting back to them?' she said. 'They'll be wondering where you are.'

'No, Jan's taken the bairn to visit his grandma. They'll not be back until after the weekend.'

She felt jealous of this woman she'd never met. He so obviously missed her. And it wasn't only the freshly ironed shirts and the meals. It was the empty bed and no one to chat to when he got home after work.

'You don't mind answering some questions about Mrs Furness? Now, I mean. It must have been a shock but I'll need a statement sometime.'

'No,' she said. 'I'd rather get it over, then I can get some sleep before the others get here. What do you want to know?'

'Everything you can tell me about her.'

I wonder if you'd say that, she thought, if your wife was at home. But she talked to him anyway, because she wanted to tell someone about Bella and what good friends they were. It was like a fairy story, she said. Bella coming out to the farm to look after Dougie's mother and falling in love with it all, with Dougie and Black Law and the hills. They'd married and they really had lived happily ever after, even after Dougie's stroke.

'Why'd she kill herself then?'

She hadn't been sure he'd been listening. It was the question which had been lying at the back of her mind all evening. 'I don't know.'

'But the note was her writing?'

17

'Oh yes. And not just the handwriting. The way the words were put together. It was like Bella talking.'

'When did you last see her?'

'November last year.'

'Well, that's it then. Anything can happen in four months.'

'I suppose it can.' Though she had not thought Bella would ever change. And Bella would realize that she'd not be able to leave it at that. She'd know Rachael would have questions, that she'd not be able to settle until she found out what lay behind it. So why hadn't she left her more to go on?

'I don't like to leave you on your own. Is there anyone you can go and stay with?'

So I can keep you company, she thought, on the drive to the road.

'I'll wait until the others arrive, then I might go to my mother's, in Kimmerston.'

She said it to get rid of him so he would realize she had family. Someone to look after her. Afterwards she thought she might go home for a few hours. She'd sort out Anne and Grace in the cottage then she'd go to see Edie. Not for comfort though. Edie wasn't that sort of mother.

Chapter Three

Instead of using her key at the ground floor door she went down the steps and banged on the kitchen window. She didn't want to appear suddenly in the kitchen from inside the house like a ghost or burglar. Edie wouldn't be expecting her back.

The door was opened, not by Edie, but by a middle-aged woman with dramatically dyed black hair, cut straight across her forehead in a Cleopatra style. She wore chunky gold earrings and a knitted tubular dress which reached almost to her ankles. The dress was scarlet, the same shade as her lipstick. There was also a child, a girl, denim-clad, bored and sulky. Rachael felt a stab of fellow feeling. The room was filled with cigarette smoke. It was very hot. The couple must have been invited to an early supper because the table showed the remains of a typically Edie meal. There were pasta bowls brought back from a holiday in Tuscany, scraps of French bread, an empty bottle of extremely cheap Romanian red. Edie was making coffee in a blue tin jug. She looked up casually. People were always banging on the kitchen window.

'Darling,' she said. 'Come in. And shut the door. It's blowing a gale.'

Rachael shut the door but remained standing. 'I have to talk to you.'

'Coffee?' Edie turned absent-mindedly. The kettle was still in her hand.

'Mother!' It was the only way she could think of to claim Edie's attention. She never called Edie that.

Edie looked at her, frowned. 'Is it urgent?'

'Yes. Actually, yes it is.'

With a competence, politeness and speed which astonished Rachael, Cleopatra and the daughter were dispatched. The coffee was never drunk.

'So sorry you had to go,' Rachael heard Edie say at the main front door as if their departure had been entirely their own idea.

When Edie returned to the kitchen Rachael had found another bottle of wine and was opening it. 'I wish you wouldn't let people smoke in here.'

'I know, dear, but she was desperate. Her husband's just run off with one of his students.'

'And you discussed that here. In front of the daughter.'

'Not directly.' She grasped for a word: 'Only eliptically. He used to teach with me in the college. I appointed him. I feel a certain responsibility.'

'Of course.' This was said with an irony which Edie perfectly recognized.

She sat opposite Rachael at the scrubbed pine table and calmly accepted another glass of wine. Edie had recently retired but she had not let herself go. Despite the radical leanings which had so embarrassed Rachael in childhood she had always thought appearances mattered. Her short hair was well cut, her skin clear. She dressed well in an ageing hippy sort of way in long skirts, ethnic padded jackets. Rachael wondered if her mother had a lover at the moment. There had always been men when she was growing up but Edie had acted with discretion which bordered on the obsessive. Those men had never been welcome in the chaotic, crowded kitchen. It had been made quite plain to them that they would never encroach on Edie's domestic life.

Edie looked up at Rachael over her glass.

'I hope,' she said carefully, 'you're not here to go over old ground.'

Meaning her father.

'No.'

'Then tell me,' Edie said very gently, 'how you think I can help.'

Rachael drank her wine in silence.

'Is it boyfriend trouble?'

'Don't be stupid. I'm not fourteen. Anyway, do you think I'd talk to you about something like that?'

'Well, yes. I hope you might.' Edie sounded regretful which made Rachael feel churlish, stupidly childish.

'Bella died,' she said. 'Last night. She committed suicide by hanging. I found her.'

'Why didn't you come back home before? Or phone? I'd have come out to you.'

'I thought I could handle it.'

'That's not the point. I'm sure you can.'

Rachael took a long time to answer.

'No,' she said. 'Not on my own. Not this time.'

'Ah.' Edie drained her wine. It left a stain on her lips and the wide front teeth which Rachael had inherited. 'Do you know, I always felt jealous of Bella. A bit. It doesn't mean I'm not sorry now. Of course not. But I resented the way you were so close, the two of you.'

'You never met her, did you?'

'That made it worse. I imagined . . . it was the way you talked about her. I thought . . .'

'That I wished she was my mum?'

'Something like that.'

'No,' Rachael said. 'But we were friends. Real, close friends.'

'If you want to talk about her I can listen all night.'

'God no.' Wasn't it typical of Edie and her friends that talking was seen as all that was needed? Throughout her childhood this house had been full of talk. She'd thought it was like a soup of words, drowning her. Perhaps that was why she liked numbers best, counting things. Numbers were precise, unambiguous.

'What then?'

'I need to know why she did it.'

'We are certain that she meant it? It couldn't have been an accident? Murder even?'

Rachael shook her head. 'The police came. And there was a note. It was her writing. And I explained to the policeman the words were put together as though she was speaking. Do you know what I mean?'

Edie nodded.

Of course, Rachael thought, you know all about words.

'She knew I was coming that night. If she had a problem she could have talked to me about it. Perhaps she thought I wouldn't help.'

'No, she wouldn't have thought that.'

'I should have kept in touch over the winter. Then

I'd have known. Do you realize I didn't even phone her?'

'Did she phone you?'

'No.'

'You do know, don't you, that guilt's a common feature of bereavement?'

'Edie!'

Edie had taught English and Theatre Studies at the sixth form college, but had also been responsible for pastoral care. She'd attended courses on counselling. The regurgitated nuggets of psychology always irritated Rachael.

'I know,' Edie said unabashed. 'Psycho babble. But it doesn't mean it isn't true.'

'Really. I don't need all that.'

'I'm not entirely sure what it is you do need.'

'Practical help. I need to find out what drove Bella to suicide. While I'm out at Black Law I can't do that. Besides, it's what you're good at. Talking. Listening. Gossip even. Someone must have some idea why she felt she had to kill herself.'

'Would she want you to do that? It seems ... an invasion of privacy.'

'She arranged for me to find her. She knew me. She knew I'd ask questions.'

'Well then, where do we start?' Edie had used the same question when, occasionally, they had taken the bus together for the long trek into Newcastle. They had stood at the Haymarket looking down Northumberland Street at the heaving shops. Rachael had always preferred open spaces and felt overwhelmed, panicky, but Edie's approach to shopping had been methodical.

'Well then, where do we start?' And she had taken out her list and organized the day: Farnons for school uniform, Bainbridge's for curtain material, lunch in the studenty café opposite the Theatre Royal, M & S for knickers and socks and back to the Haymarket for the three o'clock bus.

Again Rachael was reassured. 'I thought the funeral.'

'Who's arranging that?'

'Neville, Dougie's son. I had to let them know what had happened, though it didn't occur to me at first. I never thought of him having any connection with Bella. She didn't talk about him much. But of course he had to know about Dougie, and there's the farm to see to. They're just coming up to lambing . . .'

'And he took responsibility for the funeral.'

'Yes, he said he'd like to. I asked if he'd mind if I put a notice in the *Gazette*. She was well thought of by the other hill farmers. Some of her friends or family might see it and turn up.' She turned to Edie. 'All that time and I really knew nothing about her. I don't know if her parents are still alive, if she has brothers or sisters, even where she was born. We talked and talked about me, but about her it was only Dougie and the farm. Neville asked if there were relatives he should notify and I couldn't tell him.'

'Couldn't Dougie help?'

'I never knew about Dougie. Bella chatted to him in exactly the same way as before the stroke, but I sometimes thought she was deluding herself that he understood it all. He certainly responded to simple questions. "Do you want a drink?" "Shall I open a window?" But beyond that?' She shrugged. 'And perhaps she never told him much about her past either. He loved her so much he wouldn't have cared.'

'Where's Dougie living now?'

'A nursing home. Rosemount. Do you know it?'

'Mm. I know the night sister. I taught her son. There were problems. I was able to help a bit. So . . .'

'She owes you a favour?'

'She might be able to help a bit too?'

'I suppose you think I'm crazy,' Rachael said. They were almost at the bottom of the bottle. 'You probably think I should accept she's dead and get on with things. Why dredge up the past, right?'

'Could you do that? Just turn your back on it?'

'No.'

'Then what's the point in asking the question?'

Rachael was on her way to bed when Edie asked: 'It couldn't have anything to do with the quarry?'

'What do you mean?'

'You said she loved the hills. Could she bear a great scar cut across them, explosives, lorries. I know it's not on her land but she'd see it, wouldn't she? Every day.'

'She'd hate it but she wouldn't just give up. She'd fight it. Lie down in front of the bulldozers if she had to.'

'But if she knew, in the end, none of that would do any good?'

'How could she know that? We haven't started work yet. Until we've finished our work, until the public inquiry, no decision can be made. And it wouldn't have mattered as much as being with Dougie. In the end that was all she cared about.'

Chapter Four

Rachael worked from a large scale map. She had already chosen her survey areas using the natural boundaries shown on the map. Neither sample was on Black Law land. One, a patch close to the burn and the disused lead mine, was heavily grazed. It was farmed by one of the Holme Park tenants, almost denuded of heather. It would be easy for walking but not, she suspected, very interesting for birds. The other was a piece of heather moorland, managed for grouse. It had been leased by the Holme Park Estate to a syndicate of Italian businessmen. She suspected they would not find the shooting so enjoyable with the industrial noise of the quarry in the background, but she presumed that Slateburn Quarries had offered the estate such a tempting deal that income from the shooting rights would hardly be missed.

The lowland square was easy to plot. The Skirl formed one boundary. The other two were fences put up to keep in the sheep, which met at a right angle. The fourth was the remains of a track which led on past Baikie's, crossed the burn by a simple bridge and continued to the mine. On the map she drew lines, parallel with the burn, which crossed the survey square. On the ground these transects would be 200 metres apart. She would walk them, counting all the birds she heard or saw. This was the system known as the Kemp Methodology.

The moorland patch was less easy to define. The map showed drainage ditches, a dry stone wall, but even in good visibility she knew it would be hard to keep to the transect lines in such a featureless landscape. Some surveyors were sloppy. They seemed to think a slight variation from the map was hardly significant. Rachael was obsessive about accuracy. She despised estimated counts and counts which were hurried. She refused to work if the weather conditions would affect the outcome of the count. She would accept drizzle but never wind. Wind kept the birds low and drowned the call of the waders.

The morning of her return from Edie's she arrived too late to take a count, which had to start at dawn and be completed in three hours. It was such a still day, clear, more like June than April, that she regretted for a moment having stayed away. She had expected Anne and Grace to be out already, taking advantage of the weather to begin their own work, but they were still at Baikie's. There was the smell of bacon and coffee. Grace was in the living room working on a map stretched over the floor but Anne was sitting on a white wrought iron bench outside the kitchen door, her face turned to the sun. She waved her mug at Rachael.

'Help yourself to coffee. There should be some in the pot and it's still warm. I brought my own. Can't stand instant.' She threw a piece of bacon rind from her plate onto the grass.

'You shouldn't feed birds at this time of year,' Rachael said. 'It's not good for the young.'

'Sorry, Miss.' She grinned. Rachael felt herself blushing and turned into the kitchen. The place was a mess. The plates of the previous night's meal had not been washed. She tried to ignore it.

'I'm going up to check my moorland square,' she called to Anne outside. 'I'm not sure yet that all the boundary features are visible. Are you planning to go out?'

'I'm just working up to it.'

'You will clear this up first.' She regretted the words as soon as they were spoken. They made her sound like a girl guide leader. Anne must have heard them but she didn't answer. When Rachael walked past her on her way to the hill she was still sitting in the sun, her eyes closed but she didn't say goodbye.

On the wall by the side of the track there were three wheatears, flicking their tails to show white rumps. Each year Bella had pointed out the first wheatears. 'Black and white,' she'd said once to Rachael. 'Winter colours. It seems wrong they should come in the spring. It's the same with ring ouzel. Still, I suppose it's never far from winter up here.'

Rachael had suggested once that Bella might like to go on holiday. Somewhere hot with strong bright colours. Social services would organize respite care for Dougie. But Bella had been horrified by the suggestion. 'I couldn't leave him,' she'd said. 'I'd miss him too much. How could I enjoy myself, wondering what they were doing to him?'

'Wouldn't Neville come for a while?'

'He might. But he's not used to Dougie. It wouldn't do.'

The track crossed the stream and came to the old

lead mine. The estate had talked once of doing it up, turning it into a living museum, but nothing had come of it. Soon there would be little left to preserve. There was still a chimney but it was crumbling from the top, eaten into by the weather, so the brickwork seemed to unravel like a piece of knitting. There had been a row of cottages to house the workers but only one still had a roof. There was the smell of stale water and decay. By the door of the old engine house she saw a posy of flowers – lily of the valley and pale narcissi. She thought a child had been raiding Baikie's garden while being dragged out for a walk, then remembered she had seen flowers there on other occasions.

If Godfrey Waugh had his way this site would be the nerve centre of the new quarry. It proved, he said, that the hills had always had an industrial use too. They weren't just there for tourists to gawp at. The houses would be demolished and replaced by a structure more in keeping with the nature of the operation, a building with clean lines, made of glass and local stone. Rachael had seen an artist's impression of the proposed block. It appeared low and inconspicuous, built into the hill. Through the large windows you could see sketches of women sitting at computer terminals. There were landscaped surroundings, a belt of newly planted trees. No pictures had been shown of the quarry itself, of the blasting and the lorries and the machines with claws and diggers. There were, though, details of the plan to renovate the mine chimney. According to the PR men, it would be a symbol of continuity. Already it appeared on the company logo.

From the mine Rachael broke away from the track and took the direct climb to the top of Hope Crag.

From there she could lock onto her moorland survey square. The land sloped gently in a series of plateaux to the horizon, which was softened by woodland around Holme Park House and the village of Langholme. The keeper had been burning heather in rotation to provide a supply of new green buds for the red grouse. There were strips and patches in different stages of growth. It was the habitat she most enjoyed working. She lay on her stomach looking down on it. There was a soft westerly breeze blowing into her face and all around her was the song of meadow pipit, skylark and curlew.

She saw at once that it would be as difficult to define the survey area as she had anticipated but now she considered that only a challenge. There was a straight drainage ditch which would mark one boundary and a wall, collapsed in places, which would do as another. The rest she would have to manage with map and compass. Not many surveyors could achieve satisfactory accuracy by this method but she would.

The knowledge gave her confidence. She got up quickly and began to walk down the crag, leaning back into the slope and kicking her heels into the heather to make better progress, towards a block of conifers. There was a path through the Forestry Commission plantation which would take her almost into the Black Law farmyard. It was possible that Anne Preece was still at Baikie's working on the maps and Rachael wanted to set things straight between them. It wouldn't do to let resentment simmer. Edie, of course, would have known exactly what to say. *She* always made too much of these differences, or not enough, but still she was the project leader and it was her responsibility to sort it out.

She came down the slope at such a pace that at the bottom she had to stop for a moment to catch her breath before setting off across the damp area of juncous and cotton grass towards the trees. She crouched and stretched to ease the muscles in her legs, then turned back for a last look at the crag.

Someone was there, standing just where Rachael had been lying on her stomach minutes before. It hardly seemed possible that she had not seen them approaching. She had been looking out over the fell so they must have followed her up the path from the lead mine, but quietly, not making their presence known. Rachael was looking into strong sunlight so the figure appeared only as a silhouette next to the outcrop, almost as another finger of rock. It stood very still, apparently staring directly down at Rachael. She was reminded suddenly of the man who had been on the hill on the evening of Bella's suicide. The disturbing sensation of being watched returned.

But she had the impression that this was a woman. The shape, blocked against the sun, was of a woman with short hair, or hair pulled away from her face, wearing a full skirt over boots. For one fanciful moment Rachael thought of Bella, who'd always preferred skirts to trousers and often wore them with wellingtons around the farm. Rachael had slung her binoculars over her shoulder for the yomp down the hill. Now, after freezing for a moment, surprised by the figure, she twisted her arm out of the strap and raised them to her eyes, but in that moment of focusing the woman must have moved behind the pile of rocks. There was nothing but the crag, with a wheatear in the shadow, hopping on one of the boulders.

It must have been a walker, she thought, or Anne come to make her peace with me. Though Anne, like Grace, had been wearing jeans.

She was unsettled again when she came to the crow trap. It was built on a piece of dryer ground close to the forestry plantation, close enough for her to smell the spruce. She knew keepers hated crows – even Bella had wanted rid of them – but she thought this was a particularly horrid form of control, not for the birds which were killed but for the one which played decoy.

The trap was a large wire mesh cage with a funnel in the top. Inside a live, tame crow fluttered provocatively, inviting in another to defend its territory. Once in through the funnel there was no way out. Presumably they had to find some form of co-existence until the keeper came along to put the intruder out of its misery.

The keeper moved the trap at regular intervals. Crows were territorial creatures and wouldn't fly far, even for a fight. The last time she had seen the cage it had been on the edge of the moor near the lead mine. She had been with Peter and he had made one of his outrageous gallant jokes. Then, in her naivety, she had been flattered by them. They had seen two birds in the trap and he had said: 'Look, they're just like us. You've caught me and now there's no escape.'

She had smiled, but even then, even though she had wanted to believe him, she had known it was the other way round.

Chapter Five

Rachael was a postgraduate student at Durham University when she first met Peter Kemp. She took her first degree in Cambridge, almost as far away from Edie as she could manage, then she moved back to the north, not to be close to her mother but because the uplands had become her passion. She started by studying black grouse then transferred her interest to upland wading birds like curlew and snipe. When she met Peter she was devising a system for counting them accurately. She used Baikie's Cottage as her base. Bella had already become a friend.

It was a windy day in April. She had come into Kimmerston at the request of Bob Hewlett, English Nature Conservation Officer, who saw her project as a way of obtaining useful data on the cheap. She had come across Bob before and didn't like him much. He was a middle-aged man who dressed in tweeds. He drove a Land Rover with a couple of black Labradors in the back, looking very much the country landowner. Rachael thought he was too close to local farmers, too desperate to be accepted by them, to do his job properly. He lived in Langholme and she'd seen him, drinking in the pub, all back-slapping chums together. However, she knew better than to offend him – she might want to work for the government's conservation agency one day – and when he invited her to lunch at the White Hart to discuss her project she accepted graciously.

'I've invited Peter Kemp to join us later,' Bob said suddenly as the food arrived. 'He's doing the same sort of stuff as you for the Wildlife Trust. You might be able to help each other out.'

It was the first time she'd heard Peter's name though Bob assumed she knew who he was talking about.

The White Hart was a solid, stone-built hotel on Kimmerston's wide main street. Once it had been the only place to eat in the town. Now there was a tandoori restaurant, a pizzeria and a Chinese takeaway, and the White Hart had grown shabby. On Friday nights the public bar was a haunt for underage drinkers. Often it became rowdy, with petty skirmishes and visits by the police. During the rest of the week there was an air of genteel decay. The elderly waitresses, in their black and white uniforms, had few people to serve, even on market day, when for once the restaurant was full. The food was proudly traditional, in that the vegetables were overcooked and a brown glutinous gravy was offered with everything. When Rachael admitted to being a vegetarian there was something of a crisis. At last a leathery cheese omelette appeared.

As he mentioned Peter Kemp, Bob beamed at her across the table. His tone was that of a bucolic uncle, rather too familiar for her taste. Despite the Land Rover parked outside he had a couple of Scotches while they were waiting to order, and since then a pint to wash down the meal. Rachael decided that Peter Kemp must be new to the Wildlife Trust. She knew most of the team. She was certain that she would dislike him; she needed no help with her project. Edie would have dealt sharply with Bob's patronizing attitude – the insinuating smile, the shepherding hand on the small of her back – but Rachael always found it hard to be assertive without being rude.

She first saw Peter hovering in the doorway of the dining room. He was half hidden by a dark oak dresser which held smudged glass cruet sets and portion-controlled sachets of tartare sauce. She saw an arthritic waitress approach him to tell him that he was too late for lunch. He shook his head and gave her a lovely smile before pointing in their direction. Rachael could tell that the old lady would remember the smile for the rest of the day. He looked very young – a sixth former let out from school for the afternoon, let out, almost certainly, from a good public school. As he walked towards them he smiled with the charming diffidence which was his hallmark, but she could sense the confidence which comes with an expensive education.

He was physically fit. She could sense that too. Even crossing the floral carpet of the dining room he had a long loping stride. He arrived at the table and reached out a hand to greet Bob formally. They exchanged a few words and then he turned to her. She had to half rise in her seat to take his hand and felt awkward, at a disadvantage.

'Of course I know your name from the Bird Report,' he said. 'And from colleagues. You know, of course, that you've an impressive reputation.'

His voice was earnest, the schoolboy again, trying

to please. She knew she was being worked on, but since the smile to the waitress, she'd found it impossible to resist him.

Even as she submitted to the flattery she realized that Peter wanted something from her. He said he'd like to visit her study area and compare the methods she'd devised for her survey with his own. By the time Bob Hewlett had drunk his second pint and she and Peter had shared a pot of coffee she had invited him to Baikie's for a couple of days to watch her work. When she left the hotel she felt she was more unsteady on her feet than Bob, who was certainly not quite sober and drove off waving with the Labradors barking madly in the back.

That spring Peter spent more than a couple of days at Baikie's. In the end he was there more often than he was in the office, and he stayed most nights. His excuse was that the Wildlife Trust intended to buy an upland reserve. It probably wouldn't be in this part of the county but he needed to establish a baseline of moorland species in order to select a good area to target. She knew this was an excuse – he could use her data once the project was over – and she was delighted.

Her excuse for being taken in by him was her inexperience. When she was at university she had an affair with an older man, a lecturer of material science. It was doomed to failure. Even Rachael, despising as she did Edie's psychobabble, could tell that it was not a lover for which she was searching but a father, and Euan had been unsatisfactory on both counts. She had never before had a relationship with a man of her own age, had never even gone in much for friends of either sex, so the passion for Peter had the intensity of an adolescent crush.

Edie of course saw through him at once. Rachael made the mistake of taking him to meet her one Sunday. It was May, a humid sultry day and they had lunch in the garden. It should have been a relaxed affair but Edie took against Peter from the start. She glared into her wine glass as they made conversation across her. The more hostile she appeared the more Peter tried to charm her. Even Rachael could tell that he was coming over as flash and insincere. Later she expected a lecture about her choice in men but Edie was uncharacteristically restrained.

'A bit showy for my taste,' she said in a stage whisper as she followed Rachael into the kitchen with a tray of dirty plates. 'Never trust the showy ones.'

But it was the show which captivated Rachael and which would be her downfall. She loved the way Peter disappeared from Baikie's with talk of a meeting at Trust Headquarters, only to return at dusk with flowers and champagne. She loved dancing with him on the lawn to the music from Constance's old wind-up gramophone. No one had ever made such a fuss of her before.

She couldn't discuss this extravagance with Edie, who would disapprove of these gestures of chauvinism, even if she hadn't taken such a dislike to him. So when she needed to share her happiness Rachael went to Black Law farm for a gossip with Bella. Bella encouraged her belief in love at first sight – hadn't it happened to her and Dougie? – and followed their romance with sympathy and interest.

'What are your plans then?' she would ask. 'You will see him once the contract's over?'

'We don't talk about it much,' Rachael answered. 'We, you know, live for the minute.'

She didn't go into precise details about what living for the minute involved, though Bella would have understood. It seemed in poor taste to talk about skinny-dipping in the tarn by moonlight, making love in the heather, when Dougie couldn't walk without help. And she did have plans, secret plans which she wouldn't admit to anyone, not even Bella. These might not have included a wedding with a white frock, though suspect images of that sort did float occasionally round the edge of her subconscious, but they were about her and Peter setting up home together and having children. Edie would be horrified of course, but what Rachael really wanted was to be a proper mother in a proper family.

The first betrayal, the worst one, came two months after Peter had left the Wildlife Trust to set up his own consultancy. Rachael had been in on the scheme from the start and having completed her MSc she started working for him. She had her own desk and computer terminal in the small office which was all he could afford. She acted as receptionist, secretary and main scientist.

Now, there were no bottles of champagne and few nights of passion. She still dreamed. She understood that money was tight and that he had been under considerable stress. It couldn't have been easy to give up a steady job to go it alone. It was enough that she could be there in the crowded, chaotic office to support, that occasionally he would brush his lips over her hair and say, 'You do know, don't you, that I wouldn't be able to manage all this without you?'

Then she saw an article by him in *New Scientist*. It described a new methodology for counting upland birds. It was the methodology which she had devised, and indeed she was acknowledged in very small print at the end of the paper, along with half a dozen others, including Anne Preece. But he took the credit for it. He claimed it as his own. In a comment, welcoming the new system, the magazine's editor wrote: 'It is clear that the Kemp methodology, with its accuracy, clarity and simplicity, will become a benchmark for Upland surveys. In the future it should be the recommended system for all such work.'

Because of the article Peter was suddenly very much in demand. Now work flooded into the office and he was asked to organize seminars for other agencies. Often he asked Rachael to prepare his notes and the diagrams for the overhead projector. She did as he asked without making a fuss, though she could no longer bear for him to touch her.

She often wondered why she didn't confront him with this betrayal. Why, indeed, did she continue to work for him, supporting the business through its expansion to a new, smart office? Of course there was a practical reason. It would be hard to find such a suitable job, paying a living wage, in the north of England. But she knew that wasn't really important. It was a matter of pride. If she resigned from Kemp Associates she would have to admit to others and to herself that Peter had made a fool of her. She would have to accept the possibility that his only reason for making love to her was to steal her ideas, to concede that Edie had been right. It was better to let the world think that Peter had devised the method for counting upland birds. She was sure that by now he believed it himself.

The second betrayal came in the form of a large square envelope, which she found one morning propped on her desk. It contained an invitation to Peter's wedding. There seemed to be no spiteful intent in informing her of his marriage in this way. He presumed that she accepted the affair at Baikie's as a pleasant thing, a piece of fun. After all there had been no intimacy between them for months. She learnt from colleagues that the fiancée was called Amelia. It was Anne Preece, flitting into the office one day in the search for work, who provided more detail.

'Amelia?' she said. 'Oh, she's quite debby in a rather down-market way. Not aristocratic, not really interesting. A potential extra, you know, in the crowd scenes in *Hello!* magazine. She'd have been quite pretty if her parents had made her wear a brace.'

No one at work thought Rachael had more than a passing interest in her boss's engagement, so at last, when she felt the need to confide her misery, she made an excuse to spend a night at Baikie's. She invited Bella to supper and snuffled her way through a box of tissues and two bottles of wine. She woke with a hangover and the belief that she was free of the influence of Peter Kemp.

It was only the crow, hopping pathetically in the trap, which brought him back to mind.

Chapter Six

Rachael had planned in detail what she would say to Anne when she got back to Baikie's after her walk on the moor. 'Look, I'm sorry for being such a bossy cow. You must understand. It's my first time as project leader and I'm nervous about it. I don't want any cock-ups.'

But when she arrived at the cottage it was empty. The kitchen was tidy. The plates had been washed and dried. Grace and Anne had left details of where they would be on their hill and their estimated time of return, which was more than Rachael had done. In her irritation at finding the house in a state she'd stormed off without leaving her route information, though it was a rule which she had insisted none of them should ever break. The white sheets of paper, covered with scribbled grid references and times set squarely side by side on the table in the living room, seemed like an accusation.

Anne returned at precisely the time she'd stated. When Rachael tried to apologize for her earlier irritation Anne brushed it aside.

'Don't be daft,' she said. 'There's no need to apologize. We should be able to take it. We're adults, aren't we? Not a bunch of kids.'

This remark, which Rachael at first took as a gesture of conciliation, in the end seemed another criticism. Didn't it imply that Rachael had done just that? Treated them like children.

Her inability to find the right tone in her dealings with Anne and Grace, the feeling that she either took too much control or lost control altogether, dominated her thoughts in the next few days. It was impossible to take a consistent line. The women were so different. Anne was confident, lippy, almost reckless. Grace seemed unnaturally withdrawn. It was Grace who most worried Rachael. She seemed to have grown paler, less substantial even in the days since she arrived. She volunteered little information, except about her work. Speech had to be prised from her. She hardly ate. She picked at her food, pushing it around her plate with a fork. Rachael wondered about anorexia. Once, in desperation, when it seemed Grace had consumed nothing all day, she said, 'You must eat, you know. Especially if you're doing a lot of walking.' Then, tentatively, 'You don't have a problem, do you, about food?'

It was hard for Rachael to ask. She had been the subject of Edie's prying sympathy. Throughout her childhood and adolescence Edie had been on the lookout for signs of trauma. She had imagined bullying, drug abuse, even pregnancy. Discreet, or not so discreet, questions were asked. Occasionally leaflets about contraception appeared on Rachael's bed. So Rachael knew the value of privacy.

To her relief Grace smiled. Perhaps, after all, she was just shy. 'I've never been much of an eater. Picky I'm afraid. I've brought a supply of chocolate. You musn't worry about me. I'm fit as a lop.'

42

This was an expression Rachael hadn't heard since childhood, and then only used by old people.

And Grace did seem fit. She covered miles of riverbank every day and arrived back at the cottage at dusk showing no signs of exertion. Sometimes Rachael watched her approaching over the flat land from the Skirl burn, her pace so even that she seemed to be floating, pale in the gloom like one of the short-eared owls that hunted over the low fields near the farm.

The day before Bella's funeral Peter Kemp turned up at Baikie's Cottage. Rachael had been up at four, out on the hill at five and was back, eating breakfast, getting warm. Overnight there'd been a fresh scattering of snow on the tops. Now it was sunny, but a gusty wind had blown up on the last transect. If it had been like that when she started she wouldn't have bothered. Grace was walking a river on the Holme Park Estate. Anne was in the kitchen, filling a flask, almost ready to go out. She heard the car first, went to see who it was and called to Rachael.

'Christ Almighty! Come and look at this!'

The last thing Rachael wanted was to get out of the chair, leave the fire and her toast, but Anne wasn't always so good-humoured. It would have been churlish to ignore the request. She took her coffee and stood in her stockinged feet at the kitchen door. It was Peter, driving a brand new Range Rover with a discreet Peter Kemp Associates logo stuck to the passengers' door. Rachael hadn't seen the car before, hadn't known even that its purchase was planned, but made no comment. Anne wasn't so restrained.

'So that's why you pay your contract staff peanuts,' she said, teasing him but also making a serious point. She always felt undervalued. 'We sacrifice a living wage so the boss can swan around in a Range Rover.'

He was unoffended, grinned wolfishly. Rachael turned back into the house.

'It's all about giving the punters confidence,' she heard him say. 'You're a bright lady. You'll understand that.'

His tone was flirtatious. Rachael, who knew of Anne's reputation for wildness, promiscuity, wondered if they'd ever had an affair, if, despite Amelia, they were having one now.

'Well, as I'm just a wage slave,' Anne said, 'I'd better get on with some work. I'd hate to get the sack.'

'No chance of that, sweetie,' he replied easily. 'You're the best botanist in the county.'

If there was an answer Rachael didn't hear it. Peter came into the living room, stood with his back to the fire, blocking out the heat. 'You're not going into the field?' he said.

'I've already been. There's no point counting this late in the day. You should know that. You wrote the manual.'

He looked at her as if he didn't understand what point she was making. There were times when he could make her believe that she'd dreamt her part in the Kemp Methodology, that she was going mad. He took the other chair. 'I heard about Bella,' he said. 'I'm so sorry. That's why I came. To see how you were.'

'I'm fine.'

'No, really. I know how close you two were.'

'Really. It was a shock, but I'm fine.'

'You've no idea why she did it?'

'None.'

'I don't suppose you've heard what'll happen to the farm?'

'Dougie certainly can't manage it. Unless Neville takes it on I suppose it'll be sold. Dougie's moved into a nursing home. That'll have to be paid for.'

'What's happening over there now? They must be lambing.'

'Geoff Beck from Langholme's looking after it. I suppose Neville made the arrangements.'

It was more of an interrogation than she had been subjected to by the young policeman.

'Neville Furness. Has he been over?'

'No, I had to speak to him on the phone. He's sorting out the funeral.'

'You know he works for Slateburn Quarries?'

'I had heard.'

He turned boyish, gave her a smile. 'I don't suppose there's any chance of a coffee.'

She made him coffee but didn't offer any food. It was a trek into Kimmerston to stock up on supplies and she didn't see why they should share their rations with him. In the old days, when they were living together at Baikie's and he was still working for the trust, he'd have brought treats – fresh crusty bread from the bakery at Slateburn, pâté and Brie from the delicatessen at Kimmerston, Spanish strawberries from the supermarket, though they both knew the Costa Doñana had been drained to produce them and if they had any conscience they'd leave them alone. Today he was empty-handed and despite herself she felt cheated.

'And the project?' he asked. 'Is that going well?'

'So far. Very well.'

'Anne's a trooper of course, but Grace is settling in, is she? I've heard great things of her.'

'She certainly seems to know her subject.'

Rachael had no intention of discussing Grace's health or her state of mind with Peter. It had become a habit to reveal as little as possible. Besides, to discuss the women's problems would have seemed like telling tales.

'So we're on schedule?'

'Ahead of schedule. We've been lucky with the weather.'

'Good. That's good.'

Still he seemed reluctant to go. He sat in the tatty chair which would have looked disreputable in a student bedsit, which would certainly have no place in the flat he shared with Amelia, and clutched his empty coffee cup. She realized that he wanted to talk to her. He was building up to a confession or confidence, even to an apology. She didn't want to hear what he had to say. Not about his wife or his work or his affairs.

'Will you come to the funeral?' she asked abruptly.

'I don't know. I hadn't thought.'

'I think you should. Bella was a great help to Peter Kemp Associates.'

'Perhaps I will then.'

'And if you have queries about the farm you can ask Neville.'

'Yes.' But still he sounded uncertain.

'Look,' she said. 'I'm knackered. I could do with a couple of hours' sleep before I go out again this evening.' Though she could tell already that the wind would be too strong.

'Of course. I should go anyway. A meeting with English Nature. The possibility of more work. Good news, huh?'

Her only response was to stand up to show she expected him to leave immediately. He had left his jacket in the kitchen. It had been flung on the bench as he came in. His boots were on the doorstep. He laced them, then put on the jacket, turning up the collar. Rachael didn't bother putting on her outdoor clothes, but stood in the doorway to see him off. At the Range Rover he turned to face her and gave a sad little wave of farewell.

The car pulled away slowly and suddenly she ran after it, shouting, banging the door panel where the logo had been stuck. Even wearing the thick oiled socks the yard felt very cold under her feet. Peter braked and looked eagerly out of the window. Perhaps he thought after all he would be given the opportunity to confide in her.

'There's something I have to ask.'

'Anything, of course.'

'Did you come to see Bella, the afternoon she died?'

For a moment he was stunned. He seemed unable to speak but perhaps that was only because he had been expecting a different question.

'No,' he said at last. 'Why would I? It was your project.'

'You weren't out on the hill?'

'No. Why do you ask?'

She shook her head and stood back from the Range Rover. He hesitated and then he drove away.

She was convinced he had lied. The memory had been triggered as he stood by the car and turned to wave goodbye. It was something about his posture and the shape of the jacket with the collar pulled up. It had been Peter she had seen caught in her headlights as she crossed Black Law ford on the night of Bella's suicide. And he had lied.

Chapter Seven

Bella's remains were disposed of at the large crematorium at Kimmerston. For some reason Rachael had imagined her buried at Langholme churchyard, which was, in effect, another piece of in-bye land, with sheep grazing just on the other side of a low stone wall and Fairburn Crag in the distance. If she'd been buried, at least Rachael would have had a grave to visit. But Neville and Dougie – if Dougie had any say in the matter which she doubted – had decided on the cremation. There was piped Vivaldi and a vicar who seemed to know nothing about Bella to lead the dreary service.

The day of the funeral Grace stayed at Baikie's, though Rachael had offered her a lift into town.

'I don't mean that you should come to the crematorium. Why should you? You'd never even met Bella. But you're due some time off. Treat yourself to lunch or a browse in the bookshops. We could meet up later for a meal . . .'

But Grace had declined the offer. 'I know it's not allowed to go onto the hill without someone there to check me back in, but I've got loads to do. I mean it'll be a really good chance to look at the material I've got so far.' She'd paused, coloured. 'Besides, a friend might visit. Perhaps stay the night. You wouldn't mind, would you?'

'Oh no!' Rachael was pleased that there was someone else, that she wasn't entirely responsible for Grace's welfare. 'If you've got company we won't have to rush back.'

Though she didn't like to admit it, she hadn't been looking forward to the drive into Kimmerston with Grace, whose distracted silences deadened the conversation around her. Anne Preece could be irritating and opinionated but she was at least normal. At this thought Rachael felt a stab of guilt. She heard Edie's voice in her head: What right have you to judge? And what's normal anyway?

They arrived at the crematorium early – Rachael was incapable of being late – and they waited outside for a moment, unsure of the proper procedure. There was still a gusty wind which blew clouds across the sun and flattened the dying daffodils which had been planted along the outside wall. Rachael had visited the crematorium once before in autumn. A rare bird, a Bonelli's warbler, had turned up in the Garden of Rest. Birdwatchers from all over the country had arrived with their telescopes and tripods, mingling with bereaved relatives and irate funeral directors. Later she had described the scene to Bella, who had laughed. She remembered Bella, standing in Black Law kitchen, holding the teapot with the tannin-stained cosy, chuckling so that tea spilt over the table, and for the first time that day she felt close to tears.

Inside the chapel she chose a seat close to the aisle so she could watch the mourners. The building was almost empty. Edie arrived and squeezed in beside her, touched her hand. Rachael felt the sympathy physically. It was like someone jostling her in a queue, thrusting a face too close to hers, demanding a response. She wanted to push her mother away. She thought, I should never have gone to see her, never asked for her help.

There were a few people whom Anne recognized from Langholme. She identified them in a whisper: the postmistress and her husband, the young couple who farmed Wandylaw, tenants of the estate. Peter sat with Amelia close to the back, very smart in the expensive suit he wore for impressing potential clients. If there had been more people in the chapel Rachael would have resented Amelia's presence. Surely she had never met Bella and she seemed to be there on sufferance, though she too had dressed up. She sat at some distance from Peter and stared with an engrossed concentration at her immaculately shaped nails. As it was, Rachael was glad that there was one more person to mark Bella's passing.

'Good God!' The exclamation came involuntarily from Anne as a middle-aged couple came in. The woman had her hand on the man's arm. They seemed pleasant, ordinary. Rachael hoped that at last these were relatives of Bella's or friends from her past.

'Who is it?'

'Only Godfrey Waugh and his wife. What the hell are they doing here? He's got a nerve.'

Godfrey Waugh was a director of Slateburn Quarries, the moving force behind the development at Black Law, the reason for Anne, Grace and Rachael being in Baikie's. For their counting on the hills. He seemed mild and inoffensive to have caused such disruption.

Rachael was disappointed, felt oddly that she had to stand up for him.

'They live at Slateburn, don't they? I suppose in a way they were neighbours.'

But Anne was still fuming. 'Well, I think it's a bloody cheek.'

Rachael thought she would express her feelings more forcefully, but she had to shut up because the proceedings were starting.

Dougie was in a wheelchair pushed by Neville. Rachael thought he was not as smartly turned out as Bella would have liked. He was wearing his best suit but his shirt collar was crumpled. Whoever had shaved him had missed a patch on his cheek. His shoes could have done with a polish. Neville, in contrast, was impeccably dressed. He was a short, muscular man with hair which was the blue-black of crow's feathers and a full black beard. His shirt looked startlingly white against his dark skin and his shoes gleamed.

The vicar had already started speaking when the door banged open again. Rachael was reminded of an old, bad British movie, though whether it was a thriller or a comedy she couldn't quite say. The vicar paused in mid-sentence and they all turned to stare. Even Dougie tried to move his head in that direction.

It was a woman in her fifties. The first impression was of a bag lady, who'd wandered in from the street. She had a large leather satchel slung across her shoulder and a supermarket carrier bag in one hand. Her face was grey and blotched. She wore a knee-length skirt and a long cardigan weighed down at the front by the pockets. Her legs were bare. Yet she carried off the situation with such confidence and aplomb that they all believed that she had a right to be there. She took a seat, bowed her head as if in private prayer, then looked directly at the vicar as if giving him permission to continue.

Neville had booked a room in the White Hart Hotel and afterwards invited them all back to lunch. Anne gave her apologies, then when no one could overhear she gave Rachael a sly grin.

'You don't mind, do you? Only I do actually have better things to do with a free afternoon than stand around in the White Hart nibbling egg sandwiches, trying to avoid talking about the fact that Bella committed suicide. I mean she chose to do it, didn't she? I find it hard to feel sorry for her. I know you were mates, but there it is.'

Rachael guessed that she'd arranged to meet a man. Anne's sexual appetite was legendary, and she was wearing a little black dress and jacket which would do just as well for a discreet dinner as for the draughty crematorium. Rachael could tell she was itching to get away as soon as they were outside.

'Where shall I meet you?' she asked.

Anne hesitated. 'Look, I'm not sure what's happening. I quite fancy a night in my own bed. I'll get Jeremy to drop me off at Baikie's first thing tomorrow.'

It took Rachael a while to remember that Jeremy was Anne's long-suffering husband.

Guests at the White Hart were even thinner on the ground than at the crematorium. Godfrey Waugh stayed briefly. He had a short, intense conversation with Neville which had more, Rachael thought, to do with business than with Bella. His wife had not appeared at all.

A buffet lunch had been laid on a table against one wall. There were thick slices of cooked ham and beef, bowls of lettuce, slices of hard-boiled egg, metal ice cream bowls of a thin salad dressing which looked partly curdled. Bella's farming friends ate with relish. The hotel had provided thimble-sized glasses of sherry and whisky, but the men disappeared to the bar and returned with pints. Neville had gone to school with their sons and daughters, but they didn't treat him with the familiarity which Rachael would have expected. In contrast Edie moved easily among them, listening to the conversation, chatting, asking about children who'd been through her class at the sixth form college.

Peter and Amelia turned up eventually. There was a frostiness between them which made Rachael think they'd had a row in the car. Amelia made a show of ignoring the food, then disappeared into the ladies'.

'You see,' Peter said. 'I came. You know I always take your advice.'

Christ, Rachael thought, was I really taken in by that sort of thing?

His eyes wandered over her shoulder and she realized he was checking that they could not be overheard. 'What made you think I was at Bella's the afternoon she died?'

'Nothing. It was a silly mistake.'

He pressed her but she wouldn't say any more. At last he seemed satisfied.

Of the ugly woman with the bags there was no sign. Rachael stayed longer than she otherwise would have done, expecting the stranger to make a dramatic late entrance as she had at the crematorium. She asked around, but no one seemed to know who the woman was. Then she realized that Dougie too was missing and thought perhaps the woman was a relative of his, that they were spending some time together.

She was just about to gather up Edie to go when she was startled by a touch on the shoulder. She turned sharply to find Neville so close to her that she could see a stray white hair in his beard, smell the soap he had used.

'I'm glad you were able to come,' he said. 'You are Rachael? I wasn't sure you'd be able to face it. Not after . . .'

She interrupted him quickly, not because he seemed in the slightest embarrassed but because there was a real point to be made. 'I couldn't have missed it. We were real friends, Bella and I.'

'She used to talk about you.'

'Did she?' Rachael was surprised. She hadn't realized there'd been that much contact between Neville and Bella.

'Oh yes.' Because he was short for a man she looked almost straight into his eyes. 'Had you been in touch lately?'

'No.'

'Ah, I thought you might have some idea why . . .'

'No.'

'I was fond of her, you know. I was very young when Mum died. I was glad when Dad found someone else. I was pleased for them.'

'Of course.' Bella had never mentioned him much at all, but that hardly seemed an appropriate thing to say. 'How is your father?'

For the first time he seemed embarrassed. 'How can anyone know?'

'Bella always seemed to.'

'Did she? I thought that was self-delusion. Her way of facing it. I can't, you know. Face it. Not really. That's why I've been so bad about visiting lately.'

'Is someone from the nursing home giving him a lift?'

She hoped he might put a name to the woman with the bags but Neville said sharply: 'He's not coming here. He's gone straight back to Rosemount. They say he's better keeping to a routine.'

'I see.' Rachael hoped that Neville had at least asked Dougie if he wanted to be ferried straight back to the home. Dougie always enjoyed a party, even after his illness. They'd had a do at Baikie's at the end of her project. Peter had been there, and all the other students. One of the boys had brought a violin. Bella had wrapped Dougie up and wheeled him down the track to the cottage. Rachael could picture him, watching the dancing, his eyes gleaming, beating time with his good hand to the fiddle music.

Chapter Eight

Rachael and Edie stood outside the White Hart Hotel. Rachael's attention was distracted for a moment by a black car which drove past them up the street. She thought she recognized Anne Preece sitting in the passenger seat but didn't see the driver.

'Come home for something proper to eat,' Edie said. 'I've made soup. I thought it would be comforting.'

'Very mumsy.'

'I can do it,' Edie said grandly, 'if I want to.'

They ate the soup in the kitchen at Riverside Terrace.

'Well?' Edie said. 'What did you make of that?' Rachael imagined her asking the same question of her Theatre Studies group after a trip to the Theatre Royal in Newcastle. They would regard her with the same awkward silence which was Rachael's response now, unwilling to commit themselves, preferring something more specific.

'I'm not sure.'

'Think!' Edie could never, Rachael thought, have been anything other than a teacher. 'I mean what does it tell us?'

'Nothing,' Rachael said in frustration. 'Nothing at all.'

'Of course it does. Doesn't it seem odd that there was no one there from her past? No old school friend, no cousin.'

'There was the woman with the bags.'

'I'm not sure about her. If she was a genuine mourner why didn't she make herself known?'

'Perhaps Bella wasn't local then. The *Gazette* only goes to Kimmerston and the surrounding villages.'

'That tells us something then, doesn't it?'

'Not much.'

'In all those conversations she must have told you something about what she'd done before she turned up at the farm to look after Dougie's mum.'

'I'm not sure.' On reflection all their conversations had been one-sided. Rachael had talked about her childhood, what it had been like to be brought up by such a right-on mother as Edie, her resentment at not knowing anything about her father. Bella had listened, commented, but seldom brought her own experience into the conversation.

'Doesn't that strike you as odd?' Edie said. 'I mean, doesn't it suggest that she might have something to hide?'

'Of course not,' Rachael retorted. 'We don't all feel the need to discuss our childhood traumas with the woman behind us in the supermarket queue.'

Edie ignored the insult. 'But most of us give away some information about our family, where we went to school, work . . .'

'I think she might have gone to agricultural college,' Rachael said, 'to study horticulture. Or perhaps her parents had a market garden. She knew about gardening but she didn't enjoy it. She said she'd been put off when she was young. That's why she never bothered with a vegetable garden at Black Law. I thought it was the wind or the frost, but she said it was a luxury to buy her veg from the supermarket.'

'It's not much to go on.'

'I'm sorry. She valued her privacy. Perhaps that's not something you'd understand.'

'It's something I understand very well.' Again, unspoken, Rachael's father came between them. 'Was she married before?'

'No.'

'Why are you so certain?'

'She called Dougie her one and only true love.'

'That doesn't mean anything. People don't always marry for love.'

'Bella would.'

'Yuck! What was her maiden name? I suppose you do know that.'

'Davison.'

'And Bella? Is that short for Isabella? Any second name? So I can look in the records.'

'She signed herself I. R. Furness. I don't know what the R's for.'

'But we don't think she was local.'

'She had a local accent,' Rachael said uncertainly. 'But I had the impression that she'd lived away for a time. Perhaps she'd lost touch with people then.'

'How did she get the job at Black Law? Through the Job Centre?'

'No. Dougie put an advert in the *Gazette*. She told me about that. About seeing it and ringing him up on impulse. She did say she was desperate for work or she'd never have had the nerve. He met her at the bus stop at Langholme and brought her to the farm. It was supposed to be an interview but they ended up chatting like friends. I asked her if she didn't feel she was putting herself at risk, driving with a total stranger into the middle of nowhere. She said not once she'd seen him.' Rachael looked at her mother. 'I know. Yuck. Very romantic. But that's why I thought she'd not had any serious relationships before. She'd not had the chance to get cynical.'

'Wouldn't Dougie have taken up references?'

'I shouldn't have thought so for a minute. If he'd liked her it wouldn't have crossed his mind.'

'When was that?'

'Seven years ago. The old lady died two years later. They were married soon after. Quickly. Register Office. No fuss. That was Bella's decision. I think Dougie would have liked more of a show.'

'Why wait for Dougie's mother to die?'

'How should I know?' It came out as an ill-tempered shout. She'd had enough of talking. 'Look, I should get back.' She thought she might fit in an evening count before dusk, imagined the hill in the last of the light, the skylarks calling.

'Do you have to?'

'Why?'

'You're right. You're not the person to answer. We should speak to Dougie.'

'Grace has a friend staying. I suppose I could leave it until morning.' She could hear the reluctance in her voice. She would rather be on the hill.

'If you don't want me there I can fix up for you to go to Rosemount on your own.'

'Mother!' Rachael slapped the table with the flat of

her hand. 'Stop being so bloody understanding.' Then, after a pause, 'Don't be stupid. Of course I want you there.'

Dougie had been prepared for bed. He wore pyjamas, striped like an old-fashioned prison uniform, with Rosemount Private Nursing Home stamped in red on the collar, a thin towelling dressing gown, brown tartan slippers. The slippers had been put on the wrong feet. He had his own room, pleasant enough, looking over the garden, though it was nothing compared with the view at Black Law. It was very hot. Dougie was perspiring. Rachael had pulled off her sweater as soon as she came into the building.

Outside in the corridor there was constant noise – the clatter of a wheelchair, staff voices shouting about baths and commodes and what had happened to Mrs Price's tablets, patients, confused and distressed.

When they arrived Dougie was staring at a portable television which stood on a mock pine formica chest of drawers. The sound was so low that Rachael could hardly hear it. Dougie seemed mesmerized by the fuzzy flashing pictures.

They think he's daft, Rachael thought, and wondered angrily what Neville had told them. Yet when they went in it was clear that Dougie recognized her. The sister, who showed them into the room, was taken aback by the quick, lop-sided smile, the good hand patting the arm of the chair to indicate that Rachael should come closer.

'You've got some visitors, Mr Furness,' she said shouting, as if he had deliberately misheard her, and

Rachael thought it was the first time she had spoken directly to him. The visit had been worth it just for that.

Rachael squatted beside him, put her hand on his. 'Oh, Dougie,' she said. 'I'm so sorry.'

The sister looked at her watch, muttered something to Edie about being in her office if she was needed, and went out.

It was a strange conversation, as intensely focused as one of Edie's therapy sessions. Dougie communicated by nods, grunts, squeezes of the hand, yet they understood each other. Occasionally they were distracted by the skittering sound in the corridor of soft shoes on polished lino, a high-pitched squeal, the noise, Rachael thought, of rats in a barn, but soon they retuned to the business in hand. It came down to this: Bella had killed herself and they couldn't understand why.

'I want to find out,' Rachael said. 'Do you mind? Perhaps you would prefer she was left in peace.'

Dougie made it clear he would prefer nothing of the sort.

'I'd like to look in the house.'

He turned his head away from her and stared back at the television. At first Rachael thought she had offended him, but he clasped her fingers even tighter. It was Edie who followed his gaze, went to the chest of drawers and returned with a bunch of keys.

'Are these the Black Law keys, Dougie?'

But Rachael had already recognized them. They had hung on a cup hook in the kitchen between Dougie's Newcastle United mug and the giant yellow and green teacup from which Bella drank her coffee.

'I should tell Neville, shouldn't I, that I'll be going into the house?'

She looked at him, waiting for an answer but his concentration had gone. In the corridor there was another minor disturbance. A woman screamed in a high, thin voice: 'Go away, don't touch me. Your hands are wet. Your hands are wet!' There were running footsteps, soothing voices but Dougie seemed not to hear.

Rachael, still crouched on the floor, turned so she was speaking almost into his ear, a child whispering secrets, forcing him to pay attention.

'Tell me, Dougie, do you remember the day Bella died?'

He continued to stare at the flickering images on the television but she thought he was remembering. What did he see? Bella in the house at Black Law bending over his bed? Bella dressing up to die?

'Did anyone come to Black Law that day? I expect you heard me. I drove through the yard just as it was getting dark. All the dogs started barking. But did anyone come before that?'

He seemed lost in thought.

'Was anyone there before me, Dougie?'

She was aware of an effort of memory. He nodded.

'Inside the house?'

He nodded again.

'Did you see them? Do you know who it was? Or hear a voice you could recognize?'

Painfully he shook his head.

Chapter Nine

Overnight the wind had dropped. There was frost in the valley bottoms and beneath the dry stone walls. The smoke from Baikie's chimney rose straight into the sky.

Grace was in the kitchen making toast. She held the tiny grill pan close to the gas flame. Otherwise you could wait for hours. She was alone.

'Did your friend come?' Rachael asked. The smell of the toasting bread made her feel hungry. She'd left home deliberately, before Edie was up.

'Yesterday afternoon.'

'Stay the night?'

Grace shook her head, not just an answer to the question but a way of making it clear that no other information would be forthcoming. 'How was the funeral?' she asked. She put the toast on a plate, spread it thinly with margarine, cut it in half and offered a piece to Rachael. Rachael took it and added marmalade.

'Oh, you know.'

'I can't remember ever having been to a funeral,' Grace said. Rachael thought it was an odd way to put it. It wasn't a thing you'd forget. Then the door opened and Anne came in looking very pink and healthy like

a child bursting into the house demanding tea after playing out in the street with friends.

'I didn't hear the car,' Rachael said.

'No, I got Jem to drop me at the end of the track. I thought it looked a nice morning for a walk.'

'I've not long arrived. I must have just missed you.'

Anne grinned and Rachael thought it wasn't Jeremy who'd dropped her at the end of the track but whichever lover she'd spent the night with.

'Have you had breakfast?' Grace asked. She cut another slice from the loaf and put it under the grill. Rachael had never before seen her prepare food without prompting.

'No,' Anne said. 'I didn't seem to have time.'

Anyone that smug, Rachael thought, deserved to be gossiped about. She waited until Anne and Grace were on the hill before going into the farmhouse. She didn't want to explain what she was up to. They might have thought her morbid.

There were two doors into the house. The one Rachael had always used led straight from the yard into the kitchen. It was modern, hardwood and double-glazed with a double lock as standard. Dougie had bought the door when he had the kitchen renovated for Bella. It had been a surprise, a sort of wedding present, a new start anyway. In the old lady's day the kitchen had been small, dark and draughty, leading into a leaking scullery with a twin tub washing machine and a wringer. Bella had grumbled mildly about the twin tub. It had been before Rachael's time but she'd heard the story: 'By then there were sheets to wash most days. Ivy couldn't help herself. I had muscles like a weightlifter lugging them, soaking, into the spinner. Poor lamb. It's not the way I'd want to end up.'

After the wedding Bella had gone away for a few days – Rachael wondered now where she could have gone – and came back to find the new kitchen. Apparently she'd pointed out a photo in a magazine to Dougie, said what a picture it was and he'd copied it exactly. His mother had left him some shares and he'd blown the lot on it.

It was the washing machine which pleased Bella most though, as she said wryly to Rachael, it would have been more handy when the old lady was alive and she had bedding to do every day.

The kitchen was tidier than Rachael had ever seen it. Bella had obviously cleaned the floor just before she died. On the window sill there were plants which needed watering but she'd never bothered much about those. In the drawers and cupboards there was nothing to give a clue to her past.

Rachael moved on to the small parlour where Mrs Furness had sat in the evenings before taking to her bed. Nothing much could have changed since then. There was an upright piano, small dark wood tables with crocheted runners, framed embroidered samplers, a standard lamp with a fringed shade. The photos were of Dougie with his first wife, Neville as a small boy. In her day Ivy Furness must have been a fit and active woman. Dougie's first wife had died, quite suddenly, of a brain haemorrhage when the boy was two and Ivy had taken the family on. It occurred to Rachael that Neville must have regarded her almost as his mother. Perhaps he'd been closer to her than to

Dougie. It would be interesting to find out if he'd been more assiduous about visiting her than his father.

Dougie's first wife had been a beauty; from her Neville had inherited the black hair, the brown skin, the intense eyes. Bella had spoken of her occasionally, without jealousy.

'She was only a girl when they met, a bit wild by all accounts. Look at her picture. You can see why he fell for her.'

She was a southerner, still at art school, visiting relatives in the area. He'd bumped into her on the hill. She'd been sketching the lead mine. The completed picture still hung in the living room given pride of place over the mantelpiece.

'Don't you mind?' Rachael had once asked.

'Of course not. We both came with a history.' But her history was never discussed, and Ivy Furness's parlour revealed none of its secrets, nor did the living room with its view of the hills, and the enormous painting of the mine, a constant reminder of Dougie's first love.

There had been talk of turning Ivy's parlour into a bedroom for Dougie when he first came back from the hospital, but, as Bella said, the bathroom was upstairs and she was hardly going to wash him at the kitchen sink. In the end social services had provided a stairlift so they could keep the bedroom they'd shared since they were married, probably even before that. Bella had never been a great one for convention.

Someone must have been into the room since the night Bella died to collect Dougie's suit for the funeral. Perhaps Neville had come when they were out on the hill. Rachael hadn't heard a car. But he had taken the clothes and gone. That was all. The room still smelled of disinfectant and of Bella's perfume. Rachael searched it as meticulously as elsewhere, but without expectation of finding anything. If Bella had wanted to keep secrets from Dougie this would be the last place she'd choose.

The room which they called Neville's, the room where she'd slept off Dougie's whisky, had been stripped of everything except a single bed and a wardrobe. Her place at Edie's was still full of schoolgirl clutter. Even if she got round to buying a flat of her own she thought it would still be her room, with the curtains she'd chosen, her stencils covering the wall. This was impersonal. Nothing belonging to Neville had been left behind.

That left a third bedroom, which Rachael had never seen before. It was reached by two steps down from the landing, at the back of the house. It was small, with a sloping roof and a big cupboard containing the hot water tank. There was a narrow divan, covered with a cream quilt, still slightly crumpled as if someone had been sitting on it. By the divan was a desk, of the kind you would once have found in a schoolroom with a lift-up lid and an inkwell. Even though the surface had been sanded and painted with red gloss the scratched indentations of graffiti were still visible.

Inside the desk was a wooden box, inlaid with marquetry and mother of pearl. Once perhaps Bella had hidden it more carefully, but after Dougie's stroke there had been no need. The two steps from the landing meant he would never visit this room. Rachael took the box to the bed and opened the lid.

At first she was disappointed. It seemed to contain

the details of quite a different person, Isabella Rose Noble. There was a birth certificate in that name, dated 16 September 1942 giving the place of birth as Kimmerston, Northumberland. Next came a certificate of education dated 1963. Isabella Rose Noble had attended a teacher training college in Newcastle and was qualified to teach primary children. Only when Rachael shook a faded newspaper cutting from a brown envelope did she connect Isabella Noble with Bella Furness. At first the cutting meant nothing to her. There was an article about a child swept away by a flooded river. The body was never found. But the article was cut off in mid-sentence so she turned the paper over and read the other side.

There was an obituary taken from a local paper, dated 1970. There were two columns of print and a photograph. The man looking out at her was dark and full-faced. His name was Alfred Noble. He had died at the age of seventy, so the photograph, of a florid middle-aged man, must have been taken many years before his death.

All these details Rachael took in later. What she thought first, when she looked at the cutting, was that it was a picture of Bella. The square face, the thick dark eyebrows were the same. If the hair had been longer and if Alfred Noble had been wearing the chunky gold earrings which Bella loved, the two would have been identical. Was Alfred Noble Bella's father? If so, why had she said her maiden name was Davison?

Rachael went on to read the smaller print. Alfred Noble had died in tragic circumstances after a long illness. This was not a news report but an eulogy.

Councillor Noble had served the town of Kimmerston well for thirty years before giving up his duties. Ill health had also dictated his retirement from his position as postmaster. The funeral had taken place at the Kimmerston Methodist Church where he had served as steward. He would be much missed. He was described in the obituary as a widower but there was no mention of surviving children. Surely there would have been if Bella was his daughter, but how else could she explain the coincidence of the birth certificate, with a date which tallied with Bella's age, and the startling resemblance?

Proof was provided by another photograph, a glossy coloured one in a presentation cardboard frame. It showed twelve children aged between five and seven in a school playground. Some sat on a wooden bench, others stood behind them. There were prim girls in pigtails, tousle-haired boys with gappy grins. To one side, quite dashing in her short skirt and crocheted top, stood Bella. Written on the back in sloping handwriting was: 'Corbin County Primary School 1966. Miss Noble with Class One.'

Attached to the photo by a rusty paper clip was a handwritten letter. The address was Corbin County Primary School, Corbin, Nr Wooler, Northumberland. It was dated April 1967 and it acknowledged, with regret, Miss Noble's resignation: 'I understand you feel that family circumstances make this necessary, but trust that it will be possible for you to return to the profession in the future.'

It was signed Alicia Davison.

When Bella first met Dougie her name had been Davison. Perhaps Edie was right and Bella had been previously married. To a relative of the headmistress's for whom she was working? A son or brother? Now there was more to work on it should be possible to find out. Why had Bella kept the marriage secret?

All that was left in the box was a letter inviting Miss Noble to attend the Corbin Primary School Christmas Concert on 15 December 1969 at 7.00 p.m. Mince pies and tea would be provided. At that time then, Bella was still unmarried. There was nothing to show whether or not she attended the concert, or what had become of her between her resignation in 1967 and her appearance at the bus stop in Langholme in 1989.

It took some time for Rachael to decide what to do with the information. She felt that the box and its contents belonged to Black Law. If Neville had been inclined to snoop he'd already had the chance when he came to collect Dougie's clothes. But this was the only connection she had with Bella's past. In the end she found a circular in a brown envelope in the kitchen. She slipped the papers and photos between its pages, and returned it to the envelope. She would keep it at Baikie's until she had a chance to take it home.

She was just leaving the house when the telephone began to ring. For a while she left it, but it continued, insistent and nerve-shattering. At last she gave in and picked it up. It was a feed rep, used in these hard times to being persistent. She said Bella had left the farm without giving details. After replacing the receiver in the middle of his sales patter she phoned Edie. At first Edie pretended to be hurt, because she hadn't been included in the search of the house. Then she was gleeful. It seemed she had been right about Bella's previous marriage. And it shouldn't be hard to trace Alicia Davison, who'd once been headmistress of Corbin Primary School. Not with her contacts in County Hall. If, of course, she was still alive.

Chapter Ten

'You do realize,' Anne said, 'that she's barking.'

They were in the pub in Langholme. It had been Rachael's idea. The three of them should get away from Baikie's, have a few drinks, relax. She felt it was her responsibility that they weren't getting on. Since the funeral there had been an undercurrent of tension, a tetchiness which expressed itself in trivial gripes, explosions of bad temper. Now it had come to a head. Anne was proposing moving into the box room at the back of the cottage. It was tiny, freezing, hardly room for the bed. Because the big room with its view of the burn and the crags beyond was so much more pleasant, it had been assumed at the start of the contract that Anne and Grace would share. Rachael had a small room to herself. There was nowhere else. In the pub Anne had waited until Grace went to the phone before making her announcement. For some reason the room was very crowded and noisy. Rachael picked up that there had been a family event – a birth or an engagement. There was an air of hysterical celebration. She felt awkward conducting such a sensitive conversation in a yell.

'I thought she was getting on better. She seems happier. And at least she's been eating.'

ANN CLEEVES

'She's also awake for most of the night, prowling around.'

'I'm sorry. I didn't realize. I'll have a word.'

'Where did you get her from anyway?'

'She did a contract in Dumfries last year for a friend of Peter's. He said she was brilliant. A real find.'

Anne gave a snort of contempt. Grace returned, stared into her empty glass, didn't answer when Rachael spoke to her. They left the pub early.

Back in the cottage Anne went upstairs to move her things. They could hear her banging about. Grace went to the table in the living room which she used as a desk and began immediately to work. From the kitchen Rachael could hear her punch the buttons of a calculator. She went in. It had been a mild day and they'd not bothered to light the fire. A film of wood ash had settled on everything.

'Isn't it a bit late to start now?' Rachael said.

Grace jumped round with a start. The calculator clattered to the floor. Rachael stooped to pick it up.

'The idea was that we should all take a break. There's still a bottle of wine left from my trip into town. Shall we open it?'

'Why not?' The reply was unnaturally loud, artificially bright.

'I'll just get it. Pack that away. It'll wait until tomorrow.' My God, she thought, I sound just like Edie telling me to take it easy before A levels. There was something about Grace's passion for her subject, her intense desire for privacy which Rachael recognized. She poured the wine into the tumblers which were the only glasses to have survived a season of student washing-up, then waited for Grace to move into an easy chair before handing one to her.

'How's it going?'

'Very well.' Grace, drinking deeply, looked warily over her glass.

'The data much as you expected?'

'Pretty much.'

'I've been looking at the information you passed on last week. Was that typical?' Rachael, waiting for an answer, felt ridiculously anxious.

'I don't know. Too small a sample yet.' Grace was casual, apparently unperturbed.

'I see.' Knowing how irritated she felt when pestered about ongoing work, Rachael let that go, though the anxiety remained. 'Anne says you're not sleeping very well.'

Carefully, Grace set down the glass by her chair. 'I don't think Anne has the best interests of the project at heart,' she said seriously.

'What do you mean?'

But Grace wouldn't say.

'Are you sleeping?'

The wine which she'd drunk very quickly must have taken effect because she was almost truculent. 'As much as I need to.'

'You do know you can take the weekend off. Why don't you go home for a while? You're the only one who hasn't had a break from this place.'

'I don't need a break. I take my work seriously.' Unlike Anne Preece, she implied. 'Besides, I haven't got much of a home to go back to.' She stood up and went defiantly back to the table and her calculator.

The next day Rachael had to go into Kimmerston. A meeting had been arranged sometime before with Peter and a representative from Slateburn Quarries, to inform them of the progress of the project so far. She was reluctant to leave Anne and Grace together. They were like quarrelling children who needed an adult as peacemaker, to stop things from coming to blows.

Please be good, she wanted to say as she drove up the track.

She was surprised to find that Neville Furness was the Slateburn representative. Although she was early he was at the office before her. He and Peter were already deep in conversation. They both looked very smart, very professional in their suits. She had expected an informal meeting and was wearing her field clothes. Nothing of consequence was decided at the encounter but it seemed to drag on. She had the impression that Peter was prolonging the explanation of the methodology, making it more complicated than necessary in an attempt to impress. Afterwards he made her stay for tea. Again she felt he was building up to some confidence, and when he suggested going for a drink, she insisted on leaving. All afternoon she had been uneasy about the two women left behind in Baikie's.

She drove back in the dusk. Now the track was so familiar she could take it more quickly. She knew the best line to take so the exhaust wouldn't catch on the ruts and how to swing the car through the ford to stop the engine getting wet. On the dry stone wall by the wooden gate there was a ring ouzel, its collar crescent startlingly white against the gloom.

From the top of the bank she looked down on Black

Law and Baikie's. Black Law was still and empty. All the animals had gone, even the dogs. Without a function the buildings seemed ramshackle and pitiful. In the garden at Baikie's there was a line of washing left out, though it looked as if it might rain. Although from this angle she couldn't see the windows a square of orange light spilt onto the grass. It should have been reassuringly domestic but she realized she was driving more slowly, putting off the moment when she'd have to face the hostility between the women inside, remembering, as she always did approaching the barn, Bella's body in the torchlight.

When she went into the house she was struck first by the smell of cooking. There was nothing usually organized about meals, no cosy gathering every evening to compare notes. Rachael had suggested a rota for washing up but even that was impractical. They ate at different times. Anne seemed to survive on scrambled egg and smoked salmon. It seemed she had a friend in the Craster smokery who kept her well supplied. And Belgian chocolates which appeared from nowhere. She was always generous about sharing them. Rachael occasionally indulged. Grace seemed suspicious of the gesture.

Wandering through the living room Rachael saw that the table had been cleared of books and papers and was laid for dinner. For three. There was no sign of life. She called up the stairs, 'Hello! I'm back,' trying to keep her voice normal, unworried.

Anne appeared. She was wearing black jeans and a sleeveless top. When the fire had been lit for a while the cottage could get very warm but the top, cream silk, seemed a strange choice. It was too dressy. Rachael wondered if she'd been entertaining a guest.

'I cooked a casserole,' Anne said. 'It's all right. There's veggie for you. There's a bottle of white wine in the fridge.'

So either someone had been there, or Anne had been out for supplies. She went on, 'I thought, well, we've got to live here together, haven't we? We might as well make an effort to be chums.'

'Where is Grace?'

Anne pulled a face. 'Inconsiderate cow's not back yet. I told her I'd be cooking.'

Rachael went to the window. It was almost dark. 'She did leave her route and her ETA?'

'I suppose so. On the kitchen noticeboard. Like a good girl.'

This was a dig at Rachael who had been forced to nag her again about not leaving the details of her count. And there *was* a note in Grace's tiny, angular writing, giving the map reference of an area beyond the burn and her expected time of return at 8.30. It was about that time now.

Rachael relaxed a little. It was too early to panic. She went back to the window expecting to see Grace's pale form emerge from the long bracken, like a swimmer from the sea.

'Oh well,' Anne said. 'I suppose the food will keep. But I'm going to open the wine. Do you want one?'

'Not yet.' It seemed important to keep a clear head.

At nine o'clock she went out with a torch and followed the footpath as far as the burn. She crossed it by the footbridge and began to shout Grace's name, cupping her hands, then pausing to listen. A breeze had come up. She heard the burn, and the rustling of cotton grass and of small mammals. A hare froze, dazzled by the beam of the torch. There was no human sound, no echoing flicker of torchlight. Thick clouds had covered the moon and if it hadn't been for the water noise she would have lost her bearings completely. It would be impossible to search the area properly, even if Anne were prepared to help.

When she returned to Baikie's Anne was on her second glass of wine. She'd torn a chunk from a French loaf and was eating it hungrily to make a point. Her stockinged feet were stretched onto the hearth. 'You realize she's doing this on purpose,' she said. 'To get at me, because I said I'd cook. Well, I'll not wait much longer. I'm starving.'

'It's pitch black out there now.' Rachael couldn't keep still. She moved from the window to the kitchen door, listening, peering into the darkness.

'Don't panic, for Christ's sake. She's not that late. I bet you wouldn't worry about me. She's not a kid, you know. She's older than she looks. Nearly twenty-eight.'

For a moment Rachael was distracted. 'How do you know?'

'She'd left her passport on the dressing table upstairs. So I looked.'

Anticipating Rachael's disapproval she added, 'Well, I was curious. Aren't you? We don't know anything about her except she seems a bloody miracle worker when it comes to finding otters. If you accept her results.'

At ten o'clock Rachael went to Black Law to phone Peter Kemp.

'I didn't know you had the keys,' Anne said.

'Dougie gave me a set after the funeral. In case of an emergency.'

She reached Peter on his mobile. He seemed to be in a busy restaurant. There were shrill women's voices, the clatter of plates. At least he took the call seriously. She had been afraid he would laugh at her concern.

'Just a minute,' he said. 'I'll phone you back from somewhere quieter.'

Five minutes later the phone rang, sounding very loud in the empty house. He was brisk, assertive. He had been in touch with the mountain rescue team though he didn't think they'd do much before first light. It wasn't as if Grace had been anywhere dangerous. Not like rock-climbing or pot-holing.

'She wasn't a reckless type, was she?'

'No,' Rachael said. 'I wouldn't have thought so.'

He said it was a mild night and even if there'd been an accident she'd survive until morning, but anyway the team would soon be on its way. It was up to them to decide how to play it. A clue to his promptness came at the end of the conversation.

'The Health and Safety won't be able to get us on this, will they? All the procedures were in order?'

'Absolutely.'

'Well then, we should be able to face it out. Whatever happens.'

What happened was that six burly men turned up in a Land Rover. They were good-looking in a rugged, muscle-bound way. Anne, who had eaten a plate of casserole, finished the wine and gone to bed, would be sorry to have missed them, Rachael thought. One of the team was the doctor who had pronounced Bella dead and taken Dougie away.

'You're having a dramatic time of it,' he said, as if he envied her. Perhaps that was what being a GP was about for him. It entitled him to star in his own action movie.

They went out onto the hill just before dawn. With such a detailed record of Grace's movements they said they would easily find her. Even if she'd strayed away from her planned route there'd be no problem. The doctor carried a folded stretcher which poked out of the top of his rucksack.

Rachael watched them from her bedroom window. They didn't invite her to go with them and she didn't like to suggest it. The cloud was still thick and low, with a drizzle, so they soon disappeared. She must have dozed, although she was sitting upright in a chair, because she was suddenly aware of their return. She looked at her watch. They'd been gone for two hours. There were four of them, walking in single file. The doctor still had the poles of the stretcher poking above his shoulder but she couldn't see Grace.

She went into the kitchen and put on the kettle. Before going they had made jokes about having the tea ready on their return. The gas was so slow that she was still there when they came in. There was hardly room for them all to stand in the tiny kitchen. She could feel their heat after the walk, smell the wax on their boots.

'Did you find her?' Then this seemed a ridiculous question because Grace obviously wasn't there. 'I suppose the others are still searching.'

'We found her,' the doctor said.

'How is she?'

'She's dead.'

It was, she thought, like Bella all over again. I know now, she thought, what it's like to be mugged. You're kicked. It hurts. You think it's over, roll away, gather yourself to get up, then someone comes at you and kicks again. And all the time you know it's your own fault.

'How?'

'We can't say,' the doctor replied. 'Not yet.' As he put his arms round Rachael to support her she wondered, bitterly, if this was excitement enough for him.

Anne

Chapter Eleven

From the moment she saw Grace outside Kimmerston station Anne knew that they weren't going to get on. Something about the skinny bitch got right up her nose. Something about the way she sat there, staring straight ahead of her as if nothing in the world deserved her interest, as if she was the only person who mattered. Anne shouldn't have had to provide the taxi service in the first place. Peter had been going to do it but he'd phoned her at the last minute and turned on the charm which, according to gossip, had turned on the frigid Rachael, but which didn't work on her.

'Well,' she'd said, 'it's hardly on my way.' Because she lived in Langholme, the nearest village to the study site and Kimmerston was thirty miles away.

'Come on, Anne. You don't really mind, do you?'

'I'll be putting in a claim for the petrol.'

She hadn't felt she could refuse. Not at the moment.

She'd cut it a bit fine and was ten minutes late arriving at the station. Grace was already waiting outside. It was midday and the station was deserted, unkempt. Last year's hanging baskets were still full of brown moss and dry stalks and a couple of empty coke cans lay in the gutter. Anne thought viciously of what she'd like to do to kids who threw litter around. Grace must have realized that this was her lift but when the car pulled up she didn't move from the wrought iron bench where she was sitting. She was lost, apparently, in a world of her own. Or perhaps she just couldn't be bothered to shift her arse. Anne had to wind down the window and yell, 'Are you waiting for Peter Kemp?'

Then Grace uncoiled her long legs and stood up. Not hurrying, though Anne was waiting with the engine revving. Anne got out and opened the boot and Grace dumped in her rucksack without a word, without even a smile.

Sod you then, Anne thought, but she wore politeness automatically, like the very expensive perfume her lover provided. She held out her hand across the gear stick.

'Anne Preece,' she said. 'I'm the botanist.'

'Grace Fulwell, Mammals.'

'Not one of *the* Fulwells?' Anne said jokingly, because clearly Grace couldn't be one of *the* Fulwells or she'd have heard of her. 'Holme Park Hall? Lords of all they survey.'

Grace looked at Anne strangely.

Supercilious cow, Anne thought. She had come across people like Grace before. They got a couple of degrees then believed they were better than anyone else. It didn't help that she was a good ten years younger than Anne and now she said, 'Sorry. Why should you have heard of them if you're not local? The Fulwells are a big family in this part of the county. They own most of the Uplands. Or that's how it seems.'

'Do they?'

'Mm. They're neighbours of mine. Sort of.'

86

Grace turned away with a pained expression. 'Oh,' she said, 'I see.'

'Have you come far?'

'Just from Newcastle. Today.' Which really told Anne nothing.

On the way to Baikie's Anne tried to make conversation but was answered in monosyllables, so she, too, lapsed into silence. They were driving through Langholme when Grace suddenly sat upright. It was as if she'd woken with a start from a deep sleep.

'Where is this place?' she demanded.

Anne told her.

'Langholme?' She sounded astonished, disbelieving.

'I should know, I've lived here for ten years.'

'It's just that it's not what I expected,' Grace muttered.

'What did you expect?'

'I don't know, something smarter, I suppose. Something prettier.'

'God, where would you get that idea?'

There was nothing pretty about Langholme. The terraced houses were built along a ridge, exposed to the northerly wind. The pub's paintwork had faded as if it had been sandblasted and at the garage the petrol pumps had rusted. The place had more in common with the Durham pit villages to the south than with pictures advertising the National Park in the Northumbria Tourist brochure.

'Of course,' Anne went on, realizing at once how defensive she must sound, 'we don't actually live in the village.'

And as the road dipped past the church and a belt

87

of woodland at last provided some shelter, Anne pointed out the Priory. The marital home. The pale stone of the house was partly hidden by trees, but there was a perfect view of the garden. Anne slowed the car so Grace could admire it. Even so early in the season it was looking bloody good. It had taken ten years of hard labour but it had been worth the effort. Grace hardly looked up.

'And Holme Park Hall?' she asked. 'Where is that?'

Anne ignored her. She had to concentrate anyway on the OS map. She'd never driven to Black Law before. The other contracts she'd worked for Peter Kemp had been on the coast and she and Jeremy weren't really on socializing terms with Bella and Dougie Furness. They didn't mix in the same circles. If Bella and Dougie mixed at all. In the village they had something of the reputation of keeping themselves to themselves. Bella wasn't in the WI and she never went to church. Though thinking about that now, Anne remembered that she had seen Bella in church once.

She had a sudden picture of the woman hunched in a big coat on the back pew, her breath coming in clouds, tears streaming down her cheeks. It must have been last Christmas, the kids' Nativity play, the usual thing – out of tune 'Away in a Manger', Mary and Joseph awestruck by stardom, the angels fidgeting with their glitter wings and tinsel haloes. It was always a tear-jerker. Even Anne occasionally wondered at Christmas if she'd missed out by not having kids.

Presumably that was what had got to Bella too. By the time she'd met Dougie she must have been a bit old to think about starting a family. Though in Anne's opinion that was hardly an excuse for making a show in public, and she'd been glad when Bella had rushed away straight after the service so she'd not been forced to speak to her.

When they got to Baikie's Anne forgot all about Bella for a moment. Rachael was waiting for them. She looked exhausted, as if she'd slept in her clothes. The fire hadn't been lit so there was no hot water. Anne looked at her with irritation.

'God,' she said. 'You look dreadful!'

Rachael wiped her face with her sleeve like a snotty lad and announced to them both that Bella was dead, that she'd hanged herself in the barn. The image of the middle-aged woman in tears at the back of the church returned to Anne, and though she wasn't usually superstitious she did think it was a bit spooky that she'd pictured her so clearly on the way to the farm and wondered if it was some sort of premonition.

She didn't rush into the field the next day. She'd never been at her best in the morning and it wasn't like birds. The plants weren't going anywhere.

She'd looked at the large-scale maps and knew approximately where she wanted to site her hundred-metre squares. Peter had provided satellite landscape surveys, but they needed ground-truthing. She loved the idea of ground-truthing, the thought of bending close to the soil, of getting things right.

She walked through the farmyard quickly – she wasn't squeamish but she didn't want to be reminded of Bella swinging from a rope in the barn – and went up the track towards the ford. In the sheltered bank by the side of the track there were primroses in bud and violets and the sun felt warm on her back. From a rise in the land she had a view of the old lead mine and thought it would be interesting to survey a square close to there. Old lime spoil could encourage quite a different sort of vegetation. But today she wanted to find the area of peat bog which Peter had marked on the map as being worth surveying. She left the track and walked over the open hillside. She was out of sight of the road and the mine and the farmhouse. She couldn't even see any electricity pylons.

There was a specific way of going about the survey. It wasn't a matter of wandering over the hill with a trowel and a magnifying glass.

When she'd first got involved in this business she'd scorned the rules, thought they'd been put together by empire-building scientists who wanted to keep the amateurs out. Then Peter had sent her on a course about National Vegetation Classification and she'd started to see the point.

Each survey area was a hundred-metre square, and within that five wooden frames, each two metres square, known as quadrats, were randomly placed. You ensured a random distribution by standing in the middle of the large square and throwing the first quadrat, going to where it landed and throwing the next until all five were on the ground. The five frames provided the area for study.

Today she wouldn't have time to do more than mark out the hundred-metre square with the poles she was carrying in her rucksack but that was what she liked best, the detailed investigation, identifying the plants within the frames, recording their abundance. She loved teasing through the sphagnum moss for plants like cranberry, bog rosemary, bog asphodel, squatting so close to the ground so she could smell the peat, feel the insects on her fingers. And always hoping for something unusual, something perhaps which she'd have difficulty in identifying. Something which would put the bloody scientists in their places.

Not that there was much chance of that on this contract, she thought, pushing a pole into the ground, putting all her weight behind it because she didn't want it blowing away in the first gale. This bit of bog might be of interest but from what she knew of the rest of the estate she wasn't expecting any dramatic finds. Most of the mires had long been drained and the land farmed by the Holme Park tenants had been grazed so close by sheep and rabbits that it was as smooth and green as a billiard table. She wasn't sure why the project needed a botanist at all. But perhaps that had been Godfrey Waugh's idea.

As she straightened, the valley was filled with noise as a fighter plane from RAF Boulmer screamed overhead, so low it seemed that if she'd reached up she would have been able to feel the air move across her fingertips.

Chapter Twelve

Anne Preece first saw Godrey Waugh, Chairman of Slateburn Quarry Ltd, at a meeting held in St Mary's Church Hall, Langholme. It had been called by the developers to explain their scheme. There had, they said, been a lot of wild speculation in the press and when the villagers appreciated the real nature of the new quarry, they might actually be in favour of it.

Anne had been asked by a number of people in the village if she would attend. They seemed to feel she would have some influence in the decision-making process. Perhaps this was because she had a reputation for being lippy and standing up for herself. Perhaps it had something to do with her uncanny resemblance to Camilla Parker-Bowles. The similarity was so striking that occasionally there were rumours that she was indeed the prince's lover, incognito. Of course the idea was ridiculous. She had lived at Langholme Priory with her husband since they were married. Anne herself had always been irritated by the comparison. She could give Camilla almost ten years.

She attended the meeting, not to please her acquaintances in the village, but out of self-interest. What she loved most about the Priory was the garden and the view over the Black Law Valley. That was where the proposed quarry would be. She saw from the beginning that what was planned was essentially an industrial development. There would be new roads, arc lights, the constant sound of machinery. The noise alone would madden her. Then there was the effect on the garden. She imagined a fine silt of lime dust settling over her plants and her flowers, her raspberry canes and her vegetables, killing them slowly despite her efforts.

She tried to persuade Jeremy to go with her to the meeting. 'Think what it'll do to the value of the house,' she said. But Jeremy had decided that he had an important meeting in London so she went alone.

She sat in the front seat in the body of the hall. Although she arrived late, a chair had been left free for her because it was expected that she would speak for everyone.

The meeting was chaired by a local councillor, a solicitor from Kimmerston. Anne recognized him and gave a little wave. He ignored her and she thought his wife was probably there, sitting at the back. From the start he pushed the line that any industrial development would be good for the area because jobs were so urgently needed.

'We are losing our young people,' he announced.

Pompous prat, she thought.

She could tell from the beginning that he was trying to win the meeting, while appearing to remain impartial by mentioning vague environmental objections. At last she couldn't stand it any longer. She had come prepared. She raised her hand, a diffident gesture, and stood up, smiling sweetly.

'I wonder if I might put a question to the Chair?'

Councillor Benn looked nervous, but he could hardly refuse.

'Could you tell me where you live, Councillor Benn?'

He stuttered before replying, 'I don't think that has much bearing on this case.'

Anne looked at him. He was balding, slightly short-sighted. She thought it was just as well that he specialized in property and employment law. He would be torn apart in a criminal court.

'All the same. Humour me.' She turned slightly to face the crowd for a moment. She had always known how to play a crowd. There was a murmur of expectation. He stared back at the hall, blinking.

'I live in a village on the south side of Kimmerston. But just because I'm not local . . .'

'The village of Holystone?'

'I'm not sure what my personal details have to do with the matter in hand.' And he was so stupid that he really couldn't see. Anne felt a brief moment of conscience because he was such an easy target, but she was enjoying herself too much to stop now.

'Could I just quote from a passage in the *Kimmerston Gazette* dated July twenty-first? The headline is: HOLYSTONE RESIDENTS RISE IN PROTEST. The article is about a planning application for an open cast mine by British Coal Contractors. Could I ask you if you remember that application, Mr Benn? It was made two years ago.'

He continued to stare into the audience. Panic seemed to make him incapable of rational thought. His mouth opened, fish-like, but no words came out. She persisted, ruthlessly.

'Tell me, Mr Benn, weren't you vice chair of an

organization known as HAVOC – the Holystone Association Versus Open Cast Mining?'

This pushed him at last into coherent speech. He blustered, 'Really, I can't allow any individual to take over the meeting in this way.'

'I have proof,' she said gaily. 'There are letters from HAVOC which bear your signature to local supporters. I don't think you can deny it. And it seems very bizarre to me, Mr Benn, that you are so concerned to provide work for the youth of our community through the development of the quarry, yet so reluctant to give the same benefit to your own. I'm sure the open cast mine would have provided work too.'

She sat down. Behind her there was cheering and clapping and a couple of catcalls. It served Derek Benn right. If he'd been more even-handed in his chairing of the meeting she'd never have brought up that business of HAVOC. He hadn't given a toss about the open cast mine, hadn't even attended most of the meetings. His involvement with the group had provided an alibi, an excuse to be out of the house when he was meeting her. Good God, she thought, whatever did I see in him?

After the meeting a group of protesters went to the pub to discuss strategy. It was midsummer and still light. Anne would have preferred to be in her garden, but she followed them across the road to the Ridley Arms. Living at the Priory had given her a certain, ambiguous status within the village. A responsibility. She wasn't in the same league as the Fulwells at Holme Park. They wouldn't be expected to participate in village events, except occasionally to open the church Summer Fayre. All the same she had a standing.

They'd invited her to be St Mary's churchwarden,

for example, although she hardly ever attended church. The job seemed to go with the house. They'd thought her a stuck-up cow for refusing.

Inside the pub it was noisy and chaotic and very quickly she was forced to take charge. Some of them wanted to organize a petition. She talked them out of it. 'Look,' she said. 'Planners don't take much notice of petitions. They get them all the time. They know people sign bits of paper without reading them properly or because they don't like to say no. You should organize individual letters of protest. They carry more weight.'

When she sat down Sandy Baines, who had the garage, asked shyly if she'd like a drink.

'I'd have thought this quarry would be in your interest,' she said. 'The lorries would have to fill up somewhere, wouldn't they?'

It seemed that this idea hadn't occurred to him and she saw with amusement that as soon as he delivered her G&T, he disappeared. He had been caught up in the village's general suspicion of change and strangers. She doubted if even self-interest would make a difference to that.

She was approached next by the small man, whose name she could never remember, who lived in the modern ugly bungalow on the way into the village.

'Look,' he said. 'A few of us have been talking. We'd like you to sit on our action committee. Speak for us, like.'

He had a head the shape of a sheep's and white woolly hair. She fancied the 'like' came out as a 'baa'. She seemed to remember now that he had once been a butcher. She declined graciously. Despite her support for the project and enjoying a fight, she knew she'd soon be bored with it. Bored at least with them. She finished her drink and stood up to go.

'My husband will be wondering where I am.' Though she knew that even if Jeremy were at home he wouldn't give a shit.

Outside the pub she stood for a minute enjoying the last of the birdsong. Someone had been cooking a barbecue. She realized she was hungry and almost turned back into the pub because although Milly was a crappy landlady who understood sod-all about customer service, as Anne was some sort of heroine, she would at least have to come up with a plate of sandwiches.

Then a sleek, black car pulled up in front of her, moving out of the shadows with hardly a sound. The window was lowered with a purr. She saw Godfrey Waugh and knew then that he must have been waiting for her.

'Mrs Preece,' he said, as though he had arrived there quite by chance. 'I wonder if I might offer you a lift.'

She had recognized him at once as the owner of the quarry company. She had seen him on the platform during the meeting. He had been introduced though he had hardly spoken. When she had looked at him from the audience, stiff and uncomfortable in his subdued suit and highly polished shoes, he had reminded her of an interview candidate trying too hard to please.

'I have my own car, thank you.'

A grotty little Fiat. When she married Jeremy she had assumed there was money in the background. It hadn't quite worked out that way.

'I would very much like to speak to you. Have you eaten? Perhaps I could buy you dinner.' He was diffident, a bit like the old men in the pub.

'I'm not bribed that easily.'

'No, of course not!' He took her seriously and was shocked.

She smiled. She might look, in a bad light, like Camilla Parker-Bowles but she knew the effect that smile could have.

'Oh well,' she said. 'Why not?' By now it was too dark to do much in the garden and she was curious.

'Would you like to come with me? Or perhaps you would prefer to follow me in your own car? I was thinking of the George.'

Very nice, she thought. The George was an unpretentious hotel in the next village where the chef worked magic with local ingredients.

'No, I'd rather come with you if you don't mind bringing me back here later.'

Suddenly she didn't want him to get too close a view of the grotty Fiat. There was something about him which made her feel the need to impress. At the time she thought it was his money.

Chapter Thirteen

'Tell me about yourself,' she said. She was leaning across the dinner table, her elbows on the white cloth. There was candlelight for which she was grateful. Recently she had noticed fine lines above her upper lip and knew that she could no longer get away with sleeveless dresses. It wasn't the George Hotel but another evening, another restaurant. Godfrey Waugh had called her that morning.

'I thought we should get together again. I found the last meeting very useful. I'd like to hear any suggestions you might have for making the quarry more acceptable to the community.'

But she told him here in the restaurant she would rather discuss him.

'There's not much to tell,' he said, though she could see he was pleased to be asked. He spoke with a local accent, with a slight stutter. He was very shy. She realized at their first meeting that if it ever came to seduction, it would be down to her. She would have to be the active partner. He might be as old as she was, but there was something awkward and adolescent about him. She had been expecting a brash and vulgar businessman not a boy, and she was touched.

He continued, mumbling so she had to strain to hear him.

'I was brought up in Kimmerston. Failed the eleven-plus and went to the secondary modern. I was never much good at school. Couldn't see the point really. Not that I mucked about. I just didn't bother. When I was fifteen I left and went to work in the quarry at Slate-burn. It wasn't much of an operation then, nothing to what it is now. The old man prepared dressed stone for mantelpieces, ornamental walls, headstones, you know the sort of thing. He'd lost interest in it, the business side at least. He liked fiddling with the stone and his chisels but he couldn't be bothered chasing up unpaid bills. I got a chance to buy in. Making money always appealed to me, even when I was at school.'

He smiled at her apologetically. Perhaps he thought she was a woolly-minded environmentalist to whom money didn't matter.

'That's it really. We were able to expand. It was as much a matter of luck as anything else. Being in the right place at the right time. You know.' He stopped abruptly. 'Look, I shouldn't be going on so much about myself.' As if it was something he'd read in a magazine.

'Are you married?' she asked, thinking it was probably the advice page in his wife's magazine that he'd been reading. He wasn't wearing a ring but she thought he was married. He had the look.

He paused and she was expecting him to lie but he said: 'Yes, to Barbara. She doesn't get out much.'

'What a strange thing to say!' So strange that she pressed him to elaborate but he refused.

'I'm married,' she said at last, stretching extrava-gantly. 'And I get out all the time.'

For some reason the remark seemed to embarrass him. He didn't answer and stretched over to fill her glass. She'd drunk most of the bottle already. He'd offered to drive.

'Are you local?' he asked. He was very polite as if they'd just met. 'I mean, were you born near here?'

'Quite near.'

She hated going into her background. She'd always considered that her parents were rather horrible little people. Her father had been headmaster of a boys' prep school. Until she was old enough to go to school herself she was brought up in that atmosphere of petty tyranny and ritual, of competitive games and fake tradition. Her mother lorded it over the other wives and her father lorded it over them all.

'Where did you go to school then? The grammar, I suppose.' She was amused that this business of education seemed to matter so much to him. She rather despised people with formal qualifications but it seemed to be his way of defining them.

'Lord, no! I got sent away to a ghastly heap on the North York moors. I didn't learn a thing.'

She always described her years at the ghastly heap in this way but she knew it wasn't quite true. There was a woman who taught Biology, Miss Masterman, who had seemed as lonely and isolated as any of the girls. She was young, straight out of college, rather prickly. A Scot who would have been more at home in an inner city secondary modern than this gothic pile. Even then Anne had wondered what she was doing there. It was hard to imagine her drinking afternoon tea in the panelled Mistresses' common room with the stuffy spinsters who made up most of the staff. And she certainly seemed to prefer the company of a small set of older girls to that of her colleagues. She arranged tramps on the moors, and away from the school she seemed to relax. She carried with her a sketchbook full of pencil drawings. The lines were fine, the pictures full of detail. She sprayed them with a fixative which smelled of pear drops to prevent smudging.

Occasionally, Miss Masterman led them on fungus forays. Away from the school she encouraged the girls to call her Maggie but Anne always thought of her as Miss Masterman. They'd carry flat wicker baskets and listen with delicious horror as she recounted, in her dry Edinburgh voice, tales of people who'd taken poisoned fungus by mistake. Putting off the return to school as long as possible they would build a camp fire at dusk and fry up the edible fungi, the field mushrooms and the ink caps.

Sitting in the restaurant, watching the candle flicker, Anne could remember the smell of woodsmoke, the feel of the battered tin plates, the taste of buttery juice wiped up with crusty bread. She had learnt something from the Biology teacher. She'd learnt that she never wanted to be like Maggie Masterman, depending on adolescent girls and mushrooms for fun. And that she had a passion for plants.

'Do you work?' Godfrey asked, breaking into the memory. 'Or perhaps you have children?'

As if the two were mutually exclusive.

'No, no children. And no permanent work. Bits and pieces, you know.'

When things were tight. When Jeremy's mysterious deals failed to come off. She learnt, very soon after marriage, that Jeremy was gay in a camp, rather jolly way. Of course he knew when he married her but perhaps thought, like the old Archbishop of Canterbury, that the right girl would cure him. She was sure that no malice or spite was intended in the transaction but there were other deceits – the impression, for instance, of money. He *did* have the Priory, which had sounded grand at the time but which had turned out to be no more than a glorified farmhouse built from the stone of a Tudor chapel. And he hadn't paid for that, it had been left to him by his grandfather.

By nature Jeremy was wonderfully optimistic. He imported antiques, art, books. Usually he managed to make enough just to tide them over but recently she suspected he might even fail to do that. They never discussed finance. If she asked about money he wagged a podgy finger at her. 'Now, old girl. Leave all that to me.'

Recently there had been fewer plans for the house, less discussion about interior decoration – usually he loved talking fabric and furnishing. She wondered, not for the first time, if he was being blackmailed by one of his little boys.

But Anne resented working for money. It came hard to put in so much effort and receive so little reward. She found it demeaning. For example, she could spend a whole day landscaping someone's garden and still not be paid enough to buy this dinner. It hurt her pride to be valued so little. She found she preferred to work as a volunteer. That was how she first met Peter Kemp.

She responded to an advertisement in the *Wildlife Trust* magazine. People with botanical skills were required to help with an English Nature survey. She was sent on a course and shone. Since then she'd worked regularly for the trust as a volunteer, and loved every minute of it. It was like Miss Masterman's botanizing expectations all over again.

Sitting in the restaurant, Anne realized that Godfrey was looking at her, pleadingly.

Oh God, she thought. He wants to talk about his offspring.

'And you?' she asked with resignation. 'Do you have children?'

He replied immediately, becoming much more animated than when talking about his business. 'We've a little girl. Felicity. She's nearly ten. Very bright for her age. At least that's what we think. She's still at the village school at the moment; Barbara says the teachers there are good. Later we'll have to see . . .'

Anne yawned discreetly into the back of her hand. She almost expected him to bring out the photo which he certainly kept in his wallet. Yet this was the moment she decided she could afford to have an affair with him. He would never get *too* serious. There would be no talk of divorce, of their moving in together. He would do nothing to upset his daughter.

Now the restaurant was almost empty. It was in Kimmerston, right on the bank of the river. They were alone in an extension built almost entirely of glass. A cold green light was reflected from the water. The candle on their table provided the only pool of warmth in the room.

'Do you have to get back?' she asked. She spoke abruptly. Certainly there was no seduction in her voice. She leant forward over the table and stretched a long white hand towards him. She would never use gloves for gardening or fieldwork and was aware that her hands wouldn't stand up to close scrutiny. There was a stain on her thumb which she couldn't get rid of, they were scratched, she had to keep the nails short. But she wanted to touch him. He watched the hand slowly approaching his with fascination. When the fingers met she looked up at his face and saw that he was blushing, breathless.

'Well?'

His fingers were rough, like hers.

'I don't know.'

'Will Barbara be expecting you?'

'I could phone. Say I'd been held up.'

He was stroking the palm of her hand with his thumb. She was surprised by the effect the simple gesture had. She thought she was getting old and jaded, yet here she was, wanting this upright, middle-aged man so much that she was almost fainting.

'Why don't you do that? Because Jeremy's in London and you could come home. For a nightcap. If you'd like that.' She could hardly articulate the words.

Outside they stood for a moment hand in hand. Anne could smell the river. Although they were a long way from the coast it had traces of salt and seaweed. Across the road a car started up. For a moment it caught Godfrey's attention and she felt the hand tense. He turned his face away from the headlights. She was flattered by the reaction of guilt. Adultery obviously didn't come easily to him. It occurred to her that this might be the first time he had ever been unfaithful to his wife.

'Well?' she said. 'Will you come back with me?'

But they didn't make it home to the Priory. Their

first sexual encounter was in the back of the BMW. Godfrey pulled it off the road and parked in a farm track overhung with trees. Afterwards, lying back on the leather seats, she saw the moonlight filter through the summer foliage. She identified the trees as elder and hawthorn.

Chapter Fourteen

That summer Anne saw Godfrey regularly but secretly. She was discreet in a way which didn't come naturally to her. In the past she had flaunted her men. Jeremy had pretended he didn't mind, and perhaps he really didn't, though he liked the fiction that they were a happy couple of independent means, devoted to each other and to country pursuits. Anne was afraid that if he found out about Godfrey he would laugh. At the Marks & Spencer suits, the pretentious gold watch, the shiny shoes. Despite the company he kept, Jeremy was a snob. Godfrey was even more eager than she that the affair remain secret. He couldn't face the prospect of his wife or his child finding out that he had a lover.

Therefore, she continued as usual. It was a hot dry summer and she spent long hours working in her garden. Her forehead turned as brown as leather and her arms and neck spotted with freckles, so once she said to Godfrey, 'I look at least sixty. How can you possibly fancy me?' She expected a quip about his liking older women; instead he said, 'I don't fancy you. It's much, much more than that.' And she believed him. By the beginning of autumn she had picked the early apples, wrapped them in newspaper and stacked them in boxes at the back of the garage. And she still looked forward to the clandestine meetings.

By the autumn too, opposition to the super quarry had gathered in momentum. She continued to be involved. She liked attending meetings to which Godfrey had been invited. There was an anticipatory thrill in standing outside the door of a shabby church hall, knowing that he was inside. Sometimes she could hear his voice, low and monotonous, making a point. His points were often technical. He might not have passed exams but he carried statistics in his head and could recite them flawlessly, like a child performing a favourite nursery rhyme. She loved arguing with him in public.

The people in the action group thought she disliked Godfrey Waugh intensely.

'Come on, lass,' the man with the sheep's face said to her. 'No need to let it get personal.'

In these confrontations Godfrey was always polite. In private they never discussed the quarry. She thought he was relieved by the pretence that there was antipathy between them. His wife would never believe he could fall for such an aggressive, loud-mouthed harridan.

On one occasion she saw them together, him and Barbara. Even the child was there. Godfrey had given one of his worked-out quarries to the Wildlife Trust to form the heart of the new reserve. The pits had been flooded and turned into ponds. The director of the Wildlife Trust talked hopefully about reed beds and a wader scrape. Godfrey had donated a lot of money for planning and hides, but he had just made his official planning application for the super quarry at Black Law so there was some nervousness within the Wildlife Trust. What was Godfrey Waugh after? Did he make his donation as a pre-emptive strike in the hope of getting a soft ride over the quarry? Anne didn't know the answers to those questions, but found it hard to believe that Godfrey was that devious.

Because of suspicion about Godfrey Waugh's motives, the party to celebrate the opening of the new reserve had become a low-key event. Anne overheard one trustee, a conservative country lady in a cashmere suit, say to another: 'We had planned a marquee, but in the circumstances, well, it hardly seemed appropriate.'

It was lunchtime, early October and warmer than days in most summers. The reserve was on a lowland site. Flat fields stretched to the coast. Although a bund, built with waste from the quarry, made the sea invisible to the guests, it made its presence felt through a shimmer on the horizon, the enormous sky.

Cattle were grazing on the bank, looking down at the celebration. One pit had already been flooded, had attracted mallard, coot and moorhen.

Anne arrived late, on purpose, to avoid the speeches and joined the people who were spilling out of the visitor centre which had been converted from one of the quarry buildings. It was time apparently for the opening ceremony. A ribbon had been strung between two sickly, newly planted trees. Eventually this would be the entrance to the car park. She recognized the back of Peter Kemp's head and slipped in behind him.

'Who have they got to do the honours then?'

He turned round, startled. 'Good God, woman. You nearly gave me a heart attack.'

'So which celeb's going to cut the cord?'

109

'Godfrey Waugh's brat.' Peter pulled a face. 'Sickening, isn't it?'

'I'd heard you'd joined the fat cats yourself. Haven't you set up on your own? A consultancy, I understand.'

'Ah well, that's different.'

'Of course,' she said. 'Isn't it always?'

'You should be nice to me, Annie. I might be able to find some work for you. Proper paid work. I've got the contract for the Black Law EIA.'

'Christ!' she said. 'How did you manage that?' She was seriously impressed. 'Didn't they want to go for someone more established?'

'I'm the best, Annie. That's all they needed to know.' He paused. 'You don't want the job then?'

'I haven't got any qualifications.'

'You've got the skills though. I've been taken on to complete the report and I can employ who I like.'

She was still thinking about this, wondering in fact what Godfrey would make of it, when they were called to order. Felicity Waugh was led by her father in front of the crowd. She was a plump old-fashioned girl with hamster cheeks and long crimped hair. He handed her a pair of garden shears and she struggled to cut the ribbon. It was an awkward task because the shears were very blunt. Eventually Godfrey helped her, putting his hands over hers. There was a burst of applause.

Godfrey returned to a woman standing at the front of the crowd. This must be his wife. Anne drank a toast to the reserve in tepid white wine and looked at her.

Anne had created a fiction about Barbara Waugh. She had imagined a plump, boring woman. Godfrey would have met her at secondary school. Their domestic life would be dreary, their conversation limited. They probably hadn't had sex since the conception of the wonderchild, and according to this fiction all the couple had in common now was the daughter.

Anne saw immediately that she had misjudged the situation completely. For one thing Barbara was serious competition. She was expensively dressed, beautifully groomed. She had cheekbones some women would die for and softly permed hair. In comparison Anne felt scrawny, ill kempt.

While she was still watching, Barbara and Godfrey exchanged a few words then Barbara broke away from him and walked over the grass to Anne. For a moment Anne wondered angrily if Godfrey had, after all, told his wife about the affair. Seeing the woman had made her reassess the relationship. Perhaps he had only been bothered about secrecy so he could preserve his respectable media image. Perhaps they were one of those sick-making couples who had no secrets. She prepared herself for a scene.

But it seemed that Barbara wanted to be friendly. She smiled anxiously. Anne could sense a strain, a definite tension. The words came out too quickly. The smile was replaced by a frown, a nervous gesture which seemed habitual.

She's a neurotic cow, Anne thought triumphantly, glad to be able to pigeon-hole her, feeling superior. She thought Barbara wouldn't be much competition at all. Now that they were standing close to each other it was obvious that they were much the same age. Barbara must have been approaching forty when she had the child.

'Mrs Preece. I wondered if I could have a word . . .'

'Of course.'

'I just want to tell you how much I admire the work you do. The environment's so important, don't you think?'

It took all Anne's composure not to appear shocked. It was the last thing she was expecting. 'Oh, I do,' she said, with just a hint of pastiche. Looking over the woman's shoulder she saw Godfrey, staring at the cows in a distracted way. She could tell he was panicking.

Barbara continued earnestly, 'I just wanted to tell you that neither my husband nor I resent your opposition to the quarry at Black Law. We are fully committed to nature conservation and if the Environmental Impact Assessment comes up with any information which indicates a problem, I can assure you that the scheme won't go ahead. We wouldn't wait for a public inquiry.'

'Right.' Anne didn't know what else to say. 'Well, thank you.' She was confused because although she hadn't changed her opinion of Barbara as a neurotic cow, the woman was obviously sincere. She also found it odd that Barbara could speak with such authority about a company matter. Godfrey had never mentioned her in connection with it and Anne had imagined her a good northern wifey, staying at home and washing socks, keeping her nose out of her husband's financial affairs.

'Are you involved with your husband's business?' she asked. Perhaps Barbara went in a couple of times a week to work in the office.

'We're partners. Not that I've played an active role

since Felicity arrived, though of course Godfrey consults me. It was different in the early days. I grew up with the business. My father owned our first site at Slateburn. When we married he retired and we took it over. It wasn't easy. In fact it was a terrible strain working every hour in the day just to keep going. But looking back I suppose I enjoyed it.' She smiled. 'I enjoyed it more when a bit of money started coming in and we could catch our breath.'

She seemed lost in thought. The nervous frown returned and she twisted the paper napkin she was still holding. She looked, Anne thought, like someone rolling a joint, though that was hardly her style.

Anne wondered why Godfrey never admitted to marrying the boss's daughter. Perhaps struggling to success alone made a better story. She didn't resent that. She told stories about her own past the whole time. The truth was so unexciting.

The woman stood silently for a moment. All around them was conversation and laughter. A great deal of the tepid wine had been drunk. Above the buzz she heard Peter's voice, schoolboy clear, the diction perfect.

'Neville! Well, this has all gone very nicely, hasn't it? You must be pleased.'

Langholme was a small place so she'd heard of Neville Furness. Son of Dougie who'd gone to college and got above himself. Land agent for the Holme Park Estate and then head-hunted to join Slateburn Quarries because, word had it, he was someone who could talk with the big landowners. Soon after, the deal was announced between Godfrey and the Fulwells. She had seen him when he'd lived in one of the tied houses on the estate. She'd taken to walking her dog along the lane at a time when he often went jogging, had tried to engage him in conversation but nothing had come of it. She'd tried to find out if he had a woman, but apparently not. She was aware suddenly that Barbara Waugh was looking in the same direction. But while Anne's gaze at the dark muscular body was frankly admiring, Barbara's was hostile, even afraid.

Barbara reached out and grabbed Anne's arm.

'Come to see me,' she said, 'at Alderwhinney. That's the name of the house. We're still in Slateburn. Anyone will tell you where it is. I'd like to talk to you. Come for coffee. Or lunch. Any time. I hardly ever go out.'

It was almost a repetition of what Godfrey said when he first mentioned his wife. She didn't say goodbye. She pecked Anne on the cheek and ran back to Felicity. Anne watched with astonishment.

Perhaps I should have gone, Anne thought. She pushed in the final pole. Tomorrow she would come back with the quadrats. It might have been amusing. I suppose I could still go now, keep Barbara informed about the survey. It's not as if Slateburn's miles away. I wonder what Godfrey would make of that.

Chapter Fifteen

The next day it was pissing down with rain so they were all holed up in the cottage together. Anne suffered an hour of Rachael nagging about how this was a good opportunity to tidy up a bit, then couldn't stand it any longer. She took the grotty Fiat into Langholme. The rain was so hard that she had to stop occasionally for the windscreen wipers to push the water from the screen. She phoned Godfrey from the public call box next to the garage.

It would have been more convenient to go back to the Priory but Jeremy was there and she couldn't stand the thought of his fussing. He'd spent the last few weeks telling her that they'd have to tighten their belts. He'd even raised the possibility of selling the Priory. She'd only realized then how much the house meant to her. The thought of giving up the garden made her feel murderous. She'd nearly told him that she'd only married him for the Priory but realized in time that might be foolish. One of his famous deals might yet come off.

A boy, whose voice still seemed to be breaking, answered the phone.

'Hello! Slateburn Quarries Ltd. How may I help you?'

When Anne said she wanted to talk to Godfrey there was a pause, then some whispered conversation. She was immediately suspicious. At last the boy spoke again: 'I'm sorry, Mr Waugh isn't available just now.'

'When will he be available?'

'Not until tomorrow evening. He's at a conference.'

'Where?'

The boy sounded confused. 'I'm sorry,' he said, 'I don't know.'

It was then, in a fit of pique, that Anne phoned Barbara. She wanted to pay Godfrey back for not coming to the phone, when she was feeling so miserable. He hadn't mentioned a conference to her. First she dialled directory enquiries. That almost took the decision about phoning away from her. If the Waughs were ex-directory, which they almost certainly would be, she'd have to give up the idea. But she was put straight through and before she could have second thoughts Barbara answered, a curt 'Waugh'. It sounded so like the imitation of a dog barking that for a moment Anne was distracted. When she did speak she managed to sound as confident as if they were old friends.

'You did tell me to get in touch. I thought I'd better not just turn up. You might be busy.'

But Barbara Waugh wasn't busy. And she remembered Anne perfectly, though they had met only once several months before. She insisted that Anne come to the house now.

'Do come if you're free. Stay for lunch. It's perfect. Felicity's spending the day with a friend and Godfrey's away for two days at a conference.'

So if he's lying, Anne thought, it's to both of us.

Godfrey had never invited Anne to his house. After

all, it was one of Barbara's characteristics that she
never went out. Apparently, even if she occasionally
planned a trip shopping or to the cinema, she didn't
always go. Perhaps it was a sort of sickness. Anne
knew where the house was, all the same. She had
driven past out of curiosity, seen a rather stern modern
house built of grey stone with a grey slate roof. Anne
would have broken the harsh lines with creeper and
climbers but the Waughs' garden was conventionally
tidy. There was a bare expanse of lawn, curved borders,
coloured now by symmetrical clumps of crocus and
snowdrops, backed by more mature shrubs. The only
touch of imagination was the tree house, nailed into a
gnarled sycamore. Although the platform on which
the house was built was only about three feet from the
ground it was reached by a wooden ladder. Anne
thought Godfrey had probably built the house himself
for the Beloved Felicity. Recently she had come to
think of the child in this way, seeing the words beginning with a capital letter like an obscure saint or
martyr.

When she arrived it was still raining. The front
door opened before she left the car. Barbara was
standing there. Anne sprinted over the gravel to meet
her and stood in the hall shaking the water from her
hair. Barbara was dressed in blue denim trousers, but
not the sort of jeans Anne was wearing. These wouldn't
fade at the knee or rip at the bum. Over the trousers
she wore a navy fine wool sweater. Her face was discreetly made up and there was a hint of perfume. Anne
had considered going home to the Priory to change but
couldn't face bumping into Jeremy. Besides the jeans
she was wearing a rugby shirt and a waterproof. She

wore no make-up and her hair could have done with another application of colour tint. It was more grey than rich chestnut brown.

Anne was aware of a polished woodblock floor, a staircase with flower patterned Axminster and the smell of coffee. Barbara seemed eager and anxious at once. She was speaking quickly and Anne, shaking the water from her hair, couldn't quite make out the words. Now that she was here it didn't seem such a good idea. It had started as a bit of fun; now she wondered if she could decently make an excuse and leave. But Barbara had already led her into a large living room and was speaking, repeating perhaps what she had said in the hall.

'I'm so glad you could come. Something's been troubling me. It seemed such a lucky coincidence when you rang. You are probably the best person to talk to.' She paused then, realizing that this wasn't the stuff of normal social interchange. 'I'm sorry. This is rude. Do sit down. Would you like a drink? Sherry or coffee perhaps? I think I'd like a coffee.'

Anne, who felt very much like a drink, said she would have coffee too.

When Barbara left the room, Anne tried to compose herself. She thought she might have the nerve to see it through without too much harm. She was sitting in a comfortable room which would have been more in keeping with an older house. Nothing was shabby, but the furniture was solid, heavy, rather dark. There was a wood-burning stove. Against one wall was an upright piano. On the stand, open, a book of child's music. On another wall a pencil drawing of the Beloved Felicity was hanging. Anne wondered if Barbara had done it herself, but it was rather good and she thought not. The girl was frowning as if concentrating on a problem she had no hope of solving.

Barbara brought coffee in a Pyrex filter jug. She saw Anne looking at the drawing.

'Do you have children, Mrs Preece?'

'Anne, please. No, no children.' Without thinking she continued with the flip explanation she always gave in these circumstances. 'I never felt the need of them.'

Barbara looked horrified as if, Anne thought, a guest had farted at the dinner table, but she said immediately, 'It was so good of you to come.'

Anne poured herself a cup of coffee but she didn't reply. She thought the only subject Barbara could want to discuss with her was her relationship with Godfrey, but she sensed no hostility. Rather the reverse was true. Barbara seemed embarrassingly grateful to have her there, despite her not liking children.

'This is rather delicate.' She sat, hand poised on the coffee jug. 'It's the new quarry. I'm not sure it's a good idea.'

Anne was caught off guard. 'I'm sorry?'

'I suppose you think I'm disloyal discussing it with you when my husband's away but I'd say the same if he were here. I have said exactly the same to him. I think it's a mistake. It'll alienate too many of our customers. It's bad for our image. I was involved with this business long before Goff was. It matters to me.'

'Why do you think he's so keen?'

It wasn't a question she'd ever asked Godfrey – she wouldn't ever be able to think of him as Goff – but now she found it interesting. If she were in his place she'd want the quarry for the excitement of the development, the drama, even the confrontation. But Godfrey wasn't like her. He wasn't greedy and he never took pleasure in being the centre of attention. Perhaps it was a fear that his business might otherwise stagnate which drew him on.

Barbara, however, had other ideas. 'I don't think he is keen. Not personally. Neville Furness has persuaded him that it's the only way the business will survive.'

'Neville Furness?' Anne needed time to think.

'He works for Goff. You must have seen him at some of the public meetings, very dark.'

'Yes,' Anne said. 'I know.'

'Since Neville started working for us Goff's been restless, preoccupied. And I hardly ever see him.'

I can solve that mystery for you, Anne thought. She said, carefully, 'Do you think an employee would exert that sort of influence?'

'Not usually perhaps but . . .' She broke off and her mood suddenly changed again. 'Let's go through to lunch. You don't mind eating in the kitchen? It's only something out of the freezer. And only paper napkins I'm afraid. Would you like a glass of wine? I put some Muscadet in the fridge.'

Anne followed her. They sat at a round pine table set in the corner of the sort of kitchen featured in magazines which end up in dentists' waiting rooms. Anne took in the gleaming surfaces, the spotless Italian tiles on the floor and supposed that Barbara had a cleaning lady. She wasn't jealous though. The Priory was classier. Such cleanliness smacked of the suburbs.

She was, however, impressed by the food. The rich onion flan might have come out of the freezer but Barbara had cooked it before it went in. It was topped with tomatoes and parmesan and latticed with anchovies and olives. They ate it with a salad and warm close-textured bread which must also have been homemade. Considerable effort had gone into the preparation of this meal. Anne, who often set out to impress, if not through food, wondered what Barbara was after.

'You were talking about your husband and the company.'

Barbara drank half a glass of wine very quickly. Her face was flushed. For a moment Anne thought she would change the subject again but she took a deep breath. 'I think Neville Furness has a vested interest in the quarry being sited on Black Law. His family own the adjoining land.'

'Yes,' Anne said, 'I know.'

'And now I understand his stepmother is dead.'

'She committed suicide.'

'Did you know Bella Furness?' Barbara demanded.

'Not well. I'd met her.'

'She ran that farm. It'll pass to Neville.'

'You knew her then?' Anne wasn't surprised. In these scattered communities the Waughs and the Furnesses were almost neighbours.

'I knew of her.'

'What do you think? That Neville would sell out to Slateburn if planning permission was granted? That's why he's so keen for the quarry to go ahead? There's not much demand for hill farms otherwise.'

'I don't think he'd sell. He's too canny for that. The most convenient access is through the farmyard and he'd charge for that. Any other route in is going to mean building a new road. In effect he could almost hold Goff to ransom, charge well over the odds for allowing machinery down the track!'

'Godfrey must be aware of that danger.'

'You'd think so, yes.'

'But?' Anne wiped buttery onion juice from her plate with a piece of bread. Barbara seemed distracted by this. Felicity must already have acquired immaculate table manners.

'But where Neville Furness is concerned he seems to have lost all his business sense. I'd like to know why Goff's so willing to accept Neville's advice. It's not like my husband. He's usually a cautious man. He comes to his own decisions in his own time.'

'What exactly are you afraid of?' Reluctantly Anne pushed the empty plate aside and sat with her elbows on the table. 'Blackmail?'

Again Barbara seemed disconcerted, though whether it was by the elbows on the table or the notion of her husband being blackmailed, it was hard to say.

'No,' she said uncertainly. 'Of course not.'

That at least, Anne thought, was a relief.

'All I wanted to say,' Barbara went on, 'was that if you, or one of your team, were to find something which would have an impact on the planning inquiry, if you could recommend that after all the development shouldn't go ahead . . .' She paused. 'Well, it would certainly be in all our interests, wouldn't it?'

This was said in such a gentle, unassuming way that it wasn't until Anne was at the front door, poised to run out into the rain, that she realized that what had been going on here, if not blackmail or bribery, had certainly been some form of corruption.

Chapter Sixteen

She was driving back through Langholme when she
saw Livvy Fulwell in the Holme Park Range Rover
coming towards her. Livvy stopped abruptly and
flashed her headlights. Anne wondered for a moment
if something vital had fallen off the grotty Fiat, but it
seemed that Livvy wanted to be friendly. Anne was
surprised. They weren't usually on those sort of terms.
Of course Livvy knew who she was. They'd been introduced when Anne had first arrived at the Priory and
Livvy, newly married, had taken over the running of
the big house. Occasionally they bumped into each
other. Livvy would give her a wave from the Range
Rover if she was feeling charitable or exchange a few
words in the post office after collecting her child
benefit. But intimacy had never been encouraged.
Anne was adept at picking up social signs and knew
better, for example, than to invite the Fulwells for
dinner.

Today, however, Livvy was unusually chatty. She
got out of the Range Rover, leaving the door wide open,
though it was blocking the lane, and a toddler, strapped
in the back, was howling blue murder. Robert and
Livvy had three children and Livvy prided herself on
being a real mother. There was always some sort of

nanny in the background but Livvy had done the play-group shift, taken them to buy their own shoes, organized birthday parties. Now the two older ones were away at school, but she was always there for them in the holidays. That was the impression that was given. Anne had overheard Robert talking to Jeremy at some charity do. 'We're off to Austria. Livvy adores skiing, but she insists on taking the little buggers with us. I think she's a bloody marvel!'

Livvy was younger than her husband, still only in her early thirties. Apparently she'd been a child bride of impeccable pedigree. She had the complexion of a schoolgirl now, short curly hair which looked as if she'd just come out of the shower and a wide friendly smile which made people trust her. People who knew the family well said she was ruthless, very much the brains behind the Holme Park operation.

'I'm so glad to have seen you.' Livvy was wearing a hand-knitted cotton sweater over jeans and a Barbour. The rain had stopped and the Barbour was unzipped. There was a stain on the front of the sweater which looked as if a child had been sick. 'I've been meaning for ages to say you must come round for coffee.'

Before the start of the project Anne would have been delighted to receive this invitation. Now she wondered what Rachael would say if she accepted. The Slateburn quarry would be developed on Holme Park land. It was a joint venture. Liaising with the developers was Peter's job. Or Rachael's. Certainly not a humble contract worker's. Livvy gave one of her generous smiles.

'I wanted you to know how much we appreciate what you're doing. Robert and I both admire it. I mean the Priory seems so cosy and you've given it all up to camp out in that cottage in the hills. I mean we feel we're on the same side as you, really. Holme Park's the children's inheritance, isn't it? If you find something important up there we'd be the last people in the world to want to destroy it.'

The cries of the toddler reached a crescendo.

'Oh God, we can't talk now. I always knew we should have stopped after Harry. Two's enough for anyone. Or perhaps it comes so hard because there's such a big gap.'

But it really didn't seem to come very hard. She scooped the infant out of its child seat and fixed it onto her hip, jiggling it gently while she continued to talk. The cries subsided.

'Can you make it tomorrow? Elevenish? Or doesn't that fit in with your work?'

By now Anne was curious. Sod Rachael.

'No,' she said. 'Eleven will be fine.'

'Great!' Livvy gave another smile. This time of relief? Or of a successful mission accomplished? Then she deftly strapped in the baby and drove off, hitting the horn in farewell.

On Wednesday and Sunday afternoons Holme Park was open to the public. Anne had paid her three quid once to have a nose at the gardens, which frankly weren't up to much, but she'd never been inside. Approaching the house the following day she wasn't sure where to go. Perhaps she should go round to the back. She imagined that this coffee party would be an informal affair. They'd probably be in the kitchen, with the toddler doing something constructive and messy with paint and dogs sprawled on the floor.

But Livvy was at the front of the house chatting to a plump young woman and when Anne hesitated, not sure whether she should park in the field which the public used, Livvy waved her on. They didn't use the grand front door with the stone steps and the porticoes, but she wasn't shown into the tradesman's entrance either. There were two wings, lower, less daunting than the main house, built at right angles to it, and she was taken into the entrance hall of one of these.

'I've just asked Arabella to take the horror out for a walk,' Livvy said, 'so we can talk in peace.'

Today Livvy was more smartly dressed, though not, Anne suspected, just for her benefit. She had heard that Livvy carried out most of the business on the estate. There would be meetings. The deal with Slateburn had been her idea. Robert had worried that it might affect the shooting and hadn't been too keen. He was considered a soft touch, a financial liability.

'How's Robert?' Anne asked.

'Out on the estate. A crisis with one of the tenants. He sends his apologies. Really, he's so sorry not to be here.'

They had coffee not in the kitchen but in a pretty little sitting room. The sofa and the chairs were covered in a pale lemon fabric which would show every mark and Anne thought it unlikely that the children were allowed to play here. After Livvy had carried in the tray there was a moment of awkward silence which she must have taken as a failure on her part, because she gave one of her smiles and said apologetically, 'Crazy, isn't it, that we've got so much in common and yet that we've hardly had a chance to meet.'

Anne didn't reply.

'Anyway, I'm so interested in this survey of yours. How, exactly, does it work?'

'There are three of us,' Anne said. 'Three women.'

'Isn't that unusual?'

'Perhaps. I'm the botanist. Rachael Lambert's doing the bird work and Grace is our mammal expert.'

'Grace?'

'Grace Fulwell. No relation, I presume, but quite a coincidence.'

'Oh, there are dozens of Fulwells in the Northumberland phone book. We're a common lot. I expect we're all related one way or another too. Where does she come from?'

Livvy's voice was light but she seemed genuinely interested.

'I don't know. She's not very communicative.' Anne realized that might sound bitchy. She didn't want to give the impression that the project was falling apart. Not to Livvy Fulwell at least. 'When you live and work on top of one another like that privacy's important.'

'Oh yes!' As if a great truth had been revealed. 'I do see.'

Anne talked Livvy through the process of the survey, explained the system of the poles and the quadrats. Livvy listened intently and encouraged Anne to expand. Anne realized how the managers of shooting syndicates, the tenants and the businessmen could be persuaded to invest in her.

'And where exactly do you intend to survey?'

'I'd like to do a couple of moorland sites, the peat

bogs of course and I thought one square close to the lead mine. Sometimes the spoil changes the acidity of the soil. There might be something unusual. You don't mind?'

'God, no! Go wherever you like. Absolutely open access. I explained yesterday that I think we're on the same side.' She paused. 'I suppose it's too early to have come up with any results yet?'

'Much too early. I haven't started the detailed work yet.'

'Ah.' She seemed disappointed and Anne thought that at last she had found the reason for this invitation. Either Livvy was too impatient to wait for the full report or she was so much of a control freak that she wanted to see the results before Peter Kemp got his hands on them.

'Well, you must come again. Perhaps when you've something interesting to report.'

It was because she felt she had been manipulated, because she didn't want this confident young woman to think she'd had the conversation all her own way that Anne brought up the question of Neville Furness. She introduced the subject clumsily.

'We were talking about connections and relationships earlier. I suppose it's inevitable in a county with a population as small as this that everyone's connected somehow, but it does seem a coincidence. Neville Furness working for you then moving to Slateburn. And having an interest in Black Law Farm. More than an interest now, I suppose.'

'Isn't it dreadful!' Livvy opened her eyes wide in a gesture of shock and sympathy. She ignored Anne's point about Neville having moved from Holme Park to

Slateburn. 'Poor Neville. We do feel for him. When's the funeral?'

'Tomorrow.'

'We were wondering if we should go. To support him. But we'd never met Mrs Furness and we thought in the circumstances he might prefer just family and close friends.'

'I suppose he'll take on responsibility for the farm,' Anne said.

'I suppose he will.'

'The estate wouldn't be interested in buying it?' The idea had come to her quite suddenly. She wondered why she hadn't considered it before. 'Then if you get planning permission for the quarry you would control the access.'

'I don't know that we've even considered it,' Livvy said easily. 'That's Robert's territory not mine.'

Anne could sense that she was preparing to move the conversation on to something safer, back to the baby perhaps, or an enquiry after Jeremy's health, so she got her question in quickly.

'How did you find Neville Furness?' she asked in a gossipy, all girls together voice. 'He was your estate manager, wasn't he? I've met him a couple of times but I've never been quite sure what to make of him.'

Livvy was too wily to be thrown by that. 'Neville?' she said. 'Oh, he's a terrific bloke. A star. We were devastated to lose him.'

Then she did move the conversation back to domestic matters. The boys had just gone back to school after the Easter holidays and she was missing them like hell. Really, if there was any sort of decent day school in the area she'd have them out of that place like a shot, no matter what Robert thought.

At twelve o'clock precisely the young woman Anne had seen earlier returned. First they heard pushchair wheels on the gravel then they saw her through the long windows. The child was asleep, its arms thrown out in abandon, its mouth wide open.

'I'm sorry,' Livvy said. 'I'll have to go and retrieve the brat. It's Arabella's half day, but don't feel you have to rush off.'

'That's all right,' Anne said. 'I should get back to work.' She knew that Arabella had been told exactly when to return with the child. Livvy had allowed Anne an hour. No more.

She was reluctant to return immediately to Baikie's. Rachael would want to know where she'd been and she supposed she'd have to confess to fraternizing with the enemy. She decided to call in at the Priory, pick up her mail, throw a few things into the washing machine. Perhaps phone Godfrey's office and see if he was back from the conference.

The lane which led from Holme Park to the village had once been a private avenue bordered by trees, running through parkland up to the house. Now the fields on either side were fenced and farmed. At the end of the lane was a pair of semis, built in the twenties as suitable dwellings for senior estate workers and their families. By the side of the lane Grace Fulwell stood, staring at these houses, apparently transfixed.

Anne slowed down and pulled to a stop. Still Grace stared. She seemed not to have seen or heard the car.

Anne wound down the window, forced herself to keep her voice friendly. 'What are you doing here?'

Grace turned, came to life. 'I was walking the stretch of river through the village. I'd heard about Holme Park. Vanburgh, is it? I thought I'd take a detour to look.'

From where she stood, if she had turned and looked up the straight avenue, there was a perfect view of the house, but it wasn't Vanburgh's architecture which had Grace's interest, but these modest cottages with their tidy gardens. More specifically, it was the left-hand semi with the child's swing and the rotary washing line. Even now her eyes strayed back to it.

'Did you walk?' Anne demanded.

Grace nodded.

'It must be twelve miles from Baikie's even over the hill. You should have asked me to bring you. Or Rachael. I'm surprised she didn't offer when you told her where you were coming.'

Grace turned. There was a faint flush on her face.

'I wasn't exactly sure then, where I was going.'

'Tut tut,' Anne said. 'You naughty girl.'

But Grace seemed not to hear.

'Well, at least I can give you a lift back.'

'No,' Grace said. 'That's all right. I've not finished yet.'

So Anne left her there, still staring at the house, her eyes squinting slightly as if she were looking through a camera view finder.

Well, Anne thought. It's her funeral.

Chapter Seventeen

'Bloody hell!'

The woman coming into the crematorium chapel of rest might have tried to close the door quietly but a gust of wind caught it and blew it shut with a bang. Anne had been day-dreaming, letting the pious words wash over her, and she started as if woken suddenly from sleep. Though she had muttered the expletive under her breath she could sense Rachael's disapproval. With the rest of the congregation she turned to see the middle-aged woman appear in the aisle, apparently blown in like the door. Anne followed her progress to a pew with admiration. She seemed untroubled by the stares, the curious whispers. This woman certainly knew how to make an entrance.

Afterwards, waiting outside for Rachael, Anne saw the woman again. She evaded the other mourners, slipped past them with remarkably little effort although she had appeared so big and clumsy in the chapel. Then she let herself into a top of the Range Rover which had been parked close to the main gate for an early getaway. Not a tenant farmer then, Anne thought. Despite the poorly fitting clothes and the supermarket carrier bags this was a woman of substance. A relative of Bella's perhaps. They would have been of a similar age, could have been sisters. There was a similarity too, not of looks but expression, off-putting, secretive, rather dour.

'Was that Bella's sister?' she asked Rachael. 'The show-stopper with the bags?'

'I didn't know she had a sister.' Rachael sounded peeved as if she was the only person in the world with any right to know if Bella Furness had relatives.

'Nor do I. I was guessing. Asking.' She paused. 'Look, I'm going. I can't face a jamboree at the White Hart and it's not even as if I knew her that well. Besides, it was her choice, wasn't it? What she wanted.'

'If you wait a few minutes I'll give you a lift.'

'That'll be all right.' The crem was giving her the creeps and already she could feel one of Rachael's lectures coming on.

She had started walking along the wide pavement towards the town centre when Godfrey's car pulled up behind her. She presumed he'd got rid of his wife – perhaps she'd come in her own car – and was about to climb into the front passenger seat when she saw that Barbara Waugh was already there. It gave her the fright of her life.

'Mrs Preece, hello,' Barbara said through the open window. 'Can we give you a lift into town?' Then 'Barbara Waugh, perhaps you don't remember. We met at the opening of the Wildlife Trust Reserve.'

'Oh yes,' Anne said. 'Of course.'

Godfrey stared straight ahead over the steering wheel. It had obviously been Barbara's idea to stop. She hadn't told her husband about the cosy lunch at Alderwhinney and wanted to make sure that Anne didn't mention it either if they bumped into each other at the White Hart. That suited Anne very well. The impulsive gesture to phone Barbara already seemed childish and vindictive. She preferred Godfrey not to know about it.

'Are you going to the hotel, Mrs Preece?' Barbara asked as Anne climbed into the rear of the car. 'I gather Mr Furness has invited everyone.'

'No, I didn't know Bella very well. I only came to the funeral to give Rachael support. She's been so upset.'

'Can I take you to Langholme then? I've got my own car in town and it's not far out of my way. I'm going straight back.'

'I thought I'd spend some time in Kimmerston. Since the project started I've not had much chance . . .'

Barbara seemed disappointed and Anne was worried for a moment that she might suggest a girls' lunch out, a trip round the shops. Instead she said quickly, 'Of course, I quite understand.'

Godfrey dropped Barbara off first at the car park next to the Sports Centre.

'I'll get out here,' Anne said. 'It's not far.'

But Barbara wouldn't have it and insisted that Godfrey should take her to where she wanted to go. So she went with him to the car park in the courtyard behind the White Hart. When he went into the hotel to make, as he put it, 'at least an appearance', she sauntered across the road and down an alley to a coffee shop. She drank a cappuccino and read an old copy of *Cosmo* until he came to pick her up.

He took her for lunch to a town in the south of the county, where once there were shipyards and coal mines. This was a place where they could be sure of avoiding people who might know them. It was also a place where Godfrey seemed at home. For Anne it was like straying into a foreign country. The boarded-up shops, the litter in the street, the bare-legged women pushing mucky babies in prams, all this seemed a million miles from Livvy Fulwell and Holme Park and gave her a peculiar thrill.

Yet even here, Godfrey had found somewhere special to eat. There was a gem of a restaurant, very small and discreet, in a terrace between an old-fashioned park and the jetty where a ferry docked. The ferry carried shoppers back to a small community on the other side of the estuary. Once the terrace had housed the harbour master's offices and the small dining room, simply furnished, the walls decorated with photographs of submarines and master mariners, had the feel of the officers' mess. Now, at two o'clock, it was empty.

The owner recognized them at once and took them to their favourite table.

'A drink?' he asked. 'The usual? Are you in a hurry today?'

Sometimes they were in a hurry. It was an hour from Kimmerston and Godfrey had meetings.

'No,' Godfrey said. 'We've got all afternoon.'

So he brought them drinks, a menu and went back to his seat behind the bar and his book. He was reading *The Brothers Karamazov*. He only looked up to call over, 'The chef's on good form today. You're safe with any of the specials.'

The chef could be moody. He was an alcoholic, usually reformed, given to sudden rages. They smiled.

'I'm sorry about earlier,' Godfrey said. 'Barbara insisted.'

'That's all right.'

'She'd have been suspicious if I'd refused to stop.'

'She doesn't suspect anything, does she?' It was one explanation Anne thought for Barbara's original invitation at the Wildlife Trust Reserve. Perhaps she'd wanted a closer look at the opposition.

'No, of course not.'

'What was it like there, the . . .' She wasn't quite sure what to call it. Reception sounded like a wedding and wake was far too jolly for a finger buffet at the White Hart. 'The do.'

'All right, I suppose. I didn't stay long.'

'How was Neville bearing up?' Some of Barbara's hostility must have rubbed off because what she had intended as a simple question came out with an undercurrent of sarcasm. He seemed not to notice.

'Bella Furness was his stepmother not his mother. I don't think they were particularly close. You wouldn't expect him to be upset.'

'No,' she said. 'I'm not surprised. He always seemed a cold fish.'

'I didn't mean he didn't care. He put on a decent enough show for her.'

'Will it make any difference to your plans for the quarry? Neville being in charge of the Black Law land?'

'Why should it?'

'It'd make access a heck of a lot easier if he gives you permission to use the track.'

He studied the menu intently, frowning. For a moment she thought he wouldn't respond at all. 'I'm not sure it's altogether ethical, our discussing the quarry.' He adopted a joking tone but he was warning her off. She could understand why Barbara had felt excluded.

'What do you mean?'

'I could be influencing your results.'

'Oh yeah!' she said. 'Right. We've been having an affair for nearly a year, but a chat about Neville Furness is much more likely to influence my judgement than that. Come off it.'

'We have to be careful. Because of that.'

'I know!' She was indignant that he felt he had to say it. Then something about his voice, something about the way he looked down at the menu just as she was about to meet his eyes made her ask: 'Why? Has anyone said anything?'

'No.'

'But you think someone might have guessed?'

He shrugged.

'I've a right to know, don't you think?'

'That first time we went to the Riverside. When we came out together I thought I recognized the car on the other side of the road. We might have been seen. That's all.'

'Who by? Whose car was it?'

'Neville Furness.'

'Oh!' she cried. 'Bloody great!' Then she thought that Barbara's notion that Neville was putting pressure on Godfrey to go ahead with the quarry against his better judgement, might not be so wide of the mark. Godfrey would go along with a lot not to have his wife and child upset.

'Has Neville said anything?' she demanded.

'No.'

'Not even indirectly? He could make a fortune out of the scheme.'

'Not even indirectly.' He sounded irritated. She had never known him so cross with her.

'I'm sorry,' she said. 'What's the matter?'

'I have enough of that sort of talk at home.'

'What sort of talk?'

'Barbara thinks that Neville has too much influence over me. She's never been happy about the quarry proposal. Since we've started to flesh out the details she's become obsessed.'

'Perhaps she's right!'

'No, you don't understand. Neville's not like that.' He handed her a menu. 'Look, we should order. Rod will wonder what's going on.' Although Rod still seemed engrossed in Dostoevsky.

'What about this? Mullet baked with shallots and new potatoes.'

'Yes,' she said. 'Anything.'

They sat in silence until the food had arrived and they'd begun to eat.

'Tell me then,' she said at last. 'If Neville Furness isn't into blackmail, what *is* he like?'

'An ordinary, decent bloke. A bit lonely. A bit shy.' He smiled. She could tell he was trying to please her. 'He could do with a good woman. If he was the monster Barbara makes him out to be, do you think I'd have taken him on?'

'You might if you thought he'd be useful.'

'No,' he said quietly. 'Of course I want the business to grow. It's how I measure what I've been doing, my achievement. But not at any price.'

'Why did he leave Holme Park?'

'I don't know. I mean, not exactly. I can tell you how it happened if you're interested?'

'Yes,' she said defiantly. 'I am interested if that's OK with you.'

'I had some preliminary meetings with Robert and Olivia Fulwell about the quarry. The approach came from them. At least I think probably from her. Furness was in on some of the discussions. I was impressed. I also had the feeling that he wasn't happy. The relationship between him and Mrs Fulwell was . . . strained. I offered him a job. He accepted.'

'What did Livvy Fulwell make of that?' His calm explanation reassured her. She was starting to relax, to enjoy the idea of Godfrey poaching Neville from Livvy.

'I don't know. It was none of my business.'

An idea occurred to her. 'Do you think they'd been having an affair?'

'Like I said. None of my business.' Unusually he poured himself a second glass of wine. He looked tired. She pushed away her plate, still littered with fish bones, twigs of thyme, and reached across the table, a repeat of the gesture which had first brought them together.

'I'm sorry. I shouldn't have questioned your judgement.'

He seemed about to say something but lost his nerve at the last minute.

They spent all afternoon in the restaurant, finishing the wine then several cups of coffee. In the end Rod took their money and asked them to see themselves out. He'd long ago put up the closed signs and locked the door. Anne had the feeling again that Godfrey was building up to some confidence, but it wasn't until they were out on the street that he seemed prepared to speak.

They'd wandered into the town centre, towards the secure car park which they always used. Anne, waiting for him to spit out whatever was bothering him, saw her reflection in the window of a shop selling cut price shoes. She looked so wretchedly old that she thought: he wants to get rid of me, that's what he wanted to say. That's why he picked that fight. At just that moment he started to speak.

'It's Barbara.'

'What about her?' Anxiety made her aggressive, shrill.

'I'm not sure I can stay with her. Not indefinitely.'

'What are you saying?'

He stopped in the middle of the pavement. All around them were jostling women, kids on their way home from school. The stream of people eddied round them, took no notice. They were used to couples making a scene in the street.

'I'm asking what you feel about that.'

'I didn't mean to come between you. That wasn't my intention.'

'No. It's nothing to do with you. It's Barbara. You don't know how much I owe her . . .'

'If you hadn't married her you'd still be a craftsman, chiselling stone?'

'It's not just that.' He became impatient because he'd lost his drift. He raised his voice but still the crowds moved on, unheeding. 'What I mean is that being grateful isn't enough. What I mean is, I'd rather be with you. Not yet. When Felicity is a bit older. More independent. When this business with the quarry is settled. I need to know how you feel about that.'

It was only then that she realized he wasn't giving her the push.

'You mean openly, publicly?'

'Marriage, if you want it.'

The next morning when he left her at the end of the lane to walk down to Baikie's, she felt about fifteen again. She'd not slept. Godfrey had fallen asleep quite suddenly in the early hours and she'd lain awake listening to his quiet breathing. It was the first time they'd spent the night together. But still she felt she had the energy to work all day. And that she'd do anything Godfrey Waugh asked her to.

Chapter Eighteen

If it hadn't been for occasional trips out to meet Godfrey, that week after the funeral would have driven her demented. Being trapped in Baikie's with the two other women was worse than being back at school. She even considered moving back home despite the long drive to the survey area, but Jeremy had returned from London and seemed installed in the Priory for a long stay. He seemed chastened. Perhaps one of his love affairs had gone sour, or perhaps it was one of his business ventures, but he was in little boy mode, in need of comfort, and she didn't have the patience for it. Not now.

Rachael she could have handled. Even though Rachael was a frustrated bitch, uptight and heartless, at least she was sane. But ever since she'd come across Grace staring at the estate workers' cottages at Holme Park, Anne had realized that she was as mad as a snake. Anne wasn't given to whimsical fancies, but being woken at night by the rustling of Grace's night clothes, the padding of her feet on the bare floor, made her seriously worried. She wouldn't have put it past Grace to lose it altogether, and if someone was going to wake up with Grace's penknife through her ribs, she didn't intend it to be her.

So she told Rachael in the pub that she was going to move into the boxroom. It might not have a lock, but at least she could wedge a chair under the door and she wouldn't have to put up with Grace's midnight wanderings. The pub had been Rachael's idea. She'd been on management courses. She probably saw it as a team-building exercise. But as Grace spent all evening in the public phone box in the street outside and Anne used the opportunity to tell Rachael what she thought of Grace, it was a bit of a failure.

'Have you seen her records?' Anne demanded. She'd had a lot to drink in a short space of time, though she could tell Rachael disapproved. She needed it.

'Not yet. Not in detail.'

'We're talking fantasy here. I mean real fairy-tale time. The other day I saw her miles outside the survey area. Miles from the nearest river if it comes to that. Where did you get her from anyway?'

Rachael muttered something about it being Peter's decision. Anne thought Rachael wasn't really management material despite the courses and the degrees.

The next day she felt she needed cheering up. The vegetation classification had been going well. The quadrats in the peat bog had proved interesting. There was nothing so special that the development of the quarry would be threatened, but she'd enjoyed the variety of species there. She had a hangover and could afford to take time off.

The last time she'd seen Godfrey, he'd presented her with a mobile phone, so they could keep in touch. She hadn't told the others and when they were around she kept it switched off. There was no real reason for the secrecy – she could have said she'd bought it herself – but she knew what would happen. Rachael would consider it communal property and suggest that whoever was going furthest into the hills should borrow it as a safety measure. If Anne objected she'd be made out to be a heartless monster. Well, bugger that, she thought. If Peter Kemp wasn't such a tight bastard he'd have provided mobiles for them all. Another reason for wanting a room of her own was so that she could charge it up without anyone else seeing.

That morning Rachael drove into Kimmerston for a meeting with Peter and the developers. Grace, more together than she'd been for days, actually had breakfast with them and volunteered the information that she'd be out all day. As soon as they'd left Anne called Godfrey on her mobile.

'Can you come out to play?'

'I don't know . . .'

'You weren't planning to be at the meeting with Kemp Associates, were you?'

'I hadn't realized there was a meeting. Neville must have fixed it.'

'If Neville's as good a bloke as you say, get him to drag it out. Keep Rachael out of the way and give us longer.'

'I can't involve him.'

'Why not? If he knows already.' She paused. 'Have you got a pen?'

'Of course.'

'Write down this shopping list. You can call at Tesco's on your way over.'

'You're expecting me to come over to Black Law?'

'Why not? They're both out.'

'Well . . .' he said. 'Someone might see.'

'So what? You're entitled from time to time to look at the development site.'

'I want to see you.'

'Then come.'

When he arrived he was laden with carrier bags like a suburban husband. He seemed quite comfortable with the role. She thought he must have been shopping for Barbara. Like a suburban housewife she unpacked the groceries. He held out a polystyrene tray of chicken pieces wrapped in clingfilm.

'Shouldn't these go in the oven now, if we're going to eat them at lunchtime?'

'Are you joking? I'll do them later. I'm not wasting time cooking when I've got you to myself.'

It was a grey and misty day and she'd lit a fire. They had a picnic in front of it. She'd ordered salad, bread, a lump of Stilton, olives, chocolate.

'All the things,' she said, 'I love most in the world.'

'And me?'

'You?' she said. 'Oh, I don't think I could fall for anyone who fishes for compliments like that!' But she pushed the tub of olives out of the way and pulled him down beside her instead.

They were at the undignified stage of events. His trousers undone but not fully off, her bra unclipped but dangling from one shoulder, when Grace arrived. They heard the kitchen door open then shut and they froze. Godfrey started scrabbling for his clothes then, but it was too late. She came straight in and saw them. She stood in the doorway staring, her eyes blank, not quite focused, as if she were thinking of something else altogether.

She didn't say anything. Not even 'Sorry for

disturbing you' which Anne thought was a bit of a cheek. She just turned round and went out. Anne was tempted to let her go. What did it matter if she told the world she'd been shagging Godfrey Waugh in Baikie's cottage? Then she thought it could make things difficult, and not just for Godfrey. Anne fastened her bra and pulled on her top. In the kitchen Grace was standing, writing on a sheet of paper from out of her notebook.

'I thought you weren't coming back,' Anne said.

Grace didn't reply.

'What are you doing here anyway?'

'I'd forgotten to leave details of my route and my ETA.'

'Look,' Anne said, 'about what happened just now.'

'None of my business, is it!'

She can't have recognized him, Anne thought, or she'd have said something.

'None of my business who you mix with.' So then Anne wasn't quite sure.

'Look,' Anne said again, and even she could hear the desperation in her voice. 'He's married. With a child. No one knows about us. You won't say anything?'

Grace looked at her. Anne couldn't work out at all what the other woman was feeling. Contempt perhaps. Pity? Envy?

'No,' Grace said at last, 'I'll not say anything.'

'Thanks.' Anne was surprised at how relieved she suddenly felt. She wanted to make a gesture. 'Why don't I cook a meal later? For the three of us. Something special. It's about time we made an effort to get on. OK?'

Grace shrugged. 'OK.' She walked towards the door,

paused, gave the ghost of a smile. 'I'll let you get on then.'

For the attempt at humour, for letting her off the hook, Anne could have hugged her.

But when Anne returned to the living room Godfrey was fully dressed. His shirt was buttoned to the neck, his tie knotted.

'What are you doing? I've got rid of her.'

'What did she say?'

'Nothing. And she won't say anything.' She paused. 'And I believe her.'

'I should never have come. I told you it was a risk.'

He looked at her pathetically, reminding her of Jeremy, irritating her so much that she said: 'Anyway, I thought you wanted to go public. Isn't that what you said after the meal on the coast?'

'Not now. Not like this.' He looked around the grubby room, with the remains of the meal scattered across the floor.

'Fine,' she shouted. 'That's fine! Because I'm not into commitment either. Never have been.'

They stared at each other.

'I'm sorry.' She reached out a hand, touched the cotton of his shirtsleeve. 'Finish the wine at least. Our first row. We should celebrate.'

'No.' Then more gently, 'I'm going to walk up to the lead mine. Then if anyone recognized the car there's an excuse for me being here.'

'Who would recognize it? You're being paranoid.'

'I want to go. I want to see the site again.'

'I'll come with you then.'

'No, really, I prefer to go by myself.'

She wandered around the living room, picking up

the scraps of food, piling plates and cutlery, then she went upstairs and washed out a few things in the bathroom sink. It wasn't much of a drying day but she took them outside and pegged them on the line, thinking that from there she might see him walking back down over the hill to the cottage. She wouldn't have gone out to look specially. There was no sign of him or of Grace.

Inside again she started to prepare a casserole for the evening meal, using the ingredients Godfrey had brought. She put Annie Lennox in her cassette player and played it very loud, so when he got back he'd know she wasn't bothered about him one way or the other. She told herself it wouldn't be long before he did come back, apologetic, flushed, out of breath. She thought he must look really stupid out on the hill in the clothes he'd put on for the office this morning.

But he seemed to be away for hours and it came as a shock when at last she heard the engine of his car. She rushed out into the yard but it had driven off at great speed. She had to walk up the track and close the gate behind him. He had driven on towards the ford without bothering to stop and shut it.

Later she tried to phone him at his office, but his secretary, who must have recognized her voice, said that he wasn't taking any calls.

At first she was surprised when Grace was late back from the hill. She'd thought they'd come to an understanding, had even thought they might get on better for the remainder of the project. Then she thought Grace was making a point, letting Anne know that her co-operation couldn't be taken for granted. She tried to tell Rachael that there was probably nothing to worry about, but Rachael insisted on going out there herself, screaming and making a scene.

Later, when it got very dark and still Grace hadn't returned, Anne wondered if Godfrey had followed her and frightened her off. Usually she wouldn't have said that was in character at all – in every situation he was understated, undramatic – but today he had behaved very oddly. Rushing away without talking to her then refusing to take her calls, that wasn't like him. Anne thought it probably wouldn't have taken a lot to scare Grace off. You could tell she was pretty near the edge already. Anne could imagine her walking to the nearest road and hitching a lift back to where she'd come from. Wherever that was.

In the end she couldn't stand Rachael's melodramatics any longer. She'd put on a brave face but she was panicking about Godfrey. About losing him. She hadn't realized how much a part he'd been of her plans for the future. She went to bed and although she hadn't expected to, she went to sleep very quickly. She didn't hear the arrival of the mountain rescue team and the first she knew of Grace's death was the sound of Rachael snivelling at the bottom of the stairs, early the next morning.

Grace

Chapter Nineteen

The day after her arrival at Baikie's Grace woke suddenly. The room was filled with light and she knew she had overslept, thought with a sudden panic that she might be in trouble. She looked around the room, not sure for a moment where she was. There were bunk beds, crammed into the big room so as many students as possible could be accommodated on field trips. They had been stripped of sheets but each had a grey blanket folded at the foot. The pillows were covered with striped cases. There was a musty, institutional smell. For an instant she was reminded of another place where she had stayed and she was confused.

Then Rachael shouted up the stairs that coffee had been made if Grace wanted some.

'And what do you fancy for breakfast?'

So she jumped back to the present. She saw that one other bed in the room had been made up, and remembered Anne, picking her up from the station and driving through Langholme. She remembered the track from the road into the forest, then out onto the open hill, the feeling that emerging from the trees was like arriving in a different world. A child's fantasy, beyond the wardrobe door, a place anyway she'd dreamt of since she was little.

'Toast?' Rachael's voice was more impatient.

'Please. I'm nearly ready.'

She opened the curtains. Beyond the garden which was still in shadow, the hill was bathed in sunlight, so last year's bracken shone like copper. She pulled on her clothes and went down to the kitchen.

'I'm sorry,' she said. 'I can't have set the alarm clock.'

She was aware of Rachael looking at her, concerned, sympathetic. She had seen that look before too.

'No problem,' Rachael said. 'As long as we meet the deadline we can set our own timetable, but I thought I'd wake you. We're sure to lose days later with the weather.'

She smiled. Grace tried to respond, to be friendly too, but she felt awkward. It was more difficult with just the two of them. She wasn't used to deceit. The kitchen was so small that they had to stand very close together and she felt exposed. Last night Anne had done most of the talking. Grace had pretended to listen but mostly she'd been able to concentrate on her own thoughts. Now she drank coffee, ate toast and as soon as possible she prepared to go outside.

'Where are you going?' Rachael asked.

'I'm sorry?'

'I need to know where you're going. Health and Safety rules. I explained before.'

'Yes. Yes, of course.'

Rachael was still in the kitchen, standing because there was no room to sit, with a piece of toast in her hand. Grace put her map on the formica bench.

'I thought I'd start close to the cottage. I'll just walk

the Skirl today, get a feel for it, look out for spraints, see what the bank's like. I should be back by two.'

'Good.'

Grace saw that she had reassured Rachael, who had previously been watching her rather oddly. She should take more care. It occurred to her suddenly that Rachael looked very like an otter herself, with her chunky front teeth, the brown hair which would turn grey when she was still young, the downy lip.

'Will you take sandwiches?' Rachael asked. 'There's cheese and the bread's still OK.'

'No.' Then, seeing that more explanation was required, 'I'll get something when I get back.' In fact she'd never been much interested in food which seemed rather strange in view of her father's profession.

From the kitchen door she walked round the house, past the tractor shed and into the front garden. There was a lawn, on which apparently students played croquet in the summer, but it hadn't yet been cut. This was surrounded by bushes and shrubs. The boundary of the garden was marked by a dry stone wall. There was no gate onto the open hillside but a stile, in the form of a large boulder, on each side of the wall and an upright wooden stake beside it. There was a path, presumably flattened by students and sheep, which led through the bracken to the burn. The Skirl was as wide in some places as a river, and seemed to Grace a good place for otter. She imagined she could smell them.

She crossed the burn by a series of deep flat rocks. The water was very clear. The strong sunlight reflected from the surface dazzled her and she almost lost her footing. On the other side the bank had been cut away and a muddy beach had formed. She scrambled up the bank and began walking towards the old lead mine.

She walked along the bank slowly, looking for pulling-up places and spraints, the droppings which were distinctive because they smelled so strongly of fish. At university it had been a comprehensive study of the contents of otter spraints which had won her a First. That and her dedication. She'd never been distracted much by a social life or men. In her interview for this job Peter Kemp had said: 'There won't be much to do, you know, out there on the hills. Not in the evening. You won't be bored?'

'Oh no,' she'd said quite truthfully, not telling him of course that she had her own reasons for wanting to be part of the project.

She followed the burn from the Black Law farm land towards the estate and the old lead mine. There it was channelled into stone culverts. She presumed that once it had been used as part of the mining process. Perhaps to wash the ore or power a wheel. The boundary between Holme Park and the farm wasn't marked on the map, but she had added it in pencil, and she knew she must have got it right because past the mine where the burn opened out again, she came to a dead weasel which had been thrown into the water. Its gingery coat was perfect but it was quite stiff. Nearby she found the tunnel trap which had killed it. A spring-mounted trap had been placed in an old piece of piping in a gully and covered with stones. She couldn't find signs of any other corpses, but near to the trap there lingered the smell of rotting flesh. This must be Holme Park land because only a keeper would have gone to this much trouble. She considered blocking the entrance to the trap, but thought that would be foolish. She didn't want to draw attention to herself at this stage.

The discovery of the weasel upset her, though she couldn't quite work out why. Perhaps it was because there was no outward indication of injury. She tried to put it from her mind and continued walking but almost immediately thought she heard footsteps, splashing water, at some distance behind her. She turned round but the hill was empty. There was nowhere to hide except the old mine workings – and who would want to skulk there? So she knew she had been imagining things again.

She walked on and she began to count, though not now the traces of otter left on the bank. Now she counted the foster parents who'd cared for her, though she knew the number already. She listed them. Recently it had become an obsession to list their names. She knew it was unhealthy, this preoccupation with the past, and perhaps if she hadn't found the weasel, the sunshine and the smell of the peat would have kept the old memories away.

But perhaps not. Rachael's story of the discovery of Bella's body, white in the torchlight, had jumbled the past and the present in her mind. That was what had started the confusion. It was as if a child had shaken a jigsaw puzzle in its box. The picture was fractured. Grace's mother had committed suicide by hanging.

There had been six foster families. In the social services department this was something of a record for a child like her. At the beginning everyone was sure she would be adopted. She was pretty enough, white, only four years old. She had been well brought up and already spoke politely. She didn't have tantrums. Occasionally she wet the bed but that was only to be expected after coming in from the garden to find her mother hanging by her dressing gown cord from a light fitting. It had been sunny that morning too. The psychologist said she was very bright.

The first couple were Aunt Sally and Uncle Joe. She could hardly remember them because she was there for such a short time. It must have been emergency placement but she knew their names because they were in a scrapbook kept for her by her social worker. There were no photos.

She crossed the burn back to southern bank, this time wading, feeling the pressure of the water against the supple rubber of her expensive wellingtons. Although it was stupid she wanted to avoid the mine buildings and the tunnel trap. Out loud she said: 'Aunt Sally and Uncle Joe,' and had a brief recollection of a flowery dress, a whiff of cigarette smoke, being held on a lap against her will.

She remembered the second couple better. The plan was that they would adopt her. Recently she had returned to this memory over and over again. It was like poking a sore tooth with her tongue.

Chapter Twenty

She had been in this house for a long time, months certainly, perhaps a year. She had started school. School was a modern brick building, with large windows and grey carpet tiles on the floor. Because of the carpet they had to be very careful wiping their feet before going in. Each morning Lesley walked with her to the white wooden gates which had been pushed open to let the teachers' cars through. Lesley would go with her into the cloakroom and hang up her coat. There she would try to kiss her goodbye. In the class-room there were two boxes – one for reading books and another for packed lunches. Grace's packed lunch box was made of pink plastic and had a picture of Barbie on the side. Each day she returned a reading book. She had already moved on to the ones with orange stickers on the spines; most of the children in the class were still reading the blues.

If it rained Dave gave them a lift to school in the car and then she wore wellingtons – pink to match the lunch box – which had to be changed in the cloak-room. Lesley and Dave were her foster parents' names but she already called them mum and dad. She wanted to be the same as the other children in her class. She could be on the books with the green stickers but had slowed down so she wasn't too different.

They lived in a new house on a new estate. This too was made of brick with large windows. There was a garage which held Grace's tricycle and her doll's pram, a small patch of lawn and a rockery at the front, and a garden at the back. In the summer, Lesley said, there would be a swing. The road was still being built, and there were muddy puddles everywhere. Lesley hated the mud and so did Grace. They were both tidy individuals and so appeared perfectly matched.

That was what the social worker said when Dave and Lesley told her that they didn't want Grace to live with them any more.

'But I thought you were perfectly suited.'

Grace knew that was what she said because she was listening at the door. It was slightly open, but nobody noticed her. She must have heard Lesley explaining apologetically that they didn't think the placement was working out, but later she didn't remember that bit. She just heard the social worker say, 'She's such a sweet little thing. What's wrong with her?'

'Nothing's *wrong* with her.' Lesley and Dave looked at each other hoping the other would explain. They might just as well have said everything was wrong with her.

'You didn't phone to say there'd been any problems.' By now the social worker was getting desperate. If the placement broke down it would be considered her fault. She was a messy woman with flyaway hair. The hem of her skirt had become unstitched and her long cardigan was wrongly buttoned. Grace disapproved of this lack of order. She took great care of her clothes, especially her blue and white school dress. The woman continued: 'I mean we might have been able to help. Has she been wetting the bed again?'

'That was never a problem.' This was David. He was chief mechanic in a big garage on the main road out of town. Grace had seen him there. He wore blue overalls with his name embroidered on the chest and sometimes a blazer with gold buttons. He had come home early for this meeting. He had scrubbed his nails and put on a jacket and tie. Awkwardness had made him aggressive.

'We weren't bothered about that. Of course not. What do you think we are? Ogres? And at least it proved she was human.'

'What do you mean?' The social worker's voice rose as if she was about to cry. Even at the age of five Grace realized that, in this situation, this wasn't the right way for a responsible adult to behave.

'Look.' Dave leant forward. From her hiding place Grace could see the curve of his back. He was a very big man and from this angle he looked deformed like one of the illustrations in *Jack and the Beanstalk*, her latest reading book. Perhaps, as he had just said, he was an ogre. 'Look, we don't want to muck you about, but we've got to be straight, haven't we? I mean, better now than when all the forms have been filled out. Save you some work, eh?'

He gave a quick barking laugh. Grace understood that this was supposed to be a joke but the social worker didn't find it funny. Nor really did Dave because he continued seriously. 'We can't love her,' he said. 'We wish we could but we can't. She's so cold.

She stares at us with those eyes. She won't let us touch her. You've got to love your own kid, haven't you?' He paused. 'Perhaps it's where she comes from.'

'What do you mean? Where she comes from?' The social worker's voice was shrill, almost hysterical.

'Well, they're different to us, those people, aren't they?'

'She's a child,' the social worker said. 'She needs a family.' She didn't deny the difference. She turned towards Lesley. Dave moved and Grace saw that he wasn't an ogre at all. He too looked close to tears.

'Do you feel the same way?' the social worker asked.

'We've tried,' Lesley said. 'When you first told us about Grace we thought she'd be perfect for us, we really did. Despite the differences. And when you told us what she'd been through we expected her to be upset. We wouldn't have minded. We could have coped with bad behaviour, nightmares, tears. We thought we'd be able to help. But we can't get through to her. That's what's so dreadful. She doesn't need us.'

'You're wrong,' the woman cried. 'Don't you see she needs you just because she's so withdrawn. So self-controlled.' She paused then went on stiffly, 'But I won't try to persuade you. You must be fully committed if you want to be adoptive parents. I'm sure that was explained when you applied . . .'

The sentence was allowed to hang like a threat. Grace sensed the menace though she didn't understand exactly what the words meant.

'You're saying if we turn Grace down we won't get another one!' Dave was about to jump to his feet when Lesley put her hand on his elbow to restrain him.

'Of course not,' the social worker said, but her voice was smug. She had got her point across. 'Look,' she continued, 'don't make any hasty decisions. Give it another month. See how you feel then.'

They gave it another month. During that time Grace tried very hard. She let Dave kiss her goodnight. She let Lesley cuddle her on the sofa when they were reading their bedtime story, although the feel of the woman's soft body through her Pooh Bear nightdress almost made her gag. But all the time she was puzzling about what could make her different. She looked the same as the other children at school. Slightly skinnier, slightly browner, she supposed. Would that prevent Dave and Lesley from wanting her? In the end she came to no conclusions. And her efforts did no good. After a month she was moved to live with Aunty Carol and Uncle Jim. She didn't call them mum and dad. She knew there was no point.

Chapter Twenty-One

The next vivid memory was of going for a walk with Nan. For a while through the upheaval of changing foster parents two people stayed with her. She didn't see them often but they were a constant thread linking the various aunties and uncles. One was Miss Thorne, the social worker whom Grace had come to see now almost as a friend. Or if not a friend at least an ally. She did at least try to persuade Lesley and Dave to keep her. The other was an old woman called Nan. Grace assumed that the woman was her grandmother, though she couldn't remember being told that explicitly. But then she was told very little explicitly. The scrapbook, which was supposed to help, only confused her.

The day which specially stuck in her memory was the one when Miss Thorne took her to see Nan for the first time. There was a drive in the car. The foster parents all lived in town and this trip into the country was an adventure for Grace. She sat in the passenger seat directly behind the driver and through her window she could occasionally glimpse the sea. The town where she lived was on the coast, but there the sea was hidden behind power-station chimneys and cranes.

They drove down a road like a tunnel, covered in trees with red and brown leaves, then they took a track into a field. In the field there were three burnt-out cars and a bony piebald pony. In one corner a rusty caravan was propped up on a pile of bricks. The caravan door was opened by a fat old lady.

'I'm afraid she's a bit eccentric.' The social worker whispered as if she were talking to an adult. Grace was only eight but she understood what the word meant More loudly Miss Thorne said, 'Come on, Grace. This is Nan.'

Through the open door Grace, who hated mess at the best of times, saw black bin bags spilling over with clothes and newspapers. There was a cat standing on the cooker, the smell of cat piss and stale cat food.

'Shall I stay for a bit?' the social worker asked. Grace nodded, though she would have preferred that neither of them stayed at all.

By the time they started out on their walk the social worker had gone. It was autumn. Bundles of purple elderberries were hanging down over the river. They were so heavy that the branch was bending. She remembered plump hips, the colour of fresh blood and little haws which were a darker red, some of them shrivelled and almost black. There were blackberries. Nan ate them and offered a handful to Grace but she refused. Earlier she had seen a white maggot crawling from the overripe flesh of one. There was rose bay willow herb covered in wispy white hair, thistle heads and dead umbellifers. The umbellifers were rather taller than Grace. The stalks were brown and ribbed. She reached up and broke one. It was hollow and quite easy to break. At the top of the stalk were branches like umbrella spokes and when she snapped it the hard seeds scattered.

Then she saw a red squirrel at the top of the tree. Nan didn't point it out to her, she saw it for herself. She knew it was a squirrel because she'd seen pictures in story books, but this was the most exciting thing that had ever happened to her. She wasn't thrilled by the animal because it was cute or furry, but because it was skilful, so competent. When she first saw it, it was eating a hazelnut, holding it with its front paws and nibbling. Then it jumped from one branch to another, a huge jump which took it across the river. It judged the gap perfectly. If you were a squirrel, it seemed, it was all right to do things well. For Grace, who had to pretend at failure to be accepted at all by the other kids at school, this was a revelation.

Years later Grace could remember the red squirrel with photographic detail. It had a huge eye, whiskers and its tail was nearly black. She could see it dropping a nut into the river and the spreading ripples. She knew too, with certainty, that they didn't see otter that day, although the river was probably very good for otter.

Nan didn't speak to Grace while they were walking, though she did seem to be talking to herself. At first Grace tried to be polite.

'I'm sorry?' she said when Nan muttered. Nan turned and glared at her but didn't reply.

Grace was pleased with this response. She was fed up with people asking how she was feeling then staring at her waiting for an answer. She would prefer to watch the squirrel and the brown trout in the river.

'Did you have a nice time?' the social worker asked in the car on the way home.

'Yes, thank you.' She didn't say this just to be polite. She enjoyed the walk. She decided as an afterthought, 'I didn't understand anything Nan said though.'

'Oh,' said the social worker. Grace realized she wasn't listening. Miss Thorne often asked questions and didn't listen to the replies.

The other trips to visit Nan all followed the same pattern. The social worker would drop her off and come back later to collect her. Grace asked her once where she went on these occasions, there wasn't time to drive back to town. She said she had another client to see.

'A foster child?' Grace asked wistfully. She would like to be placed out here in the country.

'No. Someone who might like to foster one day.'

Grace would have liked to ask if that person might want to foster her but that would have been rude to the present aunt and uncle, who were trying their best.

No matter what the weather was like Grace went for a walk. She hated sitting all afternoon in the smelly caravan. Often she went by herself. Even if Nan was with her there was still little communication between the old woman and the child. Grace found that restful.

As time passed Grace became convinced that Nan was her father's mother. She could remember nothing of her father. In the scrapbook put together by the social worker there was a picture labelled 'Dad' but it meant nothing to her. There were no photographs of her mother and father together, or of them all as a family. The photograph of her father showed a tall thin man standing outside a brick house with a steeply

167

pitched slate roof. There was a storm porch which had plants growing in the window. This certainly wasn't the house where she had lived with her mother, where her mother had died. She had a perfect recollection of that house, which was flat-faced and new like many of the foster parents' homes.

It never occurred to Grace to ask her social worker about the photograph or about her father, to ask even if he was still alive. She knew that she wouldn't get a straight answer. Miss Thorne had always seemed frightened by information. She was prepared to talk about feelings, to go on about them at length, but facts disturbed her. Perhaps that was why Grace enjoyed them so much.

She came to the conclusion that the man in the photograph was related to Nan because the garden beside the brick semi-detached house in the picture was such a tip. The weeds were waist high and piles of rubbish in black plastic bags were piled in front of the garden wall. It was the black plastic which first linked Nan with her father in Grace's mind. That, and the way the man was standing, glaring out at the camera.

Nan glared at everyone, even if she wasn't particularly cross.

One day they were sitting in the sun on the caravan steps waiting for the social worker to come in the car to take her home. Grace had had a good day. She'd seen a kingfisher for the first time, and she'd tracked down its nest to a hole in the river bank. There were bluebells in the woods. She was older, in her last year at primary school. Suddenly she asked, 'Where's my dad?'

She hadn't planned the question, but she was feeling comfortable sitting there in the sunshine, relaxed after the walk, so when it came into her head she spoke it, without her usual calculation. But then she realized its significance. She watched Nan carefully. Usually Nan muttered because she had no teeth, but with some effort Grace had learnt to make sense of what she said. Today, however, Nan didn't attempt to speak.

'You do know, don't you?' It wasn't like Grace to be so persistent. She waited. A tear rolled from Nan's eye down the groove which separated her cheek from her nose and onto a stubbly upper lip, but Grace refused to be put off.

'Well?' she demanded.

Then they heard the social worker's car jolting up the track. The sun was so low that it shone straight into Grace's eyes and she couldn't see the car, except as a blurred shape, until it stopped outside the caravan. Nan wiped her eye with the hem of her apron.

On their way home the social worker asked, 'What was wrong with Nan?'

'I don't know,' Grace said truthfully.

At the time the social worker seemed to accept the reply but Grace was never taken to visit the old lady again. No explanation was given.

Chapter Twenty-Two

The following September Grace moved from primary school to the high school. This was a large establishment with more than a thousand pupils. There were three square buildings like factories, with rows of windows separated by sheets of blue and yellow plastic. In places the plastic was split, many of the windows could not be shut. Grace's first impression of the school was of a constant battle with the buildings: the heating failed, the roof leaked, cracks had been found in the gymnasium floor so there was no PE.

The lack of PE didn't bother Grace. There had been plenty of that in primary school and she was looking forward to learning new subjects. She'd been visiting the public library secretly to get an idea of what would be expected. She was especially excited by the idea of biology, physics and chemistry. When her form tutor, a harassed middle-aged man, handed her a printed timetable on the first day she ringed these subjects in red. She was in the top set in all lessons. For the last two years of junior school she had been marking time, taking care not to show off.

By that time she was living with Frank and Maureen. Before moving in with them she had a short period in an assessment centre, which for some reason was almost empty. In the centre she was subject to interviews and questions. Here, perhaps, she could have brought up the topic of her father, but she never did. She felt she wanted to discover him for herself.

With Frank and Maureen she was happier than she'd been with any of the other foster parents. Frank had been a self-employed lorry driver until back trouble had forced him to give it up. Maureen still worked as a cook in a hospital. They saw fostering as a job, a business, and this took the pressure off Grace. She didn't have to pretend to love them. They mostly took teenagers, the sort of kid no one else wanted. Now there were four, and Grace was the youngest. They lived in a four-bedroomed 1930s semi on the edge of a once respectable, but now rather neglected council estate. Grace was the only girl so she had the smallest bedroom to herself. The boys were rowdy and troublesome, all had been known to the police. Grace didn't care. She took no notice of them and shut herself in her room with her books.

The other reason for Grace's contentment at this time was a dog called Charlie. Frank and Maureen were the first of her foster parents to own a pet. Charlie was a frenetic mongrel, with wild eyes, a stray. Frank took him in with the same tolerant good nature which prompted him to open his door to delinquent boys, but amid the chaos of the house he was often neglected. Since her arrival Grace took responsibility for Charlie, who repaid her with lavish and exuberant devotion.

The first day she saw her father it was sunny. She had Biology last period and they studied the structure of the flower. She drew a diagram, neatly coloured, of petals, stamen and stigma. The biology lab was at the top of the building, a real suntrap. The others had taken off their jumpers and cardigans but Grace kept hers on. Maureen was too busy with her work in the hospital and a particularly disruptive glue sniffer to iron shirts. So Grace felt pink and a little sweaty as she humped her large bag out of school and towards the bus stop.

The man was standing on the other side of the road to the school entrance. He was dressed, inconspicuously, in jeans and a plain heavy sweatshirt. He pretended to read a newspaper and that was what made Grace notice him first. He was reading the *Guardian*. Carol and Jim, two sets of foster parents ago, read the *Guardian*. Jim taught Art and Carol was a librarian. But Frank and Maureen, and the other adults into whose homes she was occasionally invited, read the *Mirror* or the *Sun* or occasionally the *Express*. So as she waited for her bus she watched him with interest. She watched which child he was looking out for. It occurred to her that if the father read the *Guardian* the child might feel odd and isolated too. They might be friends.

But the man didn't seem to know exactly who he was waiting for. He looked over the edge of his newspaper with increasing desperation at the stream of children who flowed past. Occasionally he seemed about to ask one of them for guidance but at the last minute he lost his nerve. When her bus arrived he was still standing there. She climbed onto the bus and showed her pass, letting a crowd of pupils push past her to go upstairs. She found a seat by a window. The bus started noisily and drove straight past the man. Perhaps the diesel engine disturbed his concentration because he stared angrily after it. Then she realized that he was waiting for her. This man was older but he was the same one as had glared out at her from the photograph in the scrapbook for as long as she could remember.

She stared back, and banged on the window, hoping that he would notice her and that would provide a spark of recognition, but he had already given up. He turned away and she watched him walk down the street. That's it, she thought. I'll never see him again. She leapt to her feet and rang the bell in an attempt to stop the bus but the driver was so accustomed to naughty children playing tricks that he just turned round and swore at her.

'Please!' she cried. It was like a nightmare, watching her father disappear into the distance. But still the driver wouldn't stop.

He wasn't there the next day. She came out of school looking for him. She was certain by now that the man was her father and not just a figment of her imagination. The night before she'd taken out the scrapbook and studied the photograph. The likeness was so good that she was surprised she didn't recognize -him immediately. She let the first bus go without her, hoping that he might turn up but he didn't show.

Exactly a week after the first appearance, again after double Biology, he was there again. By now she had given him up. She had planned strategies for dealing with an appearance, but that was last week, and now she wasn't sure what to do.

She stood for a moment. The bag on her shoulder was very heavy and she stood at a list, her head tilted, so she saw him at an odd angle. Today he had no newspaper and seemed more restless, more determined. He paced up and down the pavement, occasionally approaching groups of children. Grace, who was more streetwise than many children her age, thought he'd have to watch it or he'd get himself arrested.

She waited for the lollipop lady to stop the traffic then she crossed the road. He didn't notice her because his eyes were fixed on another fair-haired girl of about her age. Grace knew her slightly. Her name was Melanie and she was very pretty.

'Excuse me.'

He turned sharply.

'I think you might be waiting for me. I'm Grace.'

He looked down at her. She stared back and waited coolly for his reaction. She wouldn't be surprised if he was disappointed, if he was hoping for someone like Melanie. He stepped back a little. He was wearing spectacles and seemed to be finding it hard to focus on her. He smiled.

'Yes,' he said. His voice was so loud and clear that people nearby turned around to look. 'Yes, of course. I can see you are.'

'Can you?'

'Oh yes. You look so like your mother.'

It was a long time since anyone had mentioned her mother. Psychologists and doctors in the assessment centre had asked about her occasionally, but they spoke tentatively, carefully. This was normal, almost joyous.

'Do I?'

'Of course you do. Hasn't anyone told you before?'

'No,' she said.

'Well, you don't look much like me, do you?'

That was certainly true. He was dark with a long, narrow face the shape of a horse's. His eyebrows, which were starting to turn grey, met over the top of his nose. Grace had been told that was a sign of madness. She hadn't believed it at the time but now she started to wonder. Not that it mattered.

'Well then,' he cried. 'What should we do? Will anyone miss you if you don't go straight back?'

She shook her head. Frank and Maureen had enough to worry about getting the boys under police curfew back in time. There weren't any other rules.

'We have supper at about seven,' she said. 'I should be home by then.'

That wasn't quite true. Supper was a flexible meal usually eaten on trays in front of the television. Anyone not around was served later from the microwave. What she meant was that Charlie usually ate at seven and if she wasn't there nobody thought to feed him.

'So we've got hours.' He tucked her hand in his arm and marched her down the wide noisy street towards the centre of town.

He seemed to know exactly where he was headed for and she thought perhaps he was taking her to his home. In the square the market was starting to pack up for the day. She came here often on Saturdays to buy cheap veg for Maureen and the stall holder called out to her, 'You all right, pet?'

Perhaps she thought it odd for her to be walking along, arm in arm, with a middle-aged man.

'Fine,' she said. She would have liked to tell her that this was her father, but by then they had moved on, across the road, down the alley by Boots and towards the harbour where the big ships carrying timber from Scandinavia docked. He stopped outside a row of houses and at first she thought this was where he lived, then she realized it was a restaurant. The door had a sign saying closed but when her father pushed it, it opened. He seemed to know the owner, who was lazily polishing glasses, because although the restaurant was obviously shut he was waved good-humouredly to a table by the bar.

He said, 'Any chance of coffee?' And when the barman nodded he added, 'And ice cream? You'd like some ice cream, wouldn't you, Grace?'

She answered that she would, though really she would have preferred coffee too.

The coffee came in a very small cup made of thick white china. There were three scoops of ice cream – strawberry, chocolate and vanilla – in a white china dish.

'Now,' he said, 'why don't you tell me what you've been up to?' He replaced the cup in its saucer and it rattled slightly. She realized then that he was nervous. He had probably been building himself up to this meeting too. The jolly good humour outside the school was an act, like Charlie bouncing playfully around a stranger he wasn't sure of.

So she took his question seriously and talked to him as she would to the social worker on one of her monthly visits, about school and how well she did in the maths test, and how difficult she found French and about the trip to the Hancock Museum in Newcastle. At first he listened intently but after a while his attention wandered. In the end he interrupted, 'I expect you're wondering why I haven't looked you up before.'

'Nan wouldn't tell me where you were.'

'You mustn't blame her.'

'Is she still there?'

'Oh, she's still in the caravan. They're trying to persuade her to move into a home before the winter. She's an embarrassment. She'll go in the end but she likes to make them sweat.'

'Them?'

'Social workers, housing officials, people who know best. My bloody family, as if it had anything to do with them.'

'But I thought she was your family.'

'What do you mean?'

'I thought she was your mother.'

He threw back his head and gave a loud laugh like a vixen barking. 'Nan? No, of course not.' Then realizing that Grace was blushing at her mistake he added gently, 'Next best thing though. She looked after me when I was little.' He looked at her across the table-cloth. 'Don't you know anything? Didn't they tell you?'

'They gave me a photograph. You standing outside a house. Lots of rubbish.'

'I remember that one!' He seemed delighted. 'That was the summer they let me stay on the estate. Before your mother rescued me.'

'From what?' She took the statement literally and was imagining robbers, pirates, hostage takers.

'From myself, of course.' He rubbed his hands and laughed. 'From myself.'

'It didn't look much like an estate. The photograph.'

She was thinking of the estate where she was living

177

with Frank and Maureen, the neat cul-de-sacs of Barrett homes which housed other foster parents. This time he seemed to understand.

'Estate's another name for the land attached to a big house,' he said. 'In this case Holme Park, Langholme.' He looked at her. 'Have you heard of it?'

She shook her head.

'You've not met Robert then. Or Mother.'

'I've only ever met Nan.'

'So that's how they played it.' He seemed shocked, but at the same time almost pleased. Grace thought it was like when someone you can't stand lives up to your worst expectations, so you can say, 'See, that's what they're like. I told you all along.'

'Who's Robert?'

'My brother.' He paused. 'My elder brother.'

'Where do you live?'

For the first time he was evasive. 'Nowhere special,' he said. 'Nowhere like Holme Park. And nowhere I could take a child.'

'I don't want you to take me. I just want to know.'

'No point, until I'm settled.'

He stood up and she followed him to the door. It was only five o'clock and she expected him to take her somewhere else. He did, after all, talk about their having hours to spend together – but outside the restaurant he shook her hand awkwardly.

'Can you make your own way home?' he asked.

She said she could.

'I'll be in touch,' he said and walked away quickly, not stopping to look back.

Chapter Twenty-Three

After waiting for four weeks without any word from her father Grace decided to take matters into her own hands. She knew that it was often necessary to force people to do the right thing. Some of the lads in Laurel Close would never attend school unless Frank took them there and watched them go in. Something about her father reminded her of a certain type of bad boy, the reckless ones who took drugs or set fire to buildings just for kicks.

At breakfast she told Maureen she'd be late home from school because she was going to a meeting of the Natural History Society. Maureen was hunched over the bench in the kitchen, spreading margarine on sliced bread to make packed lunches, as if, she often said, she didn't have enough of that to do at work all day. She turned briefly.

'That's all right, pet. I know we can trust you.'

At that Grace felt a pang of guilt because Maureen would inevitably find out that she had been lying. She'd feel hurt because Grace hadn't talked to her first.

At midday, instead of queuing up to eat her sandwiches in the school hall she slipped out to the telephone box on the main road. There was a pay phone outside the sixth form common room but she was

ANN CLEEVES

nervous to go there. The sixth formers, wearing their own clothes, talking in confident voices about music and parties, were more intimidating than the teachers.

The main road was noisy. She dialled the number she had copied from the list stuck next to the phone at home, but could hardly hear the tone. A motherly voice answered. 'Hello. Social Services. Area Six.'

'Could I speak to Miss Thorne, please.'

The social worker still called herself Miss Thorne, though Grace thought she'd married the year before. A ring had appeared and she had been mellower since, more inclined to listen. 'Who's speaking?'

'I'm sorry, I can't hear.'

'Who's speaking?' the motherly voice yelled.

'Grace Fulwell.' It seemed very strange to be shouting her own name at the top of her voice.

Miss Thorne came onto the phone almost immediately.

'Grace? Is anything wrong?'

'No.'

'Why aren't you at school?'

'It's lunchtime.'

'How can I help you?'

'I want to make an appointment to see you. Will you be in the office? Today. About four thirty.'

'I can be if it's important. But what's it all about?' Grace could hear panic in her voice, even with a lorry rumbling past. 'I thought you were settled with Maureen and Frank.'

Grace didn't answer. She banged back the receiver, hoping it would sound as if the money had run out.

She had been to the social services office before but only after some crisis, to hang around while Miss

Thorne tried to find another foster family to take her in. She had to look up the address in the phone book. It was a tall house in a tree-lined terraced street, close to the park. All the houses had been turned into offices. Grace passed solicitors, insurance agents and two firms of dentists on her way.

On previous occasions she sat by Miss Thorne's desk in the large open plan office on the top floor, but today she was taken into one of the interview rooms. It had a low coffee table and three easy chairs covered in orange vinyl. A no smoking sign was prominently displayed on the wall but Grace could see cigarette burns on the nylon carpet.

Miss Thorne was nervous. Despite being a social worker, Grace had come to the conclusion that she didn't like the unexpected. And if Grace had fallen out with Frank and Maureen she'd probably come to the end of the line where foster parents were concerned.

'Well, Grace?' she said. 'Why the mystery?'

'It's about my father.'

'Yes?'

'I do have a right to know him, don't I?' She had learnt a lot by listening to other foster children.

Miss Thorne hesitated. 'Where appropriate,' she said.

'What does that mean?'

'It's in the guidelines. Foster children should keep in touch with their natural parents, where appropriate.'

'Why isn't it appropriate for me?'

Miss Thorne seemed thrown by the question. Perhaps she thought Grace hadn't heard the word before, wouldn't understand it.

'Miss Thorne?'

'Look.' Her voice was persuasive and Grace was immediately suspicious. She looked at the woman, sitting beside her on the orange vinyl chair. Her legs were folded at the knee like a man's. She was wearing the same sort of clothes – knee-length skirts and shapeless cardigans – as when Grace first met her. She reached out and patted Grace's hand. Grace made an effort not to flinch.

'Look, we've known each other a long time and I'm not your teacher. Isn't it about time you called me Antonia?'

Grace continued staring. She knew she was being fobbed off with this chumminess, but she was intrigued by the exotic name. 'Antonia? Is that really what you're called?'

The woman nodded encouragingly, but Grace was determined not to be distracted again. She raised her voice and said firmly, 'Tell me about my father.'

Quite suddenly the social worker gave up her resistance. She caved in. 'What do you want to know?'

'Everything. From the beginning. Why wasn't he at home when my mother died?'

'Because he'd already left your mother to live with another woman.'

It seemed to Grace that she took a spiteful pleasure in the words, that she was really saying. So, you really want to know, do you? Let's see if you can handle it.

'Is that why she killed herself?'

Miss Thorne nodded. 'She left a note saying she couldn't live without him.'

Grace thought of the man who'd sat opposite her in the shadowy restaurant drinking coffee. She felt proud that her father could be the cause of such romantic passion. It didn't surprise her that she hadn't been enough to keep her mother alive.

'You mustn't blame him,' Miss Thorne said, in such a way that Grace knew that secretly she hoped Grace would. But blame was the last thing on Grace's mind. She was after facts, information.

'Is he still living with the woman?'

'No. They separated soon after your mother's death.'

'Why have you never let me see him?'

'It was never a matter of that. Of not letting!'

'What then? Not appropriate, you said. What did that mean?'

'For a long time we didn't know where he was. Your mother's death upset him. He travelled.'

'Where?'

'He worked as a diver for oil companies. I understand he was in Central America and the Middle East. We learnt that much from his family. They didn't know any more.'

'Family?'

This was a potent word and Grace was jerked back to the present. She'd been imagining her father swimming through a clear blue ocean. Foster children were always talking about families. Even Maureen's bad boys had brothers in the nick or aunties who came occasionally to take them to McDonald's. Grace had always been left out.

'Your father's brother and his mother, your grandmother. They live in a village in the country.'

'Langholme?' She had remembered all the facts passed on to her during that meeting in the restaurant. 'I guessed from something Nan said.' Grace picked some of Charlie's hairs from her pleated school skirt. 'Why didn't you tell me my family lived in Holme Park? You could have told me that.'

'We didn't want to raise expectations which couldn't be met.' Grace wasn't sure what that meant but ignored it. She had a more important question.

'Why didn't I ever see them, my gran and uncle? You took me to meet Nan.'

'They didn't want to see you. Nan did.' As soon as the words were spoken Miss Thorne seemed to regret them. Perhaps even for her, even provoked by this stubborn and demanding child, they were too hurtful. But Grace considered the idea seriously.

'They didn't know me,' she said at last.

'They felt you were your father's responsibility,' Miss Thorne said more gently. 'They never found it easy to get on with your father.'

Grace understood. 'Oh,' she said. 'They didn't want to be lumbered.'

They looked at each other and shared a rare smile of understanding.

'Is my father still abroad?' She turned away as she asked the question, casually. Of course she knew he wasn't abroad, but it would be a betrayal to let on to Miss Thorne. Besides, it was a sort of test, to see whether or not she was lying.

'No. He came back a while ago.'

'Where does he live? With his family?'

'Different sorts of places. With friends. In hostels. He moves around a lot. He's found it hard to settle.'

'Why?'

'Perhaps because he's an unsettled sort of person.'

'Like me.'

'In a way.'

Grace rubbed her finger and thumb together, releasing dog hairs which floated to the floor.

'I want to see him.'

'That might be possible. But he has problems.'

'Problem' was a euphemism much used by Maureen and Frank. Gary was a glue sniffer. Matthew took smack. Both had problems.

'Does he take drugs?'

'Not in the sense you mean.'

'What sense?'

'He's probably an alcoholic. Do you understand that?'

'Of course.' Gary's mam was an alcoholic and Grace added, 'It doesn't stop Gary seeing his mam.'

'I've said it might be possible.'

'When?'

'When I've talked to him again. And to Maureen and Frank.'

'Again?'

'I have been trying to arrange it,' Miss Thorne said defensively. 'Your father isn't always an easy person to deal with. He has his own way of doing things. I didn't want to build up your hopes only to have him disappear again.'

'I understand,' Grace said. 'Thanks.' And she did feel grateful. She'd never expected Miss Thorne to make any effort on her part.

'And you mustn't expect too much,' Miss Thorne went on. 'He wouldn't, for example, be able to have you to live with him.'

'That's all right.'

She was perfectly happy with Maureen and Frank.

ANN CLEEVES

And Charlie would miss her. She didn't want a change in her circumstances, just to know her father, to see him occasionally. To find out more about her family.

It took three weeks for Miss Thorne to arrange a meeting between Grace and her father but Grace was patient. She was enjoying school and concentrated on her work. In Biology they gave chloroform to fruit flies so they remained still long enough for the pupils to count the vestigial wings. Grace was fascinated. The girl sitting next to her was heavy-handed with the chloroform but returned the dead flies to the jar, hoping no one would notice.

Grace knew the social worker's promise hadn't been forgotten because at home Maureen and Frank discussed her father. They were very impressed that Edmund Fulwell's family lived at Holme Park. Apparently it had come as news to them too. Perhaps the social worker had remembered Dave's awkwardness, his feeling that Grace was in some way different, and thought she'd be better accepted if her wealthy connections weren't known.

'We'll have to take you there one day,' Maureen said. 'They do guided tours and there's a lovely tearoom.'

Grace and her father met at last, not in the tearoom at Holme Park, but in the front room of 15 Laurel Close. Maureen and Frank had taken the bad boys out, the ones which were left. Gary was back in the Young Offender institution. Maureen had cried when the police came to take him away.

Antonia Thorne waited in the house with Grace. Edmund Fulwell was late. Miss Thorne didn't mention that to Grace, but she could tell because the social

186

worker looked at her watch every now and then, with resignation as if it was just what she expected. Grace, waiting, didn't feel anger or fear. She was numb. She thought this must be what it felt like to be dead, then wondered if this was how her mother felt before she killed herself. Perhaps she'd been waiting for Edmund to leave his lover and come back to her with just this sort of numbness. Perhaps she'd decided she might as well be dead.

The doorbell rang. Miss Thorne gave a start and frowned. Grace thought she was annoyed because Edmund after all hadn't fulfilled her expectations. She would have preferred it if he hadn't turned up.

'I want to go,' Grace said.

She opened the door and he was standing on the doorstep, pulling a strange face so his eyebrows did definitely meet over his nose. His hands were in his overcoat pockets. It was late afternoon in October, almost dark, with a gusty wind which blew litter and dead leaves into the doorway. He stooped so his face was almost level with hers.

'So,' he said, 'you must be my lovely daughter.'

And he continued very quickly so she understood again that the previous meeting was a secret between them.

Antonia Thorne shouted in a jolly, primary school teacher's voice, 'Come along, Grace. Don't keep your father standing in the cold.'

And he came in, just as if she were the teacher and he was doing as he was told. Shrugging out of his overcoat he seemed to take up all the room in the corridor though he couldn't be much bigger than Frank.

ANN CLEEVES

The social worker left them together in the front room, though she said pointedly that she would be in the kitchen making tea if Grace needed her. She didn't close the door behind her.

'Anyone would think she didn't trust me,' he said. He laughed, then when Grace didn't join in he muttered, 'I suppose you can't blame her.'

He seemed less comfortable than when he was waiting for her outside school, more uptight. Grace, who had seen Gary's mam in various states of inebriation, thought he was probably sober today. Last time he'd had a few drinks.

'You said you'd be in touch,' she whispered.

'Yeah, look, I'm really sorry. Things haven't been easy lately. I expect she . . .' he nodded towards the open door, ' . . . explained. I needed time to sort myself out.'

She heard the self-pity in his voice and for a moment she was cross. What about me? she wanted to shout. Didn't you think of me? Then she realized it was no good. If she wanted to keep in touch with her father she wouldn't be able to make demands on him. Edmund Fulwell would need looking after.

Chapter Twenty-Four

For nearly four years Grace took responsibility for her father, though this went largely unrecognized. It was an unprecedented period of stability for them both.

One day, soon after Edmund arrived back on the scene her Biology teacher called her back after class. 'Have you ever thought of joining the Wildlife Trust? There's a junior section. I think you'd enjoy it.'

The junior section consisted of Grace and two spotty adolescent lads who refused to speak to her, but she was taken under the wing of three elderly spinster sisters. The Halifax sisters lived in a house which had remained largely unchanged since their parents' day. It was a suburb of the town which had once been very grand, housing shipowners and traders, though many of the houses had now been converted into flats. It had a library, filled with natural history books – field guides, sets of encyclopaedias and monographs.

She spent hours in the library. Although Grace had never complained of the noise in Laurel Close, very soon after meeting her the sisters invited her to use the room for homework. They said it was good for them to have someone young in the house again. Later Grace suspected this had been suggested by her Biology teacher; at the time it seemed miraculous.

When she was working the sisters left her to her own devices, except the youngest, Cynthia, who had permed hair and large squelchy bosoms. She interrupted occasionally to bring Grace cups of tea and home-baked ginger biscuits.

During the summer the Wildlife Trust organized field trips. A coach took them up the coast to look at sea birds or inland to walk in the hills. Then, for the first time, Grace plodded along pebbly river banks looking for otter spraints. Later in the season they saw bats flying into the stone barn to roost.

It was the badger watch which made the biggest impression. She sat with the Halifax sisters in a wood at dusk and waited for the badgers to emerge from a sett, their noses snuffling the air. Leading the trip was a postgraduate student who talked about her research. She knew each individual badger, how the group was organized.

When I grow up, Grace thought, that's what I'm going to do.

Occasionally she invited her father to accompany her on the Wildlife Trust excursions but he always refused.

'Na!' he said. 'I've never been much into wildlife. Except for eating it.'

Grace was already a vegetarian but she didn't rise to the bait. She suspected that food was more important to his life than she was. At least it provided him with an income. He'd started work in the little restaurant where he took her on their first meeting. He'd been at school with Rod, the owner. He was an inspirational and meticulous cook and the restaurant appeared in good food guides. Because of this Rod put up with his occasional bouts of drinking, his truculence. He also allowed Edmund to live in squalor in the flat above.

Grace continued living with Maureen and Frank in Laurel Close but she spent little time there. Before school every day she took Charlie for a walk in the park. She could already identify all the common birds there. When school was over she walked to the sisters' house, stopping on the way to have coffee with her dad – if he was there. Sometimes he was out with a woman, though seldom, she thought, with the same one more than once. In the summer she walked to the town centre from the sisters' house and caught the bus home. In the winter, when it was dark, Cynthia gave her a lift home in the sisters' ancient Rover, or Frank would pick her up. Maureen and Frank didn't seem to resent the time she spent away from home. Her Biology teacher told them that she was Oxbridge material and they said they wanted to help. Grace never seemed to have friends of her own age, but she didn't really want them.

Suddenly, in the summer before her fifth form, she noticed a change in her father. She had listened to him talking about his women before, given sympathy when it was needed but in those cases it was a matter of hurt pride, not unrequited love. This time, it seemed, it was serious. He gave up drinking. Completely. He cleaned the flat, got his hair cut. Grace asked if she could meet the woman.

'Not yet.'

'She's not married?' She didn't want him to get hurt.

'No, it's not that. She won't go out with me. Not yet. But she will, I can tell she's weakening.'

And eventually she must have weakened because when Grace called into the restaurant again he couldn't stop grinning and he couldn't sit still for a second.

'Has he been drinking?' she asked Rod. She liked Rod, who was Welsh and calm. She never found out how he ended up running this unlikely restaurant.

'No. He's been like this all day. High as a kite.'

The woman was called Sue. She ran an office supplies business from a shop on the High Street. She was much younger than him. He saw her first when he walked past the shop and he went in on impulse and bought some typing paper and a bottle of Tippex.

'Best fiver I ever spent,' he said.

Grace looked at him anxiously, like a mother watching her child embark on a first romance. She hoped it would work out for him. She'd like to pass some of the responsibility for looking after him on to Sue.

Sue was small with sleek blond hair. She wore the sort of make-up which gave her skin the shine of porcelain. She was very lively, never still, always talking and smiling and waving her hands. She and Edmund talked about things in which Grace had little interest – cinema, music, theatre. Grace wasn't jealous – it was quite a relief to spend more time in the Halifax library. She didn't find the syllabus hard but she wanted to do well in the exams. When she did see her father he was excitable, happy, full of plans.

It was at this time that his mother died.

'So,' he said to Grace on one of her occasional visits to the restaurant, 'the old bat's finally gone.'

'Can I come with you to the funeral?'

He looked at her sharply. 'I'm not going,' he said. And that was it. He wouldn't discuss it any more.

Grace was a bit disappointed. She still dreamed of meeting the family in the big house. Then she thought they must have offended her father very badly if he wouldn't attend his mother's funeral.

One Sunday in November, the day before the start of her mock exams, she received a phone call from her father. She had spent all day in the sisters' library and Maureen and Frank were making a fuss of her. They said she'd been working too hard and she needed to relax. They were sitting in front of the television drinking tea. The bad boys were out.

Frank took the call. When he came back he was frowning.

'It's your father,' he said. 'Do you want to take it?'

'Of course, why not?'

'I'm sorry, pet. I think he's been drinking.'

This was an understatement. Her father was raging drunk, just coherent enough for her to work out that Sue had dumped him. She wanted to rush round to the flat to see him but for once Frank put his foot down.

'Come on!' he said. 'He'll not even know you're there, the state he's in.'

'But he might be sick. Choke. People can die.'

'I'll go,' Frank said.

She realized for the first time what an unusually good man Frank was. The night before he'd been up until midnight sitting in the police station with one of the boys who'd been caught brawling in the youth club. All day he'd been ferrying them around – football training for one, the Halifax sisters for her. He always cooked lunch on Sundays to give Maureen a break. He looked exhausted but he was prepared to go out again. She went up to the chair where he was slumped, his feet in his slippers she gave him two Christmases ago, his sweatshirt splattered with cooking stains. She sat on the arm of the chair, put her arm round his shoulders and hugged him. It was the first intimate physical contact she'd had with another human being since she was five and trying to impress the foster parents that couldn't love her. Frank knew this was an important moment but he didn't say anything. He took her thin hand in his and squeezed it, then he got up to put on his shoes and find his car keys.

When he got back Maureen was in bed because she had to be up for the early shift the next day. Grace was waiting for him.

'How is he?'

'Well, he's had a skinful, that's for sure.' Frank was born in Liverpool and when he was tired he talked like a Scouser.

'But he is all right?'

'Oh aye, he'll be fine. Right as rain in the morning. And yes, he has been sick down the toilet. I got him to bed and he's fast asleep.'

'Frank?'

'Yes.'

'Thanks.' This time she just reached out and touched his arm. He understood, and smiled.

'Getaway,' he said. 'Now off to bed. It's an important day tomorrow. Mo and me have never had a kid go away to college before.'

At first she thought this would be a drinking bout like many others her dad had been through. For a few days he'd be dead to the world then he'd emerge,

194

sheepish and bedraggled, to apologize. She concentrated on her exams. Three days later she called into the restaurant to find Rod doing the cooking.

'It's Ed's day off,' he said. 'He's gone out.'

She thought that was a good sign. At least her father wasn't upstairs in the flat drinking whisky straight from the bottle. He'd never been a social drinker.

'Does that mean he's back with Sue?'

Rod shrugged. She took that, optimistically, to mean that things were pretty much back to normal.

Then she saw him in the town. It was the last day of the exams and the Halifax sisters had invited her to a special tea to celebrate. She was walking down the High Street with a gang of girls. She'd tagged along because there was a question in the Chemistry paper she wanted to discuss, but they weren't very interested. They were talking about a party one of the sixth formers was giving, to which most of them had been invited.

The High Street had been pedestrianized and paved with ornamental brick. Wrought iron seats had been placed, back to back, in the middle of the streets and there were tubs of plants and shrubs, long since dead and waiting to be cleared out for the winter. Her father was sitting alone on one of the benches. He was dirty, unshaven and he was crying. An empty bottle lay on its side under the bench and rolled occasionally when there was a strong gust of wind. At least the other girls, still talking about the party and which of them definitely looked old enough to get into the off-licence, didn't notice him. And Edmund was too absorbed in his own grief to see her.

She walked straight past him and on to the street

where the Halifax sisters lived. Before knocking on the door she composed herself. Cynthia had prepared a magnificent tea with smoked salmon sandwiches, meringues and gingerbread. Grace exclaimed over it and ate everything they pressed on to her.

She didn't visit her father for two days. How dare he ruin a day when she was supposed to be celebrating? Then she cracked, and went to see him after school. The town had been decorated for Christmas in a mean-spirited way, with a tall thin spruce lit by ugly white bulbs. On the door of the restaurant there was a wreath of real holly.

The restaurant was empty but Rod was behind the bar. He'd poured himself a brandy in a large round glass and seemed surprised, rather embarrassed to see her.

'Didn't that social worker tell you?'

'What?'

'Edmund's not here.'

'Where is he?'

'Look, I'm really sorry. I phoned her first thing yesterday.' There was a pause. 'He's in hospital.'

'What happened? An accident?'

'Nothing like that. Not that sort of accident.'

'What do you mean?'

'He's in St Nick's.'

St Nicholas' was the big loony-bin on the outskirts of the town. Victorian gothic surrounded by 1930s villas. Everyone had heard of it. In primary school it was the standard term of abuse. 'You should be in St Nick's, you should.'

She didn't know what to say. He came out from behind the bar.

'I'm really sorry,' he said again. 'It wasn't only the drink, you know. He was getting depressed and it wasn't only Sue. His mother's death hit him harder than he let on. I was afraid he'd do something daft. He needs time to sort himself out. I couldn't cope. He needs professional help. Something more than I could give him anyway. More than you could too.'

Chapter Twenty-Five

Miss Thorne took Grace to visit her father in hospital. Grace was reminded for a while of the times they used to visit Nan. Antonia Thorne turned up at Laurel Close in her car. Grace climbed in beside her and they drove off without a word. Even the stilted conversation which did eventually occur was much the same.

'How are things going at school?'

'Very well, thank you.' This was true. She'd been predicted an A Grade in every subject except French for her exams.

'No problems with Maureen and Frank?'

'None.'

The hospital was approached by a curving drive up a hill. The car stopped sharply, jerking Grace forward to the extent of her seat belt, when two elderly men shuffled out in front of them. Miss Thorne muttered, pulled on the handbrake and attempted a hill start. The engine stalled and she became flustered, especially when she saw a car approaching in her mirror. At the second attempt it leapt forward and she drove on.

Grace's father was being kept in Sycamore, which was one of the villas. The garden was tidy but the woodwork needed painting. The door was locked and

Miss Thorne rang the bell. Standing on the doorstep, Grace thought it didn't look like a hospital but a large suburban house. The impression was confirmed by the woman who opened the door. She looked just the sort of woman who would live in such a house. She was slim and smart, wearing a navy pleated skirt and a white blouse with a bow at the neck. It was 1985 and she reminded Grace of a young version of Margaret Thatcher.

'Yes?' The woman was friendly enough but very brisk. She made it clear she had important things to get on with.

Miss Thorne was still flustered by her problems negotiating the hill. She opened her bag, dropped a glove, stooped to pick it up.

'We're here to visit Edmund Fulwell.'

'I'm sorry.' The woman smiled graciously. 'Afternoons are the times for relatives' visits. Perhaps you could come back after lunch.'

Miss Thorne was horrified by the notion that she might be thought one of the patients' relatives. She groped again in her bag and came out with a laminated identity card.

'Actually,' she said, 'I'm a social worker. I did phone.'

Grace looked past the woman in the navy skirt. A thin girl, not much older than her, dressed in a nightdress and slippers walked down the corridor as if in slow motion. There was a smell of institutional food and cigarette smoke.

'We agreed eleven o'clock.' By now Miss Thorne was indignant.

The woman was apologetic. She introduced herself as the sister in charge of the shift. 'Edmund's doing very well,' she said, as if that would redeem her in Miss Thorne's eyes. 'The consultant's very pleased with him. We could be talking discharge in a few weeks. We don't keep them in long, these days.' She seemed to notice Grace for the first time. 'And who's this?'

'The daughter,' Miss Thorne said abruptly.

The nurse, who according to her name tag was called Elizabeth, let them in, locking the door behind them.

'Ah yes!' She sent Miss Thorne a look of great significance. 'Of course.'

In the building it was stiflingly hot. The corridor ran the length of the villa. Large painted radiators stood at regular intervals and each time they passed one they were hit by a wave of heat. Elizabeth seemed not to notice, but Antonia took off her cardigan and Grace held her anorak by its hook over her shoulder.

'You can use the interview room. It'll be quiet in there. Stan, have you seen Edmund?'

Stan, a middle-aged man in a grey overall, was washing the floor. Grace wondered idly if he were an inmate or a member of staff. He shook his head and continued to move his mop over the lino tiles.

Elizabeth pushed open the door of a large room. Chairs were lined in front of the television screen. On the television a jolly young man dressed as a clown was making a kite from brown paper and orange string. Behind him teddy bears and dolls sat on a plastic bus. The programme seemed to fascinate the audience. Grace didn't believe that her father, even when he was ill, could ever enjoy children's TV, but it was impossible to tell if he was there because a cloud of cigarette smoke hung over everything and the people were sitting with their backs to her.

'Has anyone seen Edmund?' Elizabeth asked. She used the same tone as the TV presenter. Grace thought that any minute she'd break into song with Large Ted and Jemima.

'Non-smoking lounge.'

This information was volunteered anonymously. No one turned away from the screen.

The non-smoking lounge was as large as the TV room but only two people sat there, in chairs close to a window. A pane, too small for anyone to climb out of, had been opened and let in a blast of cold air. They seemed deep in conversation. With Grace's dad was a large-boned, dark woman in cord trousers and a checked cotton shirt. As they approached Grace heard her say, 'I'm not used to all this sitting about. In the last place I was attached to the market garden. It broke your back that work, but there wasn't time to be bored.'

She wasn't at all the sort of woman Edmund would fall for, but Grace sensed an easy rapport between them which she'd never seen before in his relationships with women. With Sue especially he'd been flirtatious and devoted but never friendly.

Edmund's reply was drowned out by the repeated shout of an exotic finch, perched in a cage standing against one wall. The cage door was fastened by a huge padlock. Grace wondered if the noise of the bird irritated the patients so much that they tried to kill it. She wouldn't be surprised. Against the other wall there was a tank of tropical fish. The water was murky and green.

'You've got a visitor, Edmund,' Elizabeth said brightly.

'I'll be off then,' said the dark woman. 'Leave you in peace.'

'Thanks, Bella.'

Bella walked away quickly. When she caught Grace's eye she smiled a clear, unclouded smile. Grace was convinced she must be a nurse until Elizabeth said, 'Bella will be leaving us soon too.'

Edmund deliberately turned his back on Elizabeth. He looked up at Grace. 'Sorry about all this.'

She shook her head. He looked dreadful, worse than when he was sitting in the town centre.

'If you want to use the interview room, I'll fetch you some tea.' Elizabeth looked at her watch.

Edmund groaned. 'We're all right here if it's all the same to you. I can't stand that place. It's like a cell.' When she turned and walked away he added, just loud enough for her to hear, 'And I can't stand her either, stupid cow.'

He ignored Miss Thorne. She might as well not have been there. He talked to Grace as if they were alone in the room.

'I really fucked up this time, didn't I? I just couldn't stand the thought of being without her. And I thought you'd be better off without me to worry about.'

'You tried to kill yourself?'

'And I couldn't even manage that. Instead I'm in here with Busy Lizzie ticking me off every ten minutes to check I'm still alive.'

'I'm glad,' she said. 'That you're still alive.'

*

After that first time she was allowed to visit her father without the social worker. On Christmas Day she went there for lunch. Most of the patients had been allowed home for the holiday so Sycamore Ward was almost empty. She had considered asking Maureen and Frank if he could come to them but decided that they had enough to worry about. This group of boys were particularly troublesome and Maureen always looked tired. She'd lost weight and there were shadows under her eyes.

So Grace walked the three miles up the hill to the hospital and sat with her father at the formica bench in the dining room. Also there were Wayne, a teenage schizophrenic whose parents were embarrassed by him, and a woman whose name Grace had never been told. From an overheard conversation between other patients Grace had learnt that this woman had had a child, who had died soon after birth.

'She won't accept it, see,' the patient had said. 'They caught her in the maternity hospital, trying to walk out with a little boy.'

The two nurses on duty tried to do their best and it was quite a pleasant meal. They ate turkey which had already been plated up in the hot trolley, pulled crackers and wore paper hats. Her father had been much calmer lately and didn't even make too much fuss about the dreadful food.

After Christmas there was a period of quiet, very cold weather. She and her father, wrapped up in coats and scarves and gloves, because after the heat of the ward it felt glacial, even in the sun, went for walks in the hospital grounds. He was allowed to be away from the nurses for half an hour at a time now. She

pointed out a red squirrel in the tall trees which separated the hospital from farmland beyond.

'I saw my first one when I went for a walk with
Nan,' she said.

'Did you?' He was pleased, amused. 'Fancy you
remembering that.'

'Does she know you've been ill?'

She knew that her father had kept sporadically in
touch with Nan who'd moved at last into sheltered
accommodation.

'God, I hope not.'

He was being prepared for release. He had to attend
a group. That was what it was called – the group. It
was run by a pretty young psychologist. There was a
lot of drama and role play, lots of talking. At first
Edmund was sceptical, even antagonistic.

'Load of crap,' he said. 'I wouldn't go if I didn't
think they'd let me out quicker.'

After a while Grace thought he must be finding the
group useful, because he wouldn't miss it, even when
he was given the opportunity for a legitimate excuse.
She was curious about what went on at these sessions
but he wouldn't answer her questions in any detail. It
seemed unlike him to be so co-operative and she hoped
he hadn't fallen for the pretty young psychologist.

Usually the group met in the lounge with the
finches and the fish tank. They shut all the curtains
so no one could see in. But one day when Grace arrived
to visit her father, the time and the place of the group
had changed. They were meeting in the TV room and
it was still in session. It was cold and almost dark,
so although the corridor was curtained they hadn't
bothered with the windows facing the garden. The

therapist must have assumed that no one would venture outside.

Grace realized this by chance. She hadn't meant to pry. When Elizabeth told her Edmund wouldn't be available for at least half an hour she decided to walk to the WRVS canteen to buy him some chocolate. On her way back she saw the light from the windows falling on the unpruned rose beds. Although she knew she shouldn't look she was attracted closer, like a moth.

They had pulled the chairs into a circle, almost a huddle. Her father was sitting next to Bella, who had been released from the hospital but returned as a day patient to attend the group. Grace recognized most of them. The woman with the dead baby, who had shared Christmas lunch with them, was there too.

Bella was talking. The others were listening intently. Grace had the impression that it was a new development, Bella taking centre stage. The psychologist who was sitting on the floor because there weren't enough chairs to go round, nodded, encouraging Bella to continue. Suddenly Bella got up from her chair and moved to the middle of the circle. She stood with one hand above her head, still talking. She seemed agitated but Grace couldn't hear what she was saying. She dropped her hand to her side and began to cry. The others crowded round her. Grace saw Edmund put his arm round her and hug her.

She felt awkward about being there, pulled up the hood of her anorak because now she was very cold, and walked on round the building. She rang the doorbell and stood shivering on the doorstep for Elizabeth to let her in. When the door to the TV lounge opened and they came out, they were chatting and laughing like old friends. No one would have been able to tell that Bella had been crying. Edmund seemed preoccupied. Grace said she wouldn't stay long, soon they'd have to go into the dining room for supper. But he walked with her to the bus stop.

'Good group tonight?' she asked.

He didn't answer. 'They're letting me out next week.' He seemed almost sad.

'Will you go back to Rod's?'

'He says I can.'

'Well then.'

'It won't be easy,' he said, and though he didn't say so, she knew he was thinking about the support he'd received from the group.

'No reason why you shouldn't stay in touch.'

'No,' he said relieved, 'no.'

When she arrived back in Laurel Close there was an ambulance outside the door. Frank had had a heart attack. The ambulance crew wheeled him out on a trolley. Grace rushed through the crowd and touched his hand. Before Maureen climbed into the back of the ambulance Grace put her arm around her, and they cried together.

Frank died before he reached hospital. Grace was offered another foster family but she opted instead for the children's home. There she slept in a room with three empty beds. There were blankets folded at the foot of them and pillows in striped cases.

Chapter Twenty-Six

The memory of the room in the children's home, so similar to her room at Baikie's, jolted her back to the present. An hour had passed. She had come to one of the stone blinds built by the estate for grouse shoots, and she imagined her father's relatives crouched here, guns raised, waiting for the whirring grouse to speed overhead. They would have waxed jackets, braying voices. Her family's decision to sell this land for the quarry had only reinforced her prejudices about them.

In the days leading up to Bella's funeral, once she had finished her survey in the morning, she would walk the hills, getting her bearings. Late one afternoon she climbed Fairburn Crag. From there it was possible to look down on Holme Park House, laid out beneath her like an architect's plan. In a bend in the river was the main house, with two wings, and beyond it the formal gardens. Grace understood that the gardens were what the visitors came to see. She had never been herself. The Halifax sisters had offered to take her, had planned a jolly day out in the Rover with a picnic. They said the park was the only place in Northumberland where you could guarantee seeing hawfinch. Grace had been tempted but when Cynthia muttered something about her heritage she'd refused.

Now, looking down, she felt no connection with the house. She wouldn't have wanted to live there. Her father's bitterness seemed misplaced and she wished she hadn't been drawn into it.

She began the long walk back to Baikie's reluctantly. She hated the evenings in the cottage. She hadn't expected it to be like this. She'd known it wouldn't be easy – she'd told her father that – but she thought she might enjoy living with other women. She'd hoped for the easy camaraderie she'd experienced in the Halifax library. University had been competitive but she'd put that down to the presence of men. Here, she'd thought with three women sharing the same expertise and interest there'd be no pressure. She might even build some sort of friendship. Instead there were questions and suspicion. Anne Preece was the most intrusive.

'Fulwell?' she'd asked as soon as they'd met. 'I don't suppose you're related to Rob and Livvy at the park.'

She'd laughed so Grace had felt no obligation to answer, but the question had made her uneasy. Since arriving at the cottage, since hearing the story of Bella swinging from the beam in the barn she'd been frightened. She only felt safe when she was alone in the hills, and even then occasionally she had a sense of being followed.

When she arrived back at Baikie's it was almost dark. She hesitated on the doorstep, tempted in a moment of panic, to turn round and walk away. There was a smell of food. Rachael, in the kitchen, must have heard her boots on the yard because the door opened. Grace didn't know what to make of Rachael. Sometimes she thought she was more dangerous than Anne.

'Hi,' Rachael said. 'Come in. I was just starting to worry.'

Walking in from the clear air the smell of tomatoes, garlic and browned cheese made Grace's stomach tighten.

'I've made a veggie lasagne,' Rachael said. 'Why don't you have some? There's plenty. It's a bit late to start cooking.'

'Great. Thanks.' She didn't know what else to say.

Because it was cold they sat in the easy chairs, pulled close to the fire, with the plates on their knees. No one had bothered to draw the curtains or put on the main light. Anne was still working at the desk, with the table lamp turned onto her papers, so they sat in shadow, lit occasionally by the red flash of a spitting log.

'I've been looking at your survey results,' Rachael said. Grace felt her stomach clench again. She poked the food with her fork.

'Yes?'

'Amazing! I mean I didn't realize. This valley must have the greatest density of otters in the county. In the North of England.'

'I don't know about that. I think they've generally been underestimated.'

'When this is all over you should think about publishing.'

At this Grace looked up, wondering why Rachael was so insistent.

'Oh?'

'If you don't someone else will. You've done the work. Why shouldn't you take the credit?'

'I suppose so.' Though she knew she would never

present these figures for scientific scrutiny. She gathered up the plates and took them into the kitchen quickly, so Rachael couldn't see how little she'd eaten.

When she returned to the living room Anne had stood up and was stretching her hands towards the fire.

'I called at the post office today,' Rachael said. 'There was some mail. I should have given it to you earlier.'

She handed Grace a white envelope. It was the first letter she'd received since the project started and the other two stared at her, expecting her to open it immediately. But she folded it in two so it fitted into her jeans pocket.

Anne was equally secretive about one of the letters she'd received. She ripped the envelope open immediately as if she couldn't wait to see what was inside, skimmed the contents then stuffed the page back into the envelope.

Rachael studiously avoiding any suspicion that she was prying, read her book while this was going on, but Grace watched. She saw that the letter was handwritten but that the paper had a corporate logo at the top. Even from the brief glimpse she had convinced herself that the logo was that of Slateburn Quarries. That only added to her unease, her sense that there was no one here she could trust.

Later she tried to find the letter. When Anne was in the bathroom that night, washing her hair, Grace went through the chest where she kept her clothes, and her handbag. She even emptied the waste bin onto the floor but there was no sign of the letter. Either Anne had kept it with her or she had burnt it when no one was looking. That, in itself, Grace took to be suspicious.

Although she was awake long after the others were asleep, Grace didn't open her own letter that night. She had enough to think about. She waited until the next morning when she was out on the hill and she could see to the horizon in every direction.

The letter was from her father. He was still living and working in the restaurant and he'd been bad about keeping in touch since she'd left school. This was much longer than his usual notes. Even when she'd been at university she'd been able to tell a lot about his state of mind from the length of his contact. When he was sober and happy he kept in touch with chatty phone calls, postcards with a dirty picture on one side, and on the other gossip about Rod and work, perhaps a new recipe that had excited him. The length of this letter, even before she started reading it, made her suspect that he was depressed again and that he'd been drinking. The tone, obsessive, panicky, convinced her and made her own anxiety worse.

The letter started with a list of questions about Bella. He'd heard somehow about the suicide and he wanted to know all about it. 'How did she die?' he asked. 'Were you there when they found her?' 'Are they sure it was suicide?'

At first the questions confused her. Why should her father, even in an agitated state, care so much about the death of a middle-aged farmer's wife? Then an almost throwaway line made her understand. He had written, as if he could take it for granted. 'Of course you do remember Bella from the hospital.' Then it came back to her. For the first time she made the

211

connection between the suicide victim and Bella the patient, the central member of the therapy group in St Nicholas'. Perhaps though she'd already made the connection subconsciously and that was why the memory of her father's stay in hospital had been the subject of so many of her daydreams. It was an unsettling thought.

The letter continued: 'There was a notice in the paper about her funeral. I'd like to be there. She was a friend and I feel awful that I didn't give her more support when she needed it. But I can't face those dreary rituals and I wouldn't know what to say to her family and friends. So I thought I'd come to see you that day instead. It'll stop me brooding. I'd like to see where Bella finished up. Strange that she ended her days so close to where I started mine. Perhaps you can take me for a walk. I'll point out some of my old haunts. Don't worry about my getting there. A friend has offered to give me a lift.'

The letter ended on a strange note. 'You will take care, won't you?' She found that touching. He didn't usually worry about her. She was the one that did all the worrying. All the same it hadn't occurred to him that it might be inconvenient for him to visit her, or that after his making so many demands on her she might not want to see him.

'It would serve him right if I phoned him and told him not to bother,' she said out loud, but she knew she wouldn't do it.

She tore the letter into many tiny pieces and threw them a handful at a time up into the air and watched the wind scatter the fragments safely over the hill. Then she walked on, well outside her survey area until she came to Langholme village. She thought she would use the public phone to talk to her father, but quite by chance she stumbled on the house in the photograph, the house where her father had lived before he had married her mother.

It was much more ordinary than she'd expected, on the outskirts of the village, not very close to the big house at all, though you could see Holme Park at the end of the long straight lane. It was tidier, of course, than in her father's day. The bags of rubbish had gone. She wondered if it might be possible to dream up a plausible excuse for looking inside, but then Anne Preece arrived, intruding again with all her questions. Apparently she'd been at Holme Park drinking coffee with Livvy Fulwell. That surprised Grace, who hadn't previously had the impression that the two were good friends. It was another warning that she had to be careful.

Chapter Twenty-Seven

The day of Bella's funeral Grace saw Rachael and Anne off, then waited for her father. He appeared, surprisingly, on foot, walking down the track to Black Law with a small rucksack on his back. The track through the farmyard was a public footpath and at first she thought he was just another walker. He moved very fast, though once, as she watched, he turned to look over his shoulder. He seemed jumpy, restless. She put the kettle on because she knew he would want coffee as soon as he arrived and went out to wait for him.

'You've not walked all the way from the village?'

'I don't know why you're surprised. I'm fit for my age.'

'Not that fit.'

'All right,' he admitted. 'A friend dropped me at the gate.'

'You should have brought her down for coffee.' She had guessed that it would be a woman. Rod was his only male friend and he still had the ability to attract.

'I asked but she's a bit shy. Besides, she's got things to do. She'll wait for me up there later.'

She took him into the house. She expected comment about the state of the kitchen but he seemed too preoccupied to disapprove.

'I've seen this place from a distance but I've never been inside. A bit primitive, isn't it? But I don't suppose you mind that, do you, Gracie? You're used to roughing it.'

In the rucksack, carefully wrapped, were home-made biscuits to have with the coffee and an asparagus flan for their lunch.

'But no booze, Gracie. I hope you'll give me the credit for that.'

She thought then it would be all right. When she'd read his letter she'd worried that there'd be tears. A scene. She wasn't sure she had the energy. He insisted on a guided tour of the cottage and all the way round he was asking questions, to most of which she had no answers. He asked about Bella and Dougie and how they'd managed. About Constance Baikie and the Trust, and the students that came and the research they did.

She laid the table in the living room for lunch. He always thought food should be treated seriously. He hated picnics.

'You look as if you need feeding up,' he said, only half joking.

She managed to eat the flan. Most of it.

'I want to see where Bella lived,' he said.

'You've seen it. You walked past the farmhouse to get here.'

'I want to see it properly.'

She shrugged. It didn't seem worth fighting over. They stood in the empty yard with the house on one side, and in the other the shed where Bella brought the lambs in to ewe. It was a gusty, sunny day. The shadows of small clouds blew across the hill. Edmund went over to the shed, unbolted the top half of the door and looked in. Inside were some wooden pens, a pile of mucky straw. He turned round quickly.

'I want to go in the house,' he said.

'You can't. It's locked.'

'You must have keys. For an emergency.'

'The police locked it all up when Dougie left.'

'I need to see where she lived. She talked about it all the time but I never came here.'

'You kept in touch then?' She hadn't realized.

'A few of us from the old group met up occasionally. You know, for encouragement, support, it helps.'

'It must have done.' He still had bouts of depression but he'd never had to go into St Nick's again.

'So you can understand why I need to go inside.'

'I'm sorry,' she said, starting to lose patience. 'It's not possible. I told you I haven't got the keys.'

'We'll have to break in then.'

'Don't be daft,' Grace yelled, thrusting her face close to his in an attempt to make him see sense. 'How are you going to get away with that? And don't you think I've got enough to lose here already?'

'Yes, of course. I'm sorry.' He seemed close to tears. 'It's just that you don't realize . . . You have to have been through that sort of desperation. And then I feel responsible. Perhaps I should have guessed.'

'When did you last hear from her?'

'A few of us met in the restaurant about a month ago. Rod lets me cook for them sometimes when it's closed to the public. And I phoned her the week before she died.'

'Why?'

He seemed shocked by the question. 'It's personal. I don't want to talk about it.'

'The police might want to talk to you. Rachael said they were wanting to trace people who might have some idea why she killed herself.'

'Rachael?'

'Rachael Lambert. She's supporting the project. Bella was a friend of hers.'

'I didn't realize Bella had any friends except us.'

So much, Grace thought, for Rachael's notion that she and Bella were closer than mother and daughter. Bella hadn't even considered her worth mentioning.

'Anyway,' Edmund said suddenly, 'I wouldn't want to have anything to do with the police. Bella would hate it. She'd left all that behind long ago.'

'All what?'

But he shook his head and turned away. He walked round the house, looking in each window in turn, occasionally holding his hand between his forehead and the glass to shield the reflected light from his eyes.

'I don't know what you're expecting to find.'

'I can't tell what went on here,' he said, as if he hadn't heard her. 'What was she like?'

'How should I know?' Grace snapped. She thought it was morbid, this peering into the house of a dead woman and she was worried in case Rachael or Anne came back early and caught them at it. 'She killed herself the night before I arrived.'

'Yes,' Edmund muttered resentfully, as if somehow Grace had been responsible for that, as if her imminent arrival had been the trigger of Bella's suicide.

'Shall we go back inside then?' Grace touched his arm gently, her way of making peace with him. 'We can't do any more out here and I'm cold.'

She shepherded him back toward Baikie's. He went

without argument, and sat quietly while she made tea. Later he looked at his watch. 'I'll have to go soon. She said she'd be there about five.' She. No name. Perhaps he couldn't even remember it. Since Sue he'd tried not to get too involved.

'I'll walk up the track with you.'

'No,' he said quickly, so she thought perhaps he'd made up a fiction about this trip. Perhaps he hadn't admitted to a daughter. 'I told you she's shy.'

'I'll say goodbye here then.' They stood awkwardly in the cramped kitchen.

'So?' he asked, an attempt to fatherly good humour. Now he seemed reluctant to go. 'How's the project working out?'

'It's not easy. Doing what you ask.'

'No, well, I appreciate that. But you wouldn't want it, would you? A great scar out of the hill. On my land.' He hesitated, looked at her significantly. 'Our land.'

'I'm not even sure it'll do any good in the end.'

'What do you mean?'

'A few otters. What do they matter compared with all that money, all those jobs. That's what people'll say!'

'More than a few.' He paused again. 'According to your survey anyway. Significant numbers. That's what you promised.'

'I'm not sure I can keep that up. Rachael's already started to question my counts.'

And anyway I'm no good at lying, she thought. Not when it comes to science. To the important stuff.

'Do your best, eh? For me.'

'Yeah, well, it's a strain.'

'I know.' But he didn't know at all. Like a spoilt

toddler he couldn't recognize anything beyond his own needs, his own distress. 'Look, I'd better go.'

'Can't keep her waiting,' Grace said sarcastically.

'No.'

She went outside with him then turned in the opposite direction, towards the old mine. Deliberately she didn't turn back to wave. She sat among the debris of the mine close to the stream which seemed very fast and deep channelled in the culvert, and began to brood again. She knew it was dangerous, this obsession, this desire to find meaning and connection. She almost believed that all the events which were troubling her were linked in an elaborate web – Bella's death, Anne's hostility, the quarry, the person who seemed to be following her. And she was the spider in the centre of it, causing the events without understanding why.

At last the length of the shadows thrown by the mine building made her realize how late it was. As she walked back to the cottage in the orange evening light the exercise relaxed her and it occurred to her that she might be ill, like her father. He could be paranoid too and she'd read that such diseases could be inherited. Rather than frightening her, the thought was re-assuring. She could talk to someone. Get treatment. She probably wasn't in any physical danger at all. It was all in her head.

She kept this thought clear in her mind for two days, long enough to drop a note to her father, asking if he could arrange for her to see his doctor at St Nick's, and a letter to Antonia Thorne. The letter was unspecific. She still didn't feel sufficiently safe to commit herself to paper. She just said it would be good to have a talk. Something was worrying her. She got a lift out to Langholme with Rachael to post them. Even though the letters were sealed she was reluctant to hand them over.

Chapter Twenty-Eight

Grace only went to the pub with the others so she could use the public phone in Langholme. It wasn't so much that she had a puritan attitude to communal drinking but she hated the crowded intimacy, the jostling at the bar, feeling strangers' breath on her neck. She'd gone out occasionally with people from her hall at university so as not to seem stuck-up, and student haunts were always packed and noisy. Edmund had never suggested taking her to the pub. When he drank it was seriously, on his own behind closed doors.

Rachael must have thought Grace would resist because when she suggested the trip she said, 'Project leader's orders. You've got to come. It'll do us all good to get away from this place for a while.'

So they'd climbed into Rachael's tiny car and driven through the dark to Langholme. Grace had been a bit anxious about leaving all her work at Baikie's – with the farmhouse empty anyone could break in, but the others said she was being ridiculous. Who would drive all that way to steal a pile of papers and a couple of pairs of binoculars? And she saw that she probably was being foolish. With help she'd come to realize that.

She waited until it was almost closing time to phone her father from the call box in the street outside. In the short space of time they were in the pub Anne drank four gins and flirted with the young boys by the bar.

Grace could hear the clatter of plates, sense her father's wavering concentration.

'Well?' she shouted. 'Did you get my letter?'

'Yes.'

'Have you made me an appointment?'

'Don't be stupid. You're the most sorted-out person I know. You don't need to see a shrink.'

Only then did she realize how much she'd been relying on the doctor to provide her with a way out. She stood in the phone box, cut off from the pub by the road. A lorry went past, dazzling her with its headlights, making the small panes of glass in the old-fashioned box vibrate.

'Dad?' She'd lost concentration and was scared he'd hung up on her.

'Yes.'

'I can't carry on doing this, Dad.'

'Of course you can. It's not for much longer, is it?'

'It's too long. You don't know what it's like.'

'For me, girl. Stick it out for me. The old team, working together.'

There was a shout in the background, a crash of plates and without saying goodbye, her father replaced the receiver.

For a long time she stood where she was, trapped in the box. She couldn't face Rachael or Anne in the smoky pub. She was afraid she'd burst into tears, not of sadness but of confusion. She didn't know what to do and she'd always been able to take decisions before. Then a drunk old man came out of the pub and staggered crabwise across the road towards her, lit by a single lamp further down the street. She pushed open the heavy door and fled. She passed him on the pavement but he seemed not to see her.

In the pub Anne was back at the bar.

'You've been a long time,' Rachael said.

'I couldn't get through.'

Then Rachael told her that Anne was planning to move into the boxroom.

'I think she just needs the privacy,' she said apologetically.

'Why?' Grace demanded. 'What's she up to?' It was her way of trying to warn Rachael, but the other woman looked at her strangely and changed the conversation, so for a moment Grace wondered if they were working together, if there was a conspiracy against her.

I am going mad, she thought. Just like my father.

The next morning Rachael went off early. She said she had a meeting with Peter and the developer. Grace, who hadn't slept much, was up before her, and tried to make normal conversation. She made Rachael coffee, then watched the small car drive away, the engine straining up the hill. Back in the cottage she put bread under the grill to toast, but didn't get round to eating it because Anne appeared, still in her dressing gown, her wet hair wrapped in a towel.

'I'm on my way out,' Grace said quickly. 'I won't be back until this evening. It'll be quite late.'

Anne must have seen the bread slowly turning brown under the grill but she only shrugged and said OK.

It wasn't until midday that Grace realized she'd

rushed off in such a hurry that she hadn't left details of her proposed route at Baikie's. She didn't want to give Rachael cause to look more closely at her work so she decided to go back. She assumed that by then Anne would be out with her quadrats.

There was a car parked by the cottage and for a moment Grace was suspicious. It wasn't Peter Kemp's car and they never had other visitors. Then she thought again that she was being ridiculous. It probably belonged to someone who was looking at Black Law farmhouse and the land, a valuer or an agent.

As soon as she went into the kitchen she heard the noises in the other room, snuffling, squealing sounds. Without thinking she opened the door into the living room to look in. There was a smell of food, of smoked fish and ripe fruit, which made her feel sick. She saw Anne Preece lying on the floor with a man. His naked bottom was in the air, his trousers round his ankles, so like the pose in a smutty seaside postcard that she wondered briefly if it was a practical joke. Anne's way of getting back at her. But Anne wasn't laughing. Underneath the man but facing the door she saw Grace at once and was obviously shocked. The man had to turn to look at her. At the same time he was pulling up his underpants with one hand and bearing his weight with the other. It was quite a gymnastic feat. As soon as he turned, Grace recognized the man's face. Edmund had sent her newspaper cuttings about the Black Law development and Godfrey Waugh had featured. Grace stared at him for a moment then withdrew, shutting the door behind her.

So Anne had been in league with the opposition all along. That at least hadn't been part of her imagination. While she was considering what to make of the information she tore a page from her notebook and wrote the details of where she expected to be that afternoon.

The door opened and Anne came in, not super cool any more, but ruffled, diffident. As uncertain, Grace could see, as she was. Looking at Anne Preece, Grace decided not to pass on the information about her affair with Waugh to her father. It would have to be dealt with, but not in that way. She hated the idea of Edmund gloating over it, rolling the details round and round in his mouth as if it were an expensive brandy to be savoured.

So when Anne talked about Godfrey's wife and child she said, 'It's all right. I won't say anything.'

She spoke slowly and firmly. She wanted Anne to believe her. Anne must have done because she smiled gratefully.

'I'll cook tonight. I do a chicken casserole you'd die for.'

Grace almost reminded Anne that she was vegetarian but stopped herself in time. This was a gesture of reconciliation and she didn't want to spoil it. There'd be time for all that honesty later. Instead she smiled and said, 'I'll go. Let you get on with it.'

Walking down the track towards the disused mine she felt better than she had done since her father first entangled her in this mess.

PART TWO

Chapter Twenty-Nine

They were in Baikie's again. Waiting. There was the same smoky fire, the familiar furniture covered in dust, the moth-eaten fox leering out of the smudged glass case.

But now they sat, as self-conscious and wooden as actors in an amateur production, so the room seemed different. A stage set for a gothic thriller. A two-hander. They stared at each other waiting for something to happen, to move the action on.

A young policewoman had been detailed to sit with them and she tried her best to lift the mood. The drizzle had turned into a downpour. She looked at the rain sluicing down the windows and said cheerfully that she'd been lucky to get a job indoors. She didn't envy the rest of the team who were still out on the hill. She had a date that evening with a bloke who was drop-dead gorgeous and she couldn't think what her hair would look like after a day out there.

Rachael turned politely to answer her but unexpectedly, from the kitchen, they heard another voice, quite different, hard and authoritative.

'Don't give me that crap, Joe. Just bugger off and see to it.' Joe must have obeyed the order immediately,

ANN CLEEVES

to be already on his way outside because the next question came in a shout.

'In here, are they?'

So prepared, Anne and Rachael turned to watch her come in. She was a large woman – big bones amply covered, a bulbous nose, man-sized feet. Her legs were bare and she wore leather sandals. Her square toes were covered in mud. Her face was blotched and pitted so Rachael thought she must suffer from some skin complaint or allergy. Over her clothes she wore a transparent plastic mac and she stood there, the rain dripping from it onto the floor, grey hair sleeked dark to her forehead, like a middle-aged tripper caught in a sudden storm on Blackpool prom.

She dismissed the policewoman. 'Tea please, love.' Then she held out a hand like a shovel. Rachael stood up to take it and realized she'd seen the woman before. It was the bag lady who'd crashed into the chapel late during Bella's funeral.

'Vera Stanhope,' the woman said. 'Inspector. You'll be seeing a lot of me. More of Joe Ashworth, my sergeant, but at the moment he's out there getting wet. He's still young. Less prone to arthritis.' She stared at Rachael. 'Don't I know you?'

'I was at Bella Furness's funeral.'

'So you were. I never forget a face.' She smiled smugly. 'One of my strengths.'

'What were you doing there?' Rachael asked.

For a moment the inspector seemed affronted that Rachael had the temerity to ask. 'That was personal. Nothing to do with this business.' Then, although she didn't seem to be a woman who minded being rude she added more kindly, 'I knew Bella from years back.'

'How did you know her?'

'Like I said,' Vera's voice was brisk, 'that's personal. And your chum's lying up there with a string round her neck. More important now, wouldn't you say, to sort that out.'

I'm not sure, Rachael thought. She had been shocked by Grace's death but in this new detached state she didn't feel any personal loss. Certainly she didn't think of the zoologist as a 'chum'. Grace had drifted into their lives at Baikie's with so little emotional contact that it was hard now to think of her as ever having been alive. It was almost as if her death was inevitable, as if she had been progressing towards it since her arrival.

She realized that Vera Stanhope was waiting for an answer.

'Yes,' she said. 'Of course.'

She looked at Anne. Usually she would have expected a smart flip response to that sort of remark, but Anne seemed uncharacteristically upset and continued to stare into the fire.

'Who was the last person to see her alive?' Vera asked.

Now Anne did raise herself to speak. 'Me,' she said. 'I suppose.' She paused. 'Rachael was at a meeting in Kimmerston. Grace went into the field. I stayed here to catch up on some paperwork. Unless she met someone else while she was out...'

'Is that likely?'

'It depends where she went. One of the Holme Park keepers might have seen her from the hill. Or a hiker. Sometimes she walked all the way to Langholme.

There'd be more chance, I suppose, of someone bumping into her there.'

'What time did you see her?'

'Lunchtime. One, half past.'

'Is that when she went out, or did she come back to the cottage to eat?'

'No,' Anne said, 'she didn't do eating much. She went out early and came back to leave the details of her afternoon walk. It's a Health and Safety thing.'

Vera Stanhope had taken off her plastic mac and hung it over the glass case which held the stuffed fox, but she remained standing. Anne had seemed to be directing this conversation to the uneven hem of the inspector's dress, but now she looked up into Vera's face and asked abruptly, 'What time was she killed?'

Vera gave a laugh which turned into a choking cough. 'God knows. We don't. Not yet. And we might never be able to tell with any certainty, especially if she hadn't eaten. The scientists don't work miracles whatever they have you believe.'

'She was found so close to Baikie's that she must either have been on her way out or her way back,' Rachael said. 'Do you think she realized she was in danger and was trying to reach the cottage . . .?'

No one answered. Vera continued in her matter of fact way. 'Could she have been there all afternoon, without anyone seeing?'

'Quite easily. Even if she was near to the footpath. Midweek and in this weather there'd not have been many walkers.' Rachael turned to Anne. 'You didn't go that way? You were talking about sampling near the mine.'

'No. I was in all day. Like I said, I thought I'd tidy up the paperwork.'

'You must have been out shopping,' Rachael said then stopped, realizing she sounded inquisitorial, the school prefect again, realizing too that the inspector might make more of it than she should. She continued lamely, 'I mean the stuff for the casserole, the wine.'

'Oh yeah, but that was earlier. In the morning before Grace came back.'

'We might be able to tell from Grace's notebook about what time she was killed,' Rachael said. 'Was it with her?'

Vera ignored the question. 'How would that help?'

'She was doing timed counts. She would have written down the time the last one started.'

Vera sat down in the armchair. She pulled it closer to the fire. The mud on her feet had already begun to dry in grey streaks. Today she had with her not a collection of carrier bags but a large briefcase. The leather was so soft and old that the shape had gone and the straps had curled and it looked like a postman's sack. She took out a hard-backed notebook and jotted down a few words.

She crossed her legs giving Rachael a glimpse of white lardy flesh and leant forward with her elbows on her knees. Her face took on a more serious expression. This is it, Rachael thought, this is where the real questions start. But Vera Stanhope, despite her earlier insistence that she shouldn't forget Grace lying strangled on the hill, began to talk about herself. And she told it like a fairy story so Rachael wasn't sure if it was true.

'When I was a little girl,' she started, 'I used to come

and stay in this cottage. Occasionally. My dad would bring me. There was only my dad. I never knew my mum. She died giving birth to me. It's not a nice thing to grow up with, that. As if being born was a crime. An act of violence at least. You could say that I had an interest in crime right from the start. My profession was chosen for me.' She knew she had shocked them, but she smiled roguishly. She knew she had them hooked. Rachael thought she wanted to disconcert.

'Connie Baikie lived here then. Large, loud Connie. More like an actress than a scientist. A real drama queen. I don't know what stories you've heard about her. They'll all be true. She was famous, you know, at the time. As well known as Peter Scott. My father adored her. He was a naturalist too. Only an amateur but well respected. He was a schoolmaster by profession. I can't think he was much good at it. I knew from experience that he found children tedious and his real love was always natural history.

'So. Picture the scene. Imagine the situation. A middle-aged man landed with a small child. A frail child who suffered from allergies: asthma, eczema. Psychosomatic, no doubt but real enough at the time. Did he allow that to cramp his style? Of course not. He was an obsessive. Until I was old enough to be left alone I was dragged along too. I walked miles round here, many of them. I learnt to keep quiet and stand still.

'Then, occasionally, there were the wonderful weekends when we were invited to stay at Baikie's. There was music and dancing on the lawn. Chinese lanterns and big fires, sweets and biscuits and other grown-ups to make a fuss of me. Ladies in silk dresses

234

and fur coats wearing exotic perfume. Even the talk of plants, butterflies and animals seemed more exciting here. Whatever Constance Baikie was, whatever she became, she could put on a good show . . .'

She stopped abruptly and looked up at them. Her tone and mood changed. 'I expect you think I'm odd,' she said. 'Eccentric. Even that I'm dragging up my past for effect. That's not the case, and if I do have a reputation for eccentricity, I have one too for getting results. You couldn't have got anyone better.' She paused. 'This isn't my party piece, I don't trot it out for everybody. I'm telling you, so you know I understand what goes on here. And I haven't lost touch. You mustn't think that. I lived with my father for forty-five years. Lived with the lists and the notes and the sketches. He died a year ago, but I'm in the same house. The scientific journals still drop on the doormat every month because I haven't got round to cancelling them and sometimes I read them. Some of it must have rubbed off. I never shared his passion but at times I come close to understanding it.'

She leant back in her seat and closed her eyes. There was such a long silence that Rachael thought she had fallen asleep, imagined she and Anne sitting there for hours, too embarrassed to move. Then still with her eyes closed Vera said, 'So explain what you're doing here. I want to know all about the project and where Grace Fulwell fitted into it. Tell me about the survey so far. What you expected to find and the results you've achieved. By the time we leave this room I'm going to know as much as you do about the lass. You're going to pass on everything she told you. About her work, her friends, her family. Everything.'

There was a pause, then Anne said, with a brief return of the old spirit, 'That's all right then. That'll not take us very long. And I thought we'd be here all day.'

Chapter Thirty

That day Rachael and Anne came under varying pressure to move out of Baikie's. First, in an unprecedented show of marital devotion, Jeremy arrived to fetch Anne home. That at least was what he said he was doing there.

It was late afternoon when he arrived but the rain and the low cloud made it feel like a winter's evening. The fire had been lit all day and they had the lights on. Vera, exasperated, Rachael thought, by the paucity of the information she had gleaned, had passed them on to her sergeant. In one of the unnatural coincidences which marked the day Rachael recognized him as Joe Ashworth, the timid young man who had been sent to Black Law on the night of Bella's suicide. As he talked to them he looked occasionally out of the uncurtained window. All he said was, 'Strange, isn't it, without street lights?' But she could tell the emptiness made him uneasy.

He had with him a copy of the notes which had been taken from Grace's notebook. The notebook itself hadn't been released.

'Inspector Stanhope thought they might mean something to you,' he said. 'It seems fairly obvious to us. The last count was taken between ten and twelve.'

'And those are grid references,' Rachael said, pointing over his shoulder. 'If you check the map you'll be able to find out where she was counting.'

They spread a large-scale ordnance survey over the floor. Anne followed the blue squiggle of the burn with her finger, stopped at the edge of a settlement marked by big black squares. 'She must have walked as far as Langholme,' she said. 'The Skirl runs right at the bottom of my garden there. Look, there's the Priory. But there were no counts for the afternoon.'

And then, almost as if speaking of the Priory had conjured him up, Jeremy appeared in the room, shepherded by a constable in uniform. He stood just inside the door and Anne saw him as the others must have done. A small man, dapper and balding with the round, scrubbed face of a newly bathed baby. Although he wore jeans and a striped cotton shirt he gave the impression of smartness. To Anne and her friends he'd always been something of a joke but recently she'd sensed something else about him. A desperation which might have aroused her pity if she'd let it.

It was to fend off the possibility of pity that she mocked him now.

'My God. What on earth are you doing here? I wouldn't have thought you'd know the way.'

He looked hurt, reminding her of some of the small boys in her father's school, the ones who cried in secret and wet the bed. Then, to her relief, the moment passed and he camped up a show of righteous indignation, looking round slyly to check he had the others' sympathy. 'Actually, I have lived in Langholme longer than you. Just because I don't feel the need for a daily romp over the hills doesn't mean I don't know my way about. And, if you must know, I came because I was worried.'

She responded with the same bantering tone. 'That's not like you, Jem.' Then added more seriously, 'How did you find out what happened?'

'Because the phone's been ringing every half hour with people offering condolences. It's all over the village that you were the victim.'

She felt a terrible impulse to giggle, a hysteria which had been building up all day. 'How did you know that I wasn't?'

'I didn't at first, did I? But at least I knew there were three of you. Apparently no one else did.'

'Oh, Jem,' she said, 'I am sorry.'

'The vicar's wife brought a cake this afternoon. By that time I'd phoned the police and found out you were safe.' He paused. 'She took the cake away.'

Anne thought he would have enjoyed the role of bereaved widower. People coming around and making a fuss. He'd always loved funerals. And she was insured. Her death would have solved all his financial problems. Perhaps when he phoned the police to find out who the victim was he was disappointed to be given someone else's name. Perhaps that explained the slight air of wistfulness, the edgy uncertainty.

'What are folks in the village saying now?' Joe Ashworth asked.

'What do you mean?'

'There must be some gossip. Do they know who the girl is?'

'Don't be silly,' Anne interrupted. 'That's why he's here, isn't it, Jem? To find out those juicy details. He's worse than an old woman at gossip. Who suggested it?

Ethel Siddon from the post office?' But even as she spoke she thought that for once gossip wasn't uppermost in his mind.

'No!' He was indignant again. He said in a quiet tone, almost pleading, 'I've come to take you back to the Priory where I can look after you. You can't stay here with a madman on the loose.'

'You cannot be serious. *You*, look after me? Whoever put that nonsense in your head? You can't have dreamt it up for yourself.'

'For tonight at least,' he said. 'We need to talk about it.'

'No.' Because then she thought the murder was just an excuse to get her home. If he wanted to talk, it would be about his own problems, some scrape he'd got into. Jeremy would need a serious incentive to play the part of protective male. To spite him she went on wickedly, 'Why don't you tell the truth, Jem? You're frightened of being in the Priory on your own.'

There was a flash of panic. The schoolboy summoned to the headteacher's study. She thought, What are you scared of? She almost fell for it and agreed to go, then the old irritation returned. She'd agreed to be his wife, for Christ's sake. Not his nanny. That had never been the deal.

'Won't you come back with me?'

'No,' she said lightly, 'of course I won't. I've still got work to do. But you run off to London if you're scared. I won't mind.'

'I can't do that. I'd worry about you all the time. It wouldn't be any fun at all.' But he brightened at the prospect. She'd given him an escape route.

'Did you know Grace Fulwell?' Joe Ashworth asked.

'No.'

'You never met socially?'

'No.' Now he seemed impatient, eager to leave.

'Were you at home yesterday?'

'All day. I work mostly from home.'

But what do you do? Anne thought. Your schemes and your plans. What do they add up to?

'Miss Fulwell was surveying the burn at the bottom of your garden. A slim young woman in waterproofs and walking boots. Did you see her?'

'Of course not. I'm not like my wife, Sergeant. I don't enjoy energetic exercise for its own sake. I don't go onto the hill.'

'Could you see the burn from the house?'

'Not at this time of the year when the trees are in leaf.'

'From the garden?'

'Possibly. But the garden is Anne's domain. I never stray out there. Except perhaps on a hot sunny evening with a glass of Chardonnay before dinner.'

Chapter Thirty-One

Edie wasn't so easily fobbed off as Jeremy. Rachael ran through the rain to Black Law to phone her, prompted by Jeremy's talk of inaccurate gossip. She didn't want Edie to hear in the local news that a female conservationist had been strangled on Black Law Moor.

When Rachael told her what had happened Edie didn't immediately suggest that her daughter should move home. Her style was more subtle than that.

'Of course you'll take your own decision,' she said.

'Of course.' The sarcasm had become a habit.

'But I was going to suggest that you come home for a few days anyway.'

'Oh? Why?'

'I've tracked down Alicia Davison. The headteacher Bella worked for in Corbin. If you were staying here for a while we could go to see her.' She paused. Rachael would not respond and Edie went on, 'If you wanted me to come too that is. You might prefer to see her on your own.'

'I can't come home. Not yet. Anne's determined to stay and I can hardly leave her on her own. Besides, there's the report. It's not finished.'

'You could finish it here.'

'No. I'll have to stay.'

The police must have been in touch with Neville Furness, because they had taken over the ground floor of the farmhouse. Rachael was using the phone in Bella's bedroom. Suddenly from downstairs came the sound of smashing crockery, then explosive laughter and good-natured jeers. Vera Stanhope shouted for silence. Rachael had never known so much noise in Bella's house, but thought Bella might have liked it. She would have made sandwiches for them all, dried out their clothes.

'Edie?'

'Yes.'

'Why don't you come out here? Anne and I have decided to work as a pair on the last of the surveys. It would be useful to have someone to check us back in. To be an extra back-up. And we could still go out to see Miss Davison.'

'I could cook,' Edie said. 'Clean. That sort of thing.'

'No need to go overboard.' As far as Rachael could remember there had always been a cleaning lady to muck out at Riverside Terrace despite Edie's socialist principles. It was hard to picture her in rubber gloves.

'It's late night shopping at Tesco's. I'll stop on my way over.'

'I'll come out to the road to meet you. You'll never find it on your own at night.'

'Mm.' She hardly listened to the directions, too pre-occupied with her shopping list. Preoccupied too, Rachael thought, with planning a therapeutic strategy to get her daughter through the trauma of another bereavement.

On the way back to Baikie's Rachael saw that Peter

Kemp was there. Even in the gloom she recognized the flash new Land Rover parked by the tractor shed.

Him too, she thought. Someone else to persuade us to pack our bags and run away. I suppose it wouldn't do his reputation as an employer much good if he lost any more staff.

He had made himself quite at home. He perched on the arm of the chair where Anne was sitting, his long legs stretched towards the fire. He could have owned the place. A bottle of whisky, which he must have brought with him, stood on the mantelpiece and he had a glass in his hand. When he saw Rachael, he stood up and made to take her into his arms, but she moved awkwardly out of the way.

'What are you doing here?' she demanded.

'I was summoned.'

'What do you mean?'

'An inspector called . . .' He paused, expecting recognition of the reference. When Rachael frowned impatiently, he continued. 'Inspector Stanhope. A strange woman. Do you think she's quite sane?'

'She asked you to come here at this time of night?'

'Not exactly. Look, you might have told me what had happened to Grace . . .' And that was the nearest to any expression of sympathy they got from him. '. . . The inspector wants to see all her employment records. I explained we were a small informal organization and Grace was employed on contract but she insisted. I've dug out everything I've got.' He took an envelope file from his briefcase and fanned out three or four photocopied sheets. Rachael recognized the application form for post of temporary survey worker, a reference from the Otter Trust in Scotland, simple salary details – a bank account number and home address.

'Couldn't you have dropped them at the police station at Kimmerston?'

'I suppose I could . . .' he smiled at her like an adult humouring a truculent child, and poured her a whisky '. . . but she said she was here and it was urgent. Besides, I wanted to see how you two were getting on.'

'They've not let us onto the hill to get on with any work so there's nothing new to report.'

'I didn't mean that.' Then he realized she was joking. 'Of course not. I mean, how are you?'

'Shocked,' she said. 'What did you expect?'

'What are your plans?'

'To complete the report.'

'Is that wise?'

Anne had interrupted before he could complete the question. 'We're not being scared off, if that's what you think. We're not running away to give the developer an open field.'

'Is that what you think is going on here?' It was Vera Stanhope, standing in the doorway in the shadow. She must have let herself in through the kitchen. For a large woman she moved very quietly. Rachael supposed she'd had practice stalking animals when she'd been taken into the countryside by her naturalist father. It sounded as if she'd been bullied into standing very still and listening.

'Well,' Vera demanded. 'Do you think Grace Fulwell was killed as a corporate act of intimidation to frighten you away before you find anything of significance? Something which might persuade the Department of Environment inspector to stop the development?'

'No,' Rachael said. 'If there'd been anything special here we'd have found it already.' She looked at Anne for confirmation. 'Don't you think so?'

'Probably.'

'But there is a chance that you've missed something.' Vera walked further into the room and stood with her legs apart, looking round at them. For a moment Peter stared at her. Rachael saw a second of horror and, watching, thought: he's only used to women who take some trouble with their appearance. Even I did that for him. Then the professional charm took over and he stretched out his hand and introduced himself, offered her whisky, which she accepted with a huge Cheshire cat grin. When she repeated her question it was to him, as if she had acknowledged him as the expert.

'Well, Mr Kemp, do you think these girls have missed something?'

'I suppose there's always that chance but I doubt it. You won't find better fieldworkers anywhere than Anne and Rachael.'

'And Grace? She was good too?'

'She came highly recommended as you'll see from the reference in the file.'

'The file, yes. It was very good of you to bring it.' She looked up from her glass. 'Were you out this way any time yesterday, Mr Kemp? Checking your survey perhaps? Making sure your workers weren't slacking?'

The sudden question surprised him. 'No, I spent all day in the office. Meetings, as my secretary will tell you.'

'Then we won't need to take up any more of your time, Mr Kemp. Thank you for coming over.'

He seemed uncertain how to handle this summary dismissal.

'You might as well leave the whisky,' Vera went on. 'No doubt the lasses will be able to use it.'

As she walked him towards the outside door he muttered something which Rachael couldn't make out. They heard the roar of the diesel engine as he drove up the track.

Vera refilled their glasses and made herself comfortable. Rachael expected some comment about Peter but none came.

'Of course you must make up your own minds what you do next,' Vera said, repeating almost exactly Edie's words and meaning, as Edie had done – but I'd much prefer it if you do what I want you to.

'We're not leaving,' Rachael said. She wondered how many more times it would have to be said.

'I'm not suggesting that you should.' Vera bared her teeth in a grin. 'I'm not in any position to limit your access to the hill, except where my men are working, or to restrict your movements in any way.'

'But . . .'

'But my superiors are concerned about your safety. What would the bosses know? They spend their time in centrally heated offices, the sort of man who wouldn't venture onto the Town Moor without a compass and a stick of mint cake. They can't understand what you're doing here anyway. All they think is – two girlies on their own in the wilderness with a lunatic on the loose. You appreciate my difficulty.' She grinned and continued. 'I've been told to get you to clear off. You're in the way, an unnecessary distraction. And if anything . . .' she paused ' . . . untoward was to happen to either of you the press would have a field day.'

She drained her glass and stared pensively into the fire for a moment then went on briskly. 'So let's take it as read, shall we? I've told you to piss off and you've refused, so now it's your responsibility if you get into bother. You can't sue the Chief Constable.'

'Why are you so keen for us to stay?' Rachael asked. She could read forceful middle-aged women and knew that was exactly what Vera wanted.

'I can't see there's any danger,' Vera said briskly. 'There'll be men crawling around the hill for weeks. You'll be safer here than in the middle of town. Why jeopardize weeks of research when it's not necessary?'

'No,' Rachael said. 'There must be another reason.'

Vera shot her a look. 'You forget I've come to these hills since I was a kid. I don't want a quarry here any more than you do.'

For a moment Rachael was convinced, then it came to her that Vera Stanhope was ambitious, in the same way that Peter Kemp was ambitious. She was desperate for the investigation to succeed.

'There's more to it than that.'

'Let's just say that I don't feel it would be beneficial to my investigation if your project was abandoned.'

At first Rachael thought Vera was implying that she and Anne were suspects, that she was worried they would escape if they left the hill. Then she saw there was another explanation. 'You think the murderer might come back when he sees we've not abandoned the project. You want to use us as decoys.'

Like the crow, she thought, in the trap.

Vera appeared profoundly hurt and shocked by the suggestion.

'I couldn't do that,' she said. 'The Chief Constable would never countenance it.'

But she bared her large brown teeth in another grin.

Chapter Thirty-Two

The next day they saw little of Vera Stanhope and still the cloud was so low that there was no point trying to go out to count. By the evening Rachael thought that another day trapped in Baikie's would drive her mad and she agreed to Edie's suggestion that the following morning they should visit Alicia Davison, retired head-mistress of the school where once, according to the papers left at Black Law, Bella had been a teacher. Edie disappeared into Black Law to make phone calls.

'I don't like leaving you,' Rachael said to Anne, 'even with the police still around.'

'That's all right. I want to go into Kimmerston any-way to see a friend.'

A man, Rachael supposed, though the next morning when they set off at almost the same time there was no sign of it. No make-up or perfume. No smart clothes stashed into a rucksack to be changed into later.

Overnight the weather had changed. There was still a haze over the moor but it was warm and still. Edie had managed to contact Alicia by phone and was pleased with herself. 'I said we were researching local history. Alicia assumed it was about Corbin School. Apparently it was closed in the mid seventies. She got a bigger headship and went on to make quite a name for herself.'

She was driving and paused while she concentrated on passing a tractor. 'She sat on an advisory panel on primary education and was considered quite an expert on rural schools. She published a book on it. She never left the classroom though. I suppose she's one of those sad old spinsters who can only make relationships with small kids.'

Rachael was tempted to ask what had happened to sisterly solidarity. Edie too was a spinster who'd taught for most of her life. But she kept quiet. It was a relief to be away from Baikie's and she couldn't face a row.

When Miss Davison let them into her house it was clear she was far from sad. She was tiny, very quick and bright. Neither did she give an impression of age. She wore a grey velour tracksuit and new white training shoes and had just returned, she said, from her weekly yoga session in the village hall. Her new enthusiasm was t'ai chi but she liked to keep up her yoga too. As one got older it was good to keep supple.

She lived in a small development of smart new bungalows on the edge of a tidy village close to the A1.

She led them through the house rather apologetically. 'When I retired I dreamed of a stone cottage and a large garden but I saw that it wouldn't be practical. I've too many other interests. This suits me very well. We're all of a certain age here in Swinhoe Close. Mostly couples of course, but they seem not to mind including me. And there's one widower who's very chivalrous.' She spoke quickly with sharp, staccato phrases which came out like the repeated rhythm of bird song. 'Do sit down. We'll have the coffee presently, shall we? You don't want to talk about me. You're here to find out about the school. It'll be an interesting project. I suppose you live in Corbin. You didn't say.'

Rachael prepared to explain but Miss Davison didn't seem to expect an answer. 'I arrived at Corbin in the early sixties but the building hadn't changed, not really, since the turn of the century. My first headship. I didn't quite know what to expect. There was one large room with a curtain down the middle. The infants sat on one side of it and the juniors on the other. There were fifteen of each when I arrived and I've never taught a bigger bunch of monsters. They'd been without a head for a term and allowed to run wild. The place was heated, if that's the appropriate word, by a coke boiler in one corner, which bellowed out smoke and sulphur fumes. And on my first morning a family of bats fell out of the roof and onto my desk. The boys threw them at the girls. The girls screamed. I thought I'd come to a madhouse.' She smiled and Rachael thought she'd enjoyed every minute.

'Was Miss Noble teaching with you then?' Edie asked.

'No,' Miss Davison said sharply. 'That was later. Why do you want to know?'

'We are actually very interested in Miss Noble.'

Quite suddenly her friendliness turned to hostility.

'So that's what this is about. You're not here about the school at all. What are you? Reporters? Why can't you leave the poor woman alone after all this time. Out you go. My friend lives next door. If you don't leave quickly I'll get him to throw you out.'

Rachael was horrified at the prospect of being

forcibly ejected by an elderly widower. She didn't understand the change of mood, wondered for a moment if the woman was mad.

'Bella's dead. Miss Davison,' she said. 'I was a friend of hers. I'm still a friend of her husband's. I found your name in some of her papers. We thought you'd want to know.'

Since they had arrived there'd been conversation. Now suddenly the place seemed very quiet. It was an unusual room for an older woman, uncluttered, decorated in strong warm colours. No television but an expensive CD player and on a desk a personal computer. Glass doors led to a small garden bordered by a honey-coloured stone wall. One of the glass doors was slightly open and they heard the hum of traffic, children shouting.

'Playtime,' Miss Davison said. 'Here, at least, we've saved the village school.' Then, 'I didn't know Bella was dead. But how would I? We lost touch years ago.'

'I put a notice in the *Gazette* about the funeral.'

'I don't suppose many came,' Miss Davison said. 'I'd have been there if I'd known. But I don't read the *Gazette*. It's drivel, isn't it? And I find myself looking out for news of the children I've taught which somehow seems pathetic. As if I've never moved on.' She looked at Rachael. 'Was Bella ill for long? I wish I'd visited. I should have made more effort to find out what happened to her.'

'Bella wasn't ill,' Edie said. 'She committed suicide.'

'No!' They could see now how she must have been as a teacher. Firm, decisive, unwilling to put up with nonsense despite the gentle manner and the trilling voice. 'I don't believe it. Not now. It was all forgotten.

Then I could have believed it. Understood. But now she'd have no reason.'

'I can assure you that it was suicide,' Edie insisted triumphantly. This was her trump card. 'My daughter found the body.'

Rachael squirmed. 'That's why we're here,' she said. 'We need to know why. I was close to Bella but she never spoke about the past. I hoped you might be able to help me come to terms with it.'

God, she thought. I sound just like my mother.

Alicia remained suspicious. 'You didn't know anything about the court case?'

'Nothing.'

'It was in all the papers. You live in Kimmerston, don't you?'

'Like you,' Edie announced, 'we've never bothered much with the local press.'

Alicia looked at them with continued suspicion. 'Bella was convicted of manslaughter. She killed her father.' Still watching Rachael's face, she added more gently, 'So you really didn't know?'

'I had no idea.'

Bella, why didn't you tell me? Rachael cried to herself. I feel such a fool.

'Bella came to me straight from college. She was enthusiastic, energetic, full of ideas. The infant teacher before her was elderly, close to retirement. She was little more than a childminder. She read stories, let the children play, sang songs, but as for *teaching . . .*' she shrugged. 'I tried to suggest new ways of working but she refused to listen.

'Then Bella came and everything changed. I started to like my work again. We bounced ideas off each other.

We achieved more in the two years she was there than I've done in any other school. I thought she was enjoying it too.'

'She used your name,' Rachael said. 'That's what she called herself before she married – Bella Davison. Some sort of tribute, do you think?'

'I think I let her down. Then and later.'

'What happened?'

'Her father was a local businessman, a butcher. He owned a couple of shops and a slaughter house. Wealthy in local terms. Used to getting his own way.'

'And a councillor,' Rachael said.

'Oh yes, a councillor. Alderman Noble. He had fingers in lots of pies.' She paused. 'Forgive me. I might be a spinster but you mustn't think I dislike men in general. Alderman Noble I disliked intensely, though I never met him.

'Bella left home to go to college and said it was the best thing she'd ever done. There was a younger son who was sucked into the business and the same was expected of her. She was supposed to work in the office, to put on an apron and help out in the shop when they were busy. But Bella refused. She'd always wanted to teach.

'Then her mother died and suddenly she was expected to give up everything, her career and her new friends, to go home and care for him. He bullied her into it.'

'Was he ill?'

'He was fat and idle,' Miss Davison retorted. 'I suppose that's one form of illness.'

'Why did she do it?' Rachael asked. 'She was

independent. She'd left home once. She didn't need his approval.'

'Things were different then.'

'No,' Edie said. 'Not that different.'

'He was a bully. At first I think he convinced her that he was dying. Then he convinced her that she was fit for nothing better than running around after him. I met her six weeks before she killed him and I hardly recognized her. I told her that I'd find her work, that she could pay someone to care for him, but she'd lost all her energy and her confidence. She said she'd never be able to tell him. She couldn't face the row. She'd always been frightened of him. Now perhaps we'd think she'd been abused. Then it wasn't so unusual.' She spoke bitterly. 'A natural respect for one's elders. Something to be admired. It might have been the sixties but we didn't see much of rebellious youth in Kimmerston.

'She was charged with murder. She admitted killing him. She hit him on the back of the head with a bronze statue – a monument apparently to one of his prize bulls. She said it was the nearest thing to hand but it seemed appropriate. He'd come to look very like one of his beasts. Then she phoned for the police and waited for them to turn up. She was found guilty of manslaughter on the grounds of diminished responsibility. A period of insanity, her barrister said, caused by the stress of caring for a sick man. Though she was the sanest woman I've ever met. She was sent to a special hospital in the south, then came back to St Nicholas', the big psychiatric hospital near the coast, to prepare for her release.'

'Did you ever visit her?'

'I couldn't face it. Isn't that a terrible thing to say? It wasn't Bella I couldn't face but all those other poor people. I suppose I was afraid. She wrote to me when she was first transferred to St Nick's. She didn't ask me to visit but I'm sure that was what she wanted. Why else would she write? I let her down again. I'm not quite sure what I expected. Some nightmare image of bedlam perhaps. Howling lunatics and chains and straitjackets. I *knew* rationally it wouldn't be like that but still, I couldn't bring myself to go. I did write to her but it wasn't a warm letter. Not very encouraging. I'm not surprised she didn't get in touch when she was released.'

She stopped abruptly. A bell rang in the distance. In the school yard playtime was over. 'You said she was married. Was she happy?'

'Very,' Rachael answered. 'She must have met Dougie soon after she left hospital. He employed her to look after his elderly mother.'

'Is that what she worked as? Some sort of care assistant? After the way she'd felt about looking after her father?'

'I don't suppose she had much choice,' Edie said dryly. 'There'd hardly be a queue of schools waiting to take her on as a teacher. She had no friends or family to turn to. What else did she know?'

'Anyway, it worked out well.' Rachael thought Edie was being too hard on Miss Davison. She understood her reluctance to get involved. 'Dougie was a farmer. She loved the hills, loved him. A few years ago he had a stroke but that didn't make any difference to the way she felt about him.'

'What happened then?' Miss Davison demanded.

'What do you mean?'

'Something must have happened. Why else would she kill herself?'

'I don't know,' Rachael said. 'That was why we arranged to see you. I needed a reason. We were close friends.'

'Yet she never told you about the conviction.'

'Nothing.'

'Would she have told her husband?'

'Probably not.' If Bella hadn't felt able to confide in her, Rachael thought, she wouldn't have told anyone else.

'So perhaps the past came back to haunt her. Or someone from it.'

At first Rachael didn't understand what she meant and it was Edie who said, 'She was threatened with exposure, you mean?' She considered the idea. 'She'd created a new identity. Perhaps she'd even come to believe it. Then she met someone who recognized her. Someone who threatened to tell Dougie; even worse, to tell the authorities. She'd killed one elderly dependent man. Could they take the chance of allowing her to look after another? She couldn't face the questions, the publicity.' Edie looked at Rachael. 'It's certainly one explanation.'

Rachael agreed that it was. But Bella had been a fighter. She still believed there was more to her suicide than that. And if Bella had this secret in her life, perhaps there had been others.

Chapter Thirty-Three

As Anne drove to Kimmerston she told herself she was being a bloody fool. At this of all times, she should keep her distance from Godfrey Waugh. The relationship was complicated enough, and now, if Godfrey were to become a suspect in the murder investigation . . .

She had never been into Godfrey's office. His secretary wouldn't recognize her and it occurred to Anne that she could breeze in and demand to see him. Today, though, she wouldn't have the nerve to carry it off.

These thoughts, and others, had kept her awake for most of the night and when she parked by his office she still wasn't sure what she would do.

It was mid morning. The mist had cleared and it was already very hot. Godfrey had his offices in a functional concrete block which had been built in the 1970s, close to the river on the outskirts of the town, an attempt by the council to attract employment. Anne waited, and watched the cormorants standing on the staithes in the river.

At twelve o'clock a stream of women came out of the building to eat their sandwiches by the river. The Borders Building Society had their headquarters there and the women wore identical navy skirts and patterned polyester blouses. They lay on the grass and pulled up their skirts as far as was decent to expose their legs to the sun.

Still Anne waited. She had parked so she could watch the main entrance, and though the car was like a greenhouse she didn't go outside to sit with the others on the grass. Here she felt hidden. She hadn't committed herself to anything. She could still pull back from confronting him, from saying, 'Tell me, Godfrey, what did happen out there on the hill between you and Grace Fulwell?'

Then he was there, standing on the step just outside the big swing doors as if the bright sunlight was a surprise. He walked, head bowed, hands clasped behind his back, along the road towards the town centre. She slid out of the car and followed, not stopping even to lock the door. He would be going into Kimmerston to buy lunch. There would be a café or sandwich shop which he used regularly. She would go in after him, as if by chance, and she'd say, 'I didn't know you came here too.'

Instead he stopped before he reached the shopping area. In the angle formed by two main streets was the parish church, St Bartholomew's. The churchyard was separated from the roads by low stone walls and where they met at the corner was a wooden lych-gate; sheltered by its wooden roof was a drift of pink confetti. Godfrey went through the gate, scuffing the confetti with his feet.

Even then Anne assumed he was looking for food because that was still in her mind. The church at Langholme occasionally held open house, provided soup, bread and cheese and sent the proceeds to a third world charity. She thought something like that was happening here, though there were no posters inviting passers-by to lunch and nobody else was about. The sun and the chase down the noisy road had confused her.

But she followed him in, expecting to find bosomy ladies in flowery aprons, stalls set out at the back of the church with a tea urn and thick white china cups. The buzz of parish gossip. Instead there was silence.

She had hesitated for a moment in the deep shadow of the porch. It was cool there. In the corners more confetti had been blown. A big wedding had apparently taken place the weekend before. Then she pushed open the studded door. Sunlight streamed through the stained glass above the altar, down the aisle into her eyes. The church was still decorated by the wedding flowers – huge white and gold blooms on each window in crystal vases, and the crystal reflected the coloured light too.

At first she stood, embarrassed, thinking that she'd interrupted a service and that people were staring at her as they'd all stared at Vera Stanhope when she crashed into the crem chapel in the middle of Bella's funeral. Then her eyes adjusted to the light. She saw that she and Godfrey were the only people in the building and Godfrey hadn't even noticed her coming in.

He was sitting near the front of the church in a pew close to the aisle but he didn't seem to be praying. They had never discussed religion. She wondered if perhaps that was an explanation for his jumpiness, his change of moods towards her – he had moral qualms about adultery. But now he looked more like someone waiting for a bus than facing a spiritual crisis. He glanced nervously at his watch. Perhaps he had arranged to meet someone but then surely he would have turned occasionally to check the door and still he hadn't seen her. Even when she walked down the aisle towards him and her shoes must have made a sound on the stone floor he kept his eyes firmly fixed on the front of the church.

She slipped into the pew behind him and said conversationally, 'I never took you for the religious type, Godfrey.'

'Anne.' He spoke before turning to face her and when he did, she couldn't tell whether or not he was pleased to see her.

'Or perhaps you've got something to confess.'

'What do you mean?'

'Four days,' she said lightly. 'And you've not been in touch. Don't tell me. Let me guess. You've been busy.'

He didn't reply.

'Why did you rush off like that when you'd been on the hill?' She couldn't keep up this jokey tone any longer. 'Why didn't you come into Baikie's to say good-bye?'

'I was upset,' he said at last.

'What about? Being caught with your pants down? Or had something else happened to upset you?'

'What do you mean?'

'I need to know what happened on the hill that afternoon.'

He twisted his watch face so he could see it. The strap was loose. This was a nervous gesture she hadn't noticed before. That and his continued silence got under her skin so she shouted, 'For Christ's sake, I'm asking you if you killed Grace Fulwell!'

She sensed her voice fill the church, become muffled by echo in its corners, in the high boat-shaped roof.

'No,' he said. 'Of course I didn't kill her.' There was a trace of irritation in his voice which reassured her more than the words.

'Have the police been to see you yet?' she asked.

'Why would they?'

'Because of the quarry. They think Grace might have been killed because she'd discovered something which would stop the development going ahead.'

'God, who dreamed up that theory?'

'The inspector in charge, a woman called Stanhope.'

'You told her it was ridiculous?'

'I haven't told her anything.' She spoke slowly, giving the words extra weight.

He looked up from his watch. 'So she doesn't know I was there that day?'

'No.'

'I wasn't sure what to do. There've been television appeals asking people to come forward, anyone who was near Black Law. I was going to go. I could say I was doing a site visit. Then I thought if you hadn't told them I was there it might look strange. I suppose I could say I didn't go into the house. I could say I went straight onto the hill. What do you think?'

'For Christ's sake, Godfrey, I'm not your mother.'

'No, no, I'm sorry.'

'Did you see Grace?'

'Only in the distance. She walked too fast for me to catch her up.'

'Did you see anyone else?'

'No.' She thought she had sensed a slight hesitation, then decided she had imagined it. His panic was making her rattled too.

'There doesn't seem much point then.'

'But my car was parked in your yard. I drove down the track. Anyone might have seen it. What will the police think if someone else reports it before I do?'

'How should I fucking know!'

He looked as shocked as if she had hit him. He had never liked her swearing. Memories of the other times calmed her a bit.

'I'm sorry,' she said. 'But it is your decision, you know, it has to be!'

'I've been worried about it.'

'So have I.'

'I mean how would it look?'

Keep your cool, girl, she thought. 'You mean if Barbara found out that you'd been sneaking away for illicit picnics in the hills?'

'No,' he said impatiently. 'Not that. The press hasn't got hold of the quarry angle yet but it's only time. You can image the headlines. Conservationist killed on site of proposed new development. The planning process is slow enough. I need this project to go ahead.' He paused. 'If only I could be sure the police won't find out.'

'Well, I've told no one. Grace can't. I suppose there's an outside chance that the murderer saw you but he's hardly likely to go blabbing to the police that he was on the hill. So unless you've told anyone, how will Inspector Stanhope ever know?'

There was a moment's silence and she added, 'You haven't talked to anyone, have you, Godfrey?'

'No,' he said. 'Of course not.'

She looked at him closely but didn't push it.

'So?' she asked. 'What are you doing here anyway?'

'It's quiet. I come here sometimes when I need to get out of the office.'

'Not religious then? No hang-ups about adultery? I wondered.'

'No hang-ups at all about you.'

He stood up, straightened his tie, looked again at his watch. 'I suppose I should get back.'

'Should I slip out through the vestry door so we're not seen together?'

He smiled. 'I don't think there's any need for that.'

But outside the church, standing in the shadow of the lych-gate, he hesitated. 'I suppose you're parked in town.'

'No. By your office. I was waiting for you. How else could I know you were here?'

'Perhaps,' he said awkwardly, 'after all, we shouldn't be seen there together.'

'Why the hell not?'

'Neville Furness is in today.'

'So?'

'I told you he saw us coming out of the restaurant together. I can't afford talk at this stage.'

A sudden thought occurred to her. 'You didn't tell him about coming out to Baikie's on the afternoon Grace died?'

'No,' he said. 'Of course not.' But Anne didn't believe him. He'd felt the need to confide in someone and Neville was his right-hand man, his guru, if Barbara was to be believed. 'You walk on,' he continued. 'I'll follow in a few minutes.'

'I thought you were in a hurry to get back to the office.' She felt like a spurned adolescent, ridiculous, desperate. She put her hands on his shoulders. 'When will I see you again?'

He disentangled himself gently. 'I don't think that would be wise.'

Her head spun in disbelief. 'What do you mean? For fuck's sake, not very long ago you were talking about marriage.'

'Nothing's changed,' he said earnestly. 'Not in the way I feel about you.'

'But?'

'Until they've caught this murderer, until things are more settled, perhaps we shouldn't meet.' The words came out in a rush, and when he saw her face he added, 'For your sake, Annie. I don't want you implicated.'

She turned and started off down the street. She couldn't bear to break down and plead with him. But after a moment she stopped and shouted back, 'Tell me, Godfrey, is that you talking or Neville Furness?'

He didn't answer and she continued to walk away, expecting him to follow, to catch hold of her, or at least to call after her. When there was no response, hating herself for being so spineless, she stopped again. He wasn't even looking at her. He had gone back through the lych-gate and through the gap she saw him standing in the churchyard and staring down at one of the graves where a bunch of white lilies had been laid.

Chapter Thirty-Four

Vera Stanhope kept the women in Baikie's informed about the progress of the investigation in a way Rachael couldn't believe was usual in a murder inquiry. At first she was grateful for the stream of information. She was reassured by the bulky form of Vera, sitting in Constance's old chair, legs wide apart, hands cupped around a mug of coffee, talking. If the inspector didn't trust them she wouldn't pass on all these details, would she?

They learnt, for example, that Grace had died within a couple of hours of leaving Baikie's at lunchtime. It wasn't only the absence of afternoon counts in the notebook. The pathologist had come to the same decision.

And in one short session Vera told them more about Grace than they had gleaned in weeks of sharing a house with her. The melodramatic story of abandonment, the string of foster parents and Edmund's alcoholism seemed at odds with the pale and silent woman they remembered.

'Poor girl,' said Edie, because Edie too was allowed into the discussions. She and Vera Stanhope got on surprisingly well. She spoke regretfully, as if Grace's death had denied her the opportunity of working with a subject ripe for counselling. That, at least, was how Rachael saw it.

Vera seemed surprised that Anne didn't know more about the Fulwell family secrets. It was evening, still warm. The door into the garden had been left open and as bats dipped and clicked outside she probed the subject.

'Didn't you know there was a younger son at Holme Park? Even I know that. You must have heard. There must have been talk in the village. A wayward alcoholic whose wife committed suicide. God, the gossips would have had a field day.'

'If she killed herself when Grace was a baby it must have happened at least twenty-five years ago.' Anne seemed detached, unbothered. 'I hadn't even met Jeremy then.'

'Was he here?'

'Oh, Jem's been in Langholme for ever.'

'But I know what these villages are like,' Vera insisted. 'People still talk about the war as if it ended last week. Even if Edmund never came back to Lang- holme they would still have remembered he existed, speculated about what had become of him.'

'Not in my hearing,' Anne said lightly. 'It's not as if the Fulwells mixed socially with the rest of us. Robert didn't come into the Ridley Arms for a pint on Friday nights. Livvy never joined the women's darts team. She made a thing about her kids going to the village playgroup but I bet she never took a turn on the rota to wash out the paint pots or muck out the sandpit. There was always a nanny to do that. The Fulwells live in splendid isolation in the Hall. Nothing has really changed for generations. The villagers are involved as employees – tenant farmers, estate workers – but the private lives of the family don't really have any impact. It's still very feudal. You must know that. We all have our proper place.'

'So you didn't know Robert had a brother?'

'I think I might have heard that there was a brother, working abroad.'

'Who told you that?'

'God, I really can't remember, Jeremy probably. Does it matter? Presumably, if he's such a black sheep it was a story the family put about.'

'But you hadn't heard anything about the wife's suicide or an abandoned child?'

'No, but it's not something they'd be proud of, so they'd hardly spread it about.'

'How are they playing that part of the story now?' Vera asked.

'What do you mean?'

'As you said, it doesn't show the family in a good light. I mean, allowing Edmund's child to be fostered rather than caring for her themselves. What sort of a spin are they putting on it?' She seemed rather proud of the political jargon.

'I don't know. I've been here, haven't I, except for one day out at Kimmerston. I haven't had much of a chance to listen to gossip. Besides, I'm not a member of the ladies' darts team myself.'

All these questions convinced Rachael that Vera's apparent indiscretion in passing on information about Grace's background, information which would probably soon appear in the tabloids anyway, was a tactic. It was her way of taking the investigation forward. So she came to regard Vera's visits with suspicion. Each session was some sort of test and Vera was trying to catch them out.

The next day Vera came in when they were eating lunch. Anne and Rachael had been on the hill surveying one of Rachael's squares. It had been a good day. Outside Anne lost her pose of cynic and entertainer and Rachael found her company restful. They'd stood on the moor together and watched a goshawk fly out of the forest to swoop onto a young grouse. On the way back to Baikie's they'd passed the crow trap. Inside a different bird was hopping and flapping and pecking at the corn, but neither of them mentioned it.

It wasn't much of a lunch. As Rachael had suspected, Edie hadn't really taken to the domestic life. She had begun with enthusiasm but become bored very quickly. She had brought with her a pile of novels and seemed set on making her way through them. 'A great opportunity to catch up on some reading,' she told Rachael. Cooking got in the way. And then she took a great interest in the young police officers who were now conducting a fingertip search of the marshy land close to the burn. She knew all their names and occasionally Rachael heard her give advice about girlfriend troubles, sympathizing about the stress of the job.

This time Vera had come to tell them that Edmund Fulwell had disappeared. Edie offered her a bowl of reconstituted minestrone soup, which she accepted and she sat with them at the table, eating it with great noise and relish between questions.

'Does he know that Grace is dead?' Rachael asked.

'Oh yes. We traced him quite quickly from the information your boss brought that first night. He lives and works out on the coast. He's got a job as chef in a flash restaurant there and lives in a flat over his work. At least he did. God knows where he is now.'

'What happened?'

'Of course we went to tell him Grace was dead as soon as we found out where he was. I sent young Ashworth. He's good at the compassionate bit. If we'd known more of his history at that point perhaps we'd have been more circumspect. At least we could have arranged for someone to keep an eye on him.'

'What did Joe Ashworth make of Grace's father?' Edie asked.

'Well, he had no idea he was going to do a runner. Edmund was shocked of course, angry, guilty, but that was only what you'd expect.'

Edie nodded. 'The classic symptoms of bereavement.'

'Oh, Mother!' Rachael muttered under her breath. 'Do shut up.'

Vera continued, 'He even carried on going into work. His boss is a friend, Rod Owen. I think they were at school together. Somewhere in the south where you sign up at birth. Mr Owen told him to take off as much time as he needed, but he said he preferred to be working. It gave him something else to think about, company I suppose. And he said while he was creating in the kitchen he couldn't be drinking. Ironic really, considering what must have happened later.'

'I thought you didn't know where he is now?' Rachael said.

'We can guess,' Vera said crossly. 'Knowing his past. I've seen his medical records.'

'Bouts of alcoholism, you said,' Edie probed delicately.

'Mother!' Rachael shouted. 'You can't expect Inspector Stanhope to tell us what's in the man's medical records. They're confidential.'

'Not the details of course.' Edie was unabashed.

'I think,' Vera said, 'over the years his drinking has been a symptom of his illness, not a cause.' Then, quickly, looking at Rachael, 'That's my own interpretation. I couldn't possibly divulge . . .'

'No,' Edie agreed. 'Of course not.'

'I went to see Mr Owen yesterday. We had a long talk. He was kind enough to give me lunch. He said it wasn't up to Edmund's standard of cuisine but it was certainly acceptable to me . . .'

Anne had been wiping the last of her soup with a piece of bread, apparently taking no notice of the conversation. Now she interrupted suddenly. 'What's the name of the restaurant where Grace's dad works?'

Vera was put out to be stopped in mid flow. 'The Harbour Lights. Why?'

'Nothing. I've eaten there a few times. The owner introduced me to the chef. Grace's father. I can't even remember what he looked like now. A coincidence, that's all.'

They all stared at her but she seemed not to notice and lapsed back into a brooding silence.

'What did Mr Owen tell you?' Edie asked the inspector.

'Well . . .' Vera gathered herself up for a juicy revelation. Rachael was embarrassed by the conversation. Vera and her mother could have been two old ladies huddled for a gossip at the back of a bus. She wished she had the strength to walk out and leave them to it, but she was curious too. 'Apparently he's had bouts of depression for years, even before his wife killed herself. That's why Owen wasn't too surprised when Edmund disappeared this time. It's his standard response to stress – to walk out and drink himself into oblivion. Of course we're looking for him in case he does something stupid. In the past he's threatened suicide. He ended up in St Nick's for a couple of months when Grace was at school.'

'Oh,' Edie said. 'I wonder . . .' Then thought better of it and broke off.

'What?' demanded Vera.

'Nothing,' Edie replied. 'Nothing, I just . . .' She stopped and seemed to change tack completely. 'When we were out the other day Rachael and I went to see Alicia Davison.'

Rachael glared at her furiously. They hadn't discussed telling Vera about the trip.

'Who's she when she's at home?' Vera asked.

'She was Bella's headteacher.'

'Ah.' There was a pause. 'So you know about the court case.' She turned to Rachael. 'I couldn't tell you, could I? Not my place if Bella hadn't.'

'What was your involvement?'

'I was in uniform, new to the job, taken along as the statutory WPC in case Bella Noble broke down in tears and the blokes didn't know what to do.'

'Did she break down?'

'No.'

'Why did you go to her funeral? It must have been one case out of thousands.'

'I always felt for her. We were about the same age,

in similar circumstances. I lived with my father. He wasn't ill and he probably wasn't as much of a bully as Alderman Noble but there were certainly times when I felt like hitting him on the head with a brass statue.'

'Did you keep in touch with her?'

'No, but I saw the notice of her funeral in the paper and thought I'd go along to pay my last respects.'

'But you must have known she was married,' Edie said. 'How else would you have recognized her name in the *Gazette*?'

'She sent me an invitation to her wedding. Out of the blue, to the station. I don't know why. Perhaps she had no one else to ask.' She shrugged. 'And you get close to people in times of high drama. Perhaps that was it.'

'Did you go?'

'Yeah. I spent a quarter of an hour at the register office, signed my name and wished her luck.'

'Who was the other witness?'

'A dark young man. The husband's son by a previous marriage.'

'Neville Furness,' Edie said.

The inspector grinned. 'Did you ever think about taking up police work, Mrs Lambert? You'd have made a bloody good interviewer.'

'Miss,' Edie said automatically. 'It's Miss Lambert.'

Vera grinned again. 'Like that, is it?'

'Did you know that Bella spent time in St Nicholas' hospital in preparation for release?'

'No,' Vera said. 'I wouldn't have known that.'

'It would be interesting to find out if she was there at the same time as Edmund Fulwell.'

'Unlikely I'd have thought.'

'But if she was . . .'

'If she was, so what?' Vera was brutal. 'Bella killed herself. Grace Fulwell was strangled. Another co-incidence.'

Chapter Thirty-Five

The coincidences were too much for Anne. She dug away at them, sifted them like the soil in her quadrat. Godfrey had been a regular at the Harbour Lights restaurant where Edmund Fulwell cooked. They were, she knew, more than passing acquaintances. At one of their illicit meetings Godfrey had admitted to a hangover. This was unusual for him.

'So how did you come by that?' she'd asked, amused.

He'd told her he'd arranged to meet a business contact at the restaurant. The client hadn't arrived and he, Rod and Edmund had ended up having a bit of a session. At this session hadn't Edmund mentioned a daughter? Godfrey hadn't said. But he had stormed out of Baikie's chasing Grace up the hill. And she had died.

Anne was sitting in the garden at Baikie's as she was thinking this, sheltered by the cottage from a cool easterly breeze. Now the trees were in full leaf and the view down to the Skirl was obscured. The survey was almost over and they had time to relax. Rachael had final visits to make to two of her sites and Anne had one quadrat to check in detail – the one nearest to the mine working. She was saving that as a treat.

Once their own work was finished Rachael wanted them to complete Grace's report on the otters. She thought it wouldn't take long but Anne thought it was more complicated. She'd never trusted Grace's results.

Squinting her eyes against the sun Anne could see above the trees to the hill. The team who'd been searching there had gone but Vera and Joe were still camped out in Black Law with a small team of detectives. They'd made themselves at home there. Joe Ashworth had stuck photographs of his son all over the kitchen wall.

This afternoon Rachael and Edie were in the farm too, talking to Vera Stanhope, bending her ear about something. Bella probably. Rachael had an obsession about Bella, seemed to think the two deaths were connected. And Edie egged her on. Anne thought Edie was a hoot. She couldn't understand why Rachael complained about her. She wished her mother had been half as sympathetic.

Anne was sitting in a canvas striped deckchair. The bar was wedged in the lowest notch so she was lying almost horizontal and dozing when she heard footsteps on the path which led from the yard where they parked their cars, round the house to the front garden. She struggled to sit upright, felt suddenly nervous, vulnerable. All around her empty landscape stretched to the horizon. She hadn't heard a car but perhaps she'd been more deeply asleep than she'd realized. There was no one within shouting distance despite all Vera's claimed precautions. Edie and Rachael wouldn't be back from Black Law yet. In the brief moment of scrambling to her feet she wondered if it might be Godfrey. Perhaps he'd decided to tell the police, after all, that he'd been here on the day Grace died. Perhaps he'd come to see her.

But it wasn't Godfrey. Once she was standing she could tell that from the footsteps which were light and hurrying. It was Livvy Fulwell, trying for some reason to be friendly.

'This really is the dinkiest little house.' She backed onto the lawn, looking the house up and down. 'I've seen it from a distance during shoots but I've never actually been here. Robert has, of course. Connie held house parties and occasionally he was invited for dinner. Perhaps she hoped to convert him. She *hated* shooting. He was very young, hardly more than a boy, but I think he was in love with Connie. She was such a character.'

'Was Edmund invited too?'

'I don't know.' She gave a nervous laugh. 'Before my time. You'd have to ask Robert. Probably not. Edmund was several years younger.' She paused. 'I expect you're wondering what I'm doing here.'

They were both standing awkwardly. Anne nodded to the deckchair. 'Why don't you sit down?'

So Livvy was sprawled, at a disadvantage. Anne sat on the grass beside her.

'Perhaps you'd like some tea.'

But Livvy had her speech ready prepared. She shifted her position of gravity so she was leaning forward towards Anne, her bum poking back through the canvas.

'I just wanted to say how shocked we were. About the murder. And to say if there's anything we can do. I mean anything.'

'It's a bit late,' Anne said, 'for Grace.' Immediately

she thought that at one time she'd have been chuffed to bits just to have her here.

'Ah,' Livvy said. 'That's another thing. I wanted to explain about Grace.'

So this is it, Anne thought, remembering Vera's words. This is where we get the spin.

'You do know that it all happened long before I married Robert,' Livvy said earnestly. 'I mean I wasn't involved in any way at all.'

'Of course.'

'And Robert actually didn't have much say in the matter. The old lady was still alive then. You never met the old lady.'

It wasn't a question. Livvy had done her homework. Robert's mother had died before Anne moved to Langholme. Still a response was expected.

'No.'

'She was formidable, a real tyrant. Robert was scared of her, you know. Can you imagine being *that* scared of your own mother?' She paused, lowered her voice, spoke confidentially. 'I don't think she was terribly stable. I wouldn't say anything to Robert of course – he's very loyal – but I wonder sometimes if that's where Edmund's problems came from. They do say, don't they, that mental illness is genetic.'

'So it was Lady Fulwell who banished Edmund from the ancestral home?'

'I wouldn't put it quite like that.'

'How *would* you put it?'

'Edmund was never easy, you know. Even as a boy. Robert's told me all about him. Today we'd say he had some sort of disorder or syndrome. Then, they didn't know what to do. He was expelled from school, from

279

several schools. The only person who had any sort of control over him was a woman Robert's mother employed in the kitchen. She was quite unsuitable as a nanny but that was how she ended up because no one else would put up with him. She was half gypsy by all accounts and not very hygienic. The family found it terribly difficult. I mean, of course one loves one's children equally but it must have been hard to feel any affection for Edmund. In those days he didn't seem to be good at anything. Except getting drunk in the Ridley and chasing farmers' daughters.'

Fraternizing with the plebs, Anne thought. That wouldn't have gone down very well.

'Besides, he wasn't thrown out of the Hall. He moved into one of the estate houses because he wanted more independence. More privacy. Actually I think Robert was generous to him. He lived in that house rent free, and it was space one of the workers could have used. And he never exactly contributed to the running of the business.'

'Was Grace's mother a farmer's daughter?'

'No,' Livvy said slowly. Then: 'Didn't Grace mention any of this?'

'Nothing. I didn't know you were related. I made a joke out of it.'

'She didn't tell you even then?'

'No.'

'I wonder why she was so secretive.'

'Perhaps she was ashamed of you, so she didn't want to admit the connection,' Anne said lightly. 'You're not exactly popular, you know, among conservationists. You're selling a valuable habitat for development.' She paused, saw Livvy gather herself for the old defence about protecting the family's heritage and added hurriedly, 'So, who was Edmund's wife?'

'She was called Helen.' Livvy gave a nervous giggle. 'Actually she was the rector's daughter. Very Lawrentian. Though Robert's convinced Edmund only seduced her to make his mother cross. She was pregnant of course when they married. Only just pregnant. It didn't show. And desperately in love. According to Robert, Edmund was very dashing in a wild unkempt sort of way. She thought she could look after him, stop him drinking. She thought she'd make him settle down.'

'And did he?'

'He did for a while, surprisingly. He became almost respectable. They bought a little house near the coast. Helen thought he should move away from Langholme and make a fresh start. It was all very suburban. He even had a job of a sort. He and a friend opened a restaurant.'

'The Harbour Lights.'

'So Grace did tell you about that.'

'No, I've eaten there. I've met him. Without realizing of course who he was.'

'Ah,' Livvy said. 'I heard he went back to Rod when he stopped travelling.'

'I take it the suburban dream didn't last.'

'Oh, it did for a while. A couple of years. The family thought it was the making of him. They liked Helen. She was a docile little thing. They had her to stay at the Hall after the baby was born. And later. I wonder if Grace remembered her visits there. Perhaps not. She would have been very young.'

'So what happened?'

'Edmund had an affair. I don't know who the

woman was. I'm not even sure Robert knew. Helen took it very seriously. I suppose being brought up in the rectory had left her with old-fashioned ideas.'

'Very suburban,' Anne said.

Livvy didn't pick up the sarcasm. 'It was rather. It's usually possible to find a way of working around these things.'

Does that mean you have affairs, Anne wondered. Or perhaps Roberts does. Perhaps Arabella the nanny has taken his fancy. He could easily go for the younger woman. He married Livvy when she was still a child, though I'm hardly one to judge.

'But Helen committed suicide,' she said. Like Bella, she thought, but not like me. You wouldn't catch any man driving me to that.

'Unfortunately, yes.'

'And Edmund ran away.'

'I think actually he was very upset by what had happened. He did love Helen in his own way. And the child.'

'But not enough to look after her.'

'Men don't very often, do they, even these days.'

Nor do women of your class, Anne thought. You pay people to do that. And how much effort did my parents put into caring for me?

'Didn't Robert's mother feel any responsibility for Grace?'

'She was quite ill by then,' Livvy said evasively. 'She really didn't feel up to it.'

'Would it have been that much of a drag to have a child in the house?' Anne asked. 'It's a big place. She needn't even have seen her.'

Livvy turned away from Anne and stared towards the horizon. 'It wasn't only Grace, was it?' she said.

It took Anne a moment to realize what she was getting at. 'You mean that if Grace made her home here, the family might have to accept Edmund back too.'

Livvy nodded, pleased that she hadn't had to spell it out. 'He was terribly troublesome.'

'Has he been troublesome lately?'

'What do you mean?'

'The police say he's disappeared. I wondered if he'd turned up at the Hall.'

'Good God, no, we're the last people he'd turn to. He never got on with Robert and I don't know him.' She paused. 'Grace turned out well, didn't she, despite everything. I mean, I understand she had two degrees. Edmund must have been proud.'

'She wasn't very happy,' Anne said.

'No? Oh dear.' But the expression of regret wasn't convincing. Livvy's mind was elsewhere. With an agility that Anne envied, she extricated herself from the deckchair. 'Look, I must go. The boys are home from school for the weekend and we have such little time.'

'Thank you for coming.' It had, after all, been very interesting.

Livvy was her confident self again. 'No problem. Do get in touch if there's anything. I mean it. Any time.'

Anne walked with her to the yard and watched the Range Rover drive up the lane. When she returned to the garden Vera Stanhope had materialized in the deckchair. She sat, bare legs stretched ahead of her, eyes half closed as if she'd been there for hours. She sensed Anne approaching and turned to face her. Her shifting weight made the canvas creak like sails in a storm. Anne imagined it ripping and Vera falling in a heap on the grass.

'What did you make of that then?' Vera asked.

'How much did you hear?'

'Everything,' Vera said with satisfaction. She moved again and nodded towards the open French windows. 'From there. I saw the car pass the farm. Thought it might be interesting.'

'Was it?'

'Very. I think I can remember her Robert, you know, at those parties Constance gave. My father dragged me along. We'd be more or less the same age. But Edmund?' She seemed lost in thought.

'She is much younger than Robert,' Anne said.

Vera grinned. 'I'm not past it. Not yet. I'll get to the bottom of this.'

'I'm sure you will.'

'Do you know if Livvy Fulwell met Grace while she was living here?'

'Neither of them mentioned a meeting, but then Grace didn't say much about anything.' Anne hesitated. 'I saw her once on the estate, looking at the workers' houses on the Avenue. I suppose she was curious to see where her father had grown up.'

Vera remained recumbent, beached on the deck-chair. 'And I'm bloody curious,' she said with a surprising intensity, 'to find out where the bugger's got to now.'

Chapter Thirty-Six

While Vera sat in the sun Rachael was in Black Law farmhouse trying to convince Joe Ashworth that Bella's suicide and Grace's murder were related. The sergeant was polite but unconvinced.

'The inspector doesn't think that's a profitable line of inquiry,' he said. He'd made them tea, offered chocolate digestives but he was quite firm. 'You should know her well enough by now to realize you'll not shift her once her mind's made up.'

'OK,' Rachael said. 'So, what if it's got nothing to do with murder, but Bella was being threatened before she died? Blackmail. She met someone who recognized her, or someone from the quarry found out about the manslaughter conviction and put pressure on her. That would be a criminal case, wouldn't it?'

'It might be but there's no evidence of that. No complaint. Not our business.'

'But it could be *our* business, couldn't it?' Edie asked. 'I mean, if we were curious about what happened to a friend we could ask some questions. Inspector Stanhope couldn't object to that.'

'She wouldn't like it.'

'It wouldn't be as if we'd be treading on any toes. As she'd dropped that line of inquiry anyway.'

'God,' he said. 'Save me from forceful women.'

That was all the encouragement they needed to trace Bella's younger brother, the boy who had gone straight from school into his father's butchery business. It seemed that Alfred Noble's meat empire must have collapsed because there was no shop of that name left in Kimmerston. There was only one butcher left – a smart establishment with a large delicatessen section which catered for visitors to the holiday cottages in the National Park. The owner remembered the Nobles. 'They had three shops once. Must have been worth a fortune.'

'Did the business go bust?'

'No, he sold up just in time. Before the supermarket was built and people started getting faddy ideas about nuts and bean sprouts. It must have been after the old man died.'

'He?'

'The son. Charlie.' The butcher turned away to provide a quarter of ham off the bone and some Brussels pâté for a well-dressed woman with a southern accent. He was persuading her of the quality of his home-made sausage and Edie had to shout to get his attention. 'Do you know where the son is now?'

Rachael cringed, but he completed the transaction and then replied, 'He and his wife run the stables on the way out of town on the Langholme Road. He bought it years ago from the profit on the business.' He looked at his shop. Empty again of customers. 'It was the most sensible thing he could have done. Do you know the place I mean?'

They knew exactly. It was set back from the road in a river valley surrounded by mature woodland. They passed it every time they drove back to Baikie's.

They arrived at the stables in late afternoon. The place was overrun by girls in their early teens who had come straight from school. They seemed to be everywhere. They were humping bales of straw, pushing barrows of muck, hanging over stable doors to pat ponies' heads.

'I always wanted to ride,' Rachael said. 'You wouldn't let me.'

'I never thought it was you.' Edie was dismissive. 'Precious little madams with their jodhpurs and their gymkhanas and their pushy mums.' She looked around, taking in the Range Rovers in the car park. 'It doesn't seem to have changed.'

I'd have loved it, Rachael thought. I wouldn't have minded the snobbiness or having the wrong clothes.

The girls gathered round an instructor, clamouring for their favourite horses. She was a large young woman wearing a shapeless T-shirt. She shouted out names and the girls melted away. Rachael wandered across the yard to watch them tack up while Edie accosted the instructor.

'We're looking for Mr Noble.'

'Can I help? If you want to book lessons . . .'

'No.' Edie gave a little laugh to show how ridiculous that idea was. 'No, it's personal.'

'Oh.' The woman had probably been told to keep punters away from the boss and was still reluctant. 'He's probably in the house. I know his daughter's there.'

The house was of stone, long and low, closer to the

river, separated from the road by a large indoor school and the breeze-block rows of stables. In front of it was a cobbled yard where a BMW was parked. The door was opened by a girl of about eighteen. She had glasses on her nose and a copy of Chaucer in one hand. She spoke with the rudeness of most adolescents.

'Yes?'

'Could we speak to your father, please?'

'If it's about riding you should see Andrea in the yard.'

'No,' Edie said. 'It's not about riding.' She spoke pleasantly. She had spent her career with rude adolescents and knew better than to let them wind her up. 'If he's busy we could talk to your mother.'

'God, she won't want to see you. She's got a dinner party tonight and she's locked in the kitchen.'

'Your father then.'

'I think he's in the study. I'll see.'

They watched her disappear into the shadow, bang on a door and yell: 'Dad, there are two women to see you. I think they're selling or JWs.'

He was dark, angular. Rachael could see the resemblance to Bella but he was lankier, thinner faced. She had been expecting someone athletic and weather-beaten but he looked more like an absent-minded academic.

'Yes?' He was cross about being interrupted, only slightly less rude than his daughter.

'We're not selling anything, Mr Noble. And we won't try to convert you. My name's Edie Lambert. This is my daughter, Rachael. She was a friend of your sister's.'

'There must be a mistake. I don't have a sister.' He began to close the door.

'Not now, Mr Noble,' Edie said gently. 'But you did until recently.'

'What are you saying?'

'We're not reporters, Mr Noble. As I explained, Rachael was a friend of Bella's.'

He seemed to come to a decision. 'I don't want to talk here,' he said quietly. 'Wait outside.' He went back into the house and they heard the shout, 'Lucy, tell your mother those people from the Tourist Board have arrived. I'm taking them over to the cottages.'

On the opposite side of the cobbled yard was an older stable block, grey stone, single storey. There was evidence of recent renovation. A pile of paint tins stood outside. There was a small skip full of rubble. He led them towards the block chatting as if they were who he had claimed them to be.

'We'd wanted to expand the business for some time. In the summer we cater for a lot of tourists – beginners who want to go for a ride into the hills, even for full-days treks. We thought it would be a good idea to provide quality self-catering accommodation too. We've just raised the capital to convert these.' He paused at the door, still split like a stable's. 'This is where we started off. There was no office or indoor school then. It's taken years to grow the business to this point.'

He showed them into a kitchen with a quarry-tiled floor, separated from the living space by an oak breakfast bar.

'Very tasteful,' Edie said.

'There are four self-contained cottages.' By now he seemed convinced by his own fiction.

'When did you last see Bella?' Edie asked.

'The day before she killed my father.'

'Not the same day?'

'No, I didn't see her before I went to work. I couldn't face breakfast with Father. I still have nightmares about those family meals.' He paused. 'I didn't blame Bella, you know. You mustn't think that. If I'd been with him all day I'd have killed him.'

'But you didn't go with her to court?'

'I was supposed to be there. A witness.'

'For the prosecution?'

'I didn't volunteer! I suppose I could have refused but I was only nineteen. I did as I was told. And in the end I wasn't needed. They changed the charge from murder to manslaughter and Bella pleaded guilty to that.' He paused. 'I went to the secure hospital to visit her but she wouldn't see me. Perhaps she thought I'd betrayed her by agreeing to appear for the prosecution. I had to come all the way home.' He walked through the living area and sat down, beckoning the women to follow. 'Is Bella dead? Is that what you meant before?'

'Yes,' Edie said. 'Hadn't you heard?'

'I told you. I didn't hear anything of her. She didn't answer my letters and eventually I stopped writing. So far as I knew she was still in hospital but if she'd died there I suppose they would have informed me. I was down on all the forms as her next of kin.'

'She left hospital more than ten years ago. She married a farmer – Dougie Furness of Black Law.'

'She lived at Black Law Farm?' He gave a sad little laugh. 'I lead treks past there every summer. I might even have seen her in the distance. She must really have hated me not to have got in touch. She knew where I was. I wrote and told her when I bought the stables.'

'I think she just wanted to start again. New life, new identity.'

'I suppose I can understand that. Sometimes I just feel like running away.' He smiled. 'All this money and investment scares me. My wife's the business woman, though you wouldn't think it if you met her.'

'But you started the stables soon after your father died. Your wife wasn't involved then.'

'Then it didn't seem like a business. I enjoyed horses so I bought a stable. That was all there was to it.'

'Why did you sell the butcher shops?'

'I hated being a butcher.' Charles Noble was looking out of the small window towards the river. 'Father knew I hated it. I wanted to stay on at school. I had dreams of being a vet. I envied Bella for getting out.'

'But then she came back.'

'Yes. Poor Bella.'

'It sounds almost as if you hated your father too.'

'Oh, I did,' Charles said. 'I always had.'

There was a clatter of hoofs on cobbles as Andrea led her party of girls out on their ride.

'A week after the court case I was approached by a local businessman who made me an offer for the shops and the slaughterhouse. He wasn't interested in keeping the butchery going. He wanted to develop the property and the land. I could probably have stuck out for more but I signed at once.' Charles paused. 'He knocked down the slaughterhouse and built that office block by the river. He must have made a fortune over the years but he paid me enough to buy this place and that was all I wanted.'

'Was the business yours to sell?'

'Father left it to me, if that's what you mean. There was a will. And I was a junior partner. The old man wouldn't have liked it, but it was legal.'

'What about Bella?'

'She wasn't involved in the business but I put the profit from the sale of Father's house into a separate account in her name. She knew what I was doing. I wrote to tell her.'

'Did she ever use the money?'

'No, it's still there.'

'Weren't you ever tempted to use it yourself?'

He blinked up at Edie, hurt. 'Of course not. I hoped one day she'd get in touch.'

'Her husband's disabled. He needs constant nursing care.'

'So perhaps I could help with that.' He considered the idea, seemed pleased. 'I should have made more effort to persuade Bella to see me but I was very young. The whole business with Father had been horrible. Not just the way he died – I told you I could understand that. But all the publicity that followed. I felt hounded. Everywhere I went people were talking. I suppose I turned into a bit of a recluse. Horses were less complicated.

'Then I married and Louise, my wife, thought it would be foolish to get in touch with Bella. I'd told her about the case but she couldn't really understand what led up to it. Her attitude was – why get mixed up in it all now when people have forgotten about it. Bella could find me soon enough if she wanted to.'

'And she definitely didn't try to contact you recently?'

'No. I wish she had.'

'If she had tried to contact you but got through to your wife instead, would Louise have passed on the message?'

'Of course.' But despite the reply he seemed uncertain. 'What are these questions about?'

'Bella committed suicide, Mr Noble. We think she was troubled. No one at Black Law knew about the manslaughter charge. She was living under an assumed name when she met Dougie Furness. It occurred to us that someone might have discovered her secret, threatened her with exposure.'

'And that's why she killed herself?'

'We think it's possible.'

'I wouldn't do that to her.'

'I'm sure you wouldn't. But can you think of anyone from that time who has suddenly appeared in the area again. A friend of Bella's. Someone who might recognize her.'

He shook his head.

'You've not told Bella's story to anyone?'

'Actually, I don't often think of her now.' He looked at them over thick glasses, demanding their understanding. 'Isn't that a terrible thing to say?'

'What about your wife? Could she have mentioned it to one of her friends?'

'I don't think it's really the sort of thing they discuss at the Conservative Ladies' coffee mornings.'

'If you remember anything which might help would you mind giving me a ring?' Edie said. 'It's my home number. I'm not often there but there's an answering machine.' She lowered her voice to a stage whisper. 'You see, Rachael found the body. It was a terrible shock. I really think that only finding out what led up to the suicide will help her come to terms with it.'

Good God, Edie, Rachael thought. You were doing pretty well until then.

Chapter Thirty-Seven

That evening Edie stayed in Kimmerston. There was a meeting of an educational pressure group to which she belonged and of course she felt she was indispensable. Rachael thought anyway that the isolation of Baikie's had been getting her down. She thrived on constant phone calls, friends dropping in to weep on her shoulder or to drag her into Newcastle for a fix of culture. Anne had sometimes been up for a discussion about a play or a film, but her contribution often stopped after a discussion of the leading male's anatomy.

In the kitchen at Riverside Terrace Edie had thrown together a meal and tried to persuade her to stay too. Rachael refused – she'd brought her own car specially so she could get back and she didn't want to leave Anne on her own.

'Well, you will take care, darling, won't you?' Rachael took no notice of this. Edie's mind was elsewhere. She was already planning her speech. And she'd never been much concerned for Rachael's physical safety. While other parents stressed out about safe deliverance from parties Edie had been partying herself, assuming rightly that Rachael would have the sense to make her own way home. Edie had been bothered about more difficult things – relationships, anxieties, how Rachael felt.

Now though, standing at the top of the steps to see Rachael off, Edie repeated her warning. 'I mean it. Don't stop for anything and keep all the car doors locked. And when you get into the cottage make sure everything's bolted there too.'

So suddenly Rachael was acutely aware of a danger she had never considered before. If even Edie was worried then she should take special care. Because of this jitteriness she stopped for petrol on the main road although she still had a quarter of a tank, enough to get her to Baikie's and back several times over. When she tried to start the engine again nothing happened. She'd had a dodgy starter motor for months but hadn't had the time or the money to get it fixed. Usually all it took was pressure on the bonnet to tilt the car to unstick it but this time, though she and the woman from the petrol station bounced and rocked it, nothing happened. And of course the AA took hours to get out to her, although she played the card of being a woman on her own.

While she was waiting she phoned Black Law and told Joe Ashworth she'd be late. They weren't to worry. And if Edie phoned they should explain what had happened.

'I was just about to go home,' he said. 'There's still someone here to keep a look out for Mrs Preece. And the inspector's about somewhere. But if you like I'll hang on so I can come down the lane with you.'

She was tempted to agree. Then she thought of his wife, waiting for him. She'd have prepared a meal for him. Perhaps she'd even kept the baby up so Joe could give him a bath. And she remembered her first meeting with Joe Ashworth on the night Bella died. He'd been amazed by the work she did, astonished that a woman could survive on her own in the hills. She could hardly ask for an escort back after putting him right about that.

'Nah,' she said. 'Of course not. Besides, I don't know how long I'll be.'

It was midsummer in Northumberland and still light at ten o'clock as she sat outside the garage drinking cans of coke and waiting. By the time the car was fixed and she'd driven through the new tubular steel gate onto the hill it was midnight and black. When she got out of the car to open the gate she left the engine running and even then she fumbled with the catch in her haste to pull the gate open, because she was so worried that the car would stall.

The battery must have been low because the head-lamps didn't seem to give out much light. At first she tried to go as quickly as she could but she had to slow down because she was hitting the bank and catching her exhaust on the biggest of the ruts.

A sheep ambled into the track in front of her and she braked sharply and sat, petrified for a moment, staring into its bemused amiable face before realizing what she was looking at.

This is crazy, she thought. Don't panic. Relax. Think of something else.

So she tried to concentrate on what she and Edie had been doing that day. It wasn't too late for her to have riding lessons, was it? Just because it wasn't the sort of thing a right-on mother encouraged her child to do. And she thought of Charles Noble, who'd loved animals too when he was a boy, so much that he'd wanted to become a vet. Yet he'd been forced instead to watch the live cattle and sheep herded from the trucks after market and be turned into meat. His father's death had saved him from that. It had given him a chance to buy the stables. Charles Noble had much more of a motive for killing his father than Bella had.

She was so excited by this new idea, so thrilled as she pictured dazzling Edie with it, that when she first saw the headlights coming out of apparently open countryside directly towards the passenger door of her car, she wasn't frightened. She just thought, 'I wonder who else can be out at this time of night?'

This only lasted for a second. Then she got her brain into gear and began to work out what was happening. The car was coming towards her down the forest track, the track she had taken by mistake on her first drive to Black Law that season. She knew that the track dwindled into a footpath so the car must have been parked there. It surely couldn't be a walker who'd left a vehicle there while he spent a day in the hills. Not at this time of night. Had someone been waiting, sitting in the car, watching for her headlights through the trees? Or had they expected to have the place to themselves and been more surprised by her approach than she was by theirs?

She reached the junction before the other vehicle, then looked in her mirror to see which way it would turn. If it was being driven by country kids on an illicit joyriding trip in their parents four-wheel drive or lovers wanting romance under the moonlight, it would turn back now towards the main road and the town. But it turned the other way and began to follow her.

All right then, she told herself. There's still no need to panic. It must be one of the police officers. Out on surveillance perhaps. Or Joe Ashworth's sent someone to keep an eye out for me. Deliberately she tried to slow down. She was nearly at Black Law. She was approaching the ford. If she drove at this speed into the water she'd flood the engine, the car would stop and she'd look a fool. But if anything the car behind came faster. The driver had turned up the headlamps to full beam and when she looked into the mirror she was blinded. She couldn't see the passenger or any details of the car.

She was almost at the ford when it hit her. Her neck jerked backwards and for a moment she lost control of her steering. Instinctively she stuck her foot on the accelerator to pull away from it. The car jumped forward down the bank, hitting the water at an acute angle, bonnet down like a dive. Water sprayed the windscreen so she could see nothing. The engine hissed and steamed and then it stalled. She turned the key but nothing happened. She heard the burn eddying around her and in the distance the purr of the other car at idle.

She craned her head to look behind, expecting all the time to feel the crash of another impact. She could see nothing but the hard white light of the headlamps. She turned the ignition again but the engine was quite dead.

Into her mind ridiculously, came the image of the steward on a flight she'd once taken to the States. He had stood at the front of the plane, demonstrating, with elaborate pantomime, the brace position. She put her feet firmly on the floor of the car, where water was already seeping, and bent forward with her arms protecting her head. Behind her suddenly she heard the roar of the other car's engine. As powerful as a jet.

Nothing happened.

The engine noise increased but instead of releasing its energy to shoot down at her the car screeched backwards. At this point the track was wide. There was a place where vehicles could turn if the ford was too deep to cross. The car backed into that and screamed away. Rachael listened to it disappearing into the distance. Then everything was quiet except for the sound of water lapping around the wheel arches. Still sitting with her arms around her head she began to tremble.

She sat for twenty minutes before she accepted that she would have to walk back to the cottage. She turned the key over and over again but the car wouldn't go. By then her feet were soaking and she was cold. There were three options. She could wait until morning when Joe Ashworth or one of his cronies would come along. She could hope that Vera Stanhope would still be awake and would send out a search party. Or she could take the risk of walking. She knew it would be a risk. The car had driven away down the lane but it could have parked again in the forest track and the driver could have returned on foot.

What prompted her to action in the end was an urgent desire for a pee. No way was she going to sit there all night and wet her knickers. She unlocked the driver's door and got out, having to push against the flow of water. There was a thin sickle moon which gave a little light. She looked once back up the track but she could see no shadow and she heard no footsteps. She didn't want the inspector to see her in such a state. But she couldn't make the last few yards to the cottage. She couldn't face going past the open barn where she'd found Bella. She banged on the farmhouse kitchen door and when it wasn't immediately opened she pushed it and almost fell inside.

Vera Stanhope was sitting in the rocking chair where Bella had often sat. There was a beer can on the table beside her. She was reading a pile of papers. She wore spectacles, which Rachael had never seen before, attached to a chain round her neck. Besides the pen which she held in her fingers like a cigarette, a pencil had been tucked behind one ear.

Why doesn't she ever go home, Rachael thought. Isn't she happy there?

Then she began to cry. Vera got to her feet, took a fleecy jacket which had been folded over the back of the kitchen chair, and put it carefully around Rachael's shoulders.

Chapter Thirty-Eight

When Rachael got up the next morning Vera had already turned up at Baikie's. She stood in the kitchen with a piece of toast in one hand and a mug of Anne's filter coffee in the other. Even coming down the stairs Rachael could hear her eating.

So Vera had spent another night at Black Law. Another night working. What drove her? Ambition again. A fear of failure. Or perhaps, like Rachael, she didn't have much to go home to. A husband or lover had never been mentioned and it was hard to imagine the inspector in domestic comfort. An evening curled up on the sofa watching telly wouldn't have fitted in with the image at all.

'We didn't catch them,' Vera said. 'I thought you'd want to know.'

She'd left the kitchen door open and the room was flooded with sunlight.

'Nice day,' Rachael said. 'I should have got up early. I could have got my survey finished.'

'Plenty of time for that surely.'

'There's still Grace's stuff to check.'

'All the same. No rush.'

She doesn't want us to leave, Rachael thought. She wants us here. The crows in the trap. She wants it even more than she did before. Last night the decoy worked. Besides, if we went, there'd be no excuse for her to stay. She'd have to go home too.

'I thought we *might* get them,' Vera went on. 'There was an outside chance they'd still be in the area.'

'Not they,' Rachael said. 'There was only one person in the car.'

'Are you sure?'

'Yes, but I don't know why. An assumption perhaps. No, when he drove off there was a shape in silhouette. Only the driver.'

'Man or woman?'

'I couldn't tell.'

'Not by the size?'

'No. It was all too quick. A blurred shape. That was all.'

'There was a patrol car on the A1,' Vera said. 'It searched the lanes around Langholme, but there was no one driving like a maniac. No one at all except a lad on a motorbike and a local woman on her way home after visiting her mother. Which means he didn't panic. He had the sense to lie low somewhere until the morning.'

Rachael poured herself coffee from the Pyrex jug. It was still hot. 'Where's Anne?'

'Upstairs getting ready to go out in the field.'

'I'd better be quick then.'

'Like I said, there's no rush, is there?'

'I don't want to be here any longer than I have to.'

'No,' Vera said. 'Last night would have put the wind up anyone.' It was said in a matter of fact way but it made Rachael defensive.

'Look, I'm really sorry I was such a fool last night.

If I'd left my car as soon as the other vehicle drove off you might have caught it at the other end of the track.'

'I doubt it. Not if it was driving as fast as you say.'

'I suppose not.'

'Have you remembered anything else overnight?'

'Nothing. It was a powerful saloon. That was all I could tell.'

'Colour?'

'White. Pale anyway. Not metallic.' She paused and added bitterly, 'Pathetic, isn't it? That was probably the person who killed Grace. If I'd made more effort, got the registration number, you'd have been able to trace him.'

'Can't be helped,' Vera said breezily. 'We might be able to trace him anyway.'

'How?'

'I'm going to make some more toast. Fancy some?' She cut two thick slices of bread, put them under the grill and lit the gas. The matches were damp and it took some time to get a flame. Rachael, watching, thought it added to the performance. Vera wanted her audience on the edge of its seat.

'Go on,' she said, playing along.

'Well, it's always been a mystery how our chappie got onto the hill. At first we thought he walked from Langholme, but that's miles and we've talked to every-one who lives in the place. No one remembers a strange car parked that day. He couldn't have driven all the way down the track because Mrs Preece was here and she didn't see anyone. But if he'd parked down that forest path no one would be able to see the car from here, from the farmhouse or even from the main track. As soon as he drove down that dip he'd be hidden by trees. It's all conifers there and planted really close together.' Vera was getting more excited. 'We had a team searching the hill of course but we didn't deploy them that far into the forest. A mistake. My mistake. I've looked at the map again and the path goes on through the trees and comes out near the mine workings.'

'Close to the crow trap,' Rachael said. 'I know it.'

'I've had Joe Ashworth up there sniffing about.' The inspector bared sepia teeth in a malicious grin. 'He's not a happy bunny. I called him back here at first light.'

'That wasn't very kind.'

'Don't give me that. He had all evening on the nest. I could have called him in last night but I waited. Compassion itself, that's me. And I let him back to the farm for breakfast. He's back in the forest now though, waiting for the forensic team.'

'Has he found anything?'

'Enough to put a spring into an old detective's step. Last night certainly wasn't the first time the car had been along there. The path's sandy. There are some nice tyre tracks. And what looks like traces of paint where the car turned.'

'What colour's the paint?'

'White. Why?'

'I went along there by mistake the night I found Bella's body. I didn't attempt to turn but I made a hash of reversing. Paint from my car could be all over the place. My car's white.'

But Vera seemed determined to maintain her good humour. 'We've had rain, snow and gales since then, haven't we? I'd have thought any traces you'd left would have disappeared weeks ago. But we'll have to do a test. That's the brilliant thing about scientists. They've got tests for everything. Not so many answers but lots of tests.' She pulled a piece of bread from the grill and inspected it. It was the colour of weak milky tea. She turned it over and replaced it.

'You should get a toaster in here. I've got an old one knocking around the house somewhere. I'll donate it. My contribution to Natural History.' She looked at Rachael as if she expected gratitude for the generous gesture. 'We pulled out your car. It's in the nick in Kimmerston. More tests. There might be paint on the back bumper if the burn hasn't washed it off. Will you be able to manage until we get it back from the garage?'

'Edie'll be back soon. We can share hers.'

'She's arriving at about lunchtime. She phoned.'

'You didn't tell her what happened?'

'Not in any detail. I'm too much of a coward. I thought I'd leave that to you. She'll blame me of course.'

No, Rachael thought. She'll blame herself for once, which'll be worse.

Vera Stanhope finished her toast and licked her fingers. 'I hear you went chasing after Charlie Noble.'

'You know about that?' Rachael felt like a naughty schoolkid.

'Oh, you can't keep much from your Auntie Vera.'

'We did ask Sergeant Ashworth if it was OK.'

'No problem. It's a free country.'

'Do you know Mr Noble?'

'I met him. He was living at home when the old man was killed. Why did you go to see him?'

'We thought someone might have threatened Bella

with exposure. We thought that would explain her suicide.'

'Well, you thought wrong,' Vera said bluntly. 'At least if you had Charlie in mind as blackmailer. It wouldn't have been him. It would be far too horrid. Charlie's always avoided anything horrid. That's why he ditched butchery.'

'When did you last see him?'

'Not since the investigation.'

'That was years ago. He was hardly more than a child. He could have changed.'

'You've met him. What do you think?'

'No,' Rachael said. 'I don't think he's changed much.'

'I remember him very well. Surprisingly well after all these years. Perhaps because it was the first serious case I had any part in. I remember we talked to him in his bedroom. His hidey-hole. The old man used to bully him and that's where he escaped. Everything was very tidy. He had peculiar tastes for an adolescent. He collected books, first editions, all about animals. All wrapped in plastic covers. He looked like a school prefect though he'd been working in the business for a while by then. He kept saying it all must have been a terrible mistake, though even he couldn't pretend he was very sorry his father was dead. I got the impression that once the trial was over it wouldn't take him long to pick himself up. He certainly knew what he wanted and he wouldn't find it too hard to believe that nothing as nasty as murder had ever happened.'

'He said he tried to visit Bella in the secure hospital. She refused to see him.'

'Hmph.' Vera could have been mimicking one of Charlie Noble's horses. 'I bet he didn't try very hard.'

'Why didn't Bella invite him to her wedding then? He was her only relation.'

'She'd hardly do that if she were trying to keep her conviction secret.'

'But she invited you,' Rachael said.

'She knew I could be discreet.' Vera smiled smugly.

'Something occurred to me on the way back last night . . .' Rachael said tentatively. 'You'll probably think it's stupid but . . .'

'You're wondering if Charlie could have bashed his father's brains out?' Vera finished.

'Well, yes.' She had thought this a brainwave and was disappointed.

'My colleagues aren't all as bright as me, I'll give you that, but they're not daft.'

'Of course not. I thought . . .'

'She confessed,' Vera said.

'I know, but Charles was only seventeen, wasn't he, when his father died? Perhaps Bella was protecting him.'

'Her prints were on the statue. She was waiting in the same room when we arrived.'

'But . . .'

'He couldn't have done it anyway,' Vera said. She chuckled like a seedy stand-up comedian about to give the tag line of a dreadful gag. 'He was in his father's office at the back of the slaughterhouse. It was tiny, a portakabin. The place was packed because besides Charlie there was a manager, a secretary and a meat inspector from the Ministry of Agriculture. They all swear that he only left once that morning to go to the lav. He was only away for five minutes. Even if he'd had the bottle to kill his father he couldn't have done it.'

'Oh.'

'Nice try,' Vera said magnanimously. 'What's the next theory?'

'Not a new theory. The same one. About Bella's suicide. I still think someone threatened her with exposure, told her she wouldn't be fit to care for Dougie.'

'And who do you think would do that?' Vera had the air of a nursery teacher humouring a small child.

'There is someone. Dougie's son Neville has benefited from her death. He'll be taking over the farm.' When Vera didn't respond she went on, 'You met him at Bella's wedding.'

'Would he have known about her conviction?'

'He could have done. She'd kept a newspaper cutting, some details of her past in the farmhouse. He could have found them and followed up the leads in the same way that we did.' She paused. 'He's Godfrey Waugh's assistant. He works for Slateburn Quarries.'

'I remember him from the wedding,' Vera said. 'A good-looking young man. I wouldn't mind meeting him again.' She looked at Rachael through narrowed eyes. 'You keep your neb out. No more playing private eyes. Leave Mr Furness to me.'

Chapter Thirty-Nine

After Rachael's dramatic incident with the car on the track Vera Stanhope's methods seemed to become even more unorthodox. She took to haunting Baikie's. Rachael wondered, as their work was coming to an end, if this was a deliberate ploy to hold them up. Like a lonely host delaying the departure of dinner-party guests, she didn't want the women to leave.

Anne had noticed the tactics too, was amused but slightly unsettled by the constant presence.

'Haven't you got a home to go to?' she asked one night. It was late. She and Rachael had been out since dusk, trying unsuccessfully to catch a glimpse of an otter, and had returned to find the inspector cloistered with Edie.

'Not much of one,' Vera said. And glared, daring them to ask any more.

'Do you take all your cases so personally?'

She didn't answer that but began pacing up and down the living room. As always she was wearing sandals and they slapped against the soles of her feet.

'Look,' she said, 'I've got to find Edmund bloody Fulwell. He can't have disappeared into thin air. Someone must know where he is. I'd have expected him to turn up in a nick or in the casualty department by now'

Rachael was surprised. She had never seen Vera so intense. Perhaps Vera knew Edmund, she thought. They'd be of a similar age. Perhaps he was invited to Constance's parties too. She might even have had a teenage crush on him.

Vera continued to walk and to mutter.

'Rod Owen says he doesn't know where Edmund is and I believe him. He seems really fed up. It can't be much fun doing all the cooking. I suppose Edmund's holed up in some hostel or B & B, drinking himself silly. Or he could have run away abroad again. He's run away before when things have got too heavy for him.'

Edie had been sitting in a corner, apparently reading. She set aside her book. 'Would he be able to afford that?'

'Not on a chef's salary. But perhaps his family helped him out. You could see why they'd want him out of the way. They wouldn't like Edmund wheeled out for the press, talking about his daughter. Very tacky. Very bad for family image. Not that they'd admit to anything of course.'

The pacing and the muttering had an element of performance. She wanted them to know she was worried and the way her mind was working, but Rachael thought she already knew what she was going to do. She stopped abruptly.

'I've tracked down Grace's social worker.' Finally. You'd think she'd have come forward of her own accord, wouldn't you?' She claims she's been in France on three weeks' holiday. Nice for some.'

'What's her name?' Edie asked.

'Why?'

'I might know her. Lots of my friends work for social services.'

'Poor them.' Vera paused. 'Poor you. She calls herself Antonia Thorne. She's been married for years but didn't get round to changing her name.'

Edie shrugged. 'I don't know her.'

'You could ask around. See what your friends make of her. She's based out on the coast. I wasn't very impressed. Sounds a real wimp. One of those voices that grate. But I've not met her yet, so I suppose I shouldn't judge.'

'Heaven forbid.'

'She did say something interesting.'

Rachael sensed that now they were getting to the point of the amateur dramatics. 'Oh?' she prompted helpfully.

'She said, "I wonder if Nan's been told that Grace is dead. She'd want to know." '

'Who's Nan?'

'That's what I asked. A woman called Nancy Deakin. She worked in the kitchen at the Hall when Edmund was a kid, ended up looking after him because no one else could control him.' She looked at Anne Preece. 'Olivia Fulwell talked about her when she came round for that chat the other afternoon.'

'I remember.' Anne smiled, mimicked Livvy's affectation: ' "Half gypsy and not terribly hygienic" '

'That's the one.' Vera paused. 'The social worker took Grace to visit her a few times. I'm not sure why. Couldn't get to the bottom of that one. Antonia wittered on about the importance of a child being rooted in its own past. But it wasn't Grace's past, was it? Not really. By then Nan was camping out in an old caravan on the estate, much to the family's embarrassment. They could hardly evict her after she'd brought up Edmund single-handed. Eventually they got her to move into the almshouses in Kimmerston. Robert's a trustee.'

'Very convenient,' Anne said.

'I bet Livvy Fulwell's not been to see her to tell her Grace's dead,' Vera continued as if Anne hadn't interrupted. 'They didn't seem on visiting terms. Someone should go. It's only decent.' She fixed her bulging eyes on Anne, who stared back.

'Me? Why?'

'Well, you're almost a friend of the family's, aren't you?'

'Hardly.'

'And you did know Grace.'

'Not very well.'

'Look.' Vera Stanhope seemed to lose patience with the subtle approach. 'I'll tell you how it is. I've had everyone I can spare out looking for Edmund Fuwell. If he's drinking he's on a bloody long bender. It's starting to look as if he might have something to hide.'

'You think he killed his daughter?'

'I don't know. I don't know what to think until I find him. Nancy Deakin looked out for him in the past. It just occurred to me that he might have gone to her again if he thought he was in bother.'

'Well, send one of your chaps round to ask.'

'Oh aye. And I expect she'd tell him! We don't know much about Nancy but we do know that she can't stand anyone in authority. I doubt if even I with all my charm could get much information from her. But you could go along as Grace's friend. You could say that Grace had talked about her, that you thought she ought to be told what had happened. She might talk to you.' When there was no response she added, 'Come on now. Give me a break. What do I have to do? Get down on my knees?'

'No,' Anne said slowly. 'We'll go, Rachael, won't we?'

Rachael was startled by the question. She hadn't expected to be included. She felt like a child usually left out of games and picked suddenly for a team. She nodded.

Edie had returned to her book and still seemed absorbed. Now she spoke without looking up. 'I don't know how you get away with that sort of trick, Inspector Stanhope.'

Vera's answer was sharp and immediate. 'Because I get results, pet. And in the end that's what counts. That's all the bosses want.'

Later that night when Rachael was in bed, but had the light on, still reading, there was a knock on her door. Thinking it was Edie she didn't answer. Let Edie think she was already asleep. But the knock was repeated and Anne came in. She was wearing striped pyjamas with a drawstring and a fly. Some man's. Left behind after a night of passion.

'Sorry,' Rachael said. 'I thought it was my mother.'

'What is it between you and Edie? She seems OK.'

Usually Rachael would have shrugged, given an answer which meant nothing. And anyway Anne would be the last person she'd choose as confidante. But tonight she said, 'Because she's such a hypocrite.'

'In what way?'

'All the time I was growing up I was filled with the liberal party line. Openness. Trust. The need to talk things through. But when I asked her about stuff that was important to me the same rules didn't apply.'

'What did you want to know?'

'About my father.'

'What specifically?'

'A name would have been a start.'

'Don't you know anything about him?'

'Not a thing. And there's no way of finding out. I checked.'

'Perhaps she had a good reason.'

'Like what? He was a murderer? A lunatic? I'm not even sure I want to get in touch with him, but I'd like the chance to make the choice. I'm an adult. I don't need protecting.'

'Maybe it's no big deal. When I was a kid I'd willingly have disowned my old man, through boredom.'

'But you didn't.'

'Not quite. I left home as soon as I could but I was there when he died. Why don't you talk to her again? Explain how you feel.'

'She knows how I feel.'

'Don't you think that here, on your own territory, it might be a bit different?'

There was a pause. 'Perhaps,' Rachael said.

'Worth a try then.'

'Before we leave. Yes.'

'And tomorrow we're off to do Vera's dirty work,' Anne said.

'It looks like it.'

'She can't really think Edmund killed his daughter.' She hesitated. 'I was wondering if she was making up all that stuff about Nancy to put us off the scent. It seems as if it's an elaborate game to her but she's deadly serious. Do you think she knows who the murderer is but doesn't have the evidence to make an arrest?'

'Are you saying she suspects one of us?'

'No . . . I don't know . . . She and Edie are pretty thick. She hasn't let anything slip to her?'

'If she had,' Rachael said bitterly, 'Edie hasn't passed it on.'

'Don't worry about it then. Perhaps I've just got a suspicious nature.' Anne went out, closing the door behind her, leaving Rachael to wonder what the exchange had really been about. She switched off the bedside lamp and lay in the milky gleam of the midsummer night. Through the open window came the sound of water rattling over pebbles.

Chapter Forty

The almshouses were in the old centre of Kimmerston, reached by a narrow alley from the main street. They featured as postcards of the town and occasionally tourists wandered into the courtyard to gawp. They were listed buildings and, although not practical for wheelchairs or zimmer frames, the courtyard was still cobbled.

Rachael and Anne arrived in late afternoon. It was very hot. In the distance there was the buzz of traffic, but the courtyard was deserted. There was no noise from the grey stone houses.

Then a door opened and a small middle-aged woman emerged. She wore a striped shirt and jacket and held a shiny black handbag under her chin as she used both hands to pull to the heavy warped door and lock it. She hurried across the cobbles, stiletto heels clattering.

'Excuse me!' Anne shouted.

She stopped, turned on her heels, looked at her watch in annoyance. 'Yes?'

'We're looking for the warden.'

'You've found her but I can't stop. There's a trustee meeting and I'm late already.'

'We were hoping to speak to Nancy Deakin.'

'What do you want with her?'

'A chat, that's all. She doesn't get many visitors, does she?'

'That's not my fault.' The warden was immediately defensive. 'We've all tried but she's hardly sociable.'

'Has anyone been to see her lately?'

'I haven't seen anyone and she hasn't said. But then she wouldn't. You're welcome to have a go. Number four. Don't drink the tea.' She turned and teetered on.

It was very bright in the courtyard and when the front door of the cottage was opened a crack, at first they couldn't make out the shadowy figure inside.

'Miss Deakin?' Anne asked. 'Nancy?'

The door shut again. Anne banged on it with her fist.

'Perhaps we should go.' Rachael was embarrassed. She imagined people staring from the blank net-covered windows. Anne took no notice and hit the door again. 'We're friends of Grace's,' she shouted. 'Nancy, can you hear me?'

The door opened. Nancy Deakin was very old and here, inside this house, with its latticed windows and steep roof she looked like a witch in a children's picture book. She wore a long woollen skirt and a black cardigan with holes in the elbows. She glared at them, then spoke in a series of splutters and coughs which neither woman could understand.

'Can we come in?' Throughout the visit Anne Preece took the lead. Rachael thought the business at Baikie's had mellowed her. At one time she would have refused to do Vera Stanhope's dirty work, but here she was, her foot against the door so the old woman couldn't shut it on them again.

Nancy felt in the pocket of her cardigan and brought out a pair of enormous false teeth, covered in black fluff. She put them into her mouth and bared the teeth like a caged animal.

'That's what I said, isn't it?'

She turned and led them down a passage into a small, cluttered room haphazardly furnished by junk. It seemed that she slept and lived in this room though there was no evidence that the house was shared by another occupant. A narrow divan was covered by a blanket of different coloured knitted squares. On a frayed wicker chair was a crumpled pile of clothes topped by a black felt hat. By the window, blocking out most of the light, was a birdcage on a stand. The door of the cage was open and a blue budgie flew over their heads and came to rest on the mantelpiece.

'Grace is dead,' the old lady said, more distinctly. It was as if talking was something she had to get used to.

'You know about it.' Anne sat on the divan. 'We wanted to make sure.'

Nancy pushed the pile of clothes from the chair and sat on it. She leant back, her eyes half closed. Rachael stood for a moment just inside the door then felt conspicuous and sat on the floor with her back to the wall.

'What do you want?' Nancy demanded.

'Just that. To know you'd heard. We thought you'd want to be told. Grace mentioned you.'

'When?'

'We worked together. Out at Black Law Fell.'

'Near to the Hall then.'

'That's right.'

'I don't suppose they invited her round. I don't suppose Lady bloody high and mighty Olivia cooked her tea.'

'No,' Anne replied. 'I don't think they even knew she was there.'

'The ferret will always get the rat,' Nancy said cryptically. 'If it's got an empty belly.'

Anne and Rachael looked at each other. Sunlight slanted through the latticed window and through the bars of the birdcage, spotlighting the floating specks of dusk, an elaborate cobweb in the empty grate, the faded colours of a proggie mat.

'How did you know Grace was dead?' Anne asked.

There was another pause. Nancy looked at them, weighing them up.

'Ed comes to see me,' she said at last. 'He's the only one of them who does. The only one I'd let in.'

'The warden said you'd not had any visitors recently.'

'Huh. What would that one know? Money and meetings. That's all her job's about. And chasing after her fancy man.'

'What about Grace? Did she ever visit?'

'She's been away a lot. University. Walking. Sometimes Ed brought her.'

'Lately?'

The old woman shook her head crossly. 'I didn't expect it. She was young. She had her own life to lead. But she's always written. Wherever she's lived she's written me letters. And Edmund would read them when he came to visit. My eyes are bad. I can't see to read no more.' She glared at them, defying them to contradict this explanation.

'Did you keep the letters?'

'Why?'

'Grace was a friend. We don't have much to remember her by. If we could just have the letters for a while . . . It would be like talking to her, wouldn't it? We'd bring them back.'

'I don't throw much away,' the woman conceded.

'So we would be able to look at them?'

'I don't know. I'll think about it.'

She crashed the teeth together awkwardly and looked at them again, maliciously aware that they were frustrated by her indecision, challenging Anne to push the point.

But Anne asked, 'When did Mr Fulwell come to tell you that Grace was dead?'

'The day after it happened. He said he didn't want me to hear about it on the news, though I wouldn't because I always switch off when the news comes on the wireless. I only like the old tunes. But it was kind. He's always been like that. He don't own a car so his friend brought him.'

'Which friend? Mr Owen?'

'Don't know. Didn't see. Didn't ask him in. Only Ed.'

'Did you see the car?'

'Not from here.' Which was true, because all they could see through the window was the courtyard and an elderly man in stockinged feet who had pulled a kitchen chair onto his doorstep so he could sit in the sun.

'Did Edmund give you any details of what had happened?'

Nancy breathed down through her nose, pulling her lips back from her gums. 'Of course not. He was upset, wasn't he? And I didn't ask.'

'Do you have any ideas?'

'What do you mean?'

'About who might have killed her.'

'No . . .' She hesitated but decided not to continue.

'How did Edmund seem when he was here?'

'How do you think?' She paused again. 'He was angry.'

'Did he think he knew who'd strangled her?'

'You'll have to ask him that. Not that it's any of your business.' She held out a long finger for the budgie to perch on. Anne leant over to stroke it.

'Could we see those letters?' she asked.

'No.' Nancy's voice was firm.

'We'd like to find out a bit more about her.'

'Why?'

'I said. We were friends. We miss her. And they're a valuable record of her life.'

'They're in a box upstairs. I don't manage the stairs very well these days.'

'I'll get them.' Anne got up from the divan.

'No.' With a surprising agility Nancy stood up and moved to block the door. 'I don't want you nebbing round my things. You wait here. I'll fetch them.'

They heard her banging about in the room above them. She seemed to be muttering to herself. Then a door shut and they heard her move heavily down the stairs. They went out into the passage to wait for her there. She held in her hand not a pile of letters but one white envelope.

'This was all I could find.' She grinned so they would know she was lying.

'That's very kind.' Anne took the letter and added, 'Do you know where Edmund Fulwell is?'

'Home, I suppose.'

'No. No one's seen him for days.'

'He's always been a bit wild.'

'If he gets in touch,' Anne said, 'you should tell the police. They're worried about him.'

'No need to be worried. He can look after himself that one.'

She opened the front door to let them out. Upstairs there was a movement, a noise. They stood still, startled, and stared up the gloomy stairwell. From the shadows the budgerigar flew over the banister straight towards them. It circled as if to make its escape through the open door then landed on Nancy's shoulder. She stroked its beak and cooed.

Chapter Forty-One

The letter from Grace was dated two years previously. The address was a small town in south-west Scotland. In the envelope along with the letter was a picture postcard showing the scene of a river and meadows with a church tower in the distance. Nothing was written on the blank side of the card but the picture was marked with a cross and Grace had written over it in biro, 'This is where I camped last night.'

Rachael was moved by the picture and the scribbled note. Grace had been so odd in her last few weeks that Rachael had thought of her as a wraith moving among them causing disturbance and upset. This made her human, real. It was the sort of thing Rachael might have sent to Edie to keep her off her back.

Vera was there as they passed the card between them. She must have been waiting for their return because they had just lit the gas to make tea when they heard her thump on the kitchen door. She came in without waiting to be asked.

'Why did the old bat choose this one to give you?' she demanded. Rachael had expected the inspector to be grateful because they'd returned with a trophy but she seemed more bad-tempered than she'd been since the beginning of the investigation. According to Edie she'd been in Kimmerston all afternoon.

'She probably chose a letter at random just to get rid of us,' Anne said. 'She won't admit it but I don't think she can read.'

Vera, in truculent mood, had to contradict even this. 'I don't think so. Surely she'd keep them in some sort of chronological order and just take the one on the top. There must have been one since this. Grace might even have written from here. Did she ever write letters?'

'I never saw her but how would we know?'

'Not much of a letter, is it?' Vera held up the single sheet between her thumb and finger. 'Why do you think she bothered?'

'She probably thought of Nancy almost as family,' Edie said. 'Perhaps she saw it as a duty, like writing thank-you letters to grandparents.'

'Go on then.' Vera dropped the letter on the table in front of Anne. 'Read it out.'

Anne looked round to make sure she had their attention and began to read, like a mother telling a bedtime story.

' "Dear Nan, I went for a walk today to look for signs of otter and it reminded me of the walks you used to take me on when I was a little girl. I'm employed on contract here by the Wildlife Trust. They offered to find me somewhere to stay but I prefer to be on my own so I brought a tent and I'm camping in the field marked on the card. It's a lovely spot. The Trust had a student doing the same work before me but he left suddenly and I haven't been at all impressed by his results. There was too much guessing and not enough counting so far as I was concerned. So that means I have to walk the parts of river he's supposed to have surveyed to check his results. It would be a lot easier if everyone followed the rules. If you've been properly trained it's not difficult. I hope you're continuing to be well and you're still enjoying living in Kimmerston. Perhaps when I'm next in the area I'll come with Dad to visit." ' Anne looked up. 'It's just signed Grace. Not love, or best wishes, or anything.'

'Hardly riveting stuff,' Vera said. 'And what's the point of her writing if the old woman can't read?'

'Edmund read it to her.'

'When did she last see him?'

'He went to tell her Grace was dead. He didn't want her to hear from anyone else.'

'It sounds as if he was pretty rational then, at least.' Vera looked up at Anne. 'Did you ask her where he was?'

'Of course. She claimed not to know.'

'Did you believe her?'

Anne shrugged. 'She enjoys making mischief. I wouldn't put it past her to lie.'

Vera pushed the letter away from her in disgust. 'Well, that doesn't tell us much, does it?'

'I'm not sure,' Rachael said reluctantly.

'What?' Vera growled. 'Spit it out.'

'Anne and I have always been surprised by the results of the otter counts Grace took on the rivers in the survey area. It's never been systematically studied before but counts in similar bits of the county have never come up with anything like her figures. Since she died we've retraced some of her walks. It looks as if the counts are wildly exaggerated. There was a possibility she'd made a mistake, but this letter suggests that she was aware of the danger of overestimation so that doesn't seem very likely.'

'Exactly what are you getting at?'

Anne Preece replied, 'Either she was madder than we thought and hallucinated legions of otters marching over the Langholme Valley or she was telling porkypies.'

'Why would she do that? She's a scientist.'

'Scientists have been known to falsify records for their own reasons.'

'What sort of reasons?'

'Personal glory. Because they've been nobbled.'

'Are you saying she'd been bribed by the quarry company to exaggerate her records?'

'No,' Anne said. 'Of course not. From the quarry's point of view that would be completely counterproductive. Just the opposite to what they'd want. The purpose of the Environmental Impact Assessment is to see what effect the proposed development would have on this landscape. It's in the company's interest that we find nothing of conservation value on the site. Then they can claim at the public inquiry that the quarry wouldn't cause significant environmental damage. If the report claimed the biggest concentration of otters in the county they'd find it hard to make any sort of case for the quarry to go ahead. Otters are furry and cute. Every protest group in the country would be here waving banners.'

'So you're saying she was nobbled by the opposition?'

'I'm not saying anything.' Anne was clearly starting to get exasperated. 'I don't know what was going through her head. But from the letter it doesn't seem likely she was just mistaken.'

Edie had been listening to the exchange and asked, 'Who is the opposition?'

Usually Vera seemed to welcome Edie's contributions to these discussions, but now, still angry and frustrated, she turned on her. 'What the hell do you mean?'

Edie raised her eyebrows as if commenting on the behaviour of a spoilt child and answered calmly, 'I mean, is there an organized opposition group? A campaign HQ? People in charge? And is there any evidence that Grace knew anyone involved in it? Or any of the other conservation pressure groups? Perhaps she falsified her records out of the mistaken belief that she was serving a cause she believed in.'

Vera was chastened. 'I don't know. We can check.'

'There's a group of people in Langholme who've been fighting the development,' Anne said, 'but I don't think they've been particularly effective. And so far as I know they haven't got any of the big pressure groups on their side yet. It's more a matter of the locals worrying about a decline in house prices if there's a massive quarry on the doorstep and lorries rumbling through the village night and day. Typical nimby stuff.'

'Besides,' Rachael interrupted, 'Grace wasn't stupid. I mean, I know you think she was a bit loopy when she was here, but she must have known that in the long term that sort of fraud wouldn't work. The only reason EIAs are accepted in public inquiries is because they're considered unbiased. If inspectors were to lose faith in them conservationists would give up any voice they've got in the planning process. Grace must have realized that.'

'I think she hated doing it,' Rachael said. 'Someone must have been forcing her to lie. You've read that letter. She was obsessed about getting things right. Perhaps that's why she seemed so stressed out while she was here. She couldn't bear the pretence. I can understand. It would have driven me crazy too. I should have seen what was happening. She certainly needed to talk to someone.'

'Aye,' Vera said. 'Well, it seems she realized that.'

'How do you know?'

'I had a meeting with her social worker today. Ms Antonia Thorne. Funny sort of business that welfare work. Couldn't do it myself. I always thought you had to be a heartless sod to be a cop, but it must be worse in that line. This woman had known Grace Fulwell since she was a baby, placed her with one set of foster carers after another until she found ones that would suit. You'd have thought she'd have some sort of feeling for the girl, affection even, but once Grace went off to university she washed her hands of her. Didn't even send her a card at Christmas. You'd have thought she'd be curious at least, but apparently not. She said she'd forgotten all about her until she'd heard she was dead.'

'I think,' Edie said, 'they're trained not to get involved.'

'With a kid?' Vera shook her head. 'It seems all wrong.'

'Anyway . . .' Edie prompted.

'Anyway, when Ms Thorne got back from her holidays in the sun there was a pile of mail waiting for her. She hadn't looked at it when I spoke to her earlier in the week. One of the letters was from Grace. I suppose she had no one else to turn to. Sad, that.' She paused, lost in thought, and this time Rachael didn't think it was for dramatic effect. 'Grace said that something was bothering her. There was something she needed to discuss. Although she wasn't still officially on the social services caseload would Ms Thorne see her?'

'Oh,' Rachael was almost in tears. 'If she'd been there perhaps Grace would still be alive.'

'Couldn't someone else in the office have dealt with it?' Anne asked angrily.

'It was marked personal. It wasn't even opened.'

'Are you saying that's why Grace was killed?' Edie asked.

'To prevent her from telling anyone that she was falsifying her otter records? I must say it doesn't seem sufficiently important.'

'Motives for murder seldom are,' Vera spat back.

'In that case you need to know who put pressure on her to lie in the first place.'

'Oh, I think we know that, don't we?' Vera said. 'Who resented the crowd at Holme Park? Who wouldn't want them to make a profit out of selling land to a development company? Edmund bloody Fulwell. And he seems to have disappeared like a mirage. Like all Grace's bloody otters.'

Chapter Forty-Two

Late that evening Peter Kemp turned up, powering down the track in his new white Land Rover. Rachael had phoned him from Black Law in a moment of panic. A couple of days before Grace's death she'd passed on the preliminary otter counts. Now Rachael wanted him to know they were probably inaccurate before he made a fool of them all by going public.

Amelia, the debby wife with the big teeth, answered the phone. In the background there were voices, laughter. In explanation Amelia said, 'Just a few friends round to dinner,' and Rachael thought she and Peter never seemed to be on their own together. She told Peter it wasn't urgent, there certainly was no need to rush out to Baikie's but he seemed glad of an excuse to leave.

Although it was ten o'clock when he arrived Rachael suggested they went out for a walk. She hadn't forgotten the Sunday lunch in the house in Kimmerston and couldn't stand the thought of Edie's sneers. Besides, she hadn't been on the hill all day and was feeling restless and caged in. Outside it was still light, though the sun was down and the colour had seeped out of the heather and the old bracken. They walked in silence and, without either of them appearing to decide where to go, followed the track through the edge of the conifer plantation to the tarn, high on the moor. The pool, surrounded by reed, was full to overflowing despite the recent dry weather, and reflected the last of the light. The sky was enormous, lavender and grey streaked with gold.

This was a mistake, Rachael thought. Better to be cooped up in Baikie's with Anne flirting and Edie making snide comments, than here stirring up old memories. Because here she could forgive him the stolen work and the wife. It would have been easy to reach out and take his hand.

'Do you fancy a swim?' he said and that made things worse. It was a sort of joke, a reference to the old times when they were living on their own in Baikie's and they'd come up here after a day in the field, laughing at the shock of cold water, the peaty mud squelching between their toes as they waded out to find somewhere deep enough to swim.

She was tempted to say 'Why not?' She knew what he wanted. A bit of a fling. Confirmation that the old charm still worked. Someone to bitch to about Amelia and the drag of married life. But she wanted to forget about the case for an hour, the exhilaration of running into the tarn and the feel of his jersey as he held her. The contact that Grace hadn't had.

'No,' she said, her voice light. 'We're not here to play.' Because pretending she could be close to Peter again was like Grace pretending there were more otters in the valley than the rest of the county. It was seductive but untrue and in the end would drive her barmy.

They stood looking over the tarn. There was no

breeze, no distant sound of traffic, no aircraft. Occasionally a fish jumped silver then landed with a splash and a ring of ripples and the water lapped against the reeds, spilling out almost to their feet.

'Grace was lying,' she said.

'Are you sure? She was bloody good. Everyone said. Perhaps she picked up some clues you and Anne missed. I mean if it *were* true it would be dynamite.'

'You'd have to write a paper,' she said.

'Right!' The sarcasm eluded him altogether.

'I am sure. Quite sure. And if you publish those results in their present form I'd come out publicly to question them.'

'All right. No need to get like that. We're a team, aren't we? I wouldn't do anything without consulting you first.'

She said nothing. He had convinced himself and there was no point arguing.

He went on, 'Why did she do it?'

'Anne thinks she was just mad. The inspector thinks her father put her up to it.'

'And Edie, the great oracle. What does she think?'

'I'm not quite sure.'

'It's not like Edie to keep her mouth shut.'

He sat on the grass and clasped his knees playing the schoolboy. He looked up at her. 'And what's your theory? You're the most observant person I know. You must have some idea.'

Rachael shrugged. 'How well did you know her, Peter?'

'Not at all.'

'You must have met her before she started. Interviewed her at least. You don't employ anyone without an interview. Company policy. I should know. But she didn't come into the office, did she? I would have remembered. It was supposed to be my team. Picked by me. Then I found out a mammal person had been appointed and I had to lump it.'

'But she was good, Rache. The best. I had to snap her up while I had the chance.'

'Where did you find her?'

'Scotland. She was working for a mate. I saw her in the field and I was impressed. There wasn't any need for a formal interview. Look, I didn't mean to put your nose out of joint.'

'But you rated her. After one meeting.'

'Sure, she was shit-hot.'

Rachael stood for a moment. 'Tell me about the set-up in Scotland.'

'She was working for the Wildlife Trust, the second year of a two-year contract. She was supposed to be co-ordinating volunteer counts but she wasn't much good at delegation and ended up doing most of the work herself. Accommodation was provided for the contract staff but she didn't use it. She was the only woman. Perhaps that was it. She started off camping then found digs in a farm.'

'Did you go to poach her for the Black Law project?'

'God no. I went because it was my mate's thirtieth birthday party. She was there, but only briefly. Hardly the life and soul. The next day he arranged for her to take me out. She was coming to the end of the contract. We needed someone for the mammals at Black Law. It made sense.' He paused. 'Look, I know I should have consulted you but, as I said, she was good. Ideal. She was interested in moving closer to home. She had no ties.'

'Like me then. Lonely, ripe for the old Kemp charm.'

'I don't know what you mean.' But he seemed to take it as a sort of compliment.

'Did she fancy you? Come on, you must have been able to tell.'

It was his turn to shrug.

'I think Grace probably fancied you,' she insisted. 'Most women do. At least for a while. Is that why she agreed to start with us?'

'You're not jealous, Rache, are you?' The tone was teasing but deliberately hurtful.

She turned away as if she'd been hit and he spoke more gently. 'Look, I didn't try anything on if that's what you mean. I'd just got married, for God's sake.'

'Oh,' Rachael said angrily. 'I'm not accusing you of that. What does that matter?'

'Well then?'

'I've been trying to think who would gain by Grace's exaggerated otter counts. And it wouldn't do you any harm. It'd be a great kudos to discover the best otter patch in the county. Never mind a paper, there'd be a book in it, a TV film.'

'Are you joking? I'm being paid by Godfrey Waugh. That's the last thing he'd want.'

'So you'd have a reputation for honesty too. Mr Waugh seems quite an honourable man. Perhaps he'd welcome that. Peter the incorruptible.'

'Not so incorruptible if the fraud was discovered.'

'Then it would be Grace's mistake. Not yours.' She

paused. 'I'm not saying you asked Grace to lie. But perhaps she did it to please you.'

'You're mad,' he said. 'I don't have that sort of power. You've spent too long in the hills.'

'Yes, perhaps I have.'

She sat on the grass beside him, a gesture of apology. She'd never gone in for conspiracy theories, but still she couldn't quite let it go. 'It's not true then?'

'No, it's not true.'

She believed him. 'I'm sorry.'

They sat for a moment in silence. The light was going quickly now. They couldn't see as far as the horizon. The hills were black smudges. There was a hazy moon.

'That's all right,' he said. 'You've been under a lot of strain. But rumours like that could do me a lot of harm.'

'I know.' She continued carefully, 'But you were here on the afternoon Bella died, weren't you?'

He didn't reply.

'Peter?'

She thought he was going to lie but he saw sense, probably realizing there would be more credit in telling the truth.

'Yes, I was around that day.'

'Why didn't you tell me when I asked you before?'

'Because it was none of your business.'

'Of course it was my business.'

'No,' he said. 'This time it wasn't.'

'Why were you walking?'

'I'd been in the office all week, sitting around, eating lunches with clients. I needed the exercise.'

'*That* much exercise? Walking all the way from Langholme?'

'I didn't walk from Langholme. I'd parked the car up the track into the forest and walked through to Black Law that way. I came back over the hill.'

'The inspector thinks Grace's attacker parked his car there.'

'Well, I didn't kill Grace. I couldn't have done. For Christ's sake I was in a meeting with you at the time.'

She didn't answer and he asked roughly, 'Are you satisfied?'

'I want to know what you discussed with Bella.'

'Business, Rache. That's what I'm about now. Not conservation. Business.' He turned so his back was almost facing her. 'So I can afford the pretty wife and the nice house.'

'Don't you dare blame Amelia,' she shouted. A startled coot scuttled out of the reeds and flapped over the water.

'No,' he said quietly. 'No, that wouldn't be fair.'

She felt herself being seduced again by his sadness. She had to fight the urge to comfort him and tell him she'd make everything all right. What is wrong with us? she thought. Why do we do it? Is this how Bella felt about her little brother? Men turn pathetic and we step in to sort things out.

'I have to know what you said to Bella.' She kept her voice firm. 'I have to know if anything you said made her kill herself.'

'Of course not. What do you take me for?'

'What was it all about, Peter?'

'I've told you. Business.'

'Did someone send you there?'

'What?' The question shocked him.

'Whose business were you discussing? Yours? Godfrey Waugh's? Or were you there on behalf of Neville Furness? Doing his dirty work?'

Peter didn't answer. He stood up and pulled her to her feet, then faced her with his hands on her shoulders. 'You've got to leave this alone,' he said. 'It'll make you ill.'

'No.'

'You're a mate, but sometimes you're too fucking serious.'

He took her hand and set off down the hill. She followed, laughing despite herself, and they ran, hand in hand, Hansel and Gretel towards the lights of the cottage.

Chapter Forty-Three

The next morning, after an early count, Rachael went to Black Law farm. She wanted to tell Vera Stanhope that the survey would be finished in a week's time. It was reassuring to have this time limit. A deadline for them all.

She tapped on the kitchen door and walked in. The kettle was humming. It bubbled to a boil then switched itself off. In another part of the house a door shut. She didn't hear footsteps but suddenly Neville Furness appeared in the doorway. The way he walked softly on the balls of his feet made her think of a big cat. Rachael recovered from her surprise first.

'I'm so sorry,' she said. 'I was looking for Inspector Stanhope. I didn't realize . . .'

'She's not here.' She couldn't tell what he felt about the invasion by strangers of what was now his home. 'Nor the sergeant. They left early this morning to go to Kimmerston. They should be back at any time.'

'I'm sorry,' she said again. 'I'll try later.' She was already backing out of the door.

'No! Please.' His voice was urgent. 'I was just going to make some coffee. I suppose the police must have coffee in the place.'

'In the cupboard next to the sink.'

She stayed because she was curious. As he moved with a controlled energy about the kitchen, reaching up for mugs, squatting to lift milk from the fridge she tried to work out how old he was. Mid thirties but very fit. No grey in the dark hair. He wore jeans and an open-necked shirt. He turned suddenly to offer her a biscuit and saw her staring. He smiled and she felt herself flush as if she was in the middle of a lecherous fantasy. There was a down of dark hair on the back of his hand and black hair curled from the cuff of his shirt. He smiled again. His teeth seemed very white.

Not a cat, she thought. A wolf. And I'm Red Riding Hood.

'Come through to the other room. It's more comfortable.'

What big teeth you have, Grandma.

'Come on,' he said. 'I'll not bite.'

He led her into the room with the French windows overlooking the overgrown garden and the view of the hill. Neville seemed too restless to sit still and after a moment got up to stand in front of the huge painting of the old mine workings.

'My mother did this,' he said.

'I know, Bella told me.'

'Did she?' He seemed surprised, pleased.

'We were good friends.' She wanted to stake an allegiance.

'I'm glad. She must have needed friends. It can't have been easy looking after my father. All that work and no response.'

'There was a response,' Rachael said sharply. 'There still is . . . He understands more than people realize.'

'Oh?' He was polite but disbelieving. Perhaps it was

an attempt to hit back at him when she asked, 'Do you remember your mother?'

But he seemed delighted to have the opportunity to talk about her.

'Not very well. Nursery rhymes sung at bedtime. Some games. She loved dressing up. And they fixed a swing for me in the barn. I remember that. Swinging into the sunshine and back into the shadow. Gran fussing because she thought I'd fall and my mother laughing. There was one party I was taken to at Baikie's too. It must have been nearly Christmas, very frosty and cold. It was supposed to be a great treat, but Connie was so enormous that she terrified me. One of the smart ladies was wearing a fur coat and I cuddled into it, hiding. They all laughed.' He paced to the French windows and looked out over the hill. 'It's not much, is it?'

No. But more than I've got of my father, she thought bitterly, and made up her mind that this time she would have to pin Edie down. She deserved to know her father whatever he was like. She'd put up with enough evasion. She'd have it out with Edie before they left Baikie's. As Anne had said, this was a good place to get it sorted. Neutral ground. It would be another deadline.

'I'm sorry.' She realized that he'd been speaking. 'I was miles away.'

'I said that Dad was heartbroken when my mother died. He didn't take any interest in anything. I mean, he carried on with the farm work but I suppose that was some sort of release. It would tire him anyway so he could sleep. But he couldn't take an interest in me. It was too much of an effort. Emotional, I mean. He'd given everything he had to my mother. I could tell even then. Kids can, can't they? So I tried to keep out of the way.'

She had a picture of a boy, creeping around the house, shrinking into shadows, making no noise, and found it hard to reconcile with the image of this successful, energetic man.

'And your gran came to look after you?'

'Ivy, yes.' He turned from the window to face her. 'Did Bella tell you about that too?'

'About you and Dougie and Ivy living together. Yes.'

'They were good times. We weren't a conventional family but it worked OK. Dad found it easier when I was old enough to help on the farm. We had things to talk about then.'

'Neutral ground,' she said, echoing her thoughts about her and Edie.

'Something like that.'

'Why did you leave?'

'I left first to go to school. It's too far to travel from here to Kimmerston every day, especially in the winter, so the council run a hostel where high school kids can board during the week. I was lonely at first but I suppose it made me independent. Then I went away to college. Like you, I suppose. It's what young people do.'

'Weren't you tempted to come back?'

'Not then. I had other ambitions. Something to prove perhaps. Later, when Dad was ill and it would have been natural to take over the farm, Bella was here, doing at least as good a job as I could.'

'Did you resent her taking over?' It was an Edie-like question but he seemed not to mind. 'A bit, I suppose. Only natural, isn't it? But I'd not have had the patience to care for him like she did. As I said, we weren't that close. Because of Mum dying he could never be a touchy-feely sort of dad, even if it had been in his nature in the first place. I couldn't imagine doing all those intimate things Bella took in her stride – feeding, bathing, you know. And I couldn't imagine Dad wanting me to do it either. I suppose I could have taken over the farm, but I don't think it would have worked, the three of us together. Now though . . .' He had been talking almost to himself and, realizing suddenly that he had an audience, stopped abruptly.

'You're not thinking of farming Black Law yourself?' She was astonished. The whole encounter had been a surprise. She had thought of Neville Furness as a businessman. Ruthless, ambitious. Working first on the Holme Park Estate and then for Slateburn Quarries, he was, so far as she was concerned, one of the baddies who ravaged the countryside. A cartoon villain. It had been easy to blame him for Bella's suicide, even to suspect him of Grace's murder. Yet now he was talking so diffidently about his father, with such affection about the farm.

Watch out, girl, you're being conned, she thought. What big teeth he has. A wolf in sheep's clothing.

'It has crossed my mind to move back,' he admitted. 'It's either that or sell it and I don't think I have the heart to do that. But I'll have a look at the figures. Perhaps I'm not being realistic.'

'What about the quarry?'

'Oh, the quarry would go ahead without me. Or not, depending on the outcome of the inquiry.'

'I suppose you'd sell access to the site across Black

Law land,' she said. 'It would make more of a profit than sheep.'

'At the moment anything would make more of a profit than sheep.'

'Would you come to an arrangement with Godfrey Waugh?' she persisted

'I don't know. I still love this place. It wouldn't be the same, would it, with a main road past the kitchen door, articulated trucks rolling past every hour of the day and night.'

Don't be naive, she thought. Don't get taken in. They all tell you what you want to hear. Remember Peter Kemp.

'Do you have any idea why Bella killed herself?' she asked suddenly.

'I feel responsible in a way.'

'Do you?' It was the last thing she had expected.

'I should have realized it was all getting too much for her. Looking after Dad, the farm. Something must just have given. At least . . .'

'At least what?' she demanded.

He shook his head. Some expression of distaste on his face prompted her to complete the sentence for him. 'You were going to say that at least the violence was directed at herself and not at your father?'

'Yes,' he said. 'All right.'

'You knew about her conviction?'

'Of course.'

'When did you find out?'

So it was you, she thought. You made her kill herself. Somehow you found out and you couldn't bear the thought of her looking after your father. But again his reply surprised her.

344

'It was years ago, before they were married. I was invited to tea. This room was just the same. We sat here, drinking tea and eating walnut loaf and she said, "I think you should know. I've a conviction for manslaughter." Quite calmly, as if it was a bit of news she'd picked up at the mart.

'Then I remembered the case. It was when I was a kid but it was all over the papers and they talked about it at school. Charlie Noble had been a pupil there a couple of years before. She'd told Dad the night before, had offered to leave at once if he wanted her to. Of course he said she should stay, but she insisted on telling me too.

'I said it was up to them, their lives. That was what they expected and I'd have wanted the same response from them if it was the other way round. But it wasn't easy. I thought she was after a meal ticket.'

'She wasn't like that.' But Rachael wondered how she'd feel if Edie took up with an ex-con.

'No. I realized that later. I'd have found it hard to like her anyway at the time. She wasn't my mother. And my father seemed happy with her. Much happier than I'd ever been able to make him. I was probably glad of an excuse to disapprove.' He smiled. 'I came to terms with it when my father was ill. It would have been churlish then to keep up the icy formality. I started to visit, to stay overnight occasionally.'

So Neville's room really was Neville's, Rachael thought.

'It was true what I told you at the funeral. We did get on very well at the end.'

'I'm glad.' But she wasn't glad. She was jealous. How could Bella have confided in Neville Furness and not in her? And she wasn't even sure she believed him.

In the distance there were voices. Vera Stanhope and Joe Ashworth had returned. Even from here Rachael could sense their anger and frustration. Doors were slammed. Vera swore. It seemed the meeting in Kimmerston hadn't been a success.

'I want you to have something,' Neville said quickly. He looked at the door as if he expected Vera to burst in. 'Something of Bella's. She'd want that.'

'Oh, I don't know . . .'

'Are you allowed away from this place?'

'Of course.'

'Come to dinner with me. Not tonight, there's a meeting. Tomorrow.'

'I can't,' she said. 'My car's at the garage.'

'I'll pick you up. Of course.' He moved to the door. 'I'd better see what they want with me.'

Then she realized that Vera had summoned him to Black Law for an interview. He hadn't said he was there because he loved the place; that was the impression he'd given. She felt cheated. She had wanted to ask Vera what news she had on the car which had rammed her, but now she left immediately and went back to Baikie's to work.

Chapter Forty-Four

In the garden at the Priory Anne was weeding. She was wearing shorts and knelt on an old folded towel, standing up occasionally to stretch and move on to the next patch. The sun was hot on her back and shoulders. The weeds pulled out easily and she could shake off the sandy soil before throwing the ragwort and the groundsel into her barrow.

She had paid a man from the village to come into the garden every week to water and cut the grass but he'd done nothing else and the plants seemed to have thrived on the neglect. The place had a riotous tropical feel. There were large overblown blooms and under the fruit-net berries had ripened and dropped from bushes and canes, so as she crouched in the border she smelled decay as well as heady perfume.

And all the time she felt that the weeding was a futile gesture because she couldn't imagine being in the Priory in twelve months. Left to himself Jeremy would either allow the place to become a wilderness or he'd invite one of his arty friends up from London to consider a landscape design. She imagined that they'd pull out all the plants and devise something minimalist and oriental with gravel and strange statues.

It was Edie's idea that she should take a day off. Anne decided that she got on so well with Edie because, although she hardly liked to admit it, they were of the same generation. They were somehow less hung up than the youngsters with all their principles.

Anne had confided to Edie that the thought of leaving Baikie's to return to her life at the Priory and Jeremy was making her panic. Of course she hadn't told Edie about Godfrey but she had guessed about an affair that had gone wrong.

'The trouble is I haven't really thought it through,' Anne had said. 'While I'm here I forget that there's anything going on outside. I mean, I know we have to put up with Vera's antics but that's almost seemed like part of the survey. It's all about digging around to find answers, isn't it? But now we've got a date for leaving, well, I can't put off making decisions for much longer.'

Then Edie had said, 'Why don't you take a day off and go home? It might put things into perspective.'

Anne had taken the advice and while she squatted in the sun untangling the goosegrass and the columbine, she had been trying to sort out the more difficult mess of how to spend the rest of her life.

'You have to decide what you really want,' Edie had said. Which was all very well except that she knew that what she really wanted was Godfrey Waugh and she still wasn't sure whether or not he was a murderer.

At lunchtime Jeremy arrived home. He had interests of some description in an antique shop in Morpeth and had gone in, he said, to check that the manager had priced some new stock correctly. The manager was young and pretty.

'Roland has *no* idea,' Jeremy said. He stood on the

flagstone path, very dapper in his Ralph Lauren shirt and his St Laurent blazer, sweating slightly. He had to shout because he wouldn't venture onto the grass in case his shoes got mucky. Anne refused to stop weeding to go to him. There was something reassuring about the rhythm of stooping and pulling and of seeing the ground clear in front of her.

'I mean, he's a first-class salesman. I'll give him that. But he knows nothing about the period.'

She wondered briefly which period but knew better than to ask. Jeremy liked to lecture.

'You'll never guess,' Jeremy went on excitedly, hands flapping, a parody of himself. 'We've been invited to a do at the Hall.'

That did make her stop. She stood up, felt the muscles in her shoulders pull, the tingle where the sun had caught the back of her legs.

'What sort of a do?'

'Oh, nothing really formal. Nothing really posh. I mean, I expect everyone and his dog will be there. It's some sort of celebration for the youngest brat's birthday. But Livvy Fulwell did come here specially to ask.'

'You're such a snob, Jeremy,' she said gently.

'Darling,' he said, 'I can't help it. Are you going to stop that now and come in for lunch?'

'If you like.'

'I can't wait until you give up that dreary business in the hills. Won't it be wonderful when everything's back to normal again?' She caught the anxiety in his voice and thought that Jeremy was probably panicking too. He wasn't stupid and hated any change or disruption. He was a kind and funny man and she thought she would miss him. But it wouldn't do to stay.

'What shall we have for lunch?' She couldn't face a confrontation now, even about when they should eat. This was her day off.

'Oh God!' He was distraught. 'I didn't think. I meant to pick something up on the way back.'

'Let's go to the pub,' she said, then smiled when Jeremy pulled a face. Home-made leek pudding or jumbo sausage and chips weren't really his taste. He didn't feel at ease with the lunchtime boozers.

'Oh God,' he repeated. 'All right. If we must. But I wouldn't do it for anyone else but you.'

In the house he followed her upstairs, waited in her bedroom, shouting through the door to her when she stood in the shower. This is what it must be like, she thought, to have a clinging child who follows you everywhere. She heard his words sporadically through the sound of the water. At first it seemed he was talking about the Fulwell party again. The idea of being invited to the Hall had delighted him. She caught: 'I suppose we'll have to get it a present.'

But when she emerged, wrapped in a towel, she realized he was talking about something else.

'You will phone her, won't you? I can't face putting her off again.'

'Phone who?'

'The woman who's been trying to get in touch with you. I just said.'

She was sitting at the dressing table rubbing the towel over her hair. The sun had made it brittle and the roots needed doing. 'I didn't hear.'

'Oh God, Jeremy, talk to yourself,' he said. He was sitting on the bed behind her. She saw his reflection in the dressing table mirror, put out but trying not to show it.

'I'm sorry. Can you tell me again?'

'A woman phoned for you several times. She presumed I could get a message to you. I didn't like to tell her I hardly ever see you these days.'

'Sorry,' she repeated to keep the peace. She thought – what right's he got to make me feel guilty? He's usually in London anyway. Then, because he was still sulking, she asked, 'What's her name?'

'Barbara something. She said you'd have the number.'

'Waugh?' she asked. 'Barbara Waugh?'

'That's it.'

'What did she want?'

'Oh, she wouldn't tell me. I presumed it was girly stuff. You will phone her before you go back to that hovel in the hills?'

'I will, but not until I've eaten.'

He grimaced. 'Come on then. Let's get it over.'

She was tempted to take him into the bar where Lance, the young mechanic from the garage, would be eating boiled ham and pease pudding sandwiches with oily hands. A juke-box playing rock music tried to compete with Sky TV. Instead she took him to the lounge. There were only two other customers in the room, sitting at a table in the corner. At first they were so engrossed in conversation that they didn't see Anne and Jeremy come in. But Anne saw them immediately. It was Godfrey Waugh and Neville Furness. Godfrey had his back to her but she recognized him at once, the grey tweed sports jacket he wore when he was trying to be casual, the thinning hair. A glass of orange juice stood untouched beside his elbow. Neville was drinking beer and when he looked up from the conversation to take his glass, he saw her.

He must have said something to Godfrey, because although he didn't look round he quickly drank the juice then he stood to go. Anne wondered what they could be doing here. Perhaps another meeting with the opposition group, another concession, another bribe? Neville nodded to her as he walked past, but Godfrey, staring straight ahead, would not catch her eye.

Jeremy was farting about with menus and showed no sign that he had noticed the men. She said, 'Order me a G&T. I'm just going to the ladies.'

She caught up with Godfrey in the car park. He stood with his keys in his hand by the side of his white BMW. Perhaps he'd wanted her to catch him up, had been deliberately slow, because Neville was already driving away. She thought though, as he looked in his wing mirror before pulling out into the road, that he must have seen them.

'I can't stand this,' she said. 'What do I have to do?'
'Nothing.'
'You're saying it's over between us then?'
'No,' he said. 'No. Trust me. Not much longer.'
'When can I see you?'
'Soon.' He reached out and touched her face, stroked it from her forehead down her cheek to her chin. She felt the rough skin of his thumb and fingertips. 'You will wait?'

'I don't have much bloody choice.' To keep some remnant of pride she turned away before he did and stormed back into the pub.

The gin was on the bar, the ice already starting to melt in the glass.

'Are you all right?' Jeremy said. She must have looked pale. She felt weak and shaky.

'Fine, just too much sun.'

When she returned to the Priory, several gins later, Jeremy bullied her into phoning Barbara Waugh and she didn't have the energy to resist. At least, she thought, I know Godfrey's not there. The phone was answered by the child. Anne was thrown for a moment. She was never quite sure how to speak to children.

'Can I speak to your mother?' She realized she sounded abrupt, rude.

'Who shall I say is calling?' It was as if the girl had learnt to articulate the words at an elocution class.

When Barbara answered she was breathless. Perhaps she was worried that Anne would hang up before they had a chance to speak.

'I was in the garden. Such a beautiful day. I am so sorry to have disturbed your husband with my calls. He must think me very foolish.'

'Not at all.'

'I wonder if we could meet?' The voice seemed to break and she apologized again. 'I'm sorry but I don't know where else to turn.'

'Why not?' The gin had made Anne reckless.

'What about Thursday? Could you come here? Or if that's not convenient I could come to you.'

This from Barbara who never went out. She must be desperate, Anne thought. 'No, Thursday's fine. And you'll never find Baikie's. I can come to you. In the afternoon?'

'Oh yes.' The relief was obvious. 'You'll be able to meet Felicity. Come for tea.'

At least, Anne thought, there'll be home-made cake.

Chapter Forty-Five

When Anne returned to Baikie's that evening the effects of the gin were wearing off. She regretted having agreed to meet Barbara. She shouldn't have let Jeremy persuade her to phone in the first place. The encounter with Godfrey had been unsatisfactory but it seemed he had plans. Perhaps having afternoon tea with Barbara would cock them up? What would Godfrey think if he found out? And still she had come to no conclusion about what she should do when the project was finished.

The thoughts, jagged and unformed, danced in her mind as if she had a fever. She had spent too long in the sun and was restless and spoiling for a fight. Rachael was in the living room, working at the table. Her papers were in neatly symmetrical piles.

'Well?' Anne demanded. 'Did you tell Stanhope what we agreed? We'll stay until the weekend and no longer.'

Rachael looked up, but seemed preoccupied. 'I couldn't.'

'You promised you wouldn't go all weedy on me. An ultimatum we said. You promised you wouldn't let Stanhope intimidate you.' Anne flung her bag onto the sofa, releasing a faint cloud of dust.

'I didn't. I didn't even get the chance to talk to her. Neville Furness was there.'

'What did he want?'

'I'm not sure he wanted anything. I think Vera asked him in to answer some questions.'

'What about?'

'How on earth would I know?'

'He must be a suspect.'

'Perhaps. But Vera disappeared again this afternoon and Joe Ashworth wouldn't tell me anything.'

'Neville was in the pub in Langholme at lunchtime with Godfrey Waugh. Reporting back to his lord and master, I suppose.'

'Was he?' Anne seemed flushed and jumpy and Rachael wasn't sure what to make of the information. At one time she would have been excited by this evidence of Neville's perfidy. Now she was confused. She didn't like the thought of Neville obeying Waugh's orders. She pictured him suddenly on the hill working the sheep with a dog and found that image more pleasing. 'It's possible he won't be working for Slateburn Quarries for much longer.'

'What do you mean?'

'He was talking about coming back to Black Law to farm.'

'Has he actually handed in his notice?'

'I don't think so.'

'I bet he hasn't. You weren't taken in by that, were you?' She was pacing up and down, practically ranting. 'It's a knack he has. He tells people what they want to hear and then they trust him.'

'How do you know?'

Anne was still for a moment. 'I've met other people

who've come under the Neville Furness spell. Do you think Vera would drag him out here if he weren't involved in the murder?'

They stared at each other. Rachael was embarrassed by her impulse to rush to Neville Furness's defence. In the garden there was a burst of birdsong. Upstairs a cistern was flushed and they heard Edie's footsteps in the bathroom, water running, tuneless singing.

'He's asked me to dinner,' Rachael said. She could feel herself blushing.

'You didn't say you'd go!'

Rachael didn't reply.

'But you blame him for Bella's suicide!' Anne cried.

'I know.'

'Well then. Are you crazy?'

'Perhaps I was wrong about Neville having put pressure on Bella. She told him and Dougie about her conviction years ago, before they were married.'

'And perhaps you're deluding yourself.'

'No. Why would Neville drag the information up after all this time?'

'I don't know. Because of the quarry. Because he wants to get his hands on the farm. Anyway, you only have his word for what Bella told him. Dougie's hardly in a position to contradict. How can you know he's telling you the truth?'

Anne had come up to the table and was leaning on it, her face very close to Rachael's. Rachael turned away.

'I believed him. I didn't want to, but I did.'

The effort of keeping calm made Anne's voice

shake. 'Look, you're contemplating going out on a date with a murder suspect.'

'It's not like that. Not a date. It's just to talk, to finish the conversation we started this morning.'

'Have you told Edie? I expect she'll have something to say about it. So will Vera, for that matter.'

'What's that about Vera?' The voice resonant as a foghorn, made them turn. The Inspector must have been moving even more quietly than usual, or they were engrossed in their discussion, because she had appeared suddenly at the French windows like a character in a Whitehall farce. Her bulky form blocked out the last of the light. Rachael wondered how long she had been listening, then how many other conversations in this house had been overheard.

'Well?' Vera said jauntily. She looked tired but more cheerful. 'Was somebody taking my name in vain?' She opened the door wide, but remained outside, leaning on the frame. She was wearing one of her shapeless floral frocks, with a bottle-green fleece jacket over the top. The jacket was zipped tight and the dress was pulled over her knees. Anne turned to her, demanding support.

'Neville Furness has invited Rachael out for dinner tomorrow night. She's agreed to go. I thought you might have something to say about it.'

Vera shrugged. 'None of my business, is it?'

'But he's probably mixed up in this murder.'

'Tut, tut . . . You can't go about saying things like that. It's speculation. He's been helping us with our inquiries, that's all. No question of any charge. He can see who he likes.' Vera nodded towards Rachael. 'And so can she. She's a consenting adult.'

'You're deliberately putting her into a position of danger.'

'Don't be daft. Whatever position she gets in, she'll have put herself there. And she'll not be in much danger when we all know who she's with and where she's going. Just because you don't like the lad . . .'

Rachael listened to the argument conducted over her head. Again she felt she was part of a drama played out for the benefit of other people. Vera was clearly delighted by the development.

Rachael thought, It's just what she wanted. Neville's the crow and I'm the decoy. And Anne seems too passionate to be entirely objective. Perhaps Neville's been one of her conquests. She didn't want to linger on that thought and broke into their conversation. 'I've already said I'll go.'

'Why not?' Vera said jubilantly. 'He can afford to buy you a good dinner.'

'He's cooking at home.'

'Is he?' Vera gave a huge wink. She disengaged herself from the door frame, came into the room and shut the door. 'You and me had better have a bit of a chat.'

'What about?'

'Your after-dinner conversation. I talked to Mr Furness today but he didn't give much away. Pleasant enough but very cagey. Find out if he knows anything about Edmund. He's still probably in with the Fulwells, they might have told him something.'

'Why should I do your dirty work?'

'You won't be,' Vera spat back. 'You'll be doing your own. You're the one that started playing detective.'

'We're leaving.' Rachael felt like a defiant child.

'Next weekend. At the latest. We'll have finished our work by then.'

'Will you? So will we, I hope.' She left, almost noiselessly, the way she had come.

Rachael stood in the garden. Anne had gone to bed but Rachael seemed to have been infected by her febrile mood and didn't think she would sleep.

The grass was damp. There was a lake of mist over the flat land by the burn but the sky was clear. She heard a noise behind her and turned, startled.

'Christ, Edie, don't sneak up on me like that.'

'You shouldn't be out here on your own.'

'It's a bit late to go all protective on me.'

'Perhaps.' Edie was wearing a cream wool kaftan, a garment she had used as a dressing gown for as long as Rachael could remember. With the mist in the background she looked like a character in a low-budget horror movie – a priestess perhaps at a ritual sacrifice. She stood at Rachael's side.

'I heard you give Vera an ultimatum.'

Christ, Rachael thought, is everyone in this house earwigging?

'I thought she should know what was happening. Our work will be finished by the end of the week. There'll be no point in our staying.'

'I wonder if it'll all be over by then. The investigation, I mean.'

'She seems to think so.'

'That's what she'd like us to think.'

'But you don't?' Rachael asked. 'I couldn't stand it if he were never caught.'

'Why? Is revenge so important?' Edie's voice was detached. She could have been undertaking academic research.

'No. Not revenge. But not to know ... Don't you feel the same?'

'I never met Grace. That makes a difference.' They stood for a moment in silence then Edie said, 'In some ways I'll be sorry to leave.'

'Before we leave–' Rachael came to an abrupt stop.

'Yes?'

'I need to find out about my father.'

'Another ultimatum?'

'If you like. No. A request, that's all. Tell me about him.'

She expected the usual refusal, the party line. What do a few genes matter? Do you really need a father figure to give you an identity? Why get taken in by the patriarchal conspiracy?

'Is it really important?' Edie asked gently. Another question in her survey of moral attitudes.

'Not knowing's important. That's what I meant about Grace. And it gets between you and me.'

'I didn't realize,' Edie said. 'I've been stupid. Obviously.'

'You did what you thought was best.'

'No. I did what I thought was easiest.' She paused. 'It'll come as an anticlimax, you know. No great drama. Recently that's what prevented me from telling you.'

'All the same.'

'I have been working up to it. It was finding out about Bella, I suppose. Wondering if you imagined your father as a murderer.'

'Is he?'

'Not so far as I know.' She smiled, put her arm around Rachael's shoulder. Rachael didn't pull away as she usually would have done. It would have been churlish when Edie was prepared to make concessions.

'If we're going to talk, shouldn't we go inside?' Edie asked. 'It's getting cold.'

Perhaps it was the word 'talk' invested with all Edie's special meaning? Perhaps it was the arm round the shoulder? But Rachael suddenly got cold feet. 'You don't have to tell me now. As I said, before we leave . . .'

Edie pulled away from her daughter, looked at her. 'I was thinking it might be easier if I wrote it down,' she said. 'That way I'd have my facts straight and you'd have something to keep.'

'Yes.' Rachael was grateful. She couldn't face an emotional scene tonight. 'Yes, I'd like that.'

They went into the cottage together. Edie closed the French windows behind them and pushed in the bolt. Halfway up the stairs she stopped.

'Tomorrow you'll have to tell me all about Neville Furness,' she said. 'I want to know what he's like.'

Chapter Forty-Six

Neville Furness collected Rachael from the Riverside Terrace house in Kimmerston and Edie was there to see her off. This arrangement was agreed by Rachael but had been decided by Vera and Edie who were closeted together in the farmhouse for most of the morning.

Neville arrived exactly on time. Edie opened the door to him. Rachael had been flustered in her preparations, even more confused than she had been the day before. Did she want to attract this man or repel him? In the end she chose thin cotton trousers and a loose silk shirt. She brushed out her hair and stole mascara and eyeliner from her mother's room. Edie invited Neville in and they stood together in the hall making polite conversation until Rachael hurried down the stairs. There was something very old-fashioned in the scene below her. Edie was wearing one of her long, drop-waisted skirts and Neville, dressed in black jeans and a white collarless shirt, with his bushy beard, could have been a character from Thomas Hardy. He should have been clasping a hat under his arm. And he greeted Rachael with suitable formality, standing at a distance from her, holding out his hand. The words he directed to Edie:

'I'll make sure she gets home safely, Mrs Lambert. This must be a worrying time for you.'

'Miss Lambert,' she said automatically, but she smiled at him like a fond Victorian mamma, and stood at the top of the steps to wave them off. Rachael couldn't tell whether or not the friendliness was an act. Edie hadn't confided the subject of her conference with Vera and Rachael had refused to be a part of it. Alerted by Edie's threat that she wanted to know all about Neville, Rachael had avoided serious discussion even when they had driven together into Kimmerston. The conversation about her father hadn't been mentioned again.

She was surprised by Neville's home, which was modest, a terraced house close to the almshouses where Nancy Deakin lived. The houses fronted onto gardens, then a paved narrow path which separated the row from another similar terrace. Children were playing there and women sat in doorways watching them and shouting to each other.

There were deserted doll's prams and roller skates. At the back of the row was an alley with dustbins, where he parked. There was a gate in a high brick wall into a yard, then a door into the kitchen. The walls of the yard had been whitewashed. It contained tubs of flowers and a wrought iron table and chairs.

The house was very tidy and she sensed it was always like that. It hadn't been prepared specially for her visit. It was furnished with the simplicity of a ship's cabin with fitted wooden storage boxes and drawers.

'A drink?' he asked. He seemed nervous too.

'White wine.'

In the living room a table had been set for two. There were candles and red linen napkins.

'Perhaps you would have preferred to go to a restaurant,' he said.

'No, of course not.'

'I thought it might be easier to talk here.' She was reminded of Edie, stifled a desire to giggle, felt gauche and graceless.

He left the room for a moment and returned with a jeweller's cardboard box packed with cotton wool.

'I was looking for something of Bella's. I thought you might like this.' He pulled out a silver locket on a chain. The locket was unusual, shaped like an old threepenny piece, engraved with tiny flowers and leaves. 'It's not very valuable. Victorian probably. She said it belonged to her grandmother.' He opened it to reveal the sepia photograph of a woman with the face of a donkey and dark, swept-back hair.

'I suppose someone must have loved her,' he said.

'I remember Bella wearing it.'

'You will take it?' He fixed it for her and as he fastened the clasp she felt the down on his hand on the back of her neck.

'What did Vera want of you?' she asked suddenly.

'Vera?'

'Inspector Stanhope.'

'Questions. She implied that the murder had something to do with the development of the quarry.'

'Did it?'

'Of course not.' At first the idea seemed to amuse him, then realizing she thought the response inappropriate, he was more serious. Like her, he seemed awkward, scared of striking a wrong note. 'If anything, it makes things more difficult for the company. We need public opinion on our side. Any rumour that associates us with the death of a young survey worker will alienate it.'

'It's still "our side" then?'

'I'm still employed by the company.'

'And so am I, indirectly. At least for a few more months. The fieldwork's nearly finished. It'll take me a while to finish the report but I don't need to be at Black Law to do that.'

'What's it like working for Peter Kemp?'

'Interesting.' It was her standard response to the question.

'And do you see your long-term future there?'

She smiled. 'Are you offering me a job?' It was an off the cuff remark but she wondered immediately if there was some truth in it. Perhaps Neville had been set up by Godfrey Waugh to buy her off with a meaningless post within Slateburn Quarries – environmental officer perhaps with thirty-five grand and a car. Though even if she accepted, what would it achieve? Anyway, the report would state that the quarry would cause little significant damage.

Neville shook his head. 'If my plans go ahead I'll be in no position to offer anyone work. I'll be lucky if I can scratch together a living for myself.'

'I've been thinking recently that I might like a change,' she said. 'Perhaps I'll try to move into the voluntary sector, one of the wildlife charities. The pay wouldn't be so good . . .'

' . . . but at least you wouldn't have to consort with grubby businessmen.'

'Something like that.'

There was a break in the conversation. He lit the candles, invited her to sit at the table. She realized suddenly, with horror, that she hadn't warned him she was vegetarian. Better to plough through a meal of dead animal than make a fuss at this stage. Or would she be sick? That would be worse.

'I'm sorry.'

He was carrying a Le Creuset casserole with thick oven gloves.

'This is really stupid. I should have said. I don't eat meat.'

'Nor do I much. Mushroom risotto. OK?'

Shit, she thought. I needn't have opened my big mouth. He poured her another glass of wine.

'So what's it like to work for Godfrey Waugh?' she asked, slightly desperate.

'Interesting.'

She smiled politely. 'No, I'd like to know. Power is always intriguing, isn't it?'

There was a moment of silence. He paused with his fork halfway between his plate and his mouth. 'Perhaps you'd better ask your colleague.'

'Which colleague?'

'Mrs Preece.'

She looked at him, astounded. He wiped his mouth with his napkin and continued to eat. She couldn't make out whether the indiscretion had been a mistake, a slip of the tongue, or deliberate, some kind of warning. Later she wondered even if it was the real reason for the invitation to dinner. She didn't know what to say. At last she asked, pathetically, 'Have you lived here long?'

Perhaps he sensed some criticism about the house

or the neighbourhood because he sounded defensive. 'Since I left the estate. That all happened in a rush. I had to find somewhere quickly. It suits me well enough though and I'm not here much.'

'Where did you live when you worked for the Fulwells?'

'They gave me a house, one of those semis at the end of the Avenue. That was why I had to move so quickly when I resigned.'

'Why did you leave?'

He paused, tried to find the right words. 'It was never a very comfortable working environment. I don't think I've the right temperament for the feudal life.'

'What do you mean?'

But he shook his head.

'Did you ever meet Edmund, Grace's dad?'

'Not when I was working on the estate. The family had dropped all contact with him at that point. I think they wanted to pretend he didn't exist. But earlier, when I was growing up at Black Law, I saw him around. For us kids he was a bit of a bogeyman. Grown ups would say: "If you don't behave you'll end up like Edmund Fulwell." Without really telling us what was wrong with him.'

'So you've no idea where he is now then?' She paused. 'Look, I'm sorry. Vera Stanhope told me to ask.' The wine must have already gone to her head because the nervous giggle she had been stifling all evening came out. 'Not much of a detective, am I?'

'Does she think Edmund killed his daughter?'

'I don't know what she thinks.'

He piled plates and took them into the kitchen. They moved from the table. She sat on his IKEA sofa.

He opened another bottle of wine. Both started talking together. She gestured for him to continue.

'I'm sorry about this evening,' he said. 'I'm not very used to this sort of thing. Too busy. Out of practice.'

'No,' she replied. 'I've enjoyed it.' And realized she meant it.

He walked her home. He'd had too much to drink to drive. It wasn't late. As he led her through the front door into the small garden two boys were chasing down the path between the houses, kicking a ball around in the last of the light. Through uncurtained windows she saw flickering televisions, kids sprawling on the floor with homework. Neville seemed too solitary for this sort of communal living.

'When will you make up your mind about moving to Black Law?'

'Soon,' he said. 'There are a few things to sort out.'

'Does Godfrey Waugh know what you're planning?'

'No, I've only talked to you.'

At Riverside Terrace their pace slowed. She wondered if Edie was looking out for her from one of the upstairs windows. If so, it would be a novel experience for her. Edie, who had suggested a trip to the family planning clinic as soon as Rachael reached sixteen, would have welcomed boyfriends for breakfast, would have seen it as a healthy sign. Certainly, there would have been no need for stolen goodnight kisses on the doorstep.

'Will you come in for a coffee?' she asked.

'I don't think so.'

And then, unexpectedly, he did kiss her. She felt his beard on her lips. A real kiss, but so quick and light that it could have been a friendly gesture of farewell.

She wanted to pull him closer to make it last, but he was already walking down the street away from her.

'When will I see you?' She shouted this without worrying that her mother might be watching.

He stopped, turned, smiled. 'Soon,' he said. 'I'll be in touch.'

As she watched him walk very quickly down the street there was a movement in the shadow. It appeared to be a jogger in tracksuit and training shoes. He ran for a moment on the spot until Neville turned the corner then jogged down the street after him.

Chapter Forty-Seven

When she turned away from Neville in the street and approached the house Rachael could see Edie in the basement kitchen, silhouetted against the Chinese paper lampshade, talking on the telephone. But by the time she had opened the front door Edie had finished the conversation. She appeared at the top of the kitchen stairs, obviously excited.

This is it, Rachael thought. The inquisition. Other people's parents might be curious about their daughter's dates, but their questions were usually limited to financial status, the decor of the intended's home, marital status. Edie's questions were usually more detailed and more difficult. She wanted to know what Rachael's friends were really *like*. She probed their relationship with their parents and had been known in the past, without ever meeting the man in question, to pass judgement on his stability, his ability to empathize and even on the possibility that he was a latent homosexual.

Today, however, there were no questions. Edie scarcely even acknowledged that Rachael had been to Neville's home. Something else had caught her attention.

'Are you ready to go?' she said. 'I don't suppose we'll need coats. It's still warm, isn't it?'

'I thought you might make me a coffee.'

'No, no.' Edie was firm. 'There's no time for that. It's late as it is to go visiting.'

'Oh God, Edie. Where are you off to? Surely I don't have to come.' It must have been one of Edie's women friends on the phone, probably drunk, certainly weepy, demanding support, someone to drink with and these conversations always went on until the early hours.

'You don't *have* to but I thought you might be interested.'

'Why? Who is it?' Rachael was absent-minded, still pondering Neville Furness. She told herself it was ridiculous to be imagining herself established in the kitchen at Black Law Farm after one fleeting kiss and an evening of stilted and awkward conversation. After Peter Kemp she should know better. Her judgement was crap.

'Charles Noble,' Edie said, triumphantly.

'Who?' For a moment the name meant nothing to her. She tried to dredge up memories of men Edie had taught with at college, gentlemen callers who had all been at one time potential fathers to Rachael.

'Charles Noble. Bella's brother. He's just rung. He's been trying to phone me apparently but of course there was nobody here to take the call and he said he didn't like to leave a message on the answer machine.' Rachael didn't respond with sufficient interest and Edie shouted grumpily, 'Well, are you coming?'

Charles Noble was waiting for them in the road. He'd already unlocked the high security gates which blocked the entrance to the stable yard. The stables were lit by security lights and the shadow of the wire mesh fence was thrown across him like a cage. He was dressed in a grey tracksuit and Rachael was reminded of the jogger who had been waiting in the street outside her mother's house.

They drove through the stables and up to the house, then got out of the car and waited for Noble to padlock the security gates once more and join them. Rachael had the unnerving feeling that she was being locked inside a prison compound and experienced a moment of panic. She hoped Edie had had the sense to tell Vera Stanhope or Joe Ashworth what she'd planned to do. Otherwise no one would know they were there. From the horseboxes came the sound of horses breathing and the rustle of crushed straw, the sweet smell of muck and leather.

'I don't know why this couldn't have waited until morning,' Noble said, before he'd even got to them. Rachael could tell he was already regretting his phone call to Edie. 'Louise and I usually go to bed very early. We're busy people.'

'So are we, Mr Noble.' Edie was brisk, efficient. Good God, Rachael thought, she could be playing a detective in a TV cop show. She'd always had a weakness for watching them.

'You'd better come in then.' He, at least, seemed taken in by her air of authority and opened the front door to show them into a wide hall and on into a living room, which was tastefully furnished in a bland Marks & Spencer sort of way in terracotta and cream. The long curtains were drawn and the table lights were still switched on, but the room was empty.

'Louise must have gone to bed,' he said unhappily.

'I know she's got a hectic day tomorrow. She's organizing a charity lunch. She's very active with the Red Cross.'

'We'll have to speak to her,' Edie said. 'She did take the call from Bella after all.' Then, maliciously, 'We'll only have to come back tomorrow and we wouldn't want to interrupt her if she's having guests. It might be embarrassing.'

'You couldn't do that.'

'Oh, we could. Inspector Stanhope's very interested in Bella's suicide. You do remember Inspector Stanhope? She was one of the team investigating your father's death.'

'Wait here. I'll go and find her.'

Louise Noble was wearing silk pyjamas and a dressing gown, but hadn't yet taken off her make-up. She was an attractive woman with high cheekbones and long curly hair, copper-coloured and tied away from her face. Rachael had been expecting someone worn out and stuffy like Charles, but Louise was in her early forties and rather nervy. As she followed him into the room, she lit a cigarette.

'I was on my way to bed,' she said, not aggressively but in explanation for the dressing gown. Throughout the encounter Rachael had the impression of a little girl playing at mums and dads. The lunches, the dinners, all these seemed to be endured because they were what you did when you were grown up. It was difficult to imagine her with a child of her own, or as the power behind Charles's expansion plans.

'You'll forgive the intrusion.' Edie sat down without waiting to be asked. 'We'll try not to keep you.'

'I really don't see how I can help . . .' Louise took a

drag on her cigarette, set it carefully to rest in a glass ashtray. 'I explained to Charlie . . .'

'And I understand.' Charles patted his wife's hand.

'It wasn't that I tried to keep secrets from him. I mean his sister didn't really say anything very important. It was just that we're so settled and so happy, the three of us. And I thought, well, she'd done that terrible thing to his father, it was probably just as well to forget all about it. If she intruded into his life again he'd only get hurt.'

She patted at her eyes with a tissue. The mascara didn't smudge. Charles took her hand. He was clearly besotted.

Louise turned towards him. 'I'm sorry,' she said. 'I didn't know how I'd cope if you'd brought her here. What would I say to her? And then when you told me she'd killed herself, I didn't know how to tell you she'd phoned . . .' She looked up at Edie, wide-eyed, desperate for understanding. 'I can't see how it would have made any difference. Even if Charles had phoned her back. Even if he'd gone to see her. I mean she'd already decided to kill herself, hadn't she? Charles said she wasn't the kind of person to do anything on impulse. So it would have happened anyway. It wasn't my fault.'

Charles, stroking her hand, murmured again that of course it wasn't her fault.

'When exactly did she phone?' Edie was firm but not unkind. It was the tone she used with spoilt pupils having to come to terms with the reality of the exam system.

'I've been trying to think, haven't I, Charlie? You were at work. I was on my own here.'

'Where was your daughter?'

'Not here. Definitely not. Because if she's in I always let her answer the phone. At that age their friends phone all the time and they talk for hours, don't they, even if they only saw each other an hour ago. And then after I spoke to Bella I thought – thank God Lucy's not in because she'd probably have taken the call and then we'd have had to explain. She doesn't know, you see, about Bella and Charlie's dad.'

'Can you remember where Lucy was? That might help us to pin down a date.'

Louise sat for a moment, frowning, then her face cleared, a pantomime of enlightenment. 'It was the school trip to Newcastle to see *Macbeth* in the Theatre Royal. I'd just come in. I'd taken down a car load and another parent was going to bring them all home. The school had arranged a coach but it had been double-booked and we'd all had to turn out at the last minute. I remember because I was so flustered.'

She beamed round at them, proud of the detail of her memory. It was almost, Rachael thought bitterly, as if she expected applause. Could she really be that childish?

'Good.' Edie nodded approvingly. 'What date was that?'

'Oh God knows. It was months ago.'

'Would you have written it down? Lucy's play, I mean?'

'Fetch the wall planner from the kitchen, darling.' Louise still appeared flushed with success. 'It'll be there!'

Charles returned with a large calendar. Each page was decorated with a photograph of a horse and there was a space for notes each day. He flipped the pages. 'March the eleventh,' he said. 'Lucy wrote it in.'

'There you are then,' Louise cried. 'If she'd wanted to talk to Charles she had a week to phone back. It was the nineteenth, wasn't it, when she killed herself? But she never did.'

'No,' Charles said. 'She never did.'

'Now,' Edie interrupted calmly. 'Now, we need you to remember everything Bella said, the exact words.'

Louise frowned again. She seemed incapable of thinking without screwing up her face. 'She said, "I want to speak to Charlie Noble." Like that. Quite brusque. I was surprised because not many people call him Charlie. I thought it was someone wanting to book a ride. The stable office has a separate line but people still sometimes come through on this one. But she said it wasn't about riding. It was personal.'

Louise paused. 'Those were the words she used. "It's personal". So I told her Charlie wasn't here and asked if I could take a message. And then Bella said, "Who are you?" It sounded not rude exactly but as if she wasn't used to making polite conversation, as if she wasn't bothered what people thought.'

'And you told her,' Edie prompted.

'Yes, well, I couldn't very well not. Not without being rude myself.'

The horror of being considered rude seemed suddenly to hit her again because she looked wildly round the room and said, 'Hasn't Charles offered you a drink or something. Really, darling . . .'

'What did she say then?' Edie broke in.

'She asked me if I could pass on a message to

Charles. "Tell him it's Bella and ask him to get in touch." Something like that.'

'Did she say how Charles could get in touch with her? Did she give an address, a phone number?'

'I don't think so.' Louise seemed uncertain. 'If she had, I'd have written it down. You do, don't you, automatically? Actually, it was a bit of a shock. Charles had told me about Bella but I'd never had any contact with her. I mean, speaking to a murderer. It's bound to give you the creeps, isn't it? So I might have missed something.'

'What did she say then?'

'She told me to tell Charles not to worry. "He's quite safe." I remember that because it seemed so bizarre. I knew he was safe, here with Lucy and me. I look after him. But she repeated it twice. As if I was some sort of idiot. Her attitude annoyed me actually. That's probably why I didn't tell Charles that she'd called. I mean, I don't have to put up with that, do I?'

She looked round at them.

For a moment Charles seemed stunned. He sat with his mouth slightly open. Then he began to stroke Louise's hand again.

'No,' he murmured. 'No, of course you don't, pet.'

Chapter Forty-Eight

It was like the end of term. They were starting to pack up. In Baikie's there were cardboard boxes half filled with books and papers. Black plastic bin bags were filled with blankets which Rachael would take into Kimmerston to wash. At first Edie said she'd help tidy up and floated round ineffectually with a duster. Then she said significantly that there was something she had to write and disappeared upstairs. At least, Rachael thought, my father's come in useful for something, even if only in providing an excuse.

Vera Stanhope seemed to resent the preparations for moving out. She had spent the night at home and turned up in the middle of the morning. She prowled around Baikie's, muttering to herself and poking the bags and the boxes, then summoned Rachael into Black Law to ask her about Neville. She was even ready to pass over titbits of information in an attempt to persuade Rachael to talk.

'I've been following up Edie's idea that Edmund Fulwell and Bella might have been in hospital at the same time.'

'And?'

'They were, briefly. They overlapped in the early eighties, just before Bella was released. They were on the same ward. I'm trying to track down any members of staff who might remember them both. It's probably just a coincidence. It was years ago.'

'They might have kept in touch afterwards.'

'I suppose it's possible.' Vera was out of sorts. She had made Rachael coffee, but grudgingly, as if paying her back for her reluctance to stay on at Baikie's indefinitely. Now she made it clear that Rachael's suggestions were hardly worth considering.

'Well, we think Edmund put pressure on Grace to fight against the quarry proposal. That's what the exaggerated otter counts were about. Perhaps he still had influence over Bella and used it to persuade her to refuse access over Black Law land.' Rachael paused, considered. 'Though of course she would have done that anyway.'

'Would she?' Vera demanded. 'How do you know?'

'Well, she'd have hardly wanted a road just outside her kitchen window.'

'Perhaps she didn't have any choice.'

'I don't know what you're talking about.'

'I've asked an accountant to look over her books,' Vera said. 'And talked to her accountant. Black Law's in deep trouble.'

'Like every other hill farm in the north of England.'

'No. I mean deep trouble. She was within months of the bank taking over and making her and Dougie insolvent. She'd sold everything she could. The last Constance Baikie painting went last year. Her only hope of staying here was of doing some deal with the quarry company. And quickly. She couldn't have afforded to wait for the planning process to go through.

Didn't Neville mention that when you had your cosy chat last night?'

'He couldn't have known.'

'Of course he knew. He's been in charge of things, hasn't he, since Bella died? You're not telling me that he hasn't had a quick neb through the accounts. He's a businessman.'

Like Peter Kemp, Rachael thought. That's what he'd said the last time they'd met. *That's what I'm into now. Business. Not conservation.* Was that why Peter had come to Black Law the afternoon Bella killed herself? To do Godfrey Waugh's dirty work? Offering her the final deal to keep her and Dougie on the farm? But she couldn't face giving into him and killed herself instead.

'But she had access to money,' Rachael said suddenly. 'When Charles Noble sold his father's house after the murder he put the profit into an account for Bella. She knew about it. After all these years it would be worth a fortune.'

'Are you sure she knew about it?'

'Certain. He wrote to tell her when she was first sent to the secure hospital. He was trying to persuade her to let him in to see her.'

'Charlie told you that, did he?'

'Yes.'

'And you believed him?'

'I didn't have any reason not to.'

'How sweet.' Vera got up, rinsed her mug under the tap, clattered it violently on the draining board and returned to the table. She leant over it towards Rachael.

'How did the evening go with lover boy?'

'It was very pleasant. Thank you.'

'Did you ask about Edmund Fulwell?'

'He hasn't seen anything of him since he was a kid. The Fulwells never mention him.'

'Bugger,' Vera said thoughtfully. 'What else did you talk about over the After Eights?'

'His plans for the future.' Rachael paused. 'He's talking about resigning from the quarry, coming here and taking over the farm. Why would he do that if he knows the place is in hock to the bank?'

'Perhaps he's done his own deal with Godfrey Waugh?' Vera said. She laughed unpleasantly. 'Or perhaps he's developed his very own chat-up line?' When Rachael still looked blank she added, 'It's obvious – he's trying to impress you.'

After lunch, in an attempt to escape Vera and her mother, Rachael went with Anne to gather in the wooden quadrat frames from her survey areas. It turned out not to be much of an escape.

'How did it go last night then?'

She should have realized that Anne wouldn't let it go. 'Fine. We went to see Charles Noble. Bella tried to contact him the week before she died. His stupid cow of a wife didn't pass the message on.'

'Not that. I know about that. How did it go with Neville?'

The sun was still shining. After spending a spring in the hills Rachael was fit. She moved easily, felt she could go on for miles at the same pace without discomfort. She loved the rhythm of movement and didn't want to break it. They came to a thicket of gorse in full flower with its sweet scent of roasted coconut. After what Neville had implied the night before, Rachael had niggling questions about Anne's relationship with Godfrey Waugh, but she wasn't going to bring that up now. She might be thinking about Neville but she didn't want Anne asking about him. She didn't want words at all. All she wanted was to walk on against the breeze with the smell of gorse, damp peat and crushed heather, the sound of skylark, curlew and distant sheep.

'Well?' Anne asked.

'Fine,' she said again.

'Don't you find him really spooky?' Anne went on. 'For one thing he doesn't have any friends, does he? Not that I could tell. You said there didn't seem to be any of his mates at Bella's funeral.'

'So? I don't have many "mates"!' She lengthened her stride, tried to pull ahead but Anne kept pace with her.

'I think he gets off on power, manipulating situations behind the scenes. You know your trouble, Rache, you won't face up to things. It wouldn't surprise me if he were still working for Livvy Fulwell. The Fulwells are the people who'll get most out of the quarry. And Neville's definitely pulling Godrey Waugh's strings.'

'How do you know?' Now it was impossible to ignore the conversation. Rachael stopped abruptly. She was wearing shorts and bent to massage the muscles in the back of her legs.

'What do you mean?' Anne stopped too.

'How do you know what's going on between Neville and Godfrey Waugh? Anyone would think you had some sort of inside information.'

That shut her up at last. She walked on without answering but for Rachael the walk was spoiled.

The final quadrat to be collected was in the lime

spoil close to the mine building. From the hill they looked down on the site. With the grey block of the mine, the dark moss of conifer, the pale snake line of the burn, it was like looking down onto a map. They could see the curve in the burn where Grace's body had been found. All the debris used by the police – the blue and white tape, the plastic sheeting – had been cleared, but it had been there long enough for Rachael to pinpoint the spot accurately. Neither of them mentioned it, even when they had to walk close by.

They couldn't see the quadrat from the hill because it lay in the shadow of the engine house, next to the mill chimney.

'Someone's moved it,' Anne said as they approached. The frame looked as if it had been kicked or tripped over. 'It's just as well the survey's finished. That could really have cocked things up.'

'Perhaps it was the police?'

'No. They haven't been here for days. Besides, I brought Vera up the day the investigation started and showed her what was going on. She told them to be careful.'

'A walker then.'

'Perhaps. Some ghoul interested in seeing where the murder took place. Or a protester from Langholme wanting a closer look at the mine before it's turned into Godfrey Waugh's operations centre.'

'Or a ghost.'

'I thought you were a scientist. Never had you down as a believer in the supernatural.'

'I'm not.'

'What's with the ghosts then?'

'Nothing. A flip remark.'

'There must be more to it than that.'

'Occasionally, when I've been walking the burn I've had the feeling of somebody watching me. Or following. And I saw a woman once on top of the cairn.'

'Who was it?' Anne asked. Rachael looked at her, thinking she must be taking the piss but she seemed serious.

'I don't know. Couldn't tell.'

'You must have an overactive imagination, pet. Living with Grace was enough to give anyone the willies.'

Anne crossed the culverted stream towards the square, stone room which had once held the engine which powered the mine. She turned back towards Rachael. Reflected fragments of light from the water bounced onto her face.

'Could it have been Grace?' she asked. 'We never knew exactly where she was.'

'Perhaps.' Though Rachael knew it hadn't been Grace she had seen by the cairn that day.

The room was almost intact. It had been roofed with corrugated iron. At the mouth of the ragged rectangle where once the door had been, flowers had been laid – hothouse blooms, white daisies and huge white chrysanthemums. They were perfect. They hadn't started to wilt, despite the heat.

'It must have been a walker then,' Anne said, 'marking the spot of Grace's death. Or near enough. That's touching. Perhaps we should have thought of it.'

'There were flowers here before. The day the woman was on the cairn.'

'Your ghost again?'

'No.' Rachael was irritated. 'Of course not.'

'Well, it wasn't a ghost this time.' Anne had walked into the building. The floor was of bare earth covered by loose stone flags. 'Unless ghosts eat chocolate digestives.' Anne came back towards the door, holding up a biscuit wrapper.

'Perhaps that's why Grace was never hungry. She pigged out on chocolate.'

'It couldn't have been dropped by Grace. The police searched here and took everything they found away. It must be more recent than that.'

Anne had moved further into the room. She was poking in a corner with one of her marker canes. 'I think someone's been camping out. This looks like ashes. The remains of a campfire.'

'Wouldn't we have seen the light?'

'Not from Baikie's. Not if they stayed inside.'

'Someone's been watching us then.' Rachael backed away from the building so she was standing in sunlight and had a clear view all around her. The crow, she thought. The driver of the white car. He's been here all the time watching every move we make. He'll know when the police are in Black Law. He can see the cars moving down the track. He can see us sitting in the garden or setting out for the hill. 'Come on,' she called to Anne. 'We should go.'

But Anne seemed unaware of any danger. She lingered by the entrance, looking in. 'Unless this is where Edmund Fulwell's been holed up. Imagine him here, all the time, while Vera Stanhope's been chasing round the country after him. Though you saw a woman, didn't you? Perhaps cross-dressing is one of his vices too.'

'The woman was weeks ago.' Rachael wanted to run

back to Baikie's, couldn't understand Anne's lack of urgency.

'But Edmund's a boozer and there aren't any cans or bottles. And if it was him, where is he now?'

Chapter Forty-Nine

They found Vera in Black Law with her team. When they told her about their find at the mine she erupted into a violent and entertaining fury directed at the colleagues who stood around her.

'What's wrong with you all? You're professionals, aren't you? We thought those women might be targets but nobody bothered to go and check the only cover for miles around. Are you scared of getting your feet wet? Happy that two women have to do your dirty work for you?'

Then she gathered up Joe Ashworth, climbed over the stile at the end of Baikie's garden and strode up the path to the mine. From the cottage Anne watched them – Laurel and Hardy in silhouette – disappearing into the bright sunlight.

The incident left Anne amused but unsettled. She hadn't expected Vera Stanhope to take a biscuit wrapper and a pile of ashes so seriously. And why was Rachael like a cat on hot bricks? For the first time Anne felt unsafe. She wished she could wait for their return to hear the outcome of their investigation but it was her day for tea with Barbara Waugh and it wouldn't do to be late.

Perhaps because of Vera's response she told Rachael where she was going.

'Just in case,' she said, though she hardly expected Barbara and her daughter to hold her hostage in the gloomy and immaculate house in Slateburn.

Rachael looked at her strangely and again Anne wondered if Neville had said something about her and Godfrey.

In the sunshine the house looked as austere as it had before. The lawn had been mowed, the edges trimmed, the gravel raked. The door was opened by the child. Despite the heat she was dressed in a grey pleated skirt and a uniform sweatshirt. She was so tidy that she looked as if she was just setting off for school. Her white knee-length socks were unrumpled and stainless. Her black patent-leather sandals were shining.

'Come in,' she said. 'Mummy's expecting you.'

She stood aside to let Anne in, but seemed to regard her progress with disapproval. For a moment it occurred to Anne that even Felicity could have guessed about the affair, then she turned to wheel a large doll's pram up the hall, and the idea seemed ridiculous.

God, Anne thought. Talk about paranoid.

In the kitchen Barbara was lifting scones from a baking dish onto a wire cooling tray. She seemed flustered. The kitchen was very hot.

'I'm sorry,' she said. 'I'm running a bit late.'

Felicity must have been playing there because besides the pram there was an attaché case full of doll's clothes, a real baby's cup, bowl and spoon in blue moulded plastic on the table. Anne thought Felicity was too old to be playing with dolls. She was pale, lardy. She looked as if she could do with fresh air. What were the two of them doing on top of each other in this stifling kitchen? I suppose, she thought, if Godfrey and I get together we'll have to have the brat to stay for weekends. She'll get on my tits in an hour. I know she will.

'Felicity's been helping me to bake,' Barbara said.

'Great!' Anne smiled at the girl, who simpered back.

Not an hour, she thought, five minutes.

'Why don't you go upstairs and get changed,' Barbara said. Her voice had a pleading quality as if she was worried that the child would argue. Felicity did as she was told but at the door she stopped and pulled a face at her mother's back.

'I'm sorry to have phoned you at home,' Barbara said. 'You must think I'm very foolish.' The words were conventional enough but her voice was desperate. 'Sometimes I wonder if I'm quite sane. I didn't know who else to talk to . . .'

The sun was streaming through the window and the oven was still hot. Anne felt faint, as if she was hearing Barbara in a dream. She tried to compose an appropriate response but the woman went on.

'I've tried to talk about it to Godfrey, but he's been so strange lately. I suppose that's worried me too.'

'In what way strange?'

'Tense, jumpy. He's not sleeping properly. He often gets up and wanders around in the middle of the night. Sometimes he takes the car out. I worry that he's so overwrought that he'll have an accident. He's even started to get angry with Felicity and that's never happened before.'

She seemed close to tears. She filled a kettle at the sink and plugged it in.

'I've suggested that he should go to see a doctor,' Barbara went on. 'How can he function like that? Never sleeping. Hardly eating. But he won't listen. Not a medical problem he says. Things at work which he'll soon have sorted.'

'What about you?' Anne asked. 'How are you sleeping?'

'Not well. I have the feeling that everything's breaking down all around me and despite my effort I'm not going to be able to hold it together.' She managed a smile. 'Godfrey says I'm menopausal. He's probably right. But then men blame everything on hormones, don't they?'

'Have you thought of seeing a doctor?'

'God, no. I hate them.'

Barbara lifted the tray of scones onto a bench and began to wipe down the table with a violent scrubbing motion. Anne wished she hadn't come. She didn't want the responsibility. The woman was cracking up and she didn't want to think that it might be her fault.

'Isn't there someone you can talk to? Family? Friends?'

'Of course not. Why do you think I got in touch with you?' She stopped abruptly. 'I'm sorry. That was rude. I don't have any family and all my friends know Godfrey too.'

She made tea in a white pot. From the fridge she took out a plate of sandwiches covered in cling film and a Tupperware box of small cakes which she arranged on a doily-covered plate. The action seemed to calm her.

'I'll let Felicity have hers on a tray in front of the television,' she said. 'A treat.'

'Perhaps we could have ours outside?' Anne suggested. 'It's so hot.'

'Outside?' The idea seemed to horrify her. 'Oh, I don't think so. All those bugs.' She continued to lay the kitchen table with plates, knives and napkins. Anne moved her chair so the sun wasn't shining directly into her eyes.

'What exactly is worrying you?' she asked gently.

Barbara concentrated on spooning jam into a bowl and seemed not to hear.

'Do you know,' she said. 'After all this, that girl dying and the police at his office asking questions, Godfrey's still determined to go ahead with the quarry.'

'I suppose there's no reason why he shouldn't. Certainly nothing in our report will stop it.'

Barbara stood quite still, the jam spoon poised in mid air over the bowl. She looked up at Anne with something close to despair.

'Neville Furness will have got his way then.'

'I'm sorry,' Anne said, 'but I don't understand what Neville's got to gain from it. I don't understand why he affects you so much.' She paused. 'You're scared of him, aren't you?'

Barbara nodded, but didn't speak. Anne felt like shaking her.

'For Christ's sake, why?'

'Because of what he's doing to Godfrey.'

'You said that when I was last here but it doesn't make sense. Godfrey's the boss. There must be something that you're not telling me.'

Barbara looked at her dumbly.

'Don't bother then,' Anne said crossly. 'It's nothing to do with me anyway.'

'No,' Barbara said. 'I've got to tell someone.'

There was a movement in the hall which Barbara must have seen through the frosted glass door because she stopped. The door opened and Felicity came in. She had changed from her school uniform into pink shorts and a pink T-shirt. She was large for her age and the outfit didn't flatter her.

'I've come for my tea,' she said.

'Of course, darling. I'll put it on a tray. You can have it in front of the television.'

'I want it here with you.'

Barbara's hands, setting the tray, started to shake. 'Not today, darling. I want to talk to my friend.'

'Why can't I talk too?'

'You can,' Barbara said. Anne thought she was showing remarkable restraint. 'But not today. Here, I'll carry it into the living room for you.'

They looked at each other for a moment. Felicity seemed to consider putting up a fight but thought better of it. She scowled and followed her mother from the room.

When Barbara returned to the kitchen the impulse to confide in Anne seemed to have passed. Anne wondered irrationally if the child had some evil influence over her. She poured tea, urged Anne to eat, as if the earlier outburst had never occurred.

'You were talking about Neville,' Anne said. 'I don't understand why he's so committed to the project. What can he hope to get out of it?'

'Money, of course. That's obvious. That's why he left the Fulwells because Godfrey offered him a financial incentive. He's easily bought.' The answer came readily but Anne thought there must be more to it than that.

'Does he need money that much?'

Barbara seemed confused by the question.

'Did you know that he's talking about resigning from his job at Slateburn?' Anne said. She thought Barbara might be pleased by the information. Didn't she want Godfrey out of Neville's clutches? But it seemed to disturb her further.

'No! Where will he go?'

'He's planning to take over Black Law farm.'

'Godfrey never said.'

'Perhaps Godfrey doesn't know.'

'How did you know?'

Anne paused. 'We have a mutual friend.'

Barbara was thrown into panic. 'You won't tell Neville that you've been here? That I asked to see you?'

'Of course not.'

But Barbara was almost hysterical. 'I invited you because I wanted to ask you something specific. Now I don't know that I can. If you're a friend of Neville's.'

'I'm not a friend of Neville's.' God, Anne thought. Let me out of here. The sun had moved so it no longer shone directly into the kitchen but she felt as if she'd been locked up in the room all day.

'I can trust you, can't I?'

'Of course you can.' Apart from the fact that I've slept with your husband and I'd shack up with him tomorrow if he gave me half a chance.

'The three of you working on the report, living together in the cottage. You must have been very close.'

'I don't know,' Anne answered lightly. She had no idea where the conversation was leading. 'When you're living and working on top of each other like that it's important to keep your privacy.'

'But the girl who died, you would have known where she went, who she saw?'

'Not necessarily.'

'Did she ever meet Neville Furness?'

'Not that I knew. Why?'

Barbara didn't answer.

'What are you saying? That Grace and Neville had a relationship?'

Although there was a dishwasher under the bench Barbara left the table and filled the sink with hot, soapy water. Anne waited for a reply but Barbara was giving all her attention to the cups and plates.

Anne stood behind her. 'Do you suspect Neville Furness of killing Grace?'

Barbara rubbed the dishcloth hard inside a cup. Although it must have been clean she didn't lift it onto the draining board. She stood up to her elbows in suds.

'If you have any evidence that's what happened you must go to the police. The detective in charge of the case is a woman, Vera Stanhope. She's very sympathetic. If you like, I'll come with you.'

And how will I ever explain that one away if Godfrey and I get together, she thought.

'Barbara, are you listening to me?'

But if Barbara was listening she wasn't answering. Felicity came in with her tray. Barbara, shaking the soap from her hands, turned round from the sink and said in her normal, mumsy voice, 'Could you show

Mrs Preece out, darling? It's time for her to go and as you can see I'm rather busy.'

Anne didn't put up any resistance. She hoped never to see Barbara Waugh again.

Chapter Fifty

The birthday bash for Olivia Fulwell's youngest child was a cross between a church fête and an old-fashioned street party. As Jeremy had suspected, everyone and his dog was there. Anne wasn't sure of the age of the child or even whether it was a boy or a girl. Whenever she'd seen it, it had been wrapped up in androgynous jumpsuits.

As they prepared to set off for the party Jeremy worked himself into quite a state. Through his antique dealer friend in Morpeth he thought he had found the perfect gift – a jack-in-the-box with a grotesque carved head which sprang out of the box with a squeal. 'Not terribly expensive,' he told Anne, looking up from the floor where he squatted amidst wrapping paper, ribbon and sellotape. 'But classy, don't you think? Better than the modern tat kids get given. Something that'll stand out. But what'll I put on the label? Are you sure you can't remember the brat's name?'

'Positive.' As if she cared anyway. The last thing she wanted to do was to put on a frock and make small talk to the in-bred representatives of the local aristocracy. And it had occurred to her that Barbara and Godrey might have been invited. She wasn't sure how she'd handle that. 'Just put from Jeremy and Anne.'

'I suppose I'll have to,' he said. Then, wistfully, 'Do you think love from Jeremy and Anne would be a bit OTT?' He loved dressing up on occasions like these. His clothes, immaculately pressed, had been laid out on his bed hours before.

The whole event was set up outside. Even the toilets – discreetly signposted – were in the stable block so none of the local riff-raff would actually have to set foot in the house. Anne thought that Olivia had been lucky with the weather. Soon it would break. Pale, sulphurous clouds drifted occasionally across the sun. It was very hot and humid. The forecast had mentioned thunder.

The children sat at a long trestle-table covered with a paper cloth. They wore party hats. There must have been crackers because they all had blowers and whistles which made a noise. All the playgroup were there which seemed terribly democratic, though as far as Anne could tell only two of the parents had been invited. One was a teacher and the other the wife of a tenant farmer. The children ate sausages, crisps and vivid orange jellies made in waxed paper dishes. The parent who was a teacher, a dowdy woman with hair already grey and flat shoes, hovered behind her offspring, muttering occasionally to no one in particular about BSE and E numbers. The child, apparently unused to such unlimited amounts of chemicals and sugar, ate ravenously, oblivious to her mother and the friends who tried to talk to her.

In the middle of the table was the cake, made in the shape of a character from the latest children's cult

TV show and covered in violet icing. The name LIZZY had been picked out in Smarties. So, Anne thought, that solved the mystery of the child's gender.

For the adults there were other trestles with a buffet and a bar. The food was standard catering fare – no doubt Jeremy would be sniffy about it later. Around the park were dotted sideshows which would keep the children entertained so the adults could continue to chat and drink in peace – an inflatable bouncy castle, a roundabout of galloping horses powered by its own generator, a man who swallowed swords and ate fire.

Despite the food Jeremy was enjoying himself enormously. He seemed to know instinctively which guests had money or titles. He homed in on them and camped up shamelessly for their benefit. The jack-in-the-box had been a great success. Lizzy, it was true, had burst into tears when the lid sprang open, but then she had seemed overwrought by the whole proceedings. Olivia had loved it. She had even taken him inside to ask his opinion of a painting which had recently taken her fancy at an auction. He seemed in seventh heaven.

When Olivia was inside with Jeremy, Anne found herself standing next to Robert Fulwell. He was a big man in his fifties. Broken veins in his cheeks gave him a florid appearance as if he spent most of the time in the open air or habitually drank too much. He could have stepped out of a nineteenth-century hunting print. Now though, he stood sipping orange juice, watching the proceedings with a baffled detachment.

'What a lovely party,' Anne said.

He looked her up and down. It was as if he were

making up his mind whether she was worth expending words on. It seemed she was, but not many. 'Livvy's idea.'

He wasn't bad looking in a muscular, heavy sort of way. Perhaps he sensed her appreciation and reciprocated it, because he added, in a more friendly fashion, 'I'd have been happy just to have the family. Livvy brought the boys home from school for the weekend again.'

'That must be nice.'

'Mmm.' He seemed unsure.

'What about the rest of the family?'

He set down his glass and picked up a chicken leg from the paper plate he was holding awkwardly in his other hand. When he bit into it Anne saw that his teeth were surprisingly small and sharp, like a fox's.

'What family?'

'Doesn't Livvy have any aunts or uncles?'

'No one lives locally.'

'What about Edmund?' She wasn't sure, even then, why she provoked the confrontation. Out of boredom perhaps. To make mischief. To spite Jeremy who seemed to find nothing demeaning in playing court jester to a load of nobs.

He returned the chicken to the plate, set it deliberately on the table. For a moment she thought he intended to throw her out physically. He said calmly, 'Who are you?'

'Anne Preece. I live at the Priory. We have met a few times.'

'Do you know Edmund?'

'I knew his daughter.'

'Ah, you're one of the Environmental Impact Assessment team. I remember Livvy mentioned it.'

'You've nothing to worry about,' Anne said. 'We didn't find anything of any significance.'

'I never for a moment thought you would.' He stared out across the park, beyond the chasing children, to the hills. 'I don't care for the idea of the quarry myself, but needs must.' He looked back at her. 'What was she like, the girl?'

'Hardly a girl.'

He shrugged impatiently. 'Time passes, one forgets.'

'She was screwed up,' Anne said. 'She needed help.'

'Like her father then.'

'Did he need help?'

'All the time, but not the sort, I think, that we could give him.'

'Has he come to you for help recently?'

'We'd be the last people he'd come to.'

But Anne heard the note of regret in Robert's voice and she wasn't so sure. Livvy wouldn't have stood for it of course but perhaps Livvy hadn't known. After the violent death of Edmund's daughter, would Robert have been able to turn his brother away?

'The police are looking for him.'

'I know. They've been here. Some woman with a face like a sow. Turning up whenever she feels like it. In the middle of dinner once. As if a man would harm his own daughter. Edmund might have had problems but he'd never do that.'

He was distracted by Arabella, the nanny. She walked past wearing a white silk dress with a lace trim. It looked like a petticoat. There seemed to be no purpose in her movement apart from attracting his attention.

'Look,' he said. 'I ought to go. Must circulate.'

Bloody fool, Anne thought.

To entertain herself, as a sort of game, she began to wonder where Robert might have Edmund holed up. Not in the house. It was big enough to hide an army of younger brothers fleeing from justice, but Robert was frightened of Livvy and wouldn't want her finding out. He could have paid for his brother to stay in a guest house or hotel but recently Vera had gone public about looking for Edmund. His face had appeared on the television news and the front page of national newspapers. Wouldn't one of the other residents have recognized him? Where then?

She considered the accommodation on the estate, discounting immediately the mill house at the mine. Despite the fuss Vera had made Anne couldn't really imagine Edmund camping out there. So far as she knew all the farmers were struggling to maintain their tenancies, so it was unlikely that there was an isolated and empty farmhouse where Edmund was lying low. Perhaps Robert had chosen somewhere closer to home?

At the end of the Avenue was a pair of semi-detached houses. Anne had first realized Grace was loopy when she'd caught her staring at one of them. In one of the houses lived the keeper and his family. Janet, the keeper's wife, was a keen gardener and Anne knew her well enough to exchange a few words in the post office, to borrow the odd seed catalogue. There were two teenage children, the bane of Janet's life, with their loud music and unpleasant friends. But

Anne thought the other semi had been empty since Neville Furness's departure. The new agent was rather grand and had his own place. The houses were ugly but solidly built and there was no reason why Janet and her husband would hear a new neighbour, especially over the perpetual background noise generated in their own place.

Jeremy was in the middle of a circle of elaborately dressed elderly women. They were listening, entranced, to his stories. Occasionally one of them gave a peel of genteel laughter. Anne ignored them.

'Jem, I'm going back. I'm knackered.' The women tittered as if she were part of a double act.

'But you'll miss the fireworks. You don't want me to come?'

'No, of course not. Stay as long as you like.'

'Have you said goodbye to Olivia?'

'She's busy. I thought you could do that for me.'

'Sure.' He was delighted to have the excuse to speak to Livvy again. 'Sure.'

Anne slipped away from the crowd without being noticed. The children had finished tea and were running from one stall to another with a purposeless frenzy. They had become fractious and overexcited. On the bouncy castle boys were fighting, entangled together in a rolling ball of arms and legs, the smallest in tears. Still the adults took no notice, only shouting to make themselves heard above the noise.

Anne walked down the Avenue between the line of trees. The voices and the fairground organ faded. It was very still. Tiny thunderflies settled on her shoulders and her hair.

For once the keeper's house was quiet. Presumably

403

the family had been invited to the party. Anne looked both ways down the Avenue. There were no cars, no people. She opened the gate of the empty house and went into the garden. There were drawn curtains at the windows so she couldn't see in. She tried to remember if they'd been like that when she'd been standing here with Grace. She knocked on the front door. There was no answer and when she pushed it, it was locked. She walked round to the back of the house, to the kitchen door.

There were blinds at the kitchen window. Outside the kitchen door was a black plastic dustbin. She lifted the lid and saw empty cans of soup and beans, squashed cartons of orange and milk, beer tins. They smelled, but not as if they'd been there for months.

At the Hall they had started to let off fireworks. A rocket cracked and exploded above her head. She turned the handle of the door and pushed. It opened and she went in.

Chapter Fifty-One

Rachael could hear the fireworks from Baikie's. Although it was still light she could see the coloured stars exploding above the horizon. She had taken a mug of tea outside because the cottage seemed so hot and airless and there was something unsettling about the boxes and bags stacked in piles in the living room.

Once Constance Baikie had held state there. As cut off from the rest of the world as a ship in the middle of the ocean, she had looked on as people, dressed up in smart clothes, laughed and danced to the wind-up gramophone. Many of the players in the present drama had been present at those parties – Robert Fulwell, Neville Furness, Vera Stanhope. Now the room looked like a transit camp. The next day the cottage would be locked up, the key replaced under the stone urn and it would remain damp and empty until a group of undergraduates turned up in the summer.

Edie was restless too. She would have gone back to Kimmerston that night, but Vera and Joe Ashworth had invited themselves to the cottage for a farewell drink and she didn't want to miss out. And then she wanted to have things out with Rachael. She'd kept her word and written down the story of Rachael's father.

'It'll be an anticlimax,' she said again as she handed

over the sheets of paper, covered with round, even writing. It had become her justification for not passing on the information earlier – that it was a story so uninteresting that it hardly merited telling. 'If you imagine your father as an Edmund Fulwell, a drunken adventurer travelling the world in search of sensation, you'll be disappointed.' The last line, of course, had been rehearsed.

Rachael refused to read it while Edie was there, hovering, waiting for a reaction, so she set it on the grass next to her mug and lay back in the deckchair to watch the fireworks, pale flares in an increasingly overcast sky. As soon as Edie went inside she picked the paper up.

She only had time to read the first line – *I met your father on April Fool's Day* – when she was interrupted by Vera Stanhope and Joe Ashworth. Vera was wearing a dress of the sort of material turned into stretch settee covers and advertised in the Sunday papers. Joe looked as if he were there on sufferance. He followed behind and carried a wicker picnic basket. They had come round the outside of the cottage straight into the garden.

Inside the basket was a plaid rug which Joe spread on the grass for Vera to sit on, a number of plates covered in tin foil and bottle of champagne.

'Is there something to celebrate?' Rachael asked. Vera was in a peculiarly jolly mood and Rachael wondered even if there had been an arrest, if Vera had met the deadline she had set herself. She returned the sheets of paper, face down, on the grass. She didn't resent the interruption, realizing with surprise that she even felt relieved.

'Connie always drank champagne,' Vera said. 'It seems right to honour the tradition.' She added wickedly, 'And Joe's wife has made us a cake. Not quite the same, but a nice thought.'

'Sal makes a lovely chocolate sponge,' Joe said, seeming not to realize that he was being got at. Or too laid back to care.

'She'll be glad to have you home a bit more often.' Edie came out through the French windows with glasses, another bottle of wine and bags of crisps on a wonky tin tray.

'She'll be lucky,' Vera said. 'Just because you lot aren't here doesn't mean we won't be. She'll still have plenty of time for her baking.'

'I wonder what Miss Baikie would make of all this.' Rachael got up to move the deckchair to a more upright position.

'The murder? She'd have loved every minute. She loved a drama.' Vera seemed lost in thought. Rachael expected another reminiscence of visits with her father but none came. 'Where's Mrs Preece?'

'There's a party at the Hall.'

'Hardly decent.' Joe was shocked. 'The lass hasn't long been buried.'

'The upper classes don't go in much for decency,' Vera said. 'Well, we'll not wait for her or this bottle'll get warm. You do the honours.' She winked at the other two. 'Being as you're the only man.'

But he seemed dubious. 'I've never opened champagne before. Not the real stuff.'

'Give it here then. Don't want you spilling it.' She had the bottle between her legs, had begun to turn it carefully, when her mobile phone rang.

'Bugger it,' she said. 'Get that for me, Joe.'

He took the phone from her cardigan pocket and flipped it open. After the first words he stood up and took it inside. Vera apparently felt no curiosity. She opened the champagne with a dull pop and poured it into the glasses. 'Just a splash for Joe,' she said. 'He'll be driving.'

Rachael, sipping, looked at the sergeant inside the house, talking earnestly. She had no intimation of tragedy as she had before Grace's death. She thought he was probably talking to his wife. They were discussing what time he could reasonably expect to get home. She was passing on news of the little boy. He snapped the phone shut and came to the French windows.

'Can I have a word, ma'am?'

'What's up with you?' Vera was sitting on the rug, legs apart, skirt pulled above her knees. The glass was already empty. 'Relax, man, I'm not ready to go yet.'

'It's not that.'

'Well, what is it? Spit it out.'

He hesitated, looked at Rachael and Edie. 'There was a 999 call from Holme Park.'

'And?' She saw him looking at the other women. 'For God's sake, man, whatever it is they'll find out sooner or later.'

'A body.'

'Who?'

'No positive ID.'

She was on her feet looking down at Rachael. 'You'll have to wait,' she said. 'That's the hardest thing of all. As soon as I find out what's going on I'll send someone tell you. I promise. I'll leave Joe here until someone

can relieve him. Or do you want to go back to Kimmerston?'

'No,' Rachael said. 'We'll wait.'

'Inside then. Just in case.'

Rachael sat in Constance Baikie's chair, surrounded by
black bin bags and read about her father. At one time
she would have thought it the most important thing in
her life. Now it was a distraction and she had to force
herself to concentrate. It began to rain – large heavy
drops which rattled like shingle against the window.
She saw that they'd left the rug on the grass but Joe
wouldn't let her outside to bring it in.

PART THREE

Vera

Chapter Fifty-Two

Vera Stanhope sat on the plaid rug on the grass in front
of Baikie's, gulped champagne and remembered quite
clearly the last time she had seen Constance Baikie
alive. She was tempted to recount the event to Rachael
and Edie because she knew they liked to hear her
stories. Perhaps the taste in her mouth brought the
scene back so vividly because they had been drinking
champagne that day too. Though Constance was so ill
that they had had to hold the glass for her. They had
propped her up on the sofa with pillows but by then
she was so large that her flesh spread, jelly-like, over
the edge of it and she looked in danger of overbal-
ancing and falling off. Vera had come to the cottage
with her father. She had driven him in her car because
by that time he was getting on too. The week before
she had been working nights and she was exhausted.
A day with her father always sapped her energy but
he had been determined to make the trip and even
then, towards the end of his life, he could impose his
will on her. Besides, she didn't want him to visit Connie
on his own. It wasn't only that she was concerned for
his safety, she was worried about what he might get
up to.

Because her father had been an addict. She hadn't

explained that to the women when she told stories about her childhood in the hills. She hadn't described her growing understanding of what her father was really after when he took her walking, when he pointed out the nests of skylarks and wheatears, made her watch the peregrine swooping on its prey. Her father had been an inveterate and compulsive stealer of birds' eggs. Not in the way that a schoolchild might be. For him it was an obsession and a business. It had funded his retirement. She had come to realize, as a child, that she was there as a cover. At dangerous sites, protected by wardens and electric fences, he had even sent her in to steal the eggs.

It wouldn't have done for an ambitious young detective to see her father in court in contravention of the Wildlife and Countryside Act so she never liked him going into the hills on his own. He swore he had given up collecting but she'd never believed a word he said. Addicts always lied. And even if it was true on his own account, Connie Baikie had always been able to twist him round her little finger. She shared his compulsion. She might be too old and sick to get into mischief now but Hector, Vera's father, was devoted and would have done anything for the old woman.

The champagne had been his idea. 'A treat for the old girl,' he had said. Vera had thought he knew Connie was dying and especially wanted to keep her sweet because he had an eye on her collection. His own was extensive enough. It was kept in locked mahogany cases, each egg held safely in a nest of cotton wool in the spare room, hidden inside an ugly mahogany wardrobe. Vera was supposed not to know about this secret, though most nights he'd shut himself into the room like a dirty old man with a hoard of porn.

Connie's collection he had leered at and salivated over openly since Vera was a child. Even after the Wildlife Act it had been kept in full view. Occasionally Connie saw Vera looking at the display cabinets.

'They're quite legal,' she'd say, coughing and panting to get out the words, defying Vera to contradict her. 'Collected before the Act was passed.'

Vera, though, had seen new trays added and would have investigated the origins of the collection if it hadn't been for the Hector connection. Better not to know.

So they had been in Baikie's, drinking champagne, silently pondering over the distribution of Connie's collection after death when there had been an intrusion, a small drama which had perked up the old girl no end. According to Hector the incident had probably kept her going for several extra weeks.

A woman had run into the garden and banged on the French windows. This wasn't unusual in itself. Walkers occasionally violated Connie's privacy, asking for water, directions, even to use the lavatory. Some-times Connie was gracious, usually she sent them away with a flea in their ear. But this woman was frantic. She banged on the door, hammering with her fist so Vera was afraid she'd break the glass and cut herself.

It was spring. There had been deep snow that year, recently melted, so the burn was very full and fast flowing. Vera could hear the noise of the flood water even above the woman's hysterical words as she opened the door.

From her position on the sofa Connie couldn't quite

see into the garden and, afraid of missing out on the excitement, ordered Vera to bring the visitor into the room. Stricken, bored, she smelled entertainment. The woman was in her early thirties and seemed unsuitably kitted out for a walk in the hills. She wore make-up, leggings, white shoes with a heel. Her words tumbled out in a senseless flow.

'What is the matter, my dear?' Connie wheezed, oozing concern. 'This lady's a police officer. I'm sure she'll be able to help.'

At that the woman took Vera by the arm and dragged her outside to join the search for her baby. That was what the scene was about – a lost child. They had driven out from Kimmerston to see the little lambs. The woman whose name was Bev thought they were really cute and Gary, the new man in her life, had suggested making a day of it. They'd parked on the track just before the gate into the Black Law farmyard and had a picnic. There was a cold wind so they'd stayed in the car where the sun was lovely. They'd let Lee out to play. What harm could he come to, out here in the country? It wasn't like the town with perverts and madmen lurking behind every lamp-post. Was it?

They must have fallen asleep, Bev said. Vera, noting the tousled appearance, thought this was a euphemism for something more energetic. Then the next time they looked, Lee had disappeared.

Vera walked back with Bev to the car, reassuring her all the time that by then the two-year-old would surely have turned up again. But at the car there was no sign of him. Gary seemed a pleasant lad, genuinely distraught. He was very young. In the street he could have passed for Lee's older brother rather than a potential stepfather.

'I've shouted myself hoarse,' he said. 'And hit the horn. I don't know what else to do.'

Vera left them there, went back to Black Law and got Dougie to phone for a search party. She and Dougie walked the hill until help arrived. When she returned to Baikie's Connie insisted on having everything described to her. The boy, the boyfriend, the mother's tears. She and Hector seemed to have reached an understanding in Vera's absence, because a few days later the collection of raptors' eggs were delivered to the house in Kimmerston. They joined the stock of trays in the spare-room wardrobe. The day after her father died Vera burnt them all, without opening the cases to look, on a huge pyre in the garden, along with his notebooks.

There was no happy ending to the story of the missing toddler. Indeed there was no ending at all because the boy was never found and no body was ever recovered. There was a distressing and bizarre postscript.

A gamekeeper, apparently with an axe to grind, wrote to the local paper suggesting that Lee might have been carried off by a goshawk and fed to its young. Goshawks were vicious and dangerous and should be culled, he said. Woolly-minded conservationists should let keepers get on with their jobs.

The letter was so crazy that Vera suspected Connie might be behind it. It was the sort of joke she would have loved and she could have carried it out with Hector's help. Beverly latched onto the explanation, however, and fuelled speculation by remembering suddenly that a large powerful bird *had* been hovering overhead while Lee was playing. The national press took up the story and had a field day. The case became the English equivalent of the Australian dingo story. Beverly made enough money from photos and interviews to buy Gary a new car and take him on holiday to Cyprus.

Vera thought the little boy must have wandered off towards the burn while the adults were having it away in the car, and had been swept away by the flood water. It was the only sensible explanation. Now, drinking champagne on a sultry afternoon in midsummer, she thought it was quite a coincidence. Two deaths – because the boy must surely have died – at almost the same spot so many years apart.

She thought Rachael might be entertained by the story of the goshawk and the gamekeeper but never got a chance to tell it, because Joe Ashworth came out of the house with a serious look on his face and told them about the second murder. Beating her story, she had to admit, into a cocked hat.

Chapter Fifty-Three

In the car Vera was on the radio shrieking like a mad-woman, swearing, trying to get some fix on what was going on. No one was available to talk to her. No one who knew. It wasn't supposed to have happened like this. She'd hoped the killer would come back. She couldn't see any other way forward. But to Baikie's. To her own territory. Not in Langholme.

She veered off the road from Langholme into the Avenue and saw Anne Preece, sitting on the grass bank by the side of the lane, a grey blanket around her shoulders, a mug clasped in both her hands. It was raining and Anne's hair was lank and straight. She stared ahead of her. Vera thought she looked like a vagrant after the arrival of the soup run.

A young policeman blocked her path, recognized her and let her pass. She pulled in beside Anne, wound down the window and shouted, 'What the shit have you been up to?' Relief gave an edge of anger to her voice.

The policeman, confused, said, 'This is Mrs Preece. She found the body.'

Vera got out of the car. 'We have met.'

She ignored the policeman and sat on the grass. All her questions were directed to Anne. 'Well? I thought it was a kiddie's birthday party. I didn't think you could get up to much here.'

Anne turned her head to look up towards the house. The police had blocked the road. Cars were backed up as far as the drive and there was chaos and confusion as they tried to turn. Some people had got out of their vehicles and were gawping.

'Do you want to get into the car?' Vera asked gently.

'No.' Anne shook her head violently. 'If you don't mind, I need the air.'

'Where's your husband?'

'God knows. Probably still drinking champagne and playing to the gallery.'

'What happened?'

'I was bored. It wasn't my thing. Precocious brats and the kids not much nicer.'

Vera smiled appreciatively, nodded encouragement.

'I'd been talking to Robert. About his family. He asked about Grace and then said something about her being like her father. Their both needing help. As if he'd seen Edmund recently. So I wondered . . .'

'If he'd felt guilty enough to give him the help he needed?'

'Something like that. And I knew this house had been empty since Neville Furness left it. I mean, I didn't set out to interfere but it was on my way home and I was curious.'

'You should have told me,' Vera said. 'But I'd probably have done the same thing myself.'

'The kitchen door was unlocked.'

'Where was he?'

'In the living room, lying on the settee. At first I

thought he was just drunk. There was an empty whisky bottle on the coffee table. But drunk people make lots of noises when they're sleeping, don't they? He wasn't snoring. And he looked peaceful. I mean there wasn't any blood. Do you think he killed himself?' Before Vera could answer she added, 'I suppose it was Edmund? He looked the right sort of age but I've never met him.'

Vera looked up at the policeman who nodded.

'The brother gave a positive ID.'

'Was there anyone else in the house?' Vera asked.

'No! At least I didn't see or hear anyone. I didn't go upstairs.'

'What did you do?'

'Got out as soon as I could. I know it was stupid but I couldn't face looking at him.'

'Was there a phone in the house?'

'I didn't stop to check. I thought about it when I was outside but I couldn't go back in. I couldn't decide what would be best. I suppose it was the shock. My brain seemed to work so slowly. I banged on the door of the next house but no one was in. I didn't want to go back to the Hall to phone you. All those people drinking and laughing. So I ran to the phone box in the village and dialled 999. Then I came back here to wait.'

'What would you like to do now? We can find your husband. Take you home.'

'Oh God. I couldn't face Jeremy. Can't I go back to Baikie's? Spend the last night there as I planned?'

'I don't see why not. If you can put up with Edie fussing over you. She and Rachael are still there with Joe Ashworth. I'll get someone to give you a lift.' Vera started away then turned back. 'Did you see anyone when you went into Langholme to use the phone?'

'Why? Don't you believe me?'

'It's not that. Did you see any strangers? Anything unusual?'

Anne shook her head.

'And when you were waiting here for us to arrive?'

'A few cars passed. People leaving the party early. Mostly with kids. But not many. The fireworks had just started.'

Vera was just about to get back into her car. Then she looked at the blocked Avenue and thought she'd be better off walking.

The young policeman still stood outside the ordinary, red-brick house.

'Do you want to go in?'

'No,' she said. 'I'll keep my big feet out until the experts have finished. I'll get more out of the living.'

She interrupted Robert and Livvy Fulwell in the middle of a row. The party was almost over. A few hardened drinkers stood under a makeshift canopy formed by the roof of the partially deflated bouncy castle. They had a bottle of wine which they passed between them. The rain was already collecting in pools on the compacted ground and the staff putting down the trestles and stacking the chairs weren't happy in their work.

Nobody stopped Vera as she approached the house and she'd been there often enough to find her way around. Robert and Livvy were in the kitchen. She heard them before she saw them.

'How could you have been so fucking stupid!' Livvy

screamed. 'He was trouble. He'd always been trouble. Your mother knew that.'

'I don't think this is the time to talk like that. I think it's inappropriate, actually.' Robert was dogged but slightly defensive. 'My brother's dead, for Christ's sake. Most people might think that deserved a little sympathy.'

'Oh, come off it.' Vera had come to the open door and could see Livvy leaning back in her chair, a gesture of incredulity, as she spoke.

'He was my brother. I couldn't turn him away.'

Livvy thrust her face towards her husband's. 'Can't you see what you've done? So far we've managed to distance ourselves from that affair on the hill. But now your stupid brother's killed himself in one of our cottages. The press will be all over the place. Can't you imagine the effect that'll have on us? On the boys?'

Vera stepped forward. 'We don't know that he killed himself. Not yet. Not unless you know something I don't.'

Livvy swung round. For one glorious moment Vera thought she'd swear at her too, but she managed to restrain herself. 'Inspector Stanhope. What are you saying?'

'Nothing. Just that I don't know what happened. Can't jump to any conclusions. It might have been natural causes.'

'Is that likely?' Livvy was clutching at straws. Vera let her. She shrugged. 'He was a heavy drinker,' she said.

'Yes.' Livvy was almost composed. 'So I understand.' She stood up, scraping the chair on the quarry-tile floor. 'We were just about to have some tea, Inspector. Would you like some?'

Wine would go down a treat, Vera thought, if you've got any left. But she feigned gratitude. 'Aye,' she said, emphasizing the accent, 'tea would be champion.'

Livvy moved the kettle onto the hot plate of the Aga. It hissed.

'Don't tell me you do it yourself.' Vera went on in mock astonishment. 'I thought a place like this, there'd be servants.'

Livvy looked at her, not quite sure if she was being serious, and decided a non-committal reply would be safest.

'Oh, we're all part of a team here. Everyone's outside, clearing up. We just muck in.'

'Very nice.' Vera stretched her legs in front of her. There were dried splashes of mud from when she'd crossed the lawn. 'This must be very upsetting for you, Mr Fulwell. First your niece, then your brother and all a spit from where you live.'

'It is.' He shot a glance of recrimination at Livvy, but she took no notice.

'When did you last see your brother alive?'

'This morning.'

'You knew he was holed up there then?'

'Yes. I should have told you. Perhaps if I had . . . But I couldn't turn him away. Not after what had happened to his daughter.'

'What time did you see him?'

'I went down there twice. At ten o'clock I took him some food. Then I went back at about eleven thirty.'

'Why? Wasn't that risky? If you'd wanted to keep his

424

whereabouts secret I'd have thought you'd keep visits to a minimum.'

'It wasn't so risky during the day. The family who live next door are generally out then. But yes, I tried not to go too often. It wasn't just that I was worried I'd be seen. I didn't know what to say to him.'

'So why twice today?'

'He phoned me. Here. It was crazy. He said he was desperate for a drink. He even talked about going into the village to the pub. I thought he was making a terrible mistake hiding out from you and all along I was trying to persuade him to give himself up. But the last thing I wanted was for him to come up to the house and make a scene today.'

I bet you didn't, Vera thought. The child bride would have gone ape.

'So you took him a bottle of whisky.'

'Yes. I don't know why he was suddenly so agitated. He'd been calm until then. I'd almost talked him round.'

'You said he phoned. You'd left the phone connected?'

'Yes.'

'Could he have spoken to someone? Would that explain his changed mood?'

'He wouldn't have phoned out. At the end he was paranoid. He wouldn't have told anyone else where he was.'

Livvy set the teapot violently on the table.

'Look,' she said. 'He was mad. Mentally disturbed. Up and down like a yo-yo. That's why Robert's mother couldn't handle him. That's why he ended up being shut in St Nick's.'

Vera ignored her. 'Didn't he give you any indication why he was suddenly so upset?' she asked Robert.

'He wasn't terribly coherent and to be honest I didn't really want to know. I mean, I thought I'd done my bit by giving him a place to stay. There was lots of talk about betrayal. As I said, it verged on the paranoid.'

'Just because you're paranoid doesn't mean they're not out to get you.' Vera bared her teeth. No one else smiled. She watched Livvy pour tea into blue cups. 'You can leave mine in the pot a bit longer, pet. I like to taste what I'm drinking. Has he been staying here since he left the restaurant?'

'Good God, no.' Robert was horrified. 'I wouldn't have been able to stand the strain.'

'When then?'

'He went to Nancy Deakin's first. You asked me about her once before. I don't know exactly what made him bolt there. Something put the wind up him. When his daughter's body was first found he seemed content to stay at the restaurant.'

'You were in touch then?'

'Of course.' Robert was gruffly embarrassed. 'To offer condolences. That sort of thing. I thought he was bearing up very well.'

'Had you been in regular contact?'

'No, but at a time like that, one has to make an effort.'

'Why did he leave Nancy's?'

'The two women who'd been working with Grace went round there. They were asking questions. He thought you'd sent them, so he got in touch with me.'

'Tut, tut,' Vera said. 'Paranoia indeed. How did you get him here?'

'I picked him up in the car late one night. Nobody saw.'

'And you saw it as a short-term measure until you could persuade him to talk to us?'

'Exactly that. Yes.'

'Who knew you were helping him?'

'Nancy Deakin. I didn't tell anyone else. Not even Livvy. I couldn't have her involved.'

Haddaway and shite, Vera thought. You're scared of her.

'Could anyone have found out he was there by chance?'

'I don't know how. Everyone on the estate knew the house was empty. He wouldn't have opened the door to a salesman or visitor.' Robert paused. 'Look. There's something I want to say. I wouldn't have been prepared to help him if I'd thought he'd killed his daughter. If that's what you think then you've got it all wrong. He was devastated. He talked about it being his fault, but that didn't mean he'd strangled her. He said he should have protected her. He'd never been much of a father. And he was frightened. That's why he was in such a state this morning.'

'But the kitchen door was open. If it turns out he was killed he let his murderer in.'

'I don't care.' In the face of these two fierce women Robert had become stubborn. 'I might not have seen much of him recently but we were brothers. We grew up together and I tell you he was scared.'

Chapter Fifty-Four

It was late by the time Vera got back to Baikie's but she thought the women would still be up. They'd want to know what had happened. Not that she'd have had much to tell them even if she'd been prepared to pass the information on. The pathologist was an old friend, more willing than most of them to commit himself after a first inspection, but still he'd been tentative.

She'd caught him as he came out of the cottage on his way to his car and they stood sheltering under his large black umbrella.

'There's nothing obvious,' he said. 'He wasn't stabbed and he wasn't strangled.'

'Not like the daughter then.'

'No.'

'But you must have some idea.'

'Most likely scenario at the moment? That he'd drunk himself insensible.'

'And that killed him?'

'It made things easier for the murderer.'

'You think it was murder?'

'That's what I'm working towards.' He paused. 'My intuition. If you believe in such things.'

'I believe in yours.'

'I wouldn't be surprised to find that he'd been suffocated, smothered. You do realize I'm just thinking aloud at this stage?'

'How?'

'I'm not a clairvoyant.' But despite the words he didn't sound irritated. He stood, patiently, with the rain drumming on the umbrella. Vera thought, He's got nothing to go home to either. He asked, 'Have you been inside?'

'Not yet.'

'The house was partly furnished. Apparently it was let like that to employees. There's a three-piece suite with a few scatter cushions. One of the cushions could have done it. But there's no sign of struggle. He'd hardly have known what was happening.'

'Thanks,' she said. 'And the time of death?'

'I never like to commit myself on that.'

'I know.'

'After midday, before five o'clock. I really can't be more specific. It's only a guess.'

'Understood.'

He was a thin man in his sixties, always dark-suited and gently spoken, reassuring, like a family undertaker. He had once told Vera that he was an elder in a small Presbyterian church. So far as she knew that was the nearest he had to family. Would it be enough for him when he retired?

He walked her to her car, holding the umbrella over her, though she was already wet from her walk from the house and the drips must be going down his neck.

'I'll be in touch as soon as there's anything definite.'

'I know,' she said. Her hand brushed his as she fumbled in her bag for her keys.

As she had expected there was a light still on in Baikie's. No one had bothered to draw the curtains and she felt a flash of anger at Joe Ashworth or whoever had replaced him. The women were sitting targets like that for anyone lurking in the garden or on the hill beyond. Then she thought, but that's what I made them. That's what my strategy boiled down to in the end.

She had been so convinced that she'd been right. She'd known that the murder had something to do with the development for the quarry. She'd felt it in her bones. She'd grown up with this countryside, with people who were passionate about it and she'd thought she'd understood. She'd seen the murderer as a nutter with a strange obsession about this landscape or these women, or both. She'd thought that if they'd stayed put eventually he would come back. He wouldn't be able to resist it. But obviously she'd been wrong. She'd have to start again with an open mind. That meant work. More than she knew if she could handle.

She parked her car in the yard and went in through the kitchen. Her sandals were squelching wet so she took them off at the door and went on, leaving damp footprints on the lino. The sound of rain on the roof and windows must have drowned out the noise of her car because she surprised them. They were sitting at the table playing cards. Joe Ashworth had been replaced by a constable in uniform and he held a hand too. They turned, fixed for a moment, in the soft light of the standard lamp.

Vera crossed the room and drew the curtains over the French windows.

'That's a lot more cosy,' she said. Then: 'Is there any of that booze left? I could murder a Scotch.'

Edie poured some into a tumbler.

'Mrs Preece'll have told you what happened.'

'That Edmund's dead,' Rachael said. 'Is it all over then? He killed Grace because she wouldn't lie for him to stop the quarry, and now he's killed himself.'

'Too early to say.'

Whatever the pathologist had told her had been in confidence. She might be a gabby cow who broke more rules than she kept but that information wasn't to be passed on.

'But he couldn't have been murdered?'

They've been celebrating, Vera thought. Not with a great fuss because that wouldn't be very nice with two people dead. But they really think it's all over. Case closed. No more looking over their shoulders on the hill or in their mirrors on the road.

'Look,' she said. 'It's impossible to tell until the doctor's done all his tests. I have to assume it's a suspicious death until I hear otherwise. If I didn't I'd waste hours, even days of an investigation. So there'll be questions to ask. And no doubt you've got questions too.'

'What was he doing here?' Edie asked.

'Hiding out, though we're not sure why. We didn't really consider him as a suspect until he disappeared.'

'Guilt perhaps,' Edie said. 'If he'd killed his daughter.'

'Perhaps.' Vera looked at Anne and Rachael. She wanted them to lighten up. She felt responsible for bringing their celebration to an end. 'He was at Nancy Deakin's when you went there to talk to her.'

'No!' She had succeeded. They were amused by the old lady's duplicity. 'He must have been in the bedroom all the time. No wonder she didn't want us to go upstairs.'

'I heard a noise but I thought it was the budgie.'

'Is that why he moved on to the estate?' Rachael asked. 'Because we went to Nancy's?'

'Probably.'

'So we might have provoked his death. At least he had someone to keep an eye on him there.'

'It's not your fault,' Vera said. 'I asked you to go.' She leant across the table. They had discarded their cards which lay on the table as down-turned fans. 'Now look. I've got to carry on as if Edmund was murdered. It doesn't mean he was but that's the assumption I've got to make. Do you understand?'

They nodded.

'When Rachael suggested that Bella and Edmund might have known each other, that they might have been in hospital at the same time, I didn't take it seriously because it didn't seem relevant. Grace was the victim. Edmund had hardly had any contact with her. But now it could be more important. Perhaps Rachael was right all along. Can you remember anything Bella said which could have linked them?'

'No. How could I? I didn't even know she'd been in hospital until after her suicide.'

'I mean more recently. Anything to suggest Bella and Edmund kept in touch?'

'No, she never mentioned friends. Apart from people in Langholme who'd known Dougie for years and she wasn't close to any of them.'

'But she must have left the farm sometimes.'

'She went to Kimmerston on Wednesdays. Market day. That was when she did all the shopping. And she always had lunch out. Her little treat. Social services sent someone to sit with Dougie while she was away.'

'Where did she go for lunch when she was in town?'

'I don't know. I suppose the White Hart, like all the other farmers.'

Vera had a picture of Bella and Edmund sitting in the gloomy dining room. Surely they wouldn't have met there. Not if Bella valued her privacy. Not where they could have been seen by any of Dougie's farming friends.

'No.' Rachael interrupted her thoughts. 'There's a coffee shop in the precinct where she went. I remember her coming back one day when I was staying at Baikie's. She came in for some tea and a chat but wouldn't have a biscuit. She said she'd had the biggest meringue in the world. The coffee shop did the best she'd ever tasted.' Rachael stopped. 'This seems so trivial.'

'That's what most of my job is. Trivia. Chat and gossip. That's why I'm so bloody good at it.' It came out confidently enough but to Vera it sounded hollow. 'Tell me again what happened when you last went to see Charlie Noble.'

'We told you.'

'OK. I wasn't listening properly. It didn't seem important. Edie?'

'Bella had phoned a week before she died and got through to Charlie's wife, Louise. Louise promised to tell Charles that she'd been in touch but she didn't until much later, until after our first visit. Bella said that she'd phone back.'

433

'But they never heard from her again?'

'That's what they said.'

'Do you think they might be lying?'

'I don't know. I got the impression that Louise hadn't wanted Charlie to tell me about the call. Perhaps they both regretted it. Certainly they weren't very forthcoming. And it seems strange that Bella didn't phone back.'

Anne had been listening in silence. She stood up and seemed very thin and gaunt lit below by the lamp. Shadows fell over her face, lengthening her forehead.

'I'm sorry,' she said. 'I'm so tired. I'll have to go to bed.'

'Of course!'

'I probably won't see you tomorrow. I'm leaving early.'

'I'll be in touch,' Vera said.

'More questions?'

'Oh, there are always more questions. And you two will be going tomorrow too,' Vera said after Anne had left the room, after they'd heard her footsteps on the bare stairs. 'This place will be empty. Nothing left but Connie's ghost.' She paused awkwardly, tried to phrase her question to Rachael delicately, then decided that bluff and hearty was more her style and got to the point quicker anyway. 'Are you planning to see Mr Furness again?'

'Why?'

'Because you should know I'll be asking him more questions too.'

'What has he got to do with Edmund's death?'

'Nothing. Probably. Except that he used to live in

that house. And according to Robert Fulwell no one can remember him handing back his keys.'

There was a silence. 'We're kidding ourselves, aren't we?' Rachael said 'Edmund was murdered.'

Vera didn't answer.

Chapter Fifty-Five

Vera woke early, just before the first Edinburgh train started to growl in the distance. She waited until it had screamed past, rattling the sash windows in her bedroom, before she got up. The train hadn't woken her. She'd grown up with the trains, could remember steam, trolleys of milk churns on the platform, wicker baskets of racing pigeons delivered by old men in tweed caps.

Vera didn't know why Hector had bought this house by the railway line soon after she was born. She would never have asked him. The junction, closed long ago, had served a hamlet half a mile away and nearby farms. Their house, grey stone, small windowed, stood end on to the track. She supposed it had suited him. It was near enough to the hills for his forays after birds' eggs and then, while the trains still stopped, it was only a twenty-minute ride away from Kimmerston where he taught in the grammar school. He was solitary by nature. She couldn't imagine him on a smart new estate making conversation about the mortgage rate or the latest model of Vauxhall.

It had occurred to her as an adult that the Gregorys had attracted him there. Mr Gregory had been the stationmaster and his wife looked after Vera until she was old enough to let herself in from school and have her dad's tea ready by the time his train got in. It was possible that some arrangement had been made with Mrs Gregory before they moved. Nothing was said but Vera fancied that Mr Gregory could have been one of the brotherhood of egg collectors. He had that pedantic, meticulous way about him. And certainly Hector hadn't minded being by the railway line. She'd caught him writing down train numbers in one of his bird-watching notebooks.

Vera had liked Mrs Gregory. She was a soft, motherly woman whose children had all grown up and married. Even when Hector had stopped paying Mrs Gregory to look after her, Vera had treated the Station House as a second home. When the junction was closed and the Gregorys had moved away she'd cried, though she'd never let Hector see.

She got out of bed and opened the curtains. Her room faced away from the track over a low meadow towards the hills. Now the grass was long and mixed with buttercups and clover. The rain had stopped but everything was wet, gleaming. She looked at her watch. Six o'clock. Too early to phone Ashworth. Just.

Since the Gregorys had moved the Station House had changed hands several times. Recently a couple in their forties, vaguely New Age in character, had taken over. They'd bought the field on the other side of the lane and grew vegetables and kept animals. From her window Vera could see a tethered goat and a wire mesh chicken run. The cockerel crowed. Perhaps that was what had wakened her.

She lay in the bath and planned her day. If she hadn't been used to it the room would have depressed her. The bath had chipped and scaled enamel. The walls were white tile with greying cement. There were dead flies trapped in the frosted glass bowl which covered the light bulb. Apart from burning the contents of the spare-room wardrobe she hadn't made any changes in the house since her father's death. Plans but no changes.

By the time she was dressed it was ten to seven and she thought, Bugger it. If he's not awake by now he ought to be.

Joe Ashworth answered immediately, but with the shocked voice of someone startled in the middle of a dream.

'Didn't wake you, did I?' she said.

'Yes.' He was short. It wasn't like him to be bad-tempered.

'I thought babies got up early.'

'He's been awake all night with his teeth. We've only just got him back down.'

'Sorry,' she said. Meaning it even if it didn't sound as if she did.

'What can I do for you?'

'There are a couple of things I want to sort out this morning. Can you get over to Holme Park? Start putting together a list of the people who were there yesterday afternoon. Livvy Fulwell should have one. See if there are any names we recognize.'

'Like who?'

'Anyone connected with the quarry. Godfrey Waugh, Peter Kemp, Neville Furness. They were business acquaintances of the Fulwells. It's possible they got an invite.'

'Wouldn't Mrs Preece have mentioned seeing them?'

'I didn't ask. She was very shocked still. And there was quite a crowd milling around. She might not even have noticed.'

'Can I ask what you'll be doing?'

'Me? I'll be going out for coffee.'

The night before she'd arranged for an officer to visit Rod Owen. He'd supported Edmund more than the family and deserved to be told personally about his death. With what she thought of as great consideration she waited until after she'd finished her Shredded Wheat before phoning him. She presumed that restaurateurs kept late hours.

When he answered, however, he sounded brisk, businesslike. 'The Harbour Lights.'

She started to give her name but he seemed to recognize her voice and broke in. 'Any news?'

'Not yet. A question though. Did Edmund have a regular day off?'

'Yes. Right from the beginning. Since he started working here again after leaving hospital. He didn't have much routine in his existence but it was something he hung on to. A sort of superstition I think.'

'What day was that?'

'Wednesday.'

'Do you know what he did?'

'Not specifically but he always went out. Even if he'd been on a bit of a bender he usually managed to spruce himself up, have a shave. He'd leave the flat by about ten thirty.'

'But he worked for you all those years and never told you where he went?'

'I didn't ask. None of my business. It could have been some sort of therapy, couldn't it? Personal.'

'It must have been somewhere local because Edmund didn't drive. If it was therapy, after care, would that have been held in St Nick's?'

'He definitely didn't go to the hospital. He told me it still gave him the jitters walking past and he never wanted to step foot in the place. Actually I don't think it was anywhere in town. I saw him once in a queue at the bus stop near the harbour.'

'Do you know where the bus was going?'

'You must be joking. It was years ago. Even if I'd noticed I wouldn't remember now.'

On her way into Kimmerston, Vera passed the woman from the Station House. She was climbing over the wire mesh of the hen-run, carrying a shallow basket of eggs. She waved, then gestured a pantomime to show that she had plenty spare if Vera wanted any. The couple had rather taken Vera under their wing. She wondered if they knew what she did for a living and if they'd be quite so friendly if they found out.

The police station in Kimmerston was red brick and gloomy, set right onto the pavement opposite the bus station. There was dusty blue paint and the brass handles on the outside doors were tarnished. Vera was tempted to stop and find out the times of the buses from the harbour to Kimmerston on a Wednesday morning. She thought that from her office window she could have seen Edmund get off one of the brown and cream buses. If this was where he was heading. Which she felt in her bones that it was.

But she didn't stop. If she went into work now she'd never get away. She drove on past the police station towards the car park near the shopping precinct. It was nearly nine o'clock and the traffic was heavy. She felt her blood pressure rising, resisted the temptation to hit her horn or stick up a finger at the slick young man in the silver Mondeo who pulled out in front of her.

There was only one café in the shopping centre. Despite the delay, when she got there it was still closed. It faced into an enclosed square in the precinct. Sunlight streamed through the glass roof, formed patterns on the concrete as it shone through raindrops. There were white plastic tables and chairs on the paved square outside the shop, but they were piled one on top of the other. Patience had never been one of Vera's virtues. She rattled the locked door of the café and began to bang on the glass.

'What do you think you're doing?'

A middle-aged woman with a straight back and a fierce expression came up to her from behind.

'What does it look like?'

'We don't open until ten. There's a machine in the arcade if you're that desperate.'

'I don't want coffee,' Vera snapped. 'I want the answer to some questions.'

She showed her warrant card. The woman was unimpressed.

'Well, you should know better,' she said. 'What sort of impression does it give to the youngsters? This used to be a well-mannered town.'

Vera muttered under her breath, stamping her feet impatiently as the woman unlocked the door and followed her in.

'I might as well have a cup of coffee while I'm here,' she said. Belligerently.

'You'll have to wait until I get the machine going. Unless you can make do with instant.'

'Instant'll do.'

The woman plugged in the kettle, spooned powder into a mug. She took a green overall from a drawer and put it on, then set the steaming mug in front of Vera.

'That'll be sixty pence.'

Vera wanted to argue but thought better of it and paid up.

'It's about some of your customers.'

Despite herself the woman was curious. She stopped fidgeting with crockery in the kitchen and sat at Vera's table. 'What about them?'

'I'm interested in a woman called Bella Furness. She came in here regularly on a Wednesday.'

The woman shook her head. 'Wednesday's our busiest day and I don't know many customers by name. Not even the regulars.'

Vera took out a snap which she'd nicked from the bedroom at Black Law. 'That ring any bells?'

'Oh aye. I remember her. Every Wednesday as regular as clockwork. A toasted tuna and sweetcorn followed by a chocolate meringue. Until a couple of months ago. She hasn't been in lately. I wondered what I'd done to offend her. She was a bit on the brusque side. The sort who might take offence.'

'She died,' Vera said. 'Was she here on her own?'

'No. She usually met a gentleman friend.'

Out of her large floppy briefcase Vera took a photograph of Edmund Fulwell, the one which had been shown in the local paper requesting information and which today would be on the front page of all the nationals. The woman apparently wasn't interested in the news. At least she made no comment about having seen the photo before. 'Aye,' she said. 'That's the one.'

'When you say gentleman friend, did you have the impression that they were romantically involved?'

As she waited for an answer Vera wondered what Rachael would make of that. St Bella having a bit on the side. It could ruin her faith in human nature.

The woman considered the question. 'Hard to say. She was usually here before him. He arrived flustered as if it had been a bit of a rush. He always gave her a kiss. Only a peck on the cheek but at their age anything more wouldn't have been seemly. Still, these days . . . Folks always seem to be kissing and hugging, don't they? Even people who've only just met. So I don't really know.'

Vera contained her impatience. 'But what's your instinct? After having thought about it. You work with people all day. You must get a feel for things like that.'

She was flattered, which was what Vera had intended. 'I suppose you do. On balance then, I'd say close friends. Not lovers.' She paused. 'If anything I'd say he was more attracted to the other one.'

'What other one?'

'The other woman. She wasn't in very often – perhaps three times all together. But when she was he made a fuss of her.'

'Any idea of her name?'

'None at all.' She seemed pleased that she couldn't help.

'What did she look like?'

'She was younger than them but not that much younger. She knew how to dress if you know what I mean. Perhaps a bit overdressed. Too smart for town on a Wednesday.'

'Anything else you can tell me?'

But the woman had already lost interest. She looked at her watch. 'No,' she said. 'I can't really remember her. Just the impression that I got of her at the time.'

'But if I showed you a photo you'd be able to say whether it was the woman or not?'

'No, not a chance. Like I said, Wednesday's a busy day.'

Thanks, Vera thought, for nothing.

Chapter Fifty-Six

Vera walked back through the precinct to her car. The town was busier now, mostly with elderly people who couldn't use their bus passes until after nine o'clock. One couple stood outside the grocer's shop bickering about whether they should buy cabbage or turnip to go with their dinner.

Vera had a stab of recognition which made her stop in her tracks. For a moment the woman, overweight, aggressive, seen reflected in the shop window, looked very much like her.

What'll I do when I retire?, she thought. I'll not even have anyone to fight with.

Then a young woman pushed a buggy into her shins. Vera turned and glowered and the brief moment of despair passed.

She had intended to go back to the police station but at the last minute changed her mind and took the familiar road out of Kimmerston towards Langholme. Now that she had evidence that Bella and Edmund Fulwell had kept in touch since they'd left the hospital, she wished she'd listened more carefully when Rachael and Edie had been wittering on about the Nobles. But she thought she'd be able to rattle Charlie's cage.

The stables were quiet. A teenage girl in a green

sweater with KIMMERSTON EQUESTRIAN CENTRE emblazoned on the breast was forking mucky straw into a barrow. Two stout middle-aged women prepared to mount their horses. Vera thought it all looked very prosperous and well-ordered. There was a customers' car park, properly laid with tarmac, marked with white lines and bordered by wooden tubs full of bedding plants. Charlie had turned into a canny businessman just like his dad.

She approached the girl.

'Mr Noble?'

The girl looked at her dubiously. Vera was wearing her floral crimplene dress and her sandals. 'Do you want to book a ride?'

'I want to talk to Mr Noble.'

'I think he's in the house. But he doesn't really like being disturbed in the mornings.'

'Why? What does he get up to?'

The girl blushed, confused.

'Only joking, pet,' Vera said. 'Never mind, I'll find my own way.'

She strode on, past the newly converted stable block to the freshly painted house, thinking that if she smelled anything at all, it was money.

Charlie Noble himself opened the door. She didn't think she'd have recognized him if she'd bumped into him in the street. He was younger than her. When she'd last seen him he'd hardly looked more than a schoolboy, spotty, graceless, obviously cowed by his bully of a father. He had the same expression but now he was old, stooped, bespectacled.

'Yes?' he said crossly. He was wearing a sweater and breeches. 'I was just going out.'

'Don't you recognize me, Charlie?' she asked, hearty as a jolly aunt.

'I'm sorry . . .' He hesitated, squinting at her over his specs.

Good God, she thought. I must have aged as much as him. 'Come on, Charlie. I may have put on a few pounds but I can't have changed that much. Or perhaps you don't recognize me without the uniform? We spent a lot of time together, you and I, in that mausoleum of a house when your dad passed away. Drinking cups of tea while we waited for the bosses to get their act together.'

He stared at her. She thrust out her hand, grasped his unresisting one. 'Vera Stanhope,' she said, beaming. 'Inspector now. Only a constable then.'

'Yes.' He stepped back from her as if she was a dog you had to treat with caution. 'I remember.'

'Aren't you going to invite me in then? A cup of tea for old times' sake.'

'I was going out,' he said uncertainly.

'You must have a few minutes for a chat. And I'd like to meet your lady wife.'

She stepped past him into the house. 'Mrs Noble!' she shouted into the silence. 'You've got a visitor. Put the kettle on, pet.'

They drank filter coffee in the room where Edie and Rachael had been taken on their last visit. Louise carried it in. She was wearing a sleeveless linen dress, navy, very smart, and said breathlessly that she'd leave them to it. She was meeting some friends for lunch and she needed to get ready.

'You look ready enough to me,' Vera said. 'I'll not keep you now but I'd be grateful if you could spare me

447

a few minutes of your precious time later. Before you leave.' She smiled fondly.

Louise shot a look at her husband. 'Yes,' she said. 'Of course.' She backed out of the room and shut the door.

'What's this about?' Charles said.

'Well, I'm not just here for a chat though it's always nice to catch up on old acquaintances. It's about Bella.'

'I didn't know anything about her suicide before those women came to tell me.'

'So they said. Shocking, isn't it? All those years living just up the valley and never met.' Vera paused. 'She killed the old man for you, didn't she, Charlie?'

He stared at her in horror.

'I thought so at the time, though I was only a plod and a girl at that so who would listen to me? When I came to the slaughterhouse to tell you your dad was dead you were expecting it. But you were *very* good. Have you ever thought of joining the Kimmerston Amateur Dramatic Society? They're always short of a strong male lead. But you weren't really surprised.'

He started to splutter a response but she wouldn't allow him to speak.

'Did he beat you up when you were a kid?'

There was a silence. A nerve in his cheek twitched angrily.

'Not just when I was a kid. Until he got ill.'

'So she felt guilty for leaving you there, going away to college, being a teacher, enjoying every minute of it. And I bet you made her feel guilty. Why didn't you leave yourself?'

'I couldn't. He wouldn't let me. And I didn't have any qualifications. What could I have done?'

'Didn't have the guts,' Vera said dismissively. 'It wasn't only the old man who wanted her back, was it? It was you as well.'

'You don't know what it was like.'

'No?' She spoke softly, deliberately. 'Listen, Charlie, you understand nothing about me or what I know.'

'It was just talk, wishful thinking. I didn't really mean her to kill him.'

'Didn't you? But you planned it. And every day you put pressure on her. So she had the old man on her back all day and you all night. No wonder she cracked.' She poured herself more coffee. 'How did you know it was going to be that day?'

He stood up and stared out of the window so he had his back to her. Pretending that she wasn't there, that he couldn't hear her.

'You had such a lot to gain,' Vera went on. 'We would have thought it was you, if you'd had the opportunity. That's why it was such a good day for it to happen. You were at work with all those witnesses. Not just your colleagues, but the Ministry of Agriculture inspector. And you didn't leave your office, did you? Except for five minutes to go to the lav. Did you phone her then? Tell her that you couldn't stand any more of the old man's bullying? If something didn't happen soon you'd top yourself? And God knows why but she cared about you. Like I said, she cracked.'

He continued to look into the distance, gave no indication that he'd heard her.

'But I'm not here to discuss that now,' Vera said conversationally. 'That's all water under the bridge. No

ANN CLEEVES

one took any notice of me then. They might now, but
what point would there be in mentioning it? It's not a
crime to make a phone call.'

Charles turned back to face her. 'No,' he said. 'It's
not.'

'So why don't you get your lovely wife in for a chat
and we'll say no more about it.'

She watched him carefully as he left the room,
making sure he understood the threat implied in the
last remark.

When Louise came into the room Vera stood up as
if they'd never met before, as if it was someone else
entirely who'd brought in the coffee earlier.

'Come on, Charlie,' she said jovially. 'You make the
introductions.' When he didn't speak immediately she
went on, 'My name's Stanhope. Inspector Vera Stanhope. I want a few words about Bella Furness.'

'I've never met her.'

'You've spoken to her though, on the phone. Edie
Lambert told me.' Vera thought the Nobles were two of
a kind. Neither seemed able to face the real world.

'Only once.'

'Why don't you tell me about it?'

'It was a week before she died. It can't have had
anything to do with her suicide.'

Vera watched Louise calmly. Again she was
reminded of a girl. A child who, accused of being
naughty, covers up too eagerly, too elaborately with
lies. And yet, so far, she had been accused of nothing.
An idea formed.

'I'm surprised that she only phoned once. She said
she would call back. You'd think she'd want to speak

450

to her brother, her only relative before she died.' She turned to Charles. 'Are you certain she didn't speak to you?'

'Of course.'

And you wouldn't dare lie, Vera thought. Not with what I've got on you.

'Mrs Noble?'

The woman twisted her coffee cup in its saucer.

'I can understand why you wouldn't want to talk to the Lamberts,' Vera continued. 'Why should you? Two nosey women turning up late at night, wanting to know your business. But this is different. This is a police matter. Besides, we could always check the telephone records for the relevant dates.'

Louise looked up. 'She did phone. Later that week.'

'You didn't say.' Charles was stunned, hurt. Poor dear, Vera thought maliciously. This has all been too much for him.

'What did she want?' she asked.

'To speak to Charles. But he was away for the weekend. Some of our young riders were at a show in Richmond and he'd gone with them. I told her that. She said I'd have to do. She couldn't wait.' Louise hesitated. 'She said she needed her money.'

'What money would that be?' Vera's voice was bland.

'When he sold their father's house he put the money into an account for her.'

'In her name,' Vera said. 'Of course. Edie Lambert told me.'

'No,' Charles said. 'Not in her name. It was a separate account, but I signed for it. Of course it was meant for her.'

'Ah.'

'We hadn't heard anything from her. She'd been out of prison for years, but not bothered to get in touch. We didn't know where she was. The money was just lying there.'

'So you spent it?'

'We invested it in the business. We need to expand. Holiday cottages. A leisure complex. We've our daughter to think of. I saw it as an investment for Bella.'

It was hard to see the Nobles as ruthless business tycoons. They were too pathetic. So what had driven them? Vera thought they were like spoilt children with a bag of sweeties. They'd wanted the cash. They didn't want to share it. So they'd taken it. There was no more to it than that.

'What did you tell Bella?' she asked Louise

'That there *was* no money. What else could I say? I couldn't magic it for her out of thin air.' Louise was defensive again, sulky. 'She couldn't really have needed it. I mean, whoever's heard of a poor farmer?'

Bella was poor, Vera thought. So poor that she was desperate. She couldn't face telling Dougie that they'd have to leave the farm. And the next day she killed herself.

She kept the smile fixed on her face. 'Quite,' she said. 'We've all heard the stories about farmers. They moan about EC subsidies but they all drive new cars. Did you ever meet Bella?'

'No!' Louise was horrified by the suggestion.

'Weren't you curious? I thought you might have suggested meeting her. Not here or at the farm. Somewhere neutral. For coffee perhaps in Kimmerston.'

'Heavens, no.' Louise pulled a face. 'I found the whole thing horrid. I never wanted to hear from her again.'

'No danger of that now,' Vera said.

Chapter Fifty-Seven

Outside the police station a small group of reporters had gathered on the pavement. Vera saw them before they saw her, debated whether they could be of any use to her and decided against it. She strode through them, ignoring their calls for comments or a photograph. The momentum carried her on up the stairs, gathered Joe Ashworth from his room in her wake and landed her at last in her office. There she set her bag heavily on the desk. The flap was unfastened and the contents spilled out, papers, keys, photos, five biros and a half-eaten doughnut wrapped in clingfilm slid onto the floor. She threw the doughnut into the bin.

Leaving the rest of the debris on the floor she pressed a button on the phone and began to listen to her voicemail. Without waiting to be asked Joe Ashworth crouched in the corner and switched on the plastic kettle which stood with mugs and jars on a stained tray. He pretended not to hear the angry voice of Vera's boss, demanding to know what the hell she thought she was buggering about at and to report to him as soon as she got in. The voice was slightly querulous. The superintendent knew that he was no match for Vera. He wasn't very bright and she always had an answer.

The room was as high as it was wide, painted in pale green gloss, cell-shaped. There was one window with a frosted glass pane. It reminded Vera of a women's public lavatory yet she would have resisted moving elsewhere. It had been hers since her promotion to inspector, a refuge at least from the complaints and demands of her father. There were no pictures or plants, nothing personal, nothing to give information to the nosy bastards who were curious about where or how she lived. Ashworth was the only one of her colleagues who'd seen her home and that was when he'd dropped her off there late at night after work. She'd have liked to invite him in for a drink but hadn't wanted to embarrass him. They were already calling him teacher's pet or worse.

'I've just got in from Holme Park,' he said.

'Anything?'

'I didn't get to speak to Lord or Lady Muck.'

'Don't tell me – they're too upset for visitors.'

'Hardly. They're in a meeting.'

'Who with?'

'Slateburn Quarries at the office here in Kimmerston. Apparently it was arranged a while ago.'

'To discuss the preliminary findings of the Environmental Impact Assessment,' Vera said almost to herself. 'Probably. But I bet they'll be taking the opportunity to talk about the effect Edmund Fulwell's death will have on public opinion. I wonder if it'll be enough to stop Waugh going ahead. Livvy will be upset if he starts getting cold feet.'

'You don't like the idea of this quarry, do you?'

'What I like is neither here nor there. So, was it a wasted trip?'

'Not entirely. I had a mooch round, had a chat with all the staff I could get hold of. None of them had any idea that Edmund was hiding out in the house at the end of the Avenue. Robert must have been careful. It must be hard to keep secrets in a place like that.'

'Did you manage to speak to the keeper's wife in the house next door?'

'Yes. It's a madhouse. Kids, music, animals. Everyone shouting at each other. You could have a rock band practising and they'd not hear.'

'They didn't see anyone hanging about yesterday?'

'They were at the Hall all day helping to prepare for the party. Even the teenagers had been roped in.'

'So we're not much further forward?'

'Olivia's secretary gave me a list of the guests who were at the party. I didn't recognize anyone connected with the quarry. It was mostly friends of the family and people from the village.' He pulled a face. 'The secretary said that Olivia wanted it to be a real community event.'

'Very civic-minded. Though it doesn't make much difference to the investigation. Once the jamboree had started there'd be no witnesses in the Avenue and while the guests were arriving no one would have taken any notice of strangers. Very convenient. I wonder if that's why he was killed yesterday? In that case the murderer must have known about the party, even if he didn't attend it.' She looked down at Ashworth. 'I suppose it was common knowledge.'

'Oh aye. Apparently everyone in Langholme was fighting for an invite.'

The kettle had eventually boiled. He poured water over a tea bag in a grimy mug, poked it with a spoon until the liquid was thick and brown and stirred in whitener from the tin.

'Aren't you having one?' Vera asked.

He shook his head. 'I asked Mary Sawyer to visit Nancy Deakin. I thought . . .'

'Good choice!' Mary was unflappable, classy but not bossy. 'Any joy?'

'Nancy was heartbroken. Robert Fulwell hadn't bothered telling her Edmund was dead.'

'Did she get anything useful?'

'Lots of childhood reminiscences. Apparently Nancy's quite sane when she talks about the past. Less reliable about the present.'

Aren't we all, Vera thought. Especially if it's the past that's spooked us.

'According to Nancy, Edmund was never wanted. His mother had a hard time giving birth to Robert and didn't want to go through it again. She'd had a boy. That was enough. When Edmund was born she hardly acknowledged him. Hardly surprising he grew up a bit weird.'

'Does she know who Edmund was scared of?'

'If she does she isn't telling.' He sat across the desk from Vera. 'Go on then, what have you been up to?'

'Me? I've spent the morning doing Rachael Lambert's dirty work. I've been trying to find out why Bella Furness killed herself.' She grinned. 'It's all right, lad, I've not lost my marbles. It is relevant. Every Wednesday Edmund Fulwell caught the bus from the coast and met Bella in Kimmerston. They must have kept in touch since they were in hospital together. Only friends, I think. But close friends, confidants. Occasionally they were joined by another woman. I'd give my back teeth to know who that was. Age and description could match Anne Preece and she lived in Langholme, could have known them both. But if it was her, why didn't she tell us?'

She stopped, dreamy-eyed, lost in thought, considering wild possibilities.

'Did you find out?' Ashworth asked.

'Mmm?'

'Why Mrs Furness killed herself?'

'I think so. Though even that doesn't quite make sense. She and Dougie are broke. In danger of losing the farm. She tries to get in touch with her brother, to ask for the money he put by for her after the sale of the family home. Her money. Instead she gets through to the wife, who does a very sweet little girl lost act but who's as ruthless as they come. She tells Bella the money's been spent.'

'That makes sense. She was depending on money from her brother to bail her out. When she had to face losing the farm she hanged herself. Rachael was wrong. There was no conspiracy.'

'No. It won't work. It wasn't in character. Bella was tough. She'd survived years in the loony bin. Not complaining. Seeing it out. Then she ran that business on her own after Dougie's illness. She must have seen there were other options. Why didn't she talk to Neville? According to Rachel they'd been getting on better. He was sympathetic.'

'If he was telling the truth.'

Vera glared at him. 'Of course. I realized the possibility that he's been lying. I'm not daft, lad. But why didn't she stick it out for a few more months? If the quarry was approved she'd be able to flog the access to the mine for a fortune. It might not have appealed to have Godfrey Waugh's lorries going through the yard but it must have been better than moving into town or jumping off a bale with a rope round your neck.'

Joe Ashworth said nothing. Better to keep quiet. Vera didn't want intelligent comment at this point only an admiring audience.

She went on, 'So, there were other pressures. Something that closed down those options. Something that stopped her seeing straight.'

Still Ashworth kept his mouth shut. A mistake.

'Well?' she demanded crossly. A teacher prising an answer out of a reluctant child. 'What do you think that might have been?'

'Caring for Dougie?'

'Nonsense. She'd been doing that for years. She thrived on it.'

She paused. 'Let me give you a clue. I told you she'd been seeing Edmund Fulwell. They were friends. Close friends. They'd seen each other through some bad times.'

'And he would have hated the idea of her selling off land to Slateburn Quarry or even coming to an access agreement with Godfrey Waugh.'

'Exactly.'

'That would explain why she was under so much stress. She was desperate to stay at Black Law but Fulwell saw it as some sort of test of loyalty.'

'It's possible, don't you think?'

He didn't give a direct answer. 'Inspector, can I ask you something?'

'Of course.'

ANN CLEEVES

'How does this relate to the murder of Grace Fulwell? Or even to that of her father?'

'Piss off, Ashworth. Don't be such a smart alec. If I knew that I wouldn't be sitting here. I'd be out making an arrest.'

But the question had amused her. She chuckled into her tea.

Chapter Fifty-Eight

The psychiatrist who had been consultant at St Nicholas' Hospital when Bella Noble and Edmund Fulwell were patients had moved on to become professor of a southern university. Vera spoke to him on the telephone without much hope. He was unexpectedly human and laughed out loud at her questions.

'Good heavens, you can't expect me to remember individuals after all this time.' Not unfriendly though and not in so much of a hurry that he wouldn't let her go on.

'They weren't ordinary patients. Bella Noble came to you from a secure hospital on Merseyside to prepare for discharge. She'd killed her father. Edmund was one of the Fulwells from Holme Park.'

'I remember him. At least I remember wondering why he was slumming it on the NHS instead of being treated in a private clinic. I have some recollection of the transfer of the woman but only because it was a bureaucratic nightmare. As I recall she didn't stay long. She wasn't ill and even in those days we needed the beds. Why do you want to know?'

'They're both dead.'

'Ah.' He paused. 'I'm sorry but I can't say I'm surprised. Community care only works if there's adequate supervision. It's tough on the street. People get depressed, angry. There's always a danger of suicide or violence.'

'Bella married a farmer and seems to have lived happily, caring for him after he had a stroke. Edmund had the same job since he left the hospital.'

'Ah,' he said again. This time sheepishly. 'And I'm always telling my students not to resort to stereotypes. You've given me a text for my next lecture. I'm afraid I can't help you. Any notes will be at St Nick's.'

'I've seen them. I was wondering if there was anyone else who would remember Bella and Edmund. Someone who would have had more day to day contact than you. A nurse perhaps or a junior doctor.'

'Some of the nursing staff might still be there. Talk to the auxiliaries. In the Health Service the higher up the hierarchy you go the more time you spend in an office. The junior doctors came and went with such frequency that sometimes I couldn't even remember their names.' There was a silence while he considered. 'Better still talk to Christina. Christina Flood. She's a psychologist. St Nick's was her first permanent appointment and she was like a breath of fresh air in the place. She was interested in group work, art therapy, drama. Not all of it was useful but it was about engaging with the patients rather than hiding away from them and letting them sit around until the drugs started to work. If anyone can remember those individuals it'll be Christina.'

'Do you know where she's working now?'

Vera held her breath. The woman was idealistic, enthusiastic. It would be just her luck if she'd decided to become a missionary in Africa.

462

'Still in Northumberland. Still on the coast. She's moved on since then though. She's in charge of the Community Service based at an outpatient clinic. When you talk to her pass on my best wishes. And my admiration for sticking in there. I escaped from the patients too in the end.'

Eventually Vera tracked down Christina Flood to her home. She was on maternity leave and had given birth the evening before to a daughter. She'd just returned from hospital. The partner to whom Vera spoke on the phone had just returned from hospital. He was so full of goodwill, so proud of the new infant and his part in creating it that he would have invited the whole CID into the house but Ashworth was horrified.

'You can't intrude today,' he said. 'They'll want some time on their own. She'll not feel up to it. She only came out of the labour ward this morning.'

'That'll surely not have taken away her ability to talk.'

'Anyway, I can't think why it's so important.'

'Because something went on in that hospital that brought those two together and kept them together for years. I need to know what it was.' She looked up at him. 'You like babies. Do you want to come along?'

'No,' he said, brave for once. 'I think it's harassment and I want no part of it.' Then, as she hesitated at the door, he added, 'You're not frightened of going on your own, are you? It's only a baby. It'll not bite.'

Christina Flood lived in a narrow, three-storeyed house close to the seafront in Tynemouth. A skinny man in a scarlet, handknitted sweater opened the door to Vera. Against his shoulder he held a white, wrapped bundle. He leant forward slightly, tilting from the waist so that Vera could see the baby's face.

'Isn't she lovely?'

He seemed to find it impossible to keep still, skipping from one leg to another like an excited child but the baby slept, puckering its face occasionally as if it were dreaming. 'We haven't decided on a name yet. Chrissie wants something solid and respectable.' He seemed to take Vera's interest for granted. 'I think she's going to be outrageous. She should have something to suit.'

The ground floor of the house was one large room set up as a workshop. On a grimy central heating boiler a ginger cat slept on a blanket. There was a serious anglepoise lamp on one of the benches but that wasn't switched on and the only light came from a small dusty window, the corners in shadow. There were rows of shelves made of dull metal, racks of tools, a vice. Vera sensed a secret passion. In a room like this Hector would have met the brotherhood to inject eggs and blow them.

'What goes on here?' she asked. She was glad for a moment to escape baby talk.

'I make flutes. And repair them and other woodwind instruments.' From then on Vera saw him as a pied piper, dressed in scarlet, piping to his baby.

'Chrissie's upstairs. I've told her she should be in bed, but she'll not listen to me.' He danced on, up a flight of bare wooden stairs into a wide thin room with a view over water and down the Tyne as far as the docks at North Shields. Christina Flood sat on a green linen sofa with her legs up. She was wearing trousers and a loose white tunic. She had strong features, a square jaw, black eyebrows. Her hair was cut in a straight fringe. The room was filled with flowers and a hand-painted banner saying WELCOME HOME was strung above the window. Christina saw Vera looking at it.

'I know. What is he like? I was gone for less than twenty-four hours.' She turned to the man. 'For Christ's sake, Patrick, put her in the carrycot. Why don't you make yourself useful and get some tea?'

With one lithe movement he knelt and put the baby on its back in the basket, which stood on the floor.

'Spoilsport,' he said and left the room.

'Patrick said you wanted to talk to me about Edmund Fulwell but I'm not sure I can help. He wasn't a client of mine. Not really. He'd been stable for some time. If he did need medication he'd probably get it from his GP.'

'I've seen his recent records. I'm more interested in the time he spent in St Nick's. Do you remember working with him there?'

'Very well. It was an exciting time for me. My first chance to put my ideas and my training into practice.'

'Do you remember a patient called Bella Noble?'

'Yes. She was there at the same time. A member of the group. I've not even seen her since she was discharged.'

'But you had seen Edmund?'

'Not professionally, but Patrick and I go quite regularly to the Harbour Lights. At least we did.' She smiled at the baby. 'I don't suppose we'll be able to do that sort of thing so often now.'

'Did you know that his daughter had been murdered?'

'Yes. I'd heard that a woman had been killed near Langholme but I hadn't connected her with Edmund until Rod told us. We were in the restaurant the night after she was found. I went upstairs to see Edmund. Just to tell him how sorry I was. To offer my support.'

'Was he as you would have expected?'

'More together, I'd say. More rational. I was afraid it would start his drinking again but he was sober. I asked him if I could help in any way. He said not yet. He needed to sort things out in his own mind first. But it must all have been a brave show. When we went back a week later he'd disappeared.'

'Did you have the feeling that he knew something about Grace's death? Not that he'd killed her, I don't mean that. But some idea about what might have been the reason for it. I'm looking into a motive for his own murder. If he'd worked out who killed Grace it's possible he was murdered so he couldn't tell anyone else.'

'I suppose it's possible. I just took him to mean that he needed to come to terms with the fact that his daughter was dead. They hadn't been conventionally close but he was very fond of her. Very proud.'

'You said that Bella Noble was in the same group as Edmund. What group was that?'

'One of the first things I did when I went to St Nick's was to develop the idea of group therapy. The patients were isolated, not used to trusting people. If you've been you'll know what it's like. Everyone sitting in his own private hell staring at the telly or at those bloody fish. Bella and Edmund were in the first group. I wanted it to be a success so I chose the participants carefully. Not just those I thought would get most out of it but people who could make it work. Bella was one of those. She was solid as a rock. All the same I think she benefited as much as anyone.'

'In what way?'

'You know she killed her father?'

Vera nodded.

'She'd never talked about it. Before the trial her lawyers persuaded her to plead guilty to manslaughter. They told her hospital would be better than prison. In the secure hospital she was isolated and uncommunicative. That was one of the reasons they kept her in. At first in the group she was as silent as ever. She'd join in the exercises and give support to everyone else but she wouldn't talk about herself. Of course the others loved that. Most of us would rather have an audience than listen to other people's troubles. It was Edmund who persuaded her to tell us what had happened. He said, "You're not a stupid woman. Even if it was hell at home I don't understand why you didn't just walk away from it." '

'And Bella said it wasn't only herself she had to worry about.'

Christina looked at Vera with respect. 'You know about that?'

'Since Bella died I've had a long conversation with her brother. He won't admit to anything. Nothing we could charge him with at least, but I understand what sort of pressure she was under.'

'I didn't realize Bella was dead too.'

Vera gave an expurgated version of the story which led up to Bella's suicide. 'She and Edmund stayed friends.'

'Did they?' Christina seemed pleased. 'Couldn't he have helped her out financially? His family was loaded.'

'I don't think he saw any of their money.'

'No, I don't think he did. None of them ever came to visit him in hospital. Except Grace.'

'Did you ever meet her?'

'Not to speak to. I saw her occasionally, hovering in the distance. Waiting for him.'

'Sometimes I feel she's doing that to me. Hovering in the distance waiting for me to sort out what happened to her.'

'I'd help more if I could.'

Vera pounced. 'Could you give me a list of everyone in the group? Not now. Write it down. Names if possible and something on the background of each of them.'

'I don't know.'

'I realize it's difficult after all this time.'

'It's not that. At least not only that. In one of the boxes in the workshop there are notes. I always meant to turn them into a book. Or at least into a paper. It's more a question of confidentiality.'

'I'll come here. I won't take the list away. You knew them. Grace, Edmund and Bella. I don't want the medical details. They wouldn't mean anything. More your personal impression. A reason.'

'OK,' she said. 'OK.'

Patrick must have been listening at the door because he came in that moment with tea. He talked about flutes and folk bands and about how now he'd got a kid he'd really have to get more involved in the fight to keep music in schools. The baby stirred and

Christina started to unbutton her tunic to feed her. Hurriedly Vera said it was time to leave and that she'd see herself out. She left them, sitting together on the sofa, bickering amiably about the baby's name.

Chapter Fifty-Nine

When Vera arrived back at Kimmerston it was seven o'clock. She bought chips from the fish shop opposite the police station. The skeletal middle-aged man in the long apron behind the counter recognized her in the queue and served her first, handing the greasy parcel over the heads of the people waiting, waving away her money, saying he'd take it off her next time.

Still eating the chips she stood at the door of the big room where Joe Ashworth was working, staring glassy eyed at a computer screen.

'Where are the other buggers?' she demanded.

'Still working through the guest list from Holme Park. Lots of them were out during the day.'

'Anything?'

'No one saw anyone going into the house at the end of the Avenue. No one saw a car parked outside. There were people on foot going up to the Hall but descriptions are pretty sketchy.'

'Have you managed to contact Neville Furness yet?'

'He's been out on a site visit. And not answering his mobile.' Reluctantly he turned away from the screen. 'What about you?'

'More evidence that Bella and Edmund were very close. At the hospital they confided in each other,

470

trusted each other. But as to how relevant that is now?'
She shrugged. Rolled the chip paper into a ball and
lobbed it towards a waste bin.

'Anne Preece has been trying to get in touch with
you.'

'What for?'

'She wouldn't tell me. Implied it was women's stuff.
Anyway, she said she'll be in all evening if you want
to give her a ring.'

Vera felt more cheerful. It was a reprieve. She could
put off for several hours her return to the house by
the railway with its ghost of her father. And of herself
as a child, lonely, ugly as a bagful of nails. Once, at an
attempt at kindness, Hector had said, 'I wouldn't mind,
you know, if you'd like to bring a friend back to tea.' She
hadn't told him there was no one to ask and worried for
weeks that he would mention it again.

I should sell the place, she thought. Get out. Buy a
flat in Kimmerston. Something small and easy to
manage. Rent even. Spend the profit on a few holidays
abroad and a smart new car.

But she wouldn't. It was an impossible dream, like
winning the lottery. She was tied to the house and the
memories of it. Better the ghosts than no sense of
belonging at all. She realized that Ashworth was staring
at her, waiting for her perhaps to pick up the phone to
call Anne.

'I'll go and see her,' Vera said. 'She might have
remembered something. It's better done face to face.'

'Do you want me to come?' He put as much
enthusiasm as he could summon into the question but
she wasn't deceived.

'No,' she said. 'Go home to your babby.' She thought

of Patrick and Christina in their house overlooking the Tyne and wondered what was wrong with her. Even when she'd been younger the thought of producing kids had made her feel ill. 'The other bastards on the team'll be home already. They'll have their feet up in front of the telly. Why shouldn't you?'

He was already piling papers away into a drawer, stuffing his thermos flask into his briefcase.

'Well,' he said. 'If you're sure . . .' And he was gone before she could change her mind.

There was no reply when Vera rang the doorbell of the Priory. House martins flew into a nest under the eaves. Clouds of insects hung in the still air. Vera wandered round to the garden at the back of the house and found Anne, standing out against a border of shrubs and plants with deep red blooms. She was edging the lawn, pushing the half moon of steel into the ground with a heavy boot, slicing away the untidy turf. She was dressed in jeans and a sleeveless vest and Vera thought she was wearing well. She didn't hear Vera until the inspector was halfway across the grass and then she turned, startled. In that first unguarded moment Vera thought she was expecting someone else. Or perhaps hoping for someone else, because she seemed not only surprised but momentarily disappointed.

'There was no need to come out all this way,' Anne said. 'It's not urgent. I just phoned to make an appointment. I'd have come into Kimmerston.'

She seemed flustered and Vera thought she hadn't sorted out yet exactly what she wanted to say. She hadn't got her story straight.

'It's no problem.' Vera looked admiringly round the

garden. 'There's some work gone into this, mind. It's like something out of a Sunday paper.'

'I love it. I'd really miss it if I had to leave.'

'Is that on the cards?'

Anne straightened up. 'I don't know. The time at Baikie's was to give me a chance to sort out what I wanted. I don't seem any closer to making a decision.'

'What about your husband?'

'Jeremy? I haven't talked to him. He's got problems of his own. His business isn't doing brilliantly. Besides, I can never really take him seriously.'

'I always find it's dangerous,' Vera said, 'to underestimate anyone to that extent.'

'Do you?' Anne gave an awkward little laugh. 'What a peculiar thing to say. Jeremy wouldn't hurt a fly. He's not in this evening. Some meeting with a business contact in Newcastle. Someone who's going to make him a fortune. Apparently. Jem's always optimistic.'

'I'd like to have met him,' Vera said easily. 'But I suppose now we can chat in peace. Over a beer perhaps. If you've got any beer in the fridge. After the day I've had I could do with a drink.'

They sat in the kitchen with the back door open so they could hear the last of the birdsong outside. At the end of the garden the hill rose steeply. Its shadow edged towards them.

'Well?' Vera demanded. 'What can I do for you?' She was pouring lager carefully into a straight pint glass. 'Have you remembered anything about finding Edmund?'

'No. It's nothing like that. I'm not sure that I should say . . .'

'I could have had a beer in my own house. And

473

I've not come all this way to look at the scenery. So spit it out. It's not your place to decide what's important. You can leave that to me.'

'I wondered if you've talked to Barbara Waugh.'

'Who's she when she's at home?'

'Wife of Godfrey, the quarry boss. And a partner in the business, I think.'

'I talked to him briefly after Grace was killed to try to get a handle on that Environmental Impact report. I've had no cause to speak to the wife. Is she a friend of yours?'

'Not exactly. I met her first more than a year ago. Slateburn Quarries had put some money into a North-umberland Wildlife Trust reserve and the Waughs were there for the opening. She came up to me and started talking about the Black Law development. She must have heard that I opposed it. I was expecting an earful but she was very generous. She even invited me to her home for lunch.'

'What was all that about? Was she nobbling the opposition?'

'No. She wasn't very happy about the quarry either. She felt the company was being bumped into it.' Anne paused. 'She made allegations, all of them unspe-cific, about Neville Furness. That he was a ruthless businessman. That he had more influence on her husband than she thought was healthy. She even implied some sort of blackmail. She said that was why Godfrey was so single-minded about the Black Law development. If it was left to her she'd favour a more flexible approach.'

'She didn't say what grounds Neville might have had for blackmail?'

Anne turned away, stared out into the garden. 'No. It was all very vague.'

'Did you believe her?'

'I wasn't sure. Not then. But what reason would she have to lie?'

'Have you seen her since?'

'Just before the party at Holme Park. She'd phoned here several times the week before and left messages with Jeremy. I went to have tea. The daughter was there. Perhaps that's why she didn't talk but I think something had happened. There'd been some threat. She seemed terrified but she wouldn't tell me what was wrong.'

'Do you think her husband beats her up?'

'No!'

The answer, instant and vehement, surprised Vera. 'It does happen,' she said mildly. 'Even in the best of families.'

'I don't think that's what frightened her. I wondered if it had anything to do with Neville Furness. And now he seems to be taking an interest in Rachael . . .'

'You think I should find out what's at the bottom of it. Did you mention any of this to Rachael?'

'I tried to warn her but she's besotted.'

'Has she seen him again?'

'I think so. She phoned last night to see how I was and I thought I could hear his voice in the background.'

'Don't worry.' Vera drained her glass and set it regretfully on the table. 'Edie won't let her do anything silly.'

'Edie won't be able to stop her if she sets her mind to it.'

'I'll have a word. Find out what's going on.'

'Will you talk to Barbara Waugh?'

'Do you want me to?'

'Something was scaring her. She wouldn't tell me. She might talk to you. But don't let on I sent you.'

'So I just drop in, do I, to have a friendly chat and a cup of tea as I'm passing?'

'I told you. She's a partner in the business. Isn't that excuse enough?'

'Maybe.'

Vera sensed that Anne wanted rid of her but she was reluctant to go. There's something you're not telling me, lady, she thought. But what is it? She sat, waited.

'I thought I might go back to college,' Anne said suddenly. 'Try for a degree in environmental science. Get a real job so I can pay my own way.'

Is that all it was, Vera thought. You didn't want to admit to academic pretensions. But she wasn't convinced. 'Why not?' she said out loud. 'You might find yourself a toyboy.'

It was a flip remark because she could think of nothing better but Anne seemed embarrassed.

'Or have you already found one?'

'No,' Anne said. 'Of course not.'

'I'd better go then. Thanks for the beer.'

Anne showed her out through the house to the main door. In the hall there was a picture of Jeremy at a do, flamboyant in a silk bow tie.

At the door Vera hesitated. 'Do you ever go into that coffee shop in the precinct?'

This time she was sure Anne flushed. 'Occasionally. Why?'

476

'Bella Furness used to go in every Wednesday. At lunchtime. Did you ever meet her?'

'No. I'm sure I didn't.'

So who did you meet, Vera thought. Edmund Fulwell or someone altogether different?

At home she drank whisky because there was no beer, phoned Edie to make an appointment to see her the following day, watched an Orson Welles movie on the television and fell asleep before the Aberdeen sleeper rumbled past. As she drifted off she thought of Neville Furness. Dreaming, she confused him with a pirate she'd read about as a girl in a favourite picture book. She must have had a last moment of lucidity before sleep because she wondered suddenly why it had been so hard to pin him down for an interview.

Chapter Sixty

Conventional policing had drawn a blank. Even her boss who was a believer in persistence and routine, who was convention personified, who knew nothing else, had to admit that. By the time the team met the following morning they had contacted everyone on the Holme Park guest list but they were no further forward. It seemed that the heat and the drink had dulled the partygoers' senses. They could remember snatches of gossip – an amusing conversation with an ex-diplomat from Tokyo, a ravishing frock, a tired and emotional old woman eating strawberries – but nothing outside this social contact. Certainly nothing as prosaic as whether a car had been parked outside the semis at the end of the Avenue.

Vera's instinct was always to keep important information to herself until she was sure of it. As a young detective other people had taken credit for her work, mocked her when details hadn't checked out. Now she built a case privately, discussing it, if at all, with Ashworth. He accused her of paranoia, occasionally protecting her when her refusal to co-operate got her into bother. Now she realized secrecy wouldn't do. The team was dispirited. The troops needed something to keep them going. A story they could believe in.

'Once upon a time,' she said, grinning at their confusion because it was the last thing they expected. 'Once upon a time there were two brothers. Let's call them Robert and Edmund. Good old-fashioned English names. The elder brother was good and dutiful and did as his mother told him. As a reward he inherited the big house and the family business. He married a pretty young girl who gave him sons. The younger brother was a wastrel and a drunkard. He got a local lass pregnant and had to marry her. Then he ran away to sea. The wife committed suicide and the daughter, who if she wasn't beautiful was certainly clever, was taken away by social workers.

'Now when the younger son returned from his adventures he wasn't treated like the prodigal son in the Bible story. Nobody loved him. Nobody except his daughter and the barmy old woman who'd looked after him as a boy.' She looked up at them, asked sharply. 'With me so far?'

They nodded at her, compliant as kids in a kindergarten. They might think *she* was a barmy old woman but no one was prepared to risk a confrontation.

'I've come to realize that what Edmund loved, more than his clever daughter even, was the countryside where he grew up. He loved it so much that when his enemies planned to build a quarry there he forced his daughter to tell lies for him. They wanted to bring machines to dig out the rock and he couldn't stand the thought of it. It became an obsession.'

She paused and her audience shuffled, embarrassed, because this wasn't the way inspectors were supposed to carry on. They hoped that she'd finished. But

479

she just took a swig of the coke from a can on the desk in front of her and continued.

'Someone else was as passionate about that countryside as Edmund – the woman who farmed the land adjoining the estate. Her name was Bella Furness and her stepson was one of the wicked businessmen who wanted to dig a pit in the hillside. And surprise, surprise! Bella and Edmund knew each other. They met more than ten years ago when they were both patients in St Nick's. Both crazy people. Perhaps. They'd stayed friends ever since. Not lovers because Bella married Doug and they'd lived happily ever after. At least until Dougie had a stroke and the banks and the bailiffs gathered like birds of prey around the carcass of the farm. But very close friends.

'Perhaps Edmund confided in Bella, told her what his plans were. Who was scaring him. Perhaps if we asked she could answer all our questions and tell us who killed Edmund.' Vera stopped abruptly. The tone of her voice changed from storyteller to someone who meant business. 'But she can't, because in the spring, very inconveniently, she committed suicide.'

A hand was tentatively raised. She frowned as if annoyed to be interrupted. 'Yes?'

'Are you certain it was suicide?'

'If it wasn't, Fraser, I'd have told you.'

'Yes, ma'am.'

'So we need to find someone else to answer our questions. In the hospital a group of people met for therapy and support. Bella and Edmund were part of that group. We know that after leaving St Nick's they kept in touch and regularly had lunch together. Occasionally they were joined by another woman. We need to trace her. Without even realizing, she might know who killed Edmund and Grace. It won't be easy. She might not want to be found. Perhaps her friends and family don't even know that she spent a period in a mental hospital. But we have to talk to her.'

'Can't the hospital help?' A brave question, shouted from the back of the room.

'Their records show which patients were on each ward but not who attended the group. The psychologist who ran it is compiling a list at the moment but she's not sure where her notes are and she's got other things on her mind. In the meantime we need to work on finding the woman. Let's be subtle at first. No publicity to scare her off. No "Were you a loony in the 1980s?" posters. Talk to the people at the Harbour Lights restaurant again, to the other staff and the regulars. Perhaps our woman goes there to eat. And what about local GPs? The woman might have a recurring psychiatric problem.'

She watched them scribbling notes and thought she'd succeeded. They'd come to life. She banged on the table again and moved in front of the white flip chart. 'The other angle I want to pursue is the quarry. Somehow these deaths are linked to the bloody great hole Slateburn want to dig on the moor. These are the main movers in that business.' She began to write in unsteady capitals with a thick felt pen.

'Godfrey Waugh. He owns the company. I want to know whether the development was his idea or whether he was approached by the Fulwells. Talk to both lots of staff and see what you can find out.

'Neville Furness. Stepson of Bella. At one time he was land agent for the Fulwells. Then headhunted by

Godfrey. He did all the preliminary negotiations for the quarry but now he's gone all green and soppy. He's talking about moving back to his father's farm, even though it's in debt. Has he really converted? If not, what's he up to? For the moment you can leave him to me. I've got an appointment to see him when I leave here. But talk to the people who know him and work for him. We need everything we can get. He used to live in the house where Edmund died and word is he still has a key.

'Peter Kemp. Environmental consultant. He's changed sides too but he's gone the other way. Started off working for the Wildlife Trust and now sells his skills to big businesses. How much did he stand to gain from the quarry? How much would he lose if Waugh decided not to go ahead?'

There was a knock at the door. Vera glared at the probationer who came in. She stood nervously just inside the room.

'Yes?'

'A fax . . .' She thrust the paper at Vera, blushed and escaped.

Vera glanced at the contents. She was about to dismiss the team so she could consider its implication then thought they could do with cheering up even if it was only with a cheap laugh at someone on the edge of the inquiry. She waved the paper at them. 'This is about Jeremy Preece. Husband of Anne. He lives in Langholme in the house nearest to where Grace's body was found. We've been running checks as routine. You know how the boss likes routine. Mr Preece has a conviction for indecency. Scarborough Magistrates

Court 1990. Found lurking in the bogs on Filey seafront dressed in a sequinned top . . .'

There was laughter, a general release of tension. She shouted above the noise, 'I don't know why you're sitting there. Haven't you got work to do? Now you can add Jeremy Preece to your list too.'

Gratefully they gathered their belongings and scuttled out of the room. Only Joe Ashworth was left. He sat at the back and began slowly to clap his hands. 'Brilliant,' he said. 'A brilliant performance from start to finish. Now why don't you tell me what's really going on?'

She was flattered that he thought she knew.

Chapter Sixty-One

Vera took Ashworth with her to interview Neville Furness. Furness had been messing her around. She'd been trying to fix an interview with him since Edmund had died. She wanted to show him she meant business and the two of them turning up at his office gave that impression. Besides, on these occasions Ashworth was a useful observer. Sometimes she got carried away and he picked up signals she missed.

Slateburn Quarries took up the top floor of the office block by the river. She tried to remember what the site had looked like when old man Noble's slaughterhouse had been there, but couldn't. She was too used to the new roads. Even looking down at the river from the large window in reception she couldn't tie up her memories with the geography.

The receptionist was middle-aged, severe. She told them that Mr Furness would be with them shortly. He was tied up in a meeting. She brought them coffee.

'Does he know we're here?' Vera demanded.

The receptionist bridled. 'They said no interruptions. The meeting's scheduled to finish at eleven.'

'So you've not even told him?' Her voice must have been audible in the building society on the ground floor. It increased in volume: 'I want to see him now.'

The secretary hesitated, flushed with indignation, then went to the phone behind her desk. Almost immediately afterwards Neville Furness appeared from a corridor to their left. Vera had only seen him before at Black Law in jeans and a scuffed Barbour. In his suit and tie he seemed more formidable, not because the clothes gave him authority but because he wore them with such ease. Vera had expected him to seem out of place here. He was a farmer's son. But even summoned dramatically from his meeting he was unflustered.

'You must be a very busy man, Mr Furness,' she said ominously, not sure yet whether she wanted to provoke a fight but keeping her options open.

He led them into an office which had his name on the door. It looked over the town. 'And I know you're busy too, Inspector. I'm sorry to have kept you.'

There was a desk near the window but he pulled three easy chairs round a low coffee table and they sat there. Again she was taken by how self-assured he was. She wanted to shake him.

'You're difficult to pin down. You haven't been avoiding us?'

'Of course not. It's been a very difficult time here. Edmund's death has thrown the whole business of the quarry into question.'

'Why? It had nothing to do with him.'

'It's a matter of publicity. You know that Slateburn is working with the Fulwells on the project. Livvy is very keen to go ahead but we have the impression that Robert would rather let the matter go. At least for the moment. He sees it as a question of taste.'

'What would you think about that?'

485

He paused. 'I'm an employee of Slateburn Quarries. I'll implement whatever strategy is decided.'

'But you must have a personal view.'

'Not when I'm in this office, no.'

'I was told you were the great enthusiast. The power behind the whole scheme.'

'I don't know who told you that.' He paused again, frowning. When Vera said nothing he went on, 'It's my job to be enthusiastic.'

Vera stretched her legs. The chairs were low. They'd be comfortable enough for snoozing in but not for sitting up straight and taking notice.

'But Mr Waugh must be keen for the scheme to go ahead. He'll have invested a fortune just to get this far.'

'I think he's open-minded, he could be persuaded either way. The inquiry will cost in legal fees if we decide to go ahead. Godfrey was certainly more positive when we received a favourable Environmental Impact Assessment report. The company's sponsorship of the Wildlife Trust was a gamble. Once we'd become involved in that we couldn't afford to be seen damaging an area of conservation importance in any way.'

'Who called the meeting earlier in the week to discuss the future of the quarry?'

'The Fulwells. We wouldn't have intruded the day after Edmund's death.'

'Which particular Fulwell?' As if we don't already know, Vera thought. She narrowed her eyes and looked at him.

'Probably Olivia. Hoping that we'd exert some influence on Robert. During the meeting she accused him of having gone weedy on her.'

For the first time Neville had lost his professional cool. Vera was gleeful.

'You don't like Mrs Fulwell,' she said, keeping her voice neutral.

'Not much. When I worked for Robert she interfered. That was one of the reasons I was glad to leave Holme Park.'

'Who else was at the meeting?'

'Pete Kemp, our conservation consultant.'

Vera stretched again, stifled a yawn. The room was very warm. 'I don't suppose it matters to him one way or the other what's decided about the quarry. He'll be paid for his report whether the development goes ahead or not.'

'Oh, he's already been paid,' Furness said dryly. 'But it's not precisely true that he's nothing to gain from the development. If it does go ahead Godfrey has promised a new nature reserve close to the site. It was part of the plan. Kemp Associates would draw up the management agreement for that and provide the staff. It would be a lucrative contract.'

You don't like Peter Kemp either, Vera thought. Why's that, I wonder. It annoyed her that she couldn't make up her mind about Neville Furness. She couldn't pin him down, work out what made him tick. It was a matter of pride to her that her first impressions of people were sound. She boasted about it to Ashworth all the time. But her impressions of Furness were confused and unreliable.

'What did you do with the key to your house on the estate when you left?' she asked, hoping to shock him.

He didn't answer immediately.

'You did have a key?'

'I'm sorry,' he said. 'Obviously it's important. I'm trying to remember. I had two keys. One to the front door and one to the back. On a single ring.'

'Did you give them back to Mrs Fulwell?' It was Ashworth's first contribution.

'No. Definitely not that. I'd given my letter of resignation to Robert. I had some holiday to take so effectively I left Holme Park without notice. That was how I wanted it. I didn't want any scenes.'

'Would Mrs Fulwell have made a scene?' Ashworth asked.

'She's spoilt. Given occasionally to tantrums.'

'Was your relationship with Mrs Fulwell entirely professional?'

'On my part, certainly.'

'And on hers?'

'As I explained, she interfered.'

'She fancied you,' Vera interrupted with a chortle. 'Don't tell me she wanted a bit of rough.'

He blushed violently and for a moment she wondered if she had a handle on him. He was shy, a prude. There was no more to it than that. But then he recovered his composure so quickly that she thought she must be wrong.

'So far as I am aware,' he said stiffly, 'Robert and Livvy have a very happy marriage.'

'Let's get back to the keys then,' Vera said unabashed. 'You didn't give them to Livvy. Did you give them to Robert?'

'I don't think so. He wouldn't normally be involved in that sort of detail.'

'So you kept them then?'

'I suppose it's possible. I mean I suppose it's possible that I just forgot to give them back.'

'Where would they be? At home?'

'No, I'm starting to remember. The keys to the house at Holme Park were on the same ring as the spares for Black Law. Bella asked me to have them in case of an emergency. In case something happened to my father when she wasn't around. And I've always kept those here. I spend more time in the office than I do at home. They were certainly here when you asked for a key to get into the farmhouse after the girl was killed on the hill.'

He stood up and went to his desk. From where he was sitting Vera couldn't see him open the drawer but it didn't seem to be locked. He returned with a Wildlife Trust key ring, with three keys attached.

'These two belong to Black Law. The mortise is the front door and the Yale the back. This is for the front door of the Holme Park house.'

'What about the Holme Park kitchen door?'

'I don't know. It's not here. I could have sworn it was on the same ring.'

'When was the last time you saw it?'

'God knows. The last time I took them out was to give you the Black Law key. I suppose I see them every time I go into the desk drawer, but I don't look at them. Not in any detail.'

'Who else would have had access to your desk?'

He looked at her in surprise. 'We're very security conscious. Nobody gets into this suite of offices without a pass.'

'But your desk wasn't locked.'

'No. Nor my office. It doesn't need to be. As I've explained it's impossible for a stranger to wander in.'

'But anybody working for Slateburn or here on official business could have had access to the key.'

'I suppose so. If they'd wanted to. If they'd realized it was there.'

'Was it labelled?'

He hesitated. 'Yes. Just like this one.'

He handed her the Holme Park front door key. Attached to it was a small card tag, faded but just legible with 1 The Avenue written in cramped capitals. 'That's the official address of the house.'

'Would your secretary go into that drawer?'

'I don't think so. It's mostly personal stuff. But you can ask her.'

'Yes,' Vera said. 'We will.'

Neville Furness had remained standing. Perhaps he expected them to go but they sat where they were, silent, watching him.

'I didn't use that key,' he said quietly. 'And I hate the thought that anyone else might have used it, that through my carelessness I was responsible for Edmund's death.'

Still Vera said nothing. The silence seemed to get to him because he went on, 'It's been a hellish week. The Fulwells have made things very difficult here. We don't know where we are. If only they'd decide one way or another... We're all rather wound up.' He stopped abruptly. 'But that's not your problem. Of course you've got more serious concerns... Actually I've decided I need to get away from it for a while. I'm going to escape at the weekend, spend some time at

Black Law. It'll be all right, will it? You said your team had finished.'

Vera nodded. 'Have you seen Rachael Lambert this week?'

'Yes,' he said. 'She needs a break too. She's coming up to Black Law with me.' He paused. 'Aren't you going to ask me where I was on the day Edmund Fulwell was killed?'

'We'd have got round to it,' Vera said comfortably.

'I was here for most of the day going through the preliminary draft of the Environment Impact Assessment.'

'On your own?'

'Yes, though I wouldn't have been able to leave the building without going through reception and there's always someone there. I left the office at about four and went home to change. Godfrey had been working at home all day. He'd had Peter Kemp to see him to go over the plans for the new nature reserve at Black Law and he wanted to discuss them with me. I'd been invited to dinner but he wanted me there early so we could finish the business before we ate.'

'Did you have a pleasant evening?' Vera heaved herself out of her chair.

'Yes, thank you. Very pleasant.'

He shepherded them through reception and waited with them until the lift had arrived.

Outside she stood for a moment, imagining Neville and Rachael on their own in Black Law. If he meant Rachael harm, surely he wouldn't have told her about the trip? Or perhaps she'd just been involved in setting a very clever trap.

Chapter Sixty-Two

Vera walked from the police station to Edie's house in Riverside Terrace. It wasn't far and she needed a break from the incident room, the team frenetic, desperate for her approval, waiting for her to work miracles. She hoped that Edie would remind her of Baikie's where things had seemed clearer, that she could recapture something of the old certainties.

Edie had invited her for lunch and thinking she should make a token contribution she stopped at the small florist's in the High Street for flowers. Flowers had been left at the mine to mark the spot of Grace's death. Flowers for mourning. For remembrance. Or for celebration.

At the end of the terrace she stopped to get her breath. She didn't want to turn up at the house puffing and sweaty. A car passed her, stopped outside Edie's and Peter Kemp jumped out. He wasn't driving the white Land Rover but something sleek and sporty with a loud engine. He was in casual mode – grey cotton trousers and a green polo shirt with the company logo embroidered on the pocket. Very corporate. He leapt up the steps and hit the doorbell with his palm.

By the time Vera reached the front door Peter was inside, in the basement kitchen. She leant over the rails but though she could see the couple she couldn't tell what they were saying. Obviously, it wasn't a friendly exchange. She paused for a moment but then curiosity got the better of her and she rang the bell. When Edie opened the door she was flushed.

'Thank God,' she muttered. 'If you hadn't come I might have murdered him.'

In the kitchen beside the scrubbed pine table and chairs, there was a small sofa with an Indian cotton bedspread thrown over it. Peter Kemp had sat there when Edie left the room to answer the door. He lounged, his long legs stretched lengthways along the floor beside it so there was no room for anyone else to sit down. When he saw Vera he got slowly up to his feet.

'Inspector,' he said. 'What a surprise. And I always thought Ms Lambert was such an upright person. I hope you haven't come to make an arrest.' He looked pointedly at the flowers, drooping now. 'Ah no. I see it's a social visit.' The words came out as an accusation.

His freckles seemed very prominent against his fair skin.

'Look,' Edie interrupted. 'You'd better go. There's nothing more to say.'

He seemed about to argue but thought better of it, became instead concerned. 'You know,' he said, 'I'm very fond of Rachael. I've her best interests at heart. I wouldn't want her disappointed.'

Edie let him go first up the stairs, turned to Vera and mimed being sick behind his back. As she came back into the room they heard his car roar into life and drive away. She banged around furiously, setting the table with cutlery and whatever she could find in the fridge. Vera waited until half a loaf, a pleated ball of silver foil with a smear of boursin inside, a lump of dried-up cheddar and a couple of slices of ham had appeared before speaking. Edie was by the sink, shaking a ready prepared salad from its plastic bag into a bowl.

'What was all that about?'

'He always was an arrogant little shit,' Edie said.

'What did he want?'

'He must have heard that Rachael was thinking of applying for another job. He asked me to persuade her to stay. If he gets the contract for the new nature reserve at Black Law he's relying on her to manage it. He's scared he won't be able to run the firm without her. He's right. He wouldn't.'

'I suppose that's quite flattering.'

'But it was the way that he did it. Do you know what he said? "She ought to realize that now's probably not a good time. Prospective employers would be wary of taking on anyone who's been linked to a murder inquiry" implying that Rachael might have had some-thing to do with Grace's death.'

Vera realized that Edie was close to tears. In the fridge she'd seen a bottle of wine, three-quarters full with the cork jammed back in. She took it out, poured each of them a glass, drank, winced and wondered how long it had been there.

'Why do you want to talk to me anyway?' Edie said, still angry. 'You said you wanted to ask about Neville. If you come back this evening you can see Rachael. She'll be able to tell you everything you want to hear.'

'I understand she's besotted. That doesn't do a lot for a person's judgement.'

'Who told you that?'

'Anne Preece. I went to Langholme to see her last night.'

'She's still there then. I'm surprised. I thought she'd decided to leave.'

'Oh, she's still there,' Vera said. 'But she seems in a sort of limbo. Waiting for something to happen. You haven't any idea what she might be waiting for?'

'Some man perhaps. She's very discreet but I gather it's not a successful marriage. Still, how many are?'

Vera hacked a slice of bread from the loaf. 'Well?' she demanded. 'Is she?'

Edie, still preoccupied, looked up from her glass. 'Is she what?'

'Is Rachael besotted?'

'Definitely. I haven't seen her like this since she first started going out with that toad Peter Kemp.'

'I didn't realize she'd been involved with him.' Vera's voice was bland, vaguely curious, but her mind was whirring furiously. Another connection. Another complication.

'Before he was married. I never liked him. Perhaps that's why she stuck with him so long. To spite me. I shouldn't have made my feelings about him so plain. I could never manage tact with Rachael.'

'But she carried on working with him.'

'That was pride, I think. She didn't want to be seen to be running away.'

'According to Rachael they've more work than they can handle. And he's just given her a pay rise. To bribe her to stay, I suppose.'

'So he's not short of money?'

'Apparently not though I hear his wife has very

expensive tastes.' Edie pulled a face. 'Sorry, that was bitchy. I can't help listening to gossip.'

'Nothing wrong with gossip, pet. It's what my job's all about. What else does the gossip say?'

'That he married her for her money then discovered she wasn't as loaded as he thought. Daddy's wealthy but not very generous.' Edie drank the last of her wine. 'Rachael's not been happy at Kemp Associates for a while. I suppose Grace's death pushed her into looking actively for something else. There's a research post for the RSPB which interests her. It would be based in Wales. I know she's ready for a move but I'd miss her. Especially now. We've been getting on better lately.' Edie paused. 'And she'd miss Neville. Perhaps that's why she's taking so long to decide whether or not to go for it. Secretly she's waiting for him to sweep her away to Black Law so she can live with him happily ever after.'

'Is that likely?'

'God knows.'

'Perhaps that was what the scene with Peter was all about.'

'What do you mean?' Edie bristled again at the mention of Peter.

'That he's still fond of Rachael and he doesn't want to lose her to Neville. I suppose it's even possible that they've been having an affair. If Peter's not happy with his wife.'

'No!' Edie was horrified. 'Rachael wouldn't be so dumb. Not even as a way of getting back at me. And jealousy's such a very human emotion. I don't think Peter Kemp's capable of it.'

Neville might be though, Vera thought. But where does that take us?

'Did you know that Neville was planning to take Rachael to Black Law this weekend?'

'She has mentioned it. Once or twice. She's like a kid who's never been on holiday before.'

'And you've agreed?'

'It's not my place to agree or disagree, is it? She's an adult. Too old for a lecture on safe sex.' Edie looked at Vera thoughtfully across the table. 'Unless there's something you think I should know. Even then I can hardly invite myself up there as a watchdog or chaperone this time.'

'No.' Vera refilled both glasses. 'I suppose not. What do you make of Neville Furness?'

'I can see why Rachael's attracted.'

'Yes,' Vera said. 'So can I.'

'I hope he's not mucking her about.'

'Do you think he might be?'

'I don't think so. I think perhaps he's just very shy, very private. He doesn't give anything of himself away. I should be used to that in Rachael. I think I should trust her judgement.'

'Have you seen much of him?'

'He's very much the gentleman. Whenever he calls to take her out he makes a point of letting me know where they're going and what time he'll be back. You know they've seen each other every day since we moved back to Kimmerston.'

'I had been keeping an eye on him. Discreetly. But after Edmund's death we didn't have the men to spare.'

'Do you know where he was on the afternoon Edmund Fulwell was killed?'

'I know where he says he was. Of course we'll check. Why?'

'He used to live in that house.'

'I know.'

'Should I persuade Rachael not to go with him at the weekend? She might listen to me. As I say, we've been getting on better lately.'

'No,' Vera said quietly. 'Don't do that.'

'I'd not have her put in any danger.'

'No,' Vera said. 'Nor would I.'

Chapter Sixty-Three

Vera decided to call on the Waughs unannounced. Neville Furness had given her an excuse. She needed to check his alibi for the afternoon and evening of Edmund's death and the Waughs' house was on the way home. Almost. Even without the excuse she would have made the visit. Anne Preece had roused her curiosity. She wanted to see the family together.

She had grown up with a rosy picture of conventional life and blamed the lack of it for the fact that she'd turned out such an awkward cow. In her work though she'd hardly come across a great deal of domestic bliss and the colleagues who played most at happy families were the ones she suspected of jumping into bed with anything that moved. Living a sham. Not Ashworth though. He was the exception. He restored her faith in her childhood dream.

She timed her visit carefully for seven o'clock. Godfrey Waugh should be home from work by now. Surely this would be a time they would spend together. But when she pulled up onto the gravel drive the house was lifeless and she thought they must be out. After the thunderstorms of the week before the weather had changed again. It was warm and still and the hills seemed distant, hazy in the heat, yet none of the windows were open. She listened for the sound of a television or children shouting but everything was quiet.

After ringing the bell she turned back to look out at the garden because she expected no answer and was surprised to hear the catch being lifted, the door opening. Inside stood a woman, holding a tea towel. She wore pink rubber gloves which reached almost to her elbows. Underneath them, Vera knew, would be manicured nails. The woman smiled pleasantly enough but Vera had taken against her. Even washing pans she wore make-up. Vera had an image of her sitting at her dressing table preparing herself carefully for her husband's return from work. Through desire? Duty? Either way it was letting the side down.

'Are you Mrs Waugh?' The question came out more abruptly than Vera had intended. She found it hard to reconcile the picture of this self-confident creature with Anne Preece's description of an anxious woman, a victim, the subject of bullying.

'Yes.'

'Inspector Stanhope. I'm investigating the murder of Edmund Fulwell. Would it be possible to speak to your husband?'

'Of course.' Barbara Waugh took off a glove and held out her hand. Vera, stretching out hers, was aware of her own nails – bitten, split, slightly grubby. The woman shouted back into the house, 'Darling, it's Inspector Stanhope. She'd like to speak to you.'

It was impossible to tell what she thought of the intrusion.

Vera followed her into the hall. Through an open door she saw into a small room, brightly painted, with a shelf of toys beyond a pine desk. A girl sat in front of a computer screen. She was playing a game intently, clasping the joystick with both hands. The sound had been turned off and the aliens on the screen were being zapped, silently. A flashing green light indicated the final score and the girl's concentration was momentarily relaxed. She turned and Vera had a glimpse of a pale, rather puffy face before she had to greet Godfrey who was walking down the hall towards her.

He had changed from his office clothes and had the look of a politician who has been told to dress casually. He wore thin cord trousers and a checked open-neck shirt. If it had been colder he would have gone for a patterned sweater.

'Inspector.' He frowned. If anything, Vera thought, he seemed the more anxious of the couple though he covered it well. 'Is anything wrong?'

'No,' she said. Thinking, except that two people have been killed. A father and a daughter. Just like you and the child playing on the computer. 'It's a routine visit. I had a few questions and as I have to pass here anyway on my way home . . .'

He led her into a sitting room which smelled of beeswax polish. An oil painting of their daughter hung prominently over the fireplace. It was too accurate to be flattering but Vera muttered something polite about how pretty she was. Her dealings with Ashworth had taught her how to talk to parents. She had obviously pressed the right button because Waugh responded warmly. His voice was local but the words, carefully chosen, a little long-winded, also had something of the politician about them.

'We'd almost reconciled ourselves to being

childless, then Felicity arrived. Perhaps because it was so unexpected it was a real joy.'

Barbara, standing in the doorway, smiled too but a tension about her eyes made Vera think that the strain of caring for the child meant that for her the joy wasn't entirely undiluted. She felt a sudden sympathy for the woman and wondered if perhaps Anne Preece had been right. It was up to her, after all, if she wanted to tart herself up.

'Would you like tea, Inspector? Or coffee? Then I expect you'd like to speak to my husband alone.'

What I'd really like, Vera thought, is a beer. But she said that tea would be very nice. 'And I hope you'll be able to join us, Mrs Waugh. I'd appreciate your opinion.'

Barbara seemed pleased by this but once she'd left the room Godfrey said, 'I don't know how my wife can help you, Inspector. She stays at home and cares full time for our daughter. Since the young woman was killed on the hill she's been reluctant to leave the house on her own.'

'I thought she was a partner in your business.'

That surprised him. It was as if he had forgotten the fact. 'Officially yes, though she takes no active part.'

'How does she feel about the development of the quarry?'

Godfrey paused, gave a thin little smile. 'She has a rather sentimental view of the company, I'm afraid. Her father was a craftsman and she doesn't always understand that we've had to move on from that scale of business. It's not a cottage industry any more. We have to survive.'

'If it came to a vote would she support you?'

There was a brief frown of irritation then the smile returned.

'It would never come to a vote. What would be the point? We're the only two partners. We'll come to a decision together. Though of course there are other people involved. The present landowners – the Fulwells. Without their agreeing to lease the land the proposal would come to nothing.'

'And Neville Furness?'

'Neville's an employee. I value his judgement but he won't be involved in the final decision.'

'It's not been made then?'

He hesitated. 'No. We all felt we needed a few days to consider the matter. We're meeting again on Friday.'

He stopped abruptly as Barbara Waugh came in. She was carrying a tray and the child followed with a plate of home-made biscuits. She handed them to Vera and her father, then put the plate on a coffee table and made to leave the room without a word. Vera saw that she had three of the biscuits clasped in one hand and winked at her as she was shutting the door. The girl glared back, stonily.

'Will you be at the meeting on Friday, Mrs Waugh?' Vera asked conversationally.

'What meeting?'

'The meeting to decide whether or not the quarry should go ahead.'

Godfrey interrupted quickly. 'Barbara doesn't need to involve herself in the day to day running of the business. She leaves all that to me.'

'But I thought a decision had been made.' Barbara sat across the room from them, knees firmly together, hands clasped on her lap. Convent educated, Vera thought. I can always tell. 'Godfrey, didn't you say the plans would be dropped for the present?'

He shrugged. 'Livvy must have been putting pressure on Robert. He called this afternoon just before I left work, and said he thought it would be worth our getting together again.'

'You didn't tell me.' Suddenly she was close to losing control. 'I'm not sure I can stand all this again. The publicity. People talking.'

He leant back in his seat. In the gesture Vera sensed distaste, even a mild revulsion, but he spoke kindly. 'That's why I didn't tell you. I knew you were relieved that the project had been put on ice. And really that's still the most likely outcome. Robert isn't at all keen and he can be very stubborn.'

'Nonsense. Once Livvy Fulwell and Neville Furness get together neither of you will be able to stand up to them.'

'That's ridiculous. Neville won't even be at the meeting. He's taken Friday off. And you have to trust me to do what's best for all of us. One day this business will be Felicity's.'

He was making an effort to keep his voice even but had begun to sound irritated. Vera thought, So, that's what makes him tick. That's where the ambition comes from. He doesn't want the girl to have to struggle. And she thought of her own father whose only ambition was to collect successive clutches of eggs from every bird breeding in the county. Who'd never thought of her once.

Now Waugh seemed embarrassed. 'Look,' he said quietly. 'We'll discuss this later. The inspector doesn't want to hear all this.'

Vera reached out to dunk a biscuit in her tea. 'Don't mind me, it's fascinating. I'm just glad to get the weight off my feet.'

'How can we help you?'

'As I said. Details to check. Very boring but necessary. Neville Furness used to work in Holme Park. He lived in the house where Edmund Fulwell was killed. It seems that he still had a key to the house.'

'Neville wouldn't have killed anyone.'

'It's not a character reference I'm after, Mr Waugh. He says he was here on the evening Edmund Fulwell was killed.'

'He was. Peter Kemp had drawn up some interesting proposals for the new upland nature reserve on the Black Law site. I needed to discuss that with him. We thought it would provide positive publicity to coincide with the publication of the Kemp Associates report.'

'What time did he arrive?'

'I'm not sure. About four thirty.'

'No,' Barbara said loudly. 'Later than that. Quarter past five at the earliest. I'd just collected Felicity. She'd been at her friend's for tea. We pulled up at the same time.'

Godfrey looked at her calmly.

'Is your wife right, Mr Waugh?'

'Yes, Inspector. I believe she is.'

Barbara stood up suddenly. 'I promised I'd help Felicity with her homework. I'm sure Godfrey can help you with anything else you need, Inspector. He'll see you out.'

And she left the room before Vera could say anything. After her previous hospitality the abrupt departure was awkward, almost rude. Later Vera thought she could have called Barbara back, made some attempt to see her alone. Then she could have offered help, given her the office phone number, pushed for more information about Neville Furness. As it was she just followed Godfrey to the door and said goodbye to the girl who'd returned to the computer. Despite the talk about homework Barbara was nowhere to be seen.

Outside she paused by her car. Swifts swooped above the house weaving a cat's cradle pattern in the sky. She lingered, thinking that Barbara might find some excuse to talk to her. But, turning back, she saw the woman in an upstairs window, not looking at her at all but staring at the hill beyond.

Chapter Sixty-Four

In her house by the railway line Vera opened a bottle
of red wine and drank most of it sitting by the open
kitchen window until the colour had drained from the
hills. As the wine began to take effect she was troubled
not by doubts about the investigation but by memories
of Constance Baikie. She had a picture of the woman
as she had last seen her, lying wide and soft on her
sofa, looking out at Vera with sly black eyes. Since
her father's death she had thought of him often. With
anger, guilt, occasional flashes of reluctant affection.
He had been company. Another person to talk to.
Connie she had largely forgotten until she had walked
into Baikie's Cottage, dripping with rain, to investigate
a young woman's murder and then all the memories
had returned.

As she drained her second glass it occurred to Vera
for the first time that Hector and Connie might have
been lovers. After all she had never seen him with
another woman. Almost immediately she dismissed
the idea. Their joint passion had been for their illicit
collections, for the secret obsession which took them
out onto the hills before dawn to deprive birds of their
young, leaving the nests empty and cold. They had
shared the secret excitement. They were drawn closer

by the danger which exposed them to blackmail and threatened their reputations and careers. It had nothing to do with love or even friendship.

Then, at almost the same time as she remembered that she had not eaten since Edie's bread and cheese at lunchtime, she was struck by the thought that the murderer she was seeking could be similarly obsessive. The daughter and then the father had been killed. Like Hector taking clutches from the same nest. There was no apparent motive but evidence of meticulous planning especially before Edmund's death. Behind the killings she saw a passion as intense and irrational as that which had driven her father, clouded his judgement, ruined both their lives. Yet Hector had been quite different before his wife died. She had seen photographs of him, talking to friends, laughing. Even afterwards he had held down a respectable job until his retirement, had been considered a little eccentric, a bit of a loner, but not any sort of threat. She should be looking for someone with a secret obsession and when she understood what that was perhaps she would know why Grace and Edmund had been killed.

Her mobile phone rang. She came to her senses, thought, What a load of crap, get a grip, lady. Imagine explaining that to Ashworth and the crew.

On the phone was Christina Flood the psychologist. In the background was the sound of a flute playing something Celtic and mournful.

'I've dug out that information you wanted. You can come and get it if you like. I know it's late but we've taken to sleeping at the same time as the baby and she's definitely a night owl. We'll be up for hours.'

Vera was tempted then she saw the empty bottle

on the window sill and thought better of it. Some rules she was not prepared to break.

'I can't tonight,' she said. 'I've had a few glasses of wine. Definitely over the limit.'

Christina was surprisingly insistent. 'Why don't we bring it to you? If you don't have the stuff now, it'll have to wait until Monday. We're away for the weekend, showing off the sprog to doting grandparents.'

'Are you sure?'

'Of course. We're all wide awake. Patrick and the baby want to play.'

Vera had almost given them up and it was midnight before she saw the headlights moving down the lane towards the house. She went out to wait for them, thinking perhaps they had been lost and would need reassuring that they'd got the right place. They were in a sea blue van with the words THE MUSIC MAN stencilled in orange along the side. Christina was apologetic.

'My car wouldn't start. Flat battery. So we had to come in Patrick's.'

'I was glad you could make it.'

'Not at all. We've enjoyed the jaunt. Especially the baby.'

'We're going for a walk,' Patrick said. 'Leave you two in peace.'

'No need.'

'We want to,' he said. 'We've never done moonlight before.'

And he walked down the lane with the baby in a sling on his back and disappeared into the black shadow of the old station house.

'Did you decide on a name for her?' Vera asked.

'Miranda. Theatrical enough for Patrick but not too outrageous.'

They sat at the kitchen table drinking tea. Christina's papers were in a large box file. There were shorthand notebooks containing a jotted record of each meeting of the group, and some photocopies of patients' record sheets.

'I need these because in the notebooks I often just use first names or initials and after all this time I can't remember the backgrounds of every individual patient. But I'm still concerned about confidentiality. I promised each group that anything said would be secret.' She hesitated. 'Look, I'd like you to read the notebooks first. That way the people involved can remain anonymous. If anything strikes you as especially significant we can discuss revealing the identity of the people concerned.'

'Wouldn't it be simpler just to give me a list of the patients who attended the same group as Bella and Edmund? I can see if there's a name I recognize.'

Christina paused again, chose her words carefully. 'It might be simpler but I don't think you'd find it useful.'

'You're saying there's something relevant in these notebooks?'

'I think you should read them.'

So Vera read. Bella and Edmund were founder members of the first group. Christina had taken detailed notes of each session. Bella was referred to by first name and Edmund by initials. In the beginning it was clear that Christina was frustrated by the way the group was operating. She even considered packing the whole thing in. A male patient was dominating every discussion. He talked constantly about his destructive relationship with his mother. She'd overprotected him and became ill every time he wanted to leave her. The other patients were too polite or too apathetic to shut him up. Vera was surprised no one had thumped him.

Only in the third meeting was some progress made and then it was Edmund who had interrupted. Christina had written down his exact words.

'For Christ's sake, do you think you're the only person to have had a shitty childhood? Haven't you ever read Larkin?'

And he had gone on to talk angrily about his life at Holme Park, about the mother who was always too wrapped up in her social life and her elder son to give time to him, the succession of incompetent nannies, the restrictions and the boredom. 'There was only one person who cared for me and the rest of them treated her like shite. Just because she couldn't read or write very well.'

Nancy Deakin, Vera thought. And she cared for him until the end.

That had stimulated a more general discussion. Others had come in with halting stories of their own. There were hints of abuse and bullying. One woman had been brought up believing her mother was her sister. Another's father had thrown himself under a train.

Very jolly, Vera thought. She hoped Christina was happy in her work.

There was no mention of any contribution from Bella until the fifth session. Then, prompted by Edmund who had already befriended her, she had told the story of her father's death. It was much as Vera had expected. Charles had always made her feel guilty – she at least had escaped for a while, made friends, found a job she enjoyed. And Arthur Noble had never hit her. All his frustration had been taken out on the boy. When she returned to the family home Bella's little brother had increased the pressure relentlessly.

In her notebook Christina described the scene as Bella told her story.

It was remarkable. Until Edmund persuaded her to speak Bella had always been a passive member of the group, sometimes supporting other people but never seeking attention for herself. Now it seemed she couldn't stop talking and she moved physically into the centre of the circle. She began to act out the attack which killed her father, starting with receiving the phone call from her brother and ending with raising her arm to smack the heavy bronze onto his skull. She was in tears, saying that she should have been charged with murder and not with manslaughter. She had planned to kill him. The group gathered round to offer support.

Vera looked up briefly from the notebook. 'She could have left them to it. Gone back to teaching. She was still responsible.'

'Yes.'

'Do you think she should have got away with it?'

'Do you think she did?' Christina stood up, stretched. 'I'll make some more tea, shall I?'

When she returned with the mugs Vera was engrossed, hunched over the table frowning. Eventually she looked up furiously, pushed the notebook towards the psychologist.

'Why didn't you do something about this at the time?'

'Because I didn't believe it.'

'Didn't you recognize the story?'

'Of course. But it wasn't unusual. The patient had experienced a number of psychotic fantasies, had imagined, for example, being famous. Those were triggered by news events, movies, even TV soaps. Later we managed to control the episodes but at the time I couldn't be expected to take the story seriously.'

'How did the rest of the group respond?'

'They didn't believe it. They were sympathetic but sceptical.'

'What do you think now? Do you believe it could have been true?'

'I think it's far-fetched but you have a right to know what was claimed. That's why I'm here.'

'I'm sorry.' Vera stood up, walked to the window. There was a full moon which lit up the meadow. Patrick and the baby were silhouetted against the light.

'Could that sort of illness reoccur after a period of normality?'

'You'd need to check with a psychiatrist, but no, it wouldn't be unusual. Do you think that's what's happened here?'

'Don't you?'

'I'm not sure,' Christina said. 'As a way of surviving, these murders make perfect sense. I don't think that's madness.'

'Well, it'll not be for me to decide. Thank God.' Vera turned back into the room. 'You'll have to let me see the patient's notes. You do realize that. I have to know who this lunatic is. If it is a lunatic.'

For a moment Christina hesitated. Through the open window they heard footsteps on the lane as Patrick approached. He was singing to the baby. Some sort of lullaby.

'For Christ's sake,' Vera hissed. 'You of all people can't let this go.'

'No.' Christina took a single sheet of paper from her file and left it on the table. She went out of the house to meet Patrick. When they returned the paper was back in its file and Vera was on the telephone. The baby was fast asleep, her mouth slightly open, her head tilted back. Vera replaced the receiver.

'Will you make an arrest?' Christina asked.

'Not yet. As you said the story's too far-fetched to accept without proof. But there'll be no more killings either, I hope.'

She walked with them to the van. It was just starting to turn from moonlight to dawn. There was a pale grey flush on the horizon. In the distance a single blackbird began to sing.

'It was an obsession, wasn't it?'

'Oh yes.' Christina was cradling Miranda in one arm, sliding her into the baby seat without waking her. 'If we're right, that's exactly what it was.'

Chapter Sixty-Five

Vera's instinct was to wait. The Black Law Fells seemed empty but they were exposed. There was no way she could drive to the site without the chance of being seen by a gamekeeper, a shepherd or a walker and the last thing she wanted was a rumour in Langholme, spreading like a moorland fire, that the police were snooping around again. It was a small place. Soon everyone would know.

She spread her Ordnance Survey map on her desk. In this way Hector and Connie had planned their raids, looking for cover, the best route to the nests of ospreys or black-necked grebes, avoiding local volunteers and wardens. Again she felt she was reliving her past.

The only way she could see of getting to Baikie's and the mine without risk of being seen from a distance was to park up the track in the Forestry Commission plantation. Then she could walk out onto the hill by the crow trap. But that would be impossible. That was the way she expected the murderer to go.

It was Friday morning. After Christina and Patrick had left she'd slept, very deeply, for three hours then woken to the sound of the neighbouring cockerel and the first train. She'd phoned Edie, obviously wakened her.

'Can I speak to Rachael?'

'She's not here. She was out with Neville yesterday evening and stayed the night.' There was a pause. 'Look, she's all right. She phoned to say what was happening, gave me Neville's number. If you want I can get it for you.'

'That's all right. I've got it.'

'Has anything happened?' Now Edie was sufficiently awake to start to panic.

'No.' Vera sounded reassuring, even to her own ears. 'Will she be at work today?'

'No, she's taken a day's leave. They're going up to Black Law.'

'Of course.' As if she'd forgotten about that. 'Do you know what time they intend to set off?'

'After lunch I think. Look, do you want me to phone them? I can find out what their plans are.'

Vera considered the idea but only briefly. Better not to interfere. No one must know she was interested in Black Law today.

'No. Don't do that. Let them have a couple of days away without thinking about the investigation. I don't want to spoil things for them.'

So she sat in the green, cell-like office with the map spread across her desk, planning her campaign. Aware that time was passing, that if she wanted to get in before Rachael and Neville, she'd have to move quickly, that she might already be too late.

She hit some buttons on her phone and spoke to Ashworth, who had been sitting parked in his wife's car by the side of the road since Vera had phoned him after reading Christina Flood's file.

'Any movement?'

'Not yet.'

'I'm going to walk in, down the public footpath from Langholme like all the other ramblers. If I dress the part no one will know any difference.'

'You'll need back up.'

'You can organize that later when we know what's happening. I don't want half the force on standby without cause. I'd look a right bloody prat. There's not enough to go on.'

'Would you rather I went in?'

'Don't be daft. You don't know the way. I practically grew up in these hills.' She paused. 'I'm going now. I'll call at home on the way to change. I'll park the car near the church at Langholme. That's what all the walkers do.'

'Bit risky, isn't it?'

'I'll be careful. I'll not be seen.'

Famous last words, she thought. She picked up her bag and sailed out of the station, ignoring the officers who wanted to pass on information, and the demands to know where she was going.

'You can get hold of me through Ashworth,' she said imperiously, sweeping through the door, not even looking back to check that anyone was listening.

At home she found some walking breeches of Hector's. Usually she never wore trousers. Anything on her legs made her eczema worse and she knew she'd suffer the next day. But in them she looked different, a completely new shape and profile. A thin waterproof anorak, boots and thick socks completed the picture. She went out of the house to check that the map was in the car and the ageing hippie, trying to round up a goat in the next field, stared at her, not recognizing her at all. Vera had intended to make a flask and sandwiches but she looked at her watch and found there wasn't time. She took a packet of chocolate biscuits from the kitchen cupboard, filled a bottle of water and drove off. Only then did the woman in the field realize it must be Vera and gave a belated, rather startled wave.

Langholme was quiet. The church door was open and there was the buzz of a Hoover, then when that stopped women's voices talking about flowers. She locked her car and put the keys into the zipped jacket pocket. She walked carefully past the Priory, not looking into the garden or at any of the other cars parked outside. The road ended with a five-barred gate and a fence with a stile. She crossed it and followed the well-worn path towards Black Law, walking steadily, only turning her head from time to time to check that no one was following her.

The path crossed the hill. On the lower slopes there were dry stone walls. The grass was cropped low by sheep. When she'd walked here in her childhood she'd been fit. From Langholme to the tarn had seemed a stroll. Since then she'd eaten too many curries and Chinese carry-outs. She'd drunk too much, spent too long in her car. It was another clear, hot day and soon she was sweating and dizzy with exertion. She took off the jacket and tied it round her waist by the sleeves. Already her legs were itching like crazy.

She walked through a gap in the last crumbling wall and the path climbed steeply. The ground was more uneven. Bright green bog and tufts of juncous, curlew and skylark. But all she could see was the next place to put her boot and all she could hear was her laboured breathing. At the tarn she allowed herself to rest. She drank some water and ate a biscuit. As she licked the melted chocolate from her fingers she felt her pulse return to something like normal. A slight breeze rippled the water and dried the sweat on her face. From where she sat she could look down into the valley, to Baikie's and Black Law farmhouse and the old mine. She stood up and walked on, finding the going easier because it was downhill.

She walked straight past the mine without looking inside the engine house, without showing any interest, followed the path along the burn, then took the short detour over the stile into Baikie's garden. It was as if, suddenly, she'd stepped into a tropical wilderness. In the few days since the women had left the grass had grown and needed cutting. The sun and the rain had brought more shrubs into flower. She walked round the house, found the key and let herself in through the back door. The house smelled hot and damp like a greenhouse. In the kitchen she peeled off the walking breeches and stood, pink-fleshed, bare-legged, desperate to scratch, waiting for the kettle to boil, hoping that there would be enough instant coffee in one of the jars to see her through.

She sat upstairs in the front bedroom because from there she had a view of the valley and the burn as far as the edge of the forestry plantation and the crow trap in one direction and the old mine buildings in the other. Connie had slept here before she had become too frail and fat to climb the stairs, in a large double bed with a brocade cover. Vera had a shadowy memory of one of the parties she'd attended as a child. She'd been sent upstairs to put the visitors' coats on the bed and had been fascinated by the jars and bottles on the enormous Victorian dressing table, the alien female smell of perfume and face powder. Now the room looked like a dormitory in a youth hostel, the blankets folded at the end of the beds, the pillows in their striped cases.

At three o'clock Neville Furness and Rachael arrived. From the bedroom window Vera couldn't see the farmyard, only one side of the farmhouse and the kitchen window, but she heard the car and their voices, saw them go into the kitchen carrying boxes of supplies. She ate another biscuit and hoped that Rachael wouldn't decide to give Neville a tour of Baikie's for old times' sake. It wasn't so much the collapse of the investigation which bothered her. It was the thought of being caught, sitting here, wearing nothing below the waist but a pair of knickers and some woollen socks. But there was no sign of Rachael or Neville all afternoon. As she'd suspected it seemed they had better things to do. The only people she saw were two athletic elderly walkers who seemed to cross her field of view in minutes.

Her phone rang. It was Ashworth.

'Nothing yet,' he said. 'But you must be right. There've been preparations. The car's been packed.'

'What with?'

'A shovel. Black bin bags.'

'Ah,' she said, blew him an invisible kiss. 'Thank you, God!'

'So, can I organize the back-up now?'

'No, not yet. Wait until we know exactly what's going on.'

In the late afternoon the sun shone directly

into the bedroom window and she felt herself dozing and forced herself to keep awake. At six o'clock Neville and Rachael left the farmhouse. They walked up the hill towards the tarn and returned through Baikie's garden. They stopped for a moment under the window and Vera began to panic. She could hear them clearly but was so anxious that they'd come inside that she only took in snatches of their conversation, though it wasn't like her to pass over gossip.

'So what will you do now?' Neville asked. 'Will you try to trace your father?'

'I don't think so. He sounds a bit of a nerd. He was running a weekend drama course for teachers and that was the only time Edie met him. He already had a wife and family. He never knew about me. It's not as if I ever really felt the need of a father. I just didn't like being kept in the dark. But I've not told Edie that. I want to keep my options open. She owes me that much.'

They walked on hand in hand like a couple of kids, and the moment when Rachael might have suggested taking him inside Baikie's had passed.

Vera presumed that they returned to the farmhouse although they couldn't have gone in through the kitchen, and from where she sat there was no sign that the place was occupied. The evening sun was too strong for the need for lights in the rooms and it was too warm for a fire.

Her phone rang. Ashworth's voice was insistent and excited.

'We're on.'

'How many people?'

'Just one.'

'No need to call the cavalry then,' Vera said, stretching her legs, thinking she'd best get dressed. 'This one's ours.'

Chapter Sixty-Six

There was no movement until dusk and then it was cautious, wary, giving the impression of an animal coming out after dark to drink. Suddenly a bank of cloud had appeared and Vera could make out no detail. She saw only the shadow, slightly darker against the grey hill and then she almost dismissed it as a roe deer. She had been expecting something less subtle, more purposeful and confident.

The shape followed the line of the burn from the crow trap to the mine, stopping occasionally. Vera thought this was not through tiredness, though there would be the shovel to carry, besides a rucksack, but to watch and listen. By now it was so dark that Vera had to concentrate very hard not to miss the movement. With unusual self-doubt she wondered briefly if she should after all have asked for help, enlisted the specialists with their nightsights and tracking devices. With the technology she would have felt more in control, would have known for certain what she was seeing. Then she thought that the person moving carefully across the hill would have smelled them, knew this landscape so well that an influx of strangers, however well hidden, would have been noticed.

She had an almost superstitious sense that her prey

would pick up any movement she made, so Vera stayed where she was, quite still. She knew the destination, knew what would happen there. She had to wait because there was still no proof. It wasn't against the law to take a walk on a dark night along the burn. At one point she lost the figure completely. She held her breath, peered through the smeared glass into the gloom. Then there was a brief flash of light as a match was struck and the soft glow of candlelight marking the rectangular gap where the door of the mine building had once been.

She spoke to Ashworth, whispering at first, although there was no one to hear her.

'Where are you?'

'At the edge of the forest.'

'Move on now. I'll see you there. But quietly.'

Deliberately, slowly, Vera pulled on her trousers and laced her boots. Outside it was still warm, the air smelling of honeysuckle and crushed grass, the scents of summer afternoons. There was no wind to hide the sound of her movement. She didn't want to risk using a torch but her eyes soon got used to the grey light, the hazy shapes.

She realized as she approached the burn that she was loving every minute of it. She thought this must be how Hector and Connie felt when they raided the Lake District golden eagles, sneaking up to the site, knowing the warden was dossing nearby in his tent and that the police had promised regular patrols. They did it for this buzz.

Christ, she thought. I must be light-headed. Thinking I can understand that pair. That's what exercise does to you. And having nothing to eat all day except a packet of biscuits.

Now she could hear water – the burn where it was channelled through the culvert to power the engine which had worked the mine. There was the crunch of pebble. She thought it must be Ashworth but when she turned to look there was no movement and it was too dark to see. Tonight the moon was covered by the low, dense cloud which had rolled in like fog. From the shell of the engine room came another sound, the scrape of metal against stone and soil. Vera moved closer. She was breathing heavily after the walk from the cottage but the noise from the building reassured her that she wouldn't be heard. At last she was close enough to see.

The woman was standing with her back to the gap in the wall. She wore a long skirt over black boots. She had loosened a flagstone from the corner of the room and shifted it enough so she could dig out the soil underneath. The grave must have been shallow because already Vera saw a fragment of bone, cream as ivory, waxy in the candlelight. The woman squatted and began to scrabble at the soil with her fingers.

Vera was flattened against the outside wall of the building, looking in at an angle through the gap. All she had to do now was to wait for Ashworth. She began to relax.

Suddenly, behind her, so close that it sounded like a scream, she heard a woman's voice in exclamation. Then loud footsteps and Neville Furness shouting, 'Who is it? What's going on?'

Shit, Vera thought. That's all I need. She'd thought they'd be inside all evening shagging like rabbits.

The woman in the building stood and turned in one

movement, giving a throaty growl of astonishment. She picked up the shovel which she'd leant against the wall. She couldn't see Vera, still hidden outside, but Rachael, silhouetted in the doorway, must have been visible from the light of the candle. The woman moved forward. Before Vera could stop her she lashed out with the shovel. There was the crunch of metal against flesh and bone. Then she ran and seemed to disappear immediately into the darkness.

A second later the scene was hit like a stage by the spot of Ashworth's flashlight. Neville Furness sat on the grass cradling Rachael in his arms. She was conscious. There was blood, probably a broken nose. Vera heard her gasping with pain but thought she'd rather have Neville fussing over her than a middle-aged detective. She turned towards Ashworth, blinking in the light.

'Did anyone pass you?'

'No.'

'She's not headed back for the car then.'

'What do you want me to do?'

'Radio for assistance. We'll need medics for Rachael. Then stay here. She's mad enough to come back.'

'And you?'

'I think I know where she's heading. Friendly territory.'

As she walked off she could hear him shouting at her not to be so bloody stupid, that this was no time to play cops and robbers, they'd get her no bother before morning. But the words seemed very distant, as far away as Neville's murmurs of comfort and Rachael's stifled moans. She turned back once to say to him,

'Look, I know what I'm doing. This is familiar territory for me too.'

But he was still shouting, his mouth opening and shutting in the torchlight, and she didn't know whether or not he'd heard.

As she headed up the hill towards the tarn she felt that she did know this place. Better in the dark than she did in daylight. As a child it had always been after dusk or before dawn when she'd come here with her father. The scale seemed different – then the tarn had looked like an enormous lake – but the geography was the same. They had come here to steal the eggs of black-necked grebe. Her father had paddled into the water in thigh-length angler's waders. Connie had stood on the bank, clapping her hands in delight.

The cloud thinned slightly to let through a diffuse and milky moonlight. There were no sharp lines or edges. It was like viewing the scene darkly through a photographer's filter. At one point she thought she saw the shadow of her quarry disappearing ahead of her, but imagined it was probably her imagination, the mist playing tricks. Either the woman had run too quickly, had too big a start or Vera was quite wrong about where she was heading. Now it hardly mattered. She took the same path as she had walked that morning but without the exhaustion or irritation. She had the energy of a ten-year-old and could have gone on all night. From the top of the bank she could see the faint lights of Langholme. The pub would still be open. People would be in their homes watching television, enjoying a late, relaxed Friday night meal, drinking beer.

Then, before she could believe it she had reached the five-barred gate and the stile. There were no street lights in the lane behind the church, but there were in the village's main street, and headlights and the noise of traffic.

Above the porch door of the Priory there was a bulb – energy efficient elements – encased in a wrought iron mounting. Parked on the drive was Anne Preece's Fiat, but not Jeremy's Volvo. That didn't mean it wasn't there, tucked away for the night in the garage.

She moved closer, walking on the lawn not the drive, so her footsteps wouldn't be heard. There was a light in the room which faced the lane. It was uncurtained and the sash window was wide open. From inside came a voice, Anne Preece's, anxious but slightly tetchy, as if she had been landed with a problem which she didn't want to handle.

'You look dreadful. Whatever's the matter?'

There was a mumbled response which Vera couldn't make out, but which seemed to make sense to Anne, which seemed to knock the heart from her.

'He did that to you?' she said. 'Look, you must go to the police.'

Vera moved to the front door, turned the handle. It opened without a sound. The occupied room was to her right and that door was already open. She planted herself in the doorway, put on her jolly maiden aunt's voice.

'Who said you could never find a policeman when you needed one? At least a policewoman. I hope I'll do.'

Anne looked up. She was shocked and pale. It was a pleasant room which Vera hadn't seen on her previous visit. A comfortable sofa with lemon and white striped covers. Two chairs in the same print. Lots of plants and cut flowers. The other woman sat in one of the chairs with her head in her hands. Barbara Waugh, smartly dressed in her black skirt and jacket and her leather boots, but bedraggled, tearful, shaking.

Anne said, 'She's run away from her husband. He must have terrified her. Look at the state she's in.'

'Oh no,' Vera said. 'It's not her husband who's terrified her.' She shot an amused, rather self-satisfied look at Anne. 'If it's anyone, it's me.' And standing where she was, legs apart, hands on her hips to block the door, she cautioned Barbara Waugh, told her in a flat, indifferent voice that she was under arrest. Then she waited for Ashworth to send in the troops.

Chapter Sixty-Seven

They met at Baikie's for old times' sake, though Edie would have had them to Riverside Terrace, and Rachael, who seemed to spend most of her time in the farmhouse and was already acting as if she owned the place, had invited them there.

Edie had her doubts about the Black Law connection. She'd thought lately that Rachael cared more for the place than the man. But as she'd said to Vera she'd hardly made a success of her own personal life so it wasn't really for her to say. Rachael was even talking about having Dougie back to live with them, which Edie didn't think was healthy at all. Talk about trying to live another person's life. Rachael wasn't Bella Furness reincarnated and never would be. Thank God.

Ashworth was the only man present. Rachael had wanted to invite Neville along but Edie had put her foot down at that. 'He was never a part of it. Not really. And I'm sure you'll pass on all the details anyway.'

So they sat in the room with the stuffed fox and Connie Baikie's mountainous armchairs and they waited for Vera to tell another of her stories. Edie had lit a fire not because it was cold but because outside it was damp and drizzling and they wanted the comfort. Because it had been raining when Grace was killed.

Perhaps they drank for comfort too. Certainly by the time Vera got going there were two empty wine bottles on the table. Joe Ashworth, who would have to drive Vera home, had stuck to tea. He said he knew he was only there to be chauffeur.

Vera started with a tribute, generous for her. 'Rachael was right all along. It all started years ago when Bella and Edmund met in hospital. There was another woman on the same ward and attending the same therapy group who was being treated for depression. She'd been desperate for a child. After a number of miscarriages she'd finally given birth, but the baby died after a few hours. He was buried in St Cuthbert's churchyard. The grave is still there. She had a severe breakdown. They tried to treat her at home but on a number of occasions she went missing for days. Her husband found her out on the hill, starving and exhausted. That was when she was sectioned and forced to go into hospital.

'At the same time as one of Barbara's disappearances, a toddler disappeared. His mother and her boyfriend had brought him for an outing to the hills. It was spring and they wanted to show the boy the new lambs. While the pair were otherwise engaged the boy vanished. If you believed the local newspapers he'd been swept away by a large hawk into its eyrie. If you believed me at the time he was drowned in the Skirl which was in flood.

'In fact we were both wrong. The boy was taken by Barbara Waugh on one of her crazy moorland wanderings. We don't know what she did with him while we were searching the hill, but later she took him to the old mine and kept him as a pet, a toy, a replacement son.' Vera's voice showed no emotion. Weren't fairy tales always gruesome? But she was thinking, I was there, I could have made more effort to find him. 'We don't know yet how he died. Perhaps she killed him. Perhaps he starved to death when she was taken into hospital. At some time, either then or later, she buried him under one of the flagstones in the engine house. She tried to forget him but couldn't quite, although she had a child of her own and a husband who stuck by her.' Again, Vera kept her flat storyteller's voice but she threw a knowing look towards Anne, because investigations always dug up more than people realized. 'A husband who had been so frightened by her manic outings on the hill, never knowing where she might be, that he tried to persuade her to stay at home as much as possible. He didn't like her going out.'

'Did he know about the little boy?' Anne asked.

'He never even guessed.' Vera poured more wine. 'So Barbara put the boy's death at the back of her mind. Buried it like she'd buried the body. Sometimes she visited the mine, brought flowers, but I think she'd convinced herself by then that she wasn't responsible for his dying. Perhaps she confused him with her own son. She took flowers to his grave too. And so things would have continued if her husband hadn't decided to develop the site as a quarry. Because then there would be a risk that the grave would be discovered. The unpleasantness which she'd tidily hidden away under the engine-house floor could be brought to light. She wouldn't be able to pretend any more that it wasn't her fault. So what could she do?

'At first she encouraged the opposition. She spread rumours that her husband had come under the evil influence of Neville Furness and Olivia Fulwell. She thought that if the public inquiry came out against the quarry everything could continue as before. She wound up her old friend Edmund Fulwell about the project. He was an easy target. She played on his love of his ancestral estate and he played on Grace's affection for him to rig her otter counts.

'She put pressure on Bella too. The three of them kept in touch. Bella was in a difficult position. The farm was verging on bankruptcy. She'd hoped to get money from her brother to save it but that never materialized. Her only hope was to do a deal with the development company over access to the site. She wouldn't have liked the idea but it would have been better than losing the farm. She arranged for Peter Kemp to come to Black Law to discuss possible ways forward.'

'Someone else was there that afternoon,' Rachael said. 'Dougie heard someone.'

'Barbara. Godfrey had told her what was going on and she came to turn the screw. Blackmail. She knew what had happened when Bella's father had died, knew it had all been planned. That had come out at one of the group therapy sessions. She threatened to make the whole thing public. Bella was under so much pressure that she couldn't see straight. She told Peter she couldn't make a deal and she committed suicide.

'For a while it looked as if Barbara was safe. She thought the report would come out in her favour. After all, she'd become chummy with Anne and had indirectly nobbled Grace. Then she heard from Edmund that Grace was having cold feet. She was talking about seeing a shrink or a social worker. She couldn't face lying any more. She knew it was making her ill. I'm not sure yet if Barbara planned to kill Grace to stop her telling the truth about the otters. She says not. She says she went to the engine room as she did on Friday night to try to move the remains of the little boy's body and Grace surprised her.

'When he first heard about his daughter's death Edmund was too shocked to work out what might have happened. He stayed at his flat, carried on helping in the restaurant. Then I think he probably remembered a story Barbara had told to the group, a story nobody believed because she was mad at the time and full of fantasies. This one was about a boy she had found on the hill. A boy she'd taken for her own. Her baby.

'He panicked. It had always been his style to run away. He went into hiding. First with Nancy Deakin and then in the house on the estate. How did Barbara know he was there? A guess perhaps. He'd probably told her that he'd lived in one of those houses before he got married.

'The phone number and the back door key she got from Neville. Not directly . . .' as Rachael was about to object. 'She had access to the Slateburn offices through her husband and I think she regularly went through both their desks looking for anything which would help in her fight against the quarry. She phoned Edmund to check that he was there. And to frighten him. She knew him well enough to realize that if he was scared he'd probably start drinking. On the afternoon of the birthday party when the estate was overrun with strangers she let herself into the house. Edmund had already drunk himself into oblivion. It was easy enough.'

Rachael stretched her hands towards the fire. 'Did Barbara ram my car on the track that night?'

'Oh, yes. She was desperate. She was trying to frighten you away.' Vera paused, pulled a face. 'And one of our people stopped her. Can you believe it? She told him she was visiting her sick mother and he was taken in. The fight to stop the quarry was an obsession. Perhaps she was just trying to save herself but I think it was more than that. She saw it as a desecration of the little boy's grave.'

Vera sighed, leant back, took a deep draught of wine. Ashworth shuffled restlessly. He'd heard all this before and he had his lass to get back to and a warm bed, and at last the baby had started to sleep through the night.

Anne asked suddenly, 'What'll happen to the quarry now?'

Vera shook her head. 'I wouldn't have thought Godfrey would have much stomach for it. But you'll have to talk to him about that.'

She left the three women talking about it, so engrossed that they hardly noticed her leaving.

Ashworth drove carefully up the track and through the ford towards the forest.

TELLING TALES

The second novel in the Vera Stanhope series

After years of deadly silence, a killer re-emerges . . .

Ten years after Jeanie Long was charged with the murder of fifteen-year-old Abigail Mantel, residents of the East Yorkshire village of Elvet are disturbed to hear of new evidence proving Jeanie's innocence. Abigail's killer is still at large.

For Emma Bennett, the revelation brings back haunting memories of her vibrant best friend – and of the fearful winter's day when she discovered her body lying cold in a ditch.

As DI Vera Stanhope makes fresh inquiries, villagers are taken back to a time they would rather forget. Inevitably tensions begin to mount, but are people afraid of the killer, or of their own guilty pasts?

Turn the page to read the first chapters

Chapter One

Sitting at the bedroom window, Emma looks out at the night-time square. The wind rattles a roof tile and hisses out from the churchyard, spitting a Coke can onto the street. There was a gale the afternoon Abigail Mantel died and it seems to Emma that it's been windy ever since, that there have been ten years of storms, of hailstones like bullets blown against her windows and trees ripped from the earth by their roots. It must be true at least since the baby was born. Since then, whenever she wakes at night – to feed the baby or when James comes in late from work – the noise of the wind is there, rolling round her head like the sound of a seashell when you hold it to your ear.

James, her husband, isn't home yet, but she's not waiting up for *him*. Her gaze is fixed on the Old Forge where Dan Greenwood makes pots. There's a light at the window and occasionally she fancies she sees a shadow. She imagines that Dan is still working there, dressed in his blue canvas smock, his eyes narrowed as he shapes the clay with his strong, brown hands. Then she imagines leaving the baby, who is fast asleep, tucked up in his carrycot. She sees herself slipping out into the square and keeping to the shadows, walking across to the forge. She pushes open one of the big doors which form an arch, like the door of a church, and stands inside. The roof is high and she can see through the curved rafters to the tiles. In her mind she feels the heat of the kiln and sees the dusty shelves holding unglazed pots.

Dan Greenwood looks up. His face is flushed and there is red dust in the furrows of his forehead. He isn't surprised to see her. He moves away from the bench where he's working and stands in front of her. She feels her breath quicken. He kisses her forehead and then begins to unbutton her shirt. He touches her breasts, stroking them, so he leaves lines of red clay like warpaint. She feels the clay drying on her skin and her breasts become tight, slightly itchy.

Then the image fades and she's back in the bedroom she shares with her husband. She knows her breasts are heavy with milk, not tight with drying clay. At the same time the baby begins to grizzle and to claw blindly in the air with both hands. Emma lifts him out of the cot and begins to feed him. Dan Greenwood has never touched her and probably never will, no matter how often she dreams of it. The church clock strikes midnight. By now, James should have his ship safely into port.

That was the story Emma told herself as she sat by her window in the village of Elvet. A running commentary on her feelings, as if she was an outsider looking in. It was how it had always been – her life as a series of fairy tales. Before Matthew had been born she'd wondered if his birth would make her more engaged. There was nothing more real, was there, than labour? But now, running her little finger between his mouth and her nipple to break the suction, she thought that wasn't true. She was no more emotionally involved with him than she was with James. Had she been different before she found Abigail Mantel's body? Probably not. She lifted her son onto her shoulder and rubbed his back. He reached out and grasped a strand of her hair.

The room was at the top of a neat Georgian house, built of red brick and red tile. It was double-fronted and symmetrical with rectangular windows and a door in the middle. It had been built by a seafarer who'd traded with Holland, and James had liked that. 'We're carrying on a tradition,' he'd said when he showed her round. 'It's like keeping it in the family.' Emma had thought it was too close to home, to the memories of Abigail Mantel and Jeanie Long, and had suggested that Hull might be more convenient for his work. Or Beverley. Beverley was a pleasant town. But he'd said Elvet was just as good for him.

'It'll be nice for you to be so close to your parents,' he'd said and she'd smiled and agreed, because that was what she did with James. She liked to please him. In fact she didn't much care for Robert and Mary's company. Despite all the help they offered, they made her feel uncomfortable and for some reason guilty.

Above the rumble of the wind there came another sound – a car engine; headlights swept onto the square, briefly lighting up the church gate, where dead leaves were blown into a drift. James parked on the cobbles, got out and shut the door with a solid thud. At the same time Dan Greenwood emerged from the Old Forge. He was dressed as Emma had imagined, in jeans and the blue smock. She expected him to pull together the big double doors and fasten them with a key he kept on a ring clipped to his belt on a chain. Then he would push a heavy brass padlock through the iron rings bolted to each door and shove the hasp in place. She had watched this ritual from the window many times. Instead he crossed the square towards James. He wore heavy work boots which rapped loudly on the paving stones and made James turn round.

Seeing them together, it occurred to her how different they were. Dan was so dark that he should have been a foreigner. He could play the villain in a gothic melodrama. And James was a pale, polite Englishman. She felt suddenly anxious about the two men meeting, though there was no reason. It wasn't as if Dan could guess at her fantasies. She had done nothing to give herself away. Carefully, she raised the sash window so she could hear their words. The curtains billowed. There was wind in the room with a taste of salt on it. She felt like a child listening in to an adult conversation, a parent and teacher, perhaps, discussing her academic progress. Neither of the men had seen her.

'Have you seen the news?' Dan asked.

James shook his head. 'I've come off a Latvian container. Hull to sign off, then I drove straight home.'

'You've not heard from Emma, then?'

'She's not much one for the news.'

'Jeanie Long committed suicide. She'd been turned down for parole again. It happened a couple of days ago. They kept it quiet over the weekend.'

James stood, poised to click the fob of his car key to lock up. He was still wearing his uniform and looked dashing in an old-fashioned way, as if he belonged to the time the house was built. The brass buttons on his jacket gleamed dully in the unnatural light. His head was bare. He carried his cap under his arm. Emma was reminded of when she had once had fantasies about *him*.

'I don't suppose it'll make much difference to Em. Not after all this time. I mean it's not as if she knew Jeanie, not so much. She was very young when all that was going on.'

'They're going to reopen the Abigail Mantel case,' Dan Greenwood said.

There was a moment of silence. Emma wondered what Dan could know about all that. Had the two men discussed her on other occasions when she hadn't been watching?

'Because of the suicide?' James asked.

'Because a new witness had just come forward. It seems Jeanie Long couldn't have murdered that lass.' He paused. Emma watched him rub his forehead with his broad, stubby fingers. It was as if he was trying to rub away the exhaustion. She wondered why he cared so deeply about a ten-year-old murder case. She could tell that he did care, that he had lain awake worrying about it. But he hadn't even been living in the village then. He dropped his hands from his face. No traces of clay were left on his skin. He must have washed his hands before leaving the forge. 'Shame no one bothered to tell Jeanie, huh?' he said. 'Or she might still be alive.'

A sudden gust of wind seemed to blow the men apart. Dan scurried back to the Old Forge to close the doors. The Volvo locked itself with a click and a flash of side lights and James climbed the steps to the front door. Emma moved away from the window and sat on the chair beside the bed. She cradled the baby in one arm and held him to the other breast.

She was still sitting there when James walked in. She'd switched on a small lamp beside her; the rest of the big attic room was a pool of shadow. The baby had finished feeding and his eyes were closed, but she still held him, and he sucked occasionally in his sleep. A dribble of milk ran across his cheek. She had heard James moving around carefully downstairs, and the creaking stairs had prepared her for his entrance. She was composed with a smile on her face. Mother and child. Like one of the Dutch paintings he'd dragged her to see. He'd bought a print for the house, put it in a big gilt frame. She could tell the effect wasn't lost on him, and he smiled too, looked suddenly wonderfully happy. She wondered why she had become more attracted to Dan Greenwood who could be slovenly in his appearance, and rolled thin little cigarettes from strings of tobacco.

Gently she lifted the baby into his cot. He puckered his mouth as if still looking for the nipple, sighed deeply in disappointment but didn't wake. Emma fastened the flap in the unflattering maternity bra and pulled her dressing gown around her. The heating was on but in this house there were always draughts. James bent to kiss her, feeling for her mouth with the tip of his tongue, as insistent as the baby wanting food. He would have liked sex but she knew he wouldn't push for it. Nothing was so important to him that it warranted a scene, and she'd been unpredictable lately. He wouldn't risk her ending up in tears. She pushed him gently away. He had poured himself a small glass of whisky downstairs and still had it with him. He took a sip from it before setting the glass on the bedside table.

'Was everything all right this evening?' she asked to soften the rejection. 'It's been so windy. I imagine you out there in the dark, the waves so high.'

She had imagined nothing of the sort. Not tonight. When she had first met him she had dreamed of him out on the dark sea. Somehow now, the romance had gone out of it.

'It was easterly,' he said. 'On shore. Helping us in.' He smiled fondly at her and she was pleased that she had said the right thing.

He began to undress slowly, easing the tension from his stiff muscles. He was a pilot. He joined ships at the mouth of the Humber and brought them safely into the dock at Hull, Goole or Immingham, or he guided them out of the river. He took his work seriously, felt the responsibility. He was one of the youngest, fully qualified pilots working the Humber. She was very proud of him.

That was what she told herself, but the words ran meaninglessly through her head. She was trying to fend off the panic which had been building since she had heard the men talking on the square, growing like a huge wave which rises from nothing out at sea.

'I heard you talking to Dan Greenwood outside. What was so important at this time of night?'

He sat on the bed. He was bare chested, his body coated with fine blond hair. Although he was fifteen years older than her, you'd never have guessed, he was so fit.

'Jeanie Long committed suicide last week. You know, Jeanie Long. Her father used to be coxswain on the launch at the point. The woman who was convicted of strangling Abigail.'

She wanted to shout at him, *Of course I know. I know more about this case than you ever could.* But she just looked at him.

'It was unfortunate, a terrible coincidence. Dan says a new witness has come forward. The case has been reopened. Jeanie might have been released.'

'How does Dan Greenwood know all that?'

He didn't answer. She decided he was thinking already of other things, a tricky tide perhaps, an overloaded ship, a hostile skipper. He unbuckled his belt and stood to step out of his trousers. He folded them precisely and hung them over a hanger in the wardrobe.

'Come to bed,' he said. 'Get some sleep while you can.' She thought he had already put Abigail Mantel and Jeanie Long out of his mind.

Chapter Two

For ten years Emma had tried to forget the day she'd discovered Abigail's body. Now she forced herself to remember it, to tell it as a story.

It was November and Emma was fifteen. The landscape was shadowed by storm clouds. It was the colour of mud and wind-blackened beanstalks. Emma had made one friend in Elvet. Her name was Abigail Mantel. She had flame-red hair. Her mother had died of breast cancer when Abigail was six. Emma, who had secret dreams of her father dying, was shocked to find herself a little envious of the sympathy this generated. Abigail didn't live in a damp and draughty house and she wasn't dragged to church every Sunday. Abigail's father was as rich as it was possible to be.

Emma wondered if this was the story she had told herself at the time, but couldn't remember. What *did* she remember of that autumn? The big, black sky and the wind laden with sand which scoured her face as she waited for the bus to school. Her anger at her father for bringing them there.

And Abigail Mantel, exotic as a television star, with her wild hair and her expensive clothes, her poses and

ANN CLEEVES

her pouting. Abigail, who sat next to her in class and copied her work and tossed her hair in disdain at all the lads who fancied her. So two contrasting memories: a cold, monochrome landscape and a fifteen-year-old girl, so intensely coloured that it would warm you just to look at her. When she was alive, of course. When she was dead she'd looked as cold as the frozen ditch where Emma had found her.

Emma made herself remember the moment of finding Abigail's body. She owed Abigail that, at least. In the room in the Dutch captain's house, the baby snuffled, James breathed slowly and evenly and she retraced her footsteps along the side of a bean field, making every effort to keep the recollection real. No fantasies here, please.

The wind was so strong that she had to force out each breath in a series of pants, much as she would later be taught to do during labour before it became time to push. There was no shelter. In the distance the horizon was broken by one of the ridiculously grand church spires which were a feature of this part of the county, but the sky seemed enormous and she imagined herself the only person under it.

'What were you doing there, out on your own in the storm?' the policewoman would ask later, gently, as if she really wanted to know, as if the question wasn't part of the investigation at all.

But lying beside her husband, Emma knew that *this* memory, the memory of her mother and the police-woman, sitting in the kitchen at home discussing the